HOLY TERROR

Recent Titles by Graham Masterton available from Severn House

DOORKEEPERS

GENIUS

HIDDEN WORLD

The Jim Rook Series

ROOK

THE TERROR

TOOTH AND CLAW

SNOWMAN

SWIMMER

Anthologies

FACES OF FEAR

FEELINGS OF FEAR

FORTNIGHT OF FEAR

FLIGHTS OF FEAR

HOLY TERROR

Graham Masterton

This title first published in Great Britain 2004 by
SEVERN HOUSE PUBLISHERS LTD of
9–15 High Street, Sutton, Surrey SM1 1DF.
Originally published in the UK 1999 in mass market format only,
under the title *Plague of Angels* and pseudonym *Alan Blackwood*.
This title first published in the USA 2004 by
SEVERN HOUSE PUBLISHERS INC of
595 Madison Avenue, New York, N.Y. 10022.

British Library Cataloguing in Publication Data

Masterton, Graham, 1946-
    Holy terror
    1. Bioterrorism - Fiction
    2. Suspense fiction
    I. Title
    823.9'14 [F]

    ISBN 0-7278-6067-4

Except where actual historical events and characters are being
described for the storyline of this novel, all situations in this
publication are fictitious and any resemblance to living persons
is purely coincidental.

Printed and bound in Great Britain by
MPG Books Ltd., Bodmin, Cornwall.

For Dr Kristin Øverland.
And with very special thanks to Hilly Elvenstar,
who gave me the trance of a lifetime.

Longyearbyen, Norway, September 18 1918

It was only three o'clock in the afternoon when the steamer *Forsete* appeared through the pearly mist that hung over the docks, but already it was starting to grow dark. The sea around the *Forsete*'s bows had the sloppy, reluctant consistency of gray porridge, and Arne knew that she would have to be the last ship into Longyearbyen before they were all iced in for the winter.

He clapped his frayed gray mittens together as he waited for the *Forsete* to churn her way sideways up to the wooden wharf. His friend Tarjei stood beside him in his filthy reindeer coat, a cigarette stuck to his lip.

'How much do you bet they forgot the batteries?' said Tarjei.

'I don't care if they forgot the batteries so long as they remembered the schnapps.'

Arnulf was standing a little way away, a tall skinny scarecrow in ear-muffs. 'I don't care if they forgot the batteries *and* the schnapps, so long as they remembered to bring some women.'

7

The wharf shuddered as the *Forsete* bumped against it. Lines were thrown from her bow and her stern. They were so cold that they fell with a curious stiffness, like failed attempts at the Indian rope trick. The steamer's crew were huddled against the rails, all bundled up like the men on the shore. Nobody waved, or called out a greeting. It was 11 degrees below freezing and none of them were here because they enjoyed it.

The gangplank came down and Arne went forward to meet the *Forsete*'s captain, a stocky little white-bearded Viking in a brown woolen fisherman's hat. 'Winter's come early this year,' he remarked.

'Winter comes earlier the older I get,' the captain replied. He had deepset eyes like tiny chips of ice. 'This is going to be my last year, believe me. Half the crew have coughs and sneezes.'

'You brought the oil? And the spare parts for the generator? And the winding cable?'

The captain retrieved a crumpled manifest from his coat pocket. 'You've got all of that. Plus that tinned pork you asked for. Plus – well, something extra.' He turned back toward the steamer, where seven young men were collecting up knapsacks and cheap cardboard suitcases. 'A few more lads for underground work.'

'Never learn, will they?' said Arne, wryly. 'Still, I suppose we can use them.'

The young men came down the gangplank, one of them slipping on the ice and sitting down on his rear end. The rest of them whooped and laughed. The captain beckoned them over and introduced them to

Arne. 'This is Arne Gabrielsen, chief engineer. He was here before the war. In fact he was here before you were born. In Longyearbyen, Arne is your boss, your father, your priest and your doctor. You won't be able to survive here without Arne, so treat him with respect.'

One of the young men took off his glove and held out his hand. Arne ignored it. In this cold, he didn't take his mittens off for anything as inconsequential as a handshake. The young man was pale and he was shivering. 'Tormod Albrisgten,' he said. 'We're all from Tromso.'

'Any experience, any of you?'

'Ole worked in a quarry once. I helped out on my uncle's farm. Digging out frozen turnips, that's hard work.'

'This is different. The coal seam is very deep here, 110 meters below ground. The equipment is old, too. The company haven't been able to replace it since the war. Hey – you're not frightened already, are you? You're shaking like a leaf.'

'Just a cold, that's all. It was going round the ship.'

'Well, Arnulf will show you to one of the huts. You can light the stove and warm yourselves up.'

Arnulf grumbled, 'They could have sent us women. Just *one* woman! Just because we're miners we don't have to live like monks.'

He trudged off through the gathering gloom toward the small collection of houses and huts and warehouses that lay close to the harbor. Hesitantly, the young men shouldered their knapsacks and followed him.

Helped by the miners on the docks, the ship's crew

swung out cranes and nets to unload their cargo. They hardly spoke, except to call out, 'Watch out below!' Two old motor lorries were parked on the wharf with their engines running to keep them from seizing up. The day was fading fast, but a last ghostly light was reflected from the glacier on the other side of the bay.

The captain took out a packet of Wotan cigarettes and passed one to Arne. They stood together and smoked in silence, occasionally trudging their feet to keep warm. It was so cold that it was impossible to tell which was smoke and which was breath.

In the middle of the night, in the middle of a dream in which he came across a polar bear in the middle of the street, Arne was shaken awake.

'Arne! Arne! It's me, Tarjei! You have to come quick!'

He sat up. The only light in his bedroom came from the small tiled stove which glowed redly in the opposite corner.

'What's wrong?' he asked. 'What time is it?'

'Just gone three o'clock. There's something wrong with those boys from Tromso. They're sick.'

'They've got colds, that's all. Give them a tot of schnapps and tell them to put on an extra blanket.'

'These aren't colds, Arne. You *have* to come.'

Arne took the glass funnel off the oil lamp beside his bed and lit it. He could see at once that Tarjei was serious. Without a word he took his thick plaid shirt off the back of the chair, tugged on his pants and his huge coarse-knit sweater, and his coat.

Outside it was so cold that Arne felt as if he had
been hit in the face with a ball-peen hammer.
His shoulders hunched, he followed Tarjei across
the windswept street to the huts where most of the
unmarried miners lived. There was a small knot of
them outside the porch of the young men's hut,
carrying lamps and flashlights.

'I went in to make sure their stove was burning
properly,' said Kjell. 'Go in and see them for
yourself.'

Arne opened the door and went inside, with Tarjei
closely following him. There was a sharp smell of
woodsmoke mingled with the sharper tang of vomit.
The hut was plain, with a boarded floor and a potbel-
lied stove in the middle, and the young men were
lying in bunk beds on either side. Some of them
were silent. Others were coughing and shivering and
gasping for breath.

'What do you think it is?' asked Tarjei.

Arne leaned over the bunk of the young man
called Tormod. His face was blotchy maroon, and
his eyes were so swollen that he could barely see.

'Tormod!' said Arne. 'Tormod, can you hear me?'

'Can't – breathe—' Tormod gargled. He coughed,
and a thick gobbet of blood and phlegm landed on
his chin. 'Is – my – is – my – mother here?'

Arne untucked the blankets at the end of the bed
and lifted them up. Tormod's feet were prune-
colored. Arne dropped the blankets and stepped
away.

'What is it?' Tarjei repeated. 'Is it food poisoning?'

Arne shook his head. 'The red face, the black

11

feet. The lungs filled up. It's the Spanish influenza.'

Tarjei looked at him fearfully. 'What can we do? Supposing the rest of us have caught it?'

'We can't do anything. We'll just have to pray that it's too cold here for the disease to survive.'

He went around to the other six bunks. Four of the young men were dead already, drowned by the fluid in their lungs, and he knew that it wouldn't be long before the others succumbed. The Spanish influenza killed with unbelievable rapidity. He had heard stories of people waking up in the morning in the best of health and dropping dead in the street the same afternoon. And the disease always seemed to favor young people, like these. Arne wasn't a religious man, but as he covered their faces he commended each of their souls to God.

It was beginning to snow when the funeral procession reached the cemetery at the top of the hill, and from here the town was only dimly visible, like the town that Arne had seen in his dream.

Two jackhammers burst into a staccato duet, then stopped, then started again, then stopped. Arne had ordered that the seven bodies be buried twenty feet down, where the permafrost never thawed out, even in the middle of summer.

The pit had stopped work for the morning and nearly everybody in Longyearbyen had gathered on the hill, over 400 of them. The seven pine coffins lay side by side, decorated only with sprigs of spruce and ribbons in the Norwegian colors of red, white and blue.

Old man Hansen said a prayer, and then they sang

12

a hymn together. The snow whirled thicker and thicker, around and around, until Arne found it hard to keep his balance.

The coffins were lowered: a small steam-shovel was used to push the frozen soil into the grave. Arne walked back down the hill on his own. He had seen plenty of death in his time. Miners gassed; miners burned in firedamp explosions; miners crushed beneath tons of coal. But the speed and the invisibility of the Spanish influenza frightened him more than anything he had ever come across before.

He felt as if the wing of death were sweeping over them.

13

1

At 12:27 on August 10 the temperature in New York
City rose to 106 degrees to make it the hottest day
of the decade. All the way down Fifth Avenue the
traffic glittered in the haze, and the air was filled with
the bronze smell of automobile fumes. From up here
on 57th Street the sidewalks downtown had become
a mirage, with crowds of lunchtime shoppers bob-
bing on the surface of a shining lake.

In the back seat of his arctically air-conditioned
taxi, Conor checked his heavy stainless-steel watch
and tried to work out if it would be quicker to
walk.

'You want out?' the Palestinian cab driver asked
him, his eyes floating in the rear-view mirror. 'Makes
no difference to me, sir. You want to melt, melt.' He
turned around in his seat and added, 'I'll tell you
what about this heat. This heat defies the natural
laws of the universe.'

'Tell me about it,' said Conor. He was already
more than twenty minutes late.

'Would I make up such a thing? I took a corre-

14

spondence course. This is the start of something totally cosmic. Maybe not the end of the world. But equally just as bad.'

The traffic suddenly surged forward, horns blaring, and after a brief tussle with a bus at 55th, they arrived at last outside the gleaming display windows of Spurr's Fifth Avenue. Conor climbed out of the cab and the heat roared in his face like a lion. As he paid off the driver, he said, 'What was it? The correspondence course.'

'Oh.' The cab driver made a vigorous sawing gesture. 'Carpentry.'

In spite of the heat, Conor stood on the sidewalk for a moment watching the cab drive away. How did a correspondence course in carpentry qualify you to predict the end of the world, or something equally serious? But then, well, Jesus was a carpenter, wasn't He, and He came from Palestine, too. There was a satisfying Irish logic to that.

He pushed his way into the store's revolving door and almost collided with a highly groomed middle-aged woman in a pale lemon suit. 'Pardon me, ma'am,' he told her. She raised one eyebrow at him. 'Oh, *no*. My fault entirely.' She might almost have said, 'Take me!'

Inside the store there was a midwinter chill. He walked through the brightly lit perfumery department, between the gleaming counters with their bottles of Chanel and Giorgio and Dolce e Gabbana. From the Ted Lapidus counter, the crimson-haired Doris Fugazy gave him a flirtatious little finger-wave.

15

'Chief O'Neil? Can I *talk* to you for a moment?' she called.

'Sure, Doris. But later, if you don't mind. I'm running behind.'

It was 12:39. He had almost reached the brown steel door in back of the perfumery department when he saw that two people were waiting outside. A man and a woman. The man was carrying a black canvas holdall.

Conor approached the door, taking out his security keys. 'Anything I can do for you folks?'

They didn't answer – just stood outside the door as if they expected him to open it without delay.

'I'm sorry,' said Conor. 'I can't admit customers to the strongroom area unless they've made a prior appointment with one of the managers. You see that guy over there? The guy with the glasses? Mr Berkowitz. He'll help you.'

Still no response. Conor said, 'You do speak English? *Habla Inglese?*'

The man and the woman didn't even blink. The woman was very tall, nearly six feet, and dressed entirely in black. Her black hair was swept up like a crow's wing and her face by contrast was deathly pale, so white that it was almost silver. Her eyes were so dark that she could have been wearing black contact lenses. She was wearing a heavy distinctive perfume, like decaying roses and over-ripe fruit.

The man was two or three inches shorter than the woman. He was Latin-American, with luxuriant black curls that grew over his snowy white collar and

16

a thin black mustache that could have been drawn with an eyebrow pencil. His light houndstooth blazer hung over his shoulders so that the sleeves swung empty.

Conor said, 'You understand me? You have to have authorization to enter the strongroom. *Permiso*. It's the rules, that's all. I don't make the rules. But I have to carry them out. *Comprende?*'

The man slowly raised his right hand, almost as if he were making a blessing. He was wearing black cotton gloves, fastened at the wrist with a mother-of-pearl button. *On a day like this, with the temperature over 100?* thought Conor. *But then maybe he has a skin affliction or something like that.*

But the man took off his glove and held out his hand in greeting and there was nothing wrong with his skin at all. 'Do you know me?' he asked, and that was all.

Conor found himself standing outside the door alone. The man and the woman had both vanished. He looked around the perfumery department, totally perplexed. He was sure that—

He was sure that *what?* He just couldn't remember what he was supposed to be sure of.

He hesitated for a moment longer. He looked around at Doris but she was busy spraying perfume over a large woman in a white dress. Frowning, he unlocked the door and walked through to his office. On the left-hand side, sixteen closed-circuit television monitors were flickering, each of them showing a different part of the store. His desk was

17

on the right-hand side, with his name printed on a perspex block: CONOR T. O'NEIL, SECURITY DIRECTOR, and a blue plastic lunchbox.

But it was the digital clock on the wall that caught his attention the most. It read 13:08 – nearly a half-hour since he climbed out of the taxi.

2

He stepped back into the marble-floored corridor. What the hell had he been doing for the last twenty-nine minutes, and how come he couldn't remember them? Surely he couldn't have been standing outside the security door all that time. And where had the man and the woman disappeared to?

The corridor was deserted. To the left, at the very far end, the massive hardened-steel door which led to the strongroom was firmly shut, and the closed-circuit television camera that watched over it was still blinking its single red eye. Conor walked back to the brown security door and peered out through the window.

Business in the store was carrying on as normal. The spotlights were shining off the bald marble flooring and women in splashy summer dresses were walking backward and forward between the per-fumery counters.

Conor returned to his office. He stood by his desk for a moment, with his hand pressed over his mouth, completely disoriented. He couldn't think what had happened to him. He hadn't blacked out. He hadn't fainted.

He checked the television monitors. He scanned the entire eight-story department store floor by floor, camera angle by camera angle. He ranged through corridors, changing facilities, stairwells, restrooms. There was no sign of the man and the woman. But after twenty-nine minutes they could be anyplace at all.

'The hell,' he breathed.

He rewound the videotape that had covered his movements outside the security door, when he had first talked to the man and the woman. There were three and a half hours of surveillance, up until 12:41. He fast-forwarded it so that the shoppers scuttled around like termites. After that the tape ran totally blank, only a few blips and passing meteorites on the screen, and an unintelligible blurt of noise. He shook his head in frustration. In twenty-nine minutes, a professional gang could have stripped the store of hundreds of thousands of dollars' worth of stock.

There was no sign that he had admitted the man and the woman into his office – and even if he had, nothing appeared to have been disturbed. His computer was still languidly displaying its screen-saver – a flock of white seagulls against a dark blue sky. His desk was still mathematically laid out with three Pilot pens, a letter-opener with the crest of the New York Police Department and a ceramic-framed photograph of Lacey in a red-and-white crop-top, taken at Wild Dunes golf resort in South Carolina.

He pulled out all of his desk drawers, starting at the bottom and leaving them open, in the way that

20

an experienced police officer would. Paperclips, stationery, notebooks – all undisturbed. In the corner, his green steel locker was still locked. He opened it and took out his Smith & Wesson .38. It was still in its holster, with the stud fastened, and no ammunition had been taken from his belt. Nothing else had been stolen, either.

Nothing except time. He had lost twenty-nine minutes from the moment he had walked into the store to the moment he had looked around and realized that the man and the woman were gone. And in those twenty-nine minutes, what had he done? And, more importantly, what had *they* done?

He was still searching his locker when Darrell Bussman came in, carrying a clipboard and a raspberry donut with sprinkles on it. Darrell was the store's operations manager, plump, crimson-cheeked, like the kid who nobody ever picked for their football team. He was only 23 and he had a catastrophic taste in neckties, but his uncle Newt Bussman owned 47 per cent of Spurr's Fifth Avenue and had as much sense of humor as a hammerhead shark and those were all the vocational qualifications that Darrell had ever needed.

'Hey, Conor, what kept you?' he wanted to know, in his high, clogged-up voice. 'We had to go through the delivery schedules without you. And nobody knew when UPS was supposed to drop off the Gucci collection.'

'Accept my apologies, Darrell. The custody hearing went on for ever.

'So, what happened?'

'What do you think happened? I'm a man who cheated on his wife. I got shafted.'

'You still got visitation, though?'

'Qualified, at Paula's discretion.'

'Well, better than nothing, hunh?'

'You think so? You don't know Paula.'

'Listen, how about getting UPS to pick up those Rolex watches the same time they deliver the necklaces?'

'OK. Good idea.'

Darrell stopped and looked around the office, at the open locker and the open drawers.

'Hey, Conor, you're not – ah – *clearing your desk* here, are you?'

'No, no, everything's fine. I was looking for something, that's all.'

'Must have been pretty damned lost.'

Conor stood up straight. 'To tell you the truth, I had a kind of strange experience, and I was just making sure that everything was OK.'

'You had a strange experience? Don't tell me. You were abducted by Cardassians. No, stranger than that. My uncle came in and offered you a raise.'

'This isn't a joke, Darrell. This is for real. I can't even begin to work out what happened.'

'You saw ghosts, right? They always said that Spurr's Fifth Avenue was haunted. A woman with no head who walks around the hat department. Get it? A woman with no head who—'

'Unh-hunh. These two characters weren't ghosts. A man and a woman. A tall woman, dressed in black, and a kind of Cuban-looking guy.'

'Hey! No kidding! I saw them, too!' Darrell

nodded his head as if he were never going to stop. 'They were in luggage.'

'*You* saw them?'

'For sure. They walked up to me and asked me something. They said—'

Darrell opened his mouth and then he closed it again. He lowered his clipboard and pressed the heel of his hand against his forehead. 'Isn't that stupid? I don't know what they said. I really can't remember.'

'Try, Darrell. This could be critical.'

'I'm sorry, Conor. I just can't remember. Still, it couldn't have been anything much, right? One minute they're talking to me and the next minute, piff, they're gone.'

'When did this happen?'

'Oh . . . forty minutes ago, maybe a little less. Thirty-five, maybe.'

'I wish you'd called me.'

'I did call you as a matter of fact, just to see if you were back. You didn't answer. But anyway, what are you worried about? They didn't say anything, they didn't *do* anything. Not that I can remember, that is.' He took an anxious bite out of his donut, and then another, and then another.

'I think we'd better check the strongroom,' said Conor.

'The strongroom? What the hell for?'

'I want to make sure that nothing's missing, that's all.'

'How could anything be missing?' said Darrell, his mouth crammed.

'I don't know. What happened to you up in luggage, that exact same thing happened to me, too,

23

only I didn't lose a few seconds. I lost twenty-nine minutes.'

'Twenty-nine minutes? Are you serious?'

'I met them outside the security door and that's the last I remember. That's why we have to check the strongroom.'

Darrell lifted his mountainous gold Rolex. 'Conor, I'd love to, but I'm real busy right now. And – come on – anybody who wanted to break into that strongroom would need an M60 tank. You didn't see any M60 tanks pass by your door, did you?'

'Darrell, indulge me, will you?'

'For Christ's sake, Conor. We have alarms, we have infra-red sensors, we have cameras, we have time locks. Neither of us can open the strongroom on our own and I sure as hell wasn't here, was I? You had a memory lapse, that's all. It could have been the heat.'

Conor tried to be patient. It wasn't easy to be patient with a short podgy boy with his mouth full of donut and silhouettes of hula girls on his necktie. 'Help me out here, Darrell, and let a suspicious old chief of security put his mind at rest. I've got this gut feeling, that's all.'

'Conor, do you realize the magnitude of what we're talking about here? The *magnitude*? We're probably talking about more than a billion bucks' worth of stuff here, Conor. We're talking about stuff that belongs to customers like Mrs George Whitney IV, and Harold D. Hammet. If you have any kind of gut feeling, I think you'd better start praying that it was something you ate.'

★　　★　　★

Conor crossed the office and lifted down the print that the police department had given him when he resigned. It was Norman Rockwell's famous painting of a young runaway boy perched on a stool in a 1950s diner, next to a fat, benign cop. It hadn't been given to him without irony.

Concealed behind the print was a small wall-safe. Conor punched out four numbers and then Darrell immediately punched out four more. If the second batch of numbers weren't keyed into the safe in sixty seconds, it would automatically lock and stay locked. The door opened. Inside the safe were two shoulderless safe keys. Conor took one out and Darrell took the other.

Together they walked down to the strongroom door, with Darrell's rubber shoe-soles squelching on the marble floor.

'I should be in beachwear by now,' Darrell complained. He prodded at his mobile phone but there was no signal down here, under reinforced concrete ceilings.

They reached the strongroom door. Again they had to punch out an eight-figure security code, four figures each. Then they had to insert their keys and turn them simultaneously. The closed-circuit television camera swiveled on its perch like an inquisitive gray parrot.

They stepped inside. The strongroom was coldly lit, about fifty feet long and fifteen feet wide, with rows and rows of bronze-painted deposit boxes on either side and three more rows along the center. This was where some of Spurr's wealthiest customers preferred to keep certain items of jewelry and bearer bonds and videotapes and whatever else they didn't want even their banks or their spouses to know about. In the last century, Spurr's Fifth Avenue had been of service to Jay Gould the railroad swindler, among many others; and its more recent clients had been Jacqueline Kennedy Onassis and Pamela Harriman.

Conor walked along the aisles, jingling his keys and running his eyes up and down the tiers of boxes to make sure that all the key slots were in the horizontal (locked) position, and that none of them was missing.

'Anything your side?' he asked Darrell.

'Nothing. That gut feeling of yours was probably gas. It's all that health food that Lacey gives you.'

Conor checked the last row of boxes. They were all locked, but he still couldn't shake the feeling that something was wrong. 'I guess I was imagining things, that's all.'

Darrell gave him a damp slap on the shoulder, like an affectionate seal. 'That's why we took you on, Conor. You've got imagination, as well as muscle. You don't get much of that in the security business, believe me.'

3

Conor went back to his office and stared at his salad like a recovering alcoholic staring at a bottle of Perrier water. In his blue plastic lunchbox there was a big red apple and a muesli bar, too. Lacey was trying to give his alimentary canal a daily workout. She was twelve years younger than him and her father had died of colon cancer, and so he couldn't really blame her. But there were days when he would have traded six weeks of his life for a turkey and beef brisket sandwich from the Carnegie Deli on Seventh Avenue, six inches thick, with a pickle on the side. And gravy.

He poked at his salad and then he put it back in the box and closed the lid. He felt seriously worried. Something strange had happened, something that seemed to defy the laws of physics. *Not the end of the world, but something equally bad.* Conor had an Irish sense of reality: in other words he believed that there were always two sides to every argument, but that every side had more than one side, and even those sides had their different sides to them. But he didn't believe in anything that defied the laws of physics, or any other laws for that matter.

He didn't have many friends these days, but those that had stayed loyal to him would have described him as the most complicated of all the straightforward men they had ever met. He believed in justice, absolutely, but he didn't necessarily believe that justice was best achieved by being either logical or ethical.

His complexity didn't show in his face. He had inherited his father's height and his broad Kerry features, with his eyes as green as the sea off Ballinskelligs Bay and the deep O'Neil cleft in his chin 'when your great-great-great-grandfather enraged one of the Tuatha Dé Danann, the fairies, and was struck with a tiny silver ax'. However, he hadn't inherited his father's freckle-spattered Irish complexion. His gorgeous Sicilian mother had given him her thick wavy black hair and her grace of movement and her open sensuality, too. At parties, other men's wives would make a point of catching his eye, and holding it.

He had been born 37 years ago into a celebrated dynasty of New York police officers. His older brother Gerald had become a successful bedding salesman ('World of Throws') but there had never been any question that Conor would be one of the finest of the Finest. He had graduated with honors from the Police Academy with only one blemish on his record, a disciplinary matter involving a female fingerprint expert. At the age of 26, in an undercover operation that had nearly cost him his life, he had almost single-handedly broken the Barocci crime family. By the time he was 30 he was the youngest captain of detectives in the city's history – confident, charismatic, with his pretty young well-connected wife Paula and their three-year-old daughter, Fay.

But a little over three years ago, John 'Three Fingers' Negrotti had been shot nineteen times in the barber shop of Loew's New York, right opposite the 17th Precinct, and that shooting had changed Conor's life for ever. There had been lots of blood, heaps of menthol shaving foam, but no witnesses. At first it was thought that Negrotti was the victim of a classic contract hit. But Conor had unique contacts with the Mafia Commission – the unofficial association of leading Mafia families. Gradually, he had begun to uncover the existence of a secret death squad made up of New York police officers. They called themselves the Forty-Ninth Street Golf Club. For more than six years they had been forcing the Mafia in Manhattan and Brooklyn and Queens to pay them hundreds of thousands of dollars every week. If they didn't, they would be executed without warning, their wives and children, too.

As Conor's investigation plowed up more and more evidence of extortion, torture and murder, he and his family were threatened with every kind of terrible retribution. They were going to firebomb his apartment. They were going to kidnap his daughter. They were going to castrate him and mail his genitals to David Letterman. Paula and Fay had to be guarded round the clock. By the time the case of the Forty-Ninth Street Golf Club came to court, his marriage was wrecked by strain and fear. Paula had taken Fay and gone to Darien to live with her WASPish parents.

In the witness stand, an accused detective named

William Sykes protested that the Golf Club were 'simply doing their job, only a little more so'. He justified their extortion of Mafia profits by saying that 'stealing money that's already stolen doesn't make it any more stolen than it was in the first place'.

But it was the *capo di capos*, Luigi 'The Artist' Guttuso, who made the court's scalps prickle. In what was little more than a whisper, he said, 'I was brought up never to show no fear to no man. Never. Some lowlife threatens to cut off your hands with a sausage-slicer and what do you do? You spit in his eye. But I have to impress on Your Honor that me and my family was mortally afraid of the Forty-Ninth Street Golf Club. Captain O'Neil has lifted that fear, regardless of the personal consequences. For that reason, I'm proud to call him my honorary brother.'

Nine members of the Forty-Ninth Street Golf Club were convicted on seven sample counts of extortion and five sample counts of homicide in the first degree. Between them, they were sentenced to 369 years in jail. Conor had cleaned up one of the worst scandals in the police department's history, and the *New York Post* hailed him as a hero. But Luigi Guttuso's 'honorary brother' speech and the naked hostility of his fellow officers finished his career. He resigned the morning after the trial; but before he could write out his resignation letter, he had to remove the dead sewer rat fastened to his blotter with a six-inch nail.

Conor opened up a yellow legal pad and took a pencil out of the shamrock-decorated mug which

Lacey had given him for St Patrick's Day. Tentatively, he began to sketch the man and the woman he had encountered outside the security door. He wasn't very good at drawing. His art teacher had told him that he drew people like walking mattresses and horses like ironing boards, and it took four or five attempts before he managed to produce two reasonable likenesses. He even had to stick his tongue out, the way he used to do in grade school. But the finished result wasn't too far off. He felt that he had caught the woman's feline face and her upswept hair; and even though the man's forehead was too bulgy, he definitely had that Copacabana look. Underneath, Conor wrote *August 10, 12:27 p.m. Who??? And What??? And Why???*

His deputy Salvatore Morales came into the office. 'Brinks-Mat called in. They just passed 34th Street. They should be here in less than five minutes.'

Conor stood up. Even after seven and a half weeks, he still felt uncomfortable with Salvatore. Salvatore was impeccably smart and well pressed and efficient. His mustache was always clipped and his fingernails were always buffed and he always smelled (discreetly) of lavender water. In his eleven-and-a-half-year career at Spurr's Fifth Avenue he had detained more shoplifters than the rest of the security staff put together. When Bill Hardcastle the last chief security officer had retired, Salvatore had naturally expected to step straight into his shoes.

Spurr's board of directors, however, had been urged by their public-relations people to take on 'Manhattan's Crusading Cop'. When Conor was awarded the job, Spurr's had even taken out advertisements in the Sunday papers, with a photograph of Conor in his police dress uniform, and the headline NEW YORK'S FINEST . . . STORE. Conor was embarrassed. Lacey thought it was wonderful. But Salvatore must have felt like going down on his hands and knees that Sunday and eating cat litter. Conor hadn't yet found the right moment to talk to him, to straighten their relationship out, and Salvatore was always so formal that it was almost impossible to start up a casual conversation.

'Sal – before you go – did you see anybody unusual in the store today?'

'Unusual in what way, sir?'

'Unusual like this.' Conor pushed his legal pad across the desk. 'Very well dressed. She's tall, he's small.'

Salvatore picked up the pad and studied it. 'I don't know, sir. What context?'

'Forget about the context. Context is 90 per cent to blame for witness misidentification. They see a guy in a line-up, witnesses immediately assume that he must have done something.'

'Sir, I was six years with Metro-Dade sheriff's department, Florida.'

'I know that, Sal. I know your qualifications. I'm just asking you if you ever saw these people before.'

'Respectfully, sir, maybe we could use a police artist.'

Conor looked at him steadily for a long time. 'You're saying what?'

'I'm saying . . . it's hard to make any kind of identification, that's all.'

'In what respect?'

Salvatore laid the pad back on Conor's desk. 'In the respect that these customers look like two chickens.'

Conor had to hand it to Salvatore. His lips didn't twitch, even infinitesimally. Conor picked up the pad and stared at it for a moment, breathing noisily through both nostrils. As worried as he was, he needed a lot of extra oxygen to stop himself from laughing.

'You don't think you might have seen them, though? These, ah, chickens?'

Salvatore was about to answer when his phone played the first four bars of 'Swanee River', the Florida state song. 'Excuse me, sir,' he said, and took it out of his pocket. 'Spurr's Fifth Avenue security, Deputy Chief Security Officer Salvatore Morales speaking.' He kept looking at Conor as he said, 'Yes. Unh-hunh. OK. I'll be right out.'

'Listen, Sal—' Conor began, but Salvatore said, 'Brinks-Mat have arrived, sir. I don't want to keep them waiting.'

'All right. We'll talk about these two jokers later. But in the meantime, you can ease off on the "sir".'

Salvatore said, 'If I was in your position, sir, I would expect everybody to call me "sir". To be called "sir", that means you have earned something, that you have worked for it.'

And I haven't? thought Conor, remembering the night beneath the Brooklyn Bridge when the Pratolini brothers had stamped on the small of his back and almost paralyzed him for life.

*   *   *

33

Salvatore went out to deal with the Brinks-Mat delivery and Conor made a call home. It took Lacey over a minute to answer.

'I'm sorry, my darling,' she said. 'I was right up on top of the stepladder, painting the ceiling.'

'Well, I'm glad that one of us doesn't mind climbing stepladders, otherwise our walls would only be painted halfway up.'

'You know, you should talk to Bryan about your vertigo. Do you know that he counseled the Great Bardini once, when he lost his nerve on the high wire?'

'I must be the only person I know who needs a lifestyle counselor to remodel his home.'

'Oh, no, you're not. Jennie Feinstein does Tantric meditation before she chooses her cushion covers.'

'I thought Tantric meditation was all about sex.'

'It is. And you should see her cushions.'

Conor pried opened the lid of his lunchbox and looked at his apple. He was starting to feel hungry again. Lacey said, 'How did you get on in court?'

He told her. She listened, but all she said was, 'That woman, I don't know.' She didn't give him any sympathy about Fay. She knew that it hurt too much, like poking a loose filling.

He said, 'Listen, I'll see you at six. I thought we could eat out tonight, seeing as you've been painting all day.'

'No, let's stay in. I'm cooking French tonight.'

'Don't tell me. Rare *entrecôte* steak with potatoes baked in cream, and rum baba for dessert?'

'Unh-hunh. Chard stalks in cheese sauce, followed by organic rhubarb yogurt.'

34

'You're going to kill me, with all this healthy food.'

He was still talking when Salvatore reappeared in his office doorway. Salvatore's eyes were wide and his face looked sweaty and colorless and tight, like a shiny gray balloon.

'Sal?' said Conor.

'Um, put down the phone, sir,' said Salvatore, clearing his throat.

'What? What are you talking about?'

'Please put down the phone, sir. Don't say one more word.'

Conor hesitated. He could hear Lacey saying, *'Hello? Conor? Conor, what's happening?'* He could sense that something was badly wrong. He covered the mouthpiece with his hand and slowly returned the telephone to its cradle. Then he sat back, keeping both hands on the desk.

Salvatore stepped into the office. Right behind him came a wide-shouldered black man in a khaki Brinks-Mat uniform that barely buttoned up over his chest. He reminded Conor of Mike Tyson, but with tinier eyes and inkier skin and an ethnic haircut with swirly patterns shaved into the sides. He was holding a huge nickel-plated .44 automatic up to the back of Salvatore's head. He pushed Salvatore across to the chair in front of the TV monitor screens and said in a thick, slow, gravelly voice, 'Sit down. Don't move. Don't say jack shit.'

4

Salvatore awkwardly sat down. The black man prodded his forehead with the barrel of his gun. 'You want to stay alive, you stay right where you are. And you—' he said, turning to Conor, 'you don't get cute with me, pushing no alarm button or nothing. We hear one siren outside, we see one single cop, this guy's brain's going to be wallpaper.'

'We?' said Conor.

'Me and my associate. He's on his way right now.' The black man's forehead was studded with pearls of sweat and he was in a state of strongly suppressed panic, like an actor with stage fright.

'You got a name?' Conor asked him. 'My name's Conor, and this is Sal.' First and immediate rule of survival in a hostage situation: personalize yourself, make it more difficult for your captor to shoot you because he knows who you are.

The black man said, 'You want my name? You're putting me on. You want my address and my telephone number, too?'

Conor said, 'I hope you realize that the chances of your getting away with this are just about zilch.

Look over there. You're on *Candid Camera*.'

'We know what we're doing, man. You look after the security and we'll take care of the robbery. First thing you can do is give me your gun. Take it out ultra careful with two fingers and lay it on the floor.'

Conor did as he was told. His heart rate had quickened, but he was trying to keep calm. He kept a pump-action shotgun taped to the underside of his desk, and three more revolvers in various hiding places around the office. It was a precaution he had always taken, ever since the days of the Forty-Ninth Street Golf Club. His grandfather had always told him: they don't give out medals for inferior firepower.

The black man kicked Conor's gun out of reach.

'Now you going to do something, man. You going to call the other guy, the guy you need to open the strongroom door. You going to sound *cool*, man. You going to sound so laid back. You going to say, come down here, man, there's some rich old bitch who wants to check out her jewels.'

Conor said, 'I have to warn you, this is very badly advised. If you steal any one of those safety-deposit boxes, you're going to have people after you who can afford five million dollars just to have you tracked down, and their property returned, and your body minced up and fed to every pig in Iowa.'

'Just do what you're fucking told,' said the black man, and screwed the muzzle of the pistol into Salvatore's ear.

Conor picked up the phone and punched out Darrell's number. He had to wait nearly thirty seconds before an irritable Darrell picked up. 'Yes?

What? I'm in the middle of a display meeting here.'

'Darrell, Mrs Hammerlich just came in. She needs access to the strongroom.'

'Jesus on a bicycle, Conor. Didn't she make an appointment?'

'I don't think the wife of the owner of the third largest petroleum refiner in the United States needs an appointment, do you?'

'All right, all right. Give me a couple of minutes, will you?'

'It has to be *now*, Darrell.'

There was a moment's pause. The black man cocked back the hammer of his automatic and gave Conor a look which said: *Don't push me to do this, because I just might.*

Darrell said, 'O-*kay*, then, if old Ma Hammerlich is making a song and dance about it.'

'Song and dance? Believe me, Darrell, *Showboat* has nothing on this.'

Conor put down the phone. 'He's coming. Give him a couple of minutes to get down here.'

'I'm warning you, man. If he don't come, and if he don't come quick . . . your deputy here is going to be losing his head.'

The door swung open again and a thin, bespectacled white man came in, wearing a matching Brinks-Mat uniform. He had cropped blond hair and oddly colorless eyes and his face could have been seraphic if it hadn't been so scarred and knocked about. A shop-soiled Angel Gabriel. He was carrying an Uzi sub-machine pistol close to his chest.

'Good job, Ray,' he told the black man cheerfully. 'How long before the lardass gets here?' He had a whispery, cigarette-parched voice, with a strong north-eastern accent. Boston, or Lynn, or even Marblehead.

'Give him time,' Conor volunteered. 'He's coming down from the fifth floor, and he's not exactly a natural athlete.'

The Angel Gabriel peered at him, and then a grin cracked across his face. 'You're the guy, right? You're the guy who bust all those cops. I ought to shake your hand.'

The black man Ray looked at his watch and then he looked at Conor. 'Two minutes, you got it? That's all I'm going to give him.'

'Hey – don't tell me your former colleagues in the police department haven't put a price on your ass,' said the Angel Gabriel, circling the office. 'What do you reckon they'd pay me if I shot you now?'

'You won't shoot me now because you'd never get into the strongroom.'

The Angel Gabriel sat on the edge of Conor's desk and jabbed the muzzle of his Uzi into Conor's breastbone. His breath smelled of tobacco and something strange, like licorice root. The only indications that he was stressed were his widely dilated pupils and his quick, shallow breathing. 'I have a little list here,' he said, reaching left-handed into the breast pocket of his uniform and producing a folded sheet of paper. 'And I'll tell you what we're going to do. As soon as the lardass shows, we're going to open up the strongroom. Then we're going to remove all of the safe deposit boxes on my little list, and we're going to wheel them out to our truck. After that we're going to drive away, and we're going to be

39

taking your deputy with us. If we don't get clear away, your deputy is going to be dead meat. And don't try complaining to Brinks-Mat. This particular collection is what you might call unauthorized.'

Conor looked him straight in the eye. 'Don't sweat it. You won't catch me trying to stop you.'

'Oh, really? I thought you were supposed to be the chief security officer around here.'

'I am. But what do I care if some rich old widow loses a million or two? Not worth getting killed for.'

'That doesn't sound at all like the man who broke the Forty-Ninth Street Golf Club.'

'There's a subtle difference, my friend. The man who broke the Forty-Ninth Street Golf Club was a cop. Being a cop, that's a *calling*. Being a security officer, that's a *job*.'

'Well, I guess. But some people take their jobs more seriously than others, don't they? How seriously do you take *your* job, Mr O'Neil?'

The black man Ray checked his watch yet again. He was standing directly in front of Conor's desk, and Conor had thought of discharging his shotgun right into his knees. But the chances of missing were too high, and Ray still had his automatic an inch away from Salvatore's ear. Apart from that, Conor would never be able to reach the .22 in the drawer beneath the TV monitor screens before Gabriel cut him to bits with his Uzi. Six hundred rounds a minute.

The door opened and Darrell came bustling in, looking annoyed.

'What the hell's going on here, Conor? Where's Mrs Hammerlich?'

40

Gabriel stood up and lifted his Uzi so that Darrell could see it clearly. 'Mrs Hammerlich couldn't make it so we came in her place. My friend and me would like to take a look inside your strongroom, if you don't mind. Just to make sure that Mrs Hammerlich's property is locked up good and tight, where no unscrupulous thieves can get at it.'

'Conor, what's going on here?' said Darrell, in disbelief. 'Is this a *robbery*?'

Conor nodded. 'I'm sorry, Darrell. I guess it has all the makings.'

'Well, what – well, what—'

'I can't do anything,' said Conor. 'Neither can you. We'll just have to co-operate, that's all.'

'But what – the strongroom! The stuff we've got in there! Uncle Newt's going to—! Bearer bonds! Uncut diamonds!'

'Darrell . . . one human life is worth any amount of bearer bonds or uncut diamonds. And why don't you give these guys a shopping list, while you're at it?'

'But for Christ's sake, Conor, what's it going to do to the business? Who's going to leave any of their property here if we allow these, these, these—'

'Don't say it,' said the Angel Gabriel. 'You might annoy me and I might have to blow your head off, too. Now move that oversized butt and let's have that strongroom opened up.'

'Conor?' Darrell appealed. But Conor grimly shook his head. It took perfect timing to deal with a hostage situation, and this wasn't the time. He turned to the Angel Gabriel and said, 'I have to get the strongroom keys out of the wall-safe.'

41

'Go ahead. But let me see where your hands are; and take it real, real easy.'

The Angel Gabriel backed away from Conor's desk. He crossed the office and without hesitation he took down the Norman Rockwell print and propped it against the wall. Conor approached the safe and punched out his four-digit number immediately but Darrell stayed where he was, his arms folded, his lower lip sticking out, looking belligerent.

'Come on, lardass,' said the Angel Gabriel. 'You only have sixty seconds and then the safe locks itself for good.'

'And then what will you do? Kill me?'

'You've got it in one. Now come over here and finish up the goddamn code.'

Darrell stayed defiant. But Conor said, 'Darrell . . . believe me, I have experience of situations like this. If we don't open this safe, they're going to shoot us.'

'That's right, Darrell,' the Angel Gabriel added. He pulled back the Uzi's cocking-handle and pointed the muzzle directly at Darrell's face. 'Just think about it. That stuff in the strongroom, it's only stuff, and it's not even *your* stuff. Do you really want to *die* for it?'

Darrell looked at Conor, and Conor gave him an encouraging nod. With only nine seconds to spare he stepped up to the safe and punched out the remaining numbers. Then he stepped back again and said, 'Uncle Newt's going to have me gelded for this. I mean *gelded*.'

Conor opened the safe. He took one key and passed the other to Darrell. He didn't say anything but he gave Darrell a long, serious look which warned him not to treat these men lightly. He didn't think they were sudden, psychopathic killers; but you never knew what could happen under extreme tension.

'Come on, move,' the Angel Gabriel snapped.

Ray stayed in the office with Salvatore. Conor and Darrell accompanied the Angel Gabriel down to the strongroom door. The closed-circuit television camera turned to watch them as Conor punched out his numbers. The Angel Gabriel must have noticed it but he didn't make any attempt to hide his face. Darrell tapped his numbers as slowly as he could, and he hesitated before he turned his key. 'Come on, lardass,' the Angel Gabriel urged him. 'I don't have the rest of my natural life to do this.'

'Will you please stop calling me that? I had enough of that at school.'

The strongroom door swung open. They stepped inside and their footsteps echoed. 'Wheel that trolley over here,' the Angel Gabriel ordered. 'Yes, you, lardass.'

Darrell brought over the small green trolley which they used for pushing safety deposit boxes around. 'OK,' said the Angel Gabriel. 'I want you to stack the following number boxes onto the trolley. And do it quick.'

He rapidly read out a list of fifteen numbers. Conor and Darrell located the boxes, pulled them out, and loaded them onto the trolley. Conor hadn't been working at Spurr's long enough to know the owner of every box, but there was one that he remembered from his very first week. Box number

334, which had been visited by Davina Gambit, who was in the middle of an acrimonious divorce from her husband Jack Gambit, the property billionaire. The box was very light, which probably meant that it contained letters, or bonds. In fact all the boxes were very light. The Angel Gabriel probably knew exactly what he was looking for.

When they were finished, Darrell pushed the trolley out of the strongroom. It had one squeaky wheel. Conor closed the strongroom door behind them and relocked it. 'Now it's out to the truck, gents, and we'll be saying *muchas gracias* and *adiós*.'

Conor thought: heart rate's up. Adrenalin's beginning to surge. I don't have very much longer to stop them from getting away. At the same time, I daren't risk anybody's life.

They reached his office. Ray was still standing there with his automatic pressed against Salvatore's ear.

'You ready?' he asked, jumpily.

The Angel Gabriel laid his hand on Conor's shoulder with unexpected intimacy. 'What the plan is now, we walk out through the store and you stay close to make sure that everything goes right. When we leave the store, you come back here to your office and you sit here for one hour exactly and you don't call nobody, not even your proctologist. When we're free and clear, I'll call you; and tell you where you can pick up your deputy safe and well.

'But don't try to be smart. We don't want Salvatore to end up as *menudencias*, do we?' *Menudencias* was Spanish for variety meats.

Darrell wheezed, 'My uncle's going to have your

44

nuts, you know that. You know how much money he's got? You're going to be *eunuchs* after this!' Conor was amazed at his nerve.

The Angel Gabriel patted Darrell's fiery cheek. '*Che sarà sarà*, lardass. Now let's get going.'

Conor opened the security door, and stepped out first. Darrell followed him, pushing the trolley. The Angel Gabriel came next, his Uzi loosely concealed inside his unbuttoned tunic. Then came Salvatore and Ray.

'Come on,' said the Angel Gabriel.

They began to walk between the shining displays of Nina Ricci and Guerlain. The air was chilly but heady with perfume, and in the background the store's music system played a loud and glutinous version of 'Moon River'.

'Keep going,' said the Angel Gabriel. 'Not too fast.'

They were passing the Giorgio counter when Doris Fugazy flapped out, 'Chief O'Neil! Chief O'Neil!'

'Who the fuck's this witch?' hissed the Angel Gabriel.

'Chief O'Neil, what I was going to tell you was, we're holding a charity cookout Sunday afternoon and I was so hoping that you and Mrs O'Neil would care to come along – well, I'm *so* sorry, not Mrs O'Neil but your lovely significant other. It's going to be so much fun, I'm sure you'll enjoy yourselves, both of you.'

'Get rid of her. For Christ's sake get rid of her *now*.'

'Doris . . .' said Conor. 'I'm kind of tied up right

45

now. Let me talk to you about it later.'

'You *will* do your best to come, won't you? It's all in aid of the Gulf War Veterans' Fund and the children's playgroup.'

'*Get rid of her, will you?*'

'Doris . . . this is kind of a difficult time. These guys have to get these safety deposit boxes out to their armored truck. You know, security stuff.'

'Oh, I'm sorry. But I thought if I told you now it would give you and Mrs O'Neil – well, I could bite off my tongue, *not* Mrs O'Neil but—'

A red light flashed and reflected off the revolving doors. Conor saw it and the Angel Gabriel must have seen it too, because he said, 'What? What was that?'

Another red light flashed, and then another.

'Shit!' said the Angel Gabriel. 'There's cops outside!'

Conor thought: please God, no. But then he thought of the way in which he had put the phone down on Lacey, and what Lacey would have done next. Call the cops, of course. She was a trained TV reporter. It would have been her first instinct.

He turned to the Angel Gabriel and said, 'It's nothing, it's probably nothing. Just a passing ambulance. For God's sake, whatever you do, for your own sake, don't lose your cool.'

'Don't lose my cool?' the Angel Gabriel raged. 'Don't lose my fucking cool? What else am I supposed to do?'

Another red light flashed and this time Conor knew for sure that the store was surrounded.

'You see that?' said the Angel Gabriel. 'That was no passing ambulance.'

46

Conor said, '*Don't lose your cool!* You want to survive this, put your guns on the floor and hold up your hands.'

'Are you crazy? *What?* Are you totally crazy?'

'I'm not just talking about you!' Conor retorted. 'There are innocent people here!'

The Angel Gabriel pulled open his tunic and brandished his Uzi. 'Who's innocent? Who's innocent? I don't see anybody innocent!' Doris gasped and put up her hands. Another woman screamed as if she'd been scalded. The Angel Gabriel pointed the gun within a quivering inch of Conor's nose and said, 'We're walking out. You understand me? That's all we're doing. We're walking out. You can't stop me. The police can't stop me. Even God can't stop me.'

But at that moment, everything began to unravel. Conor could see what was going to happen but he was powerless to stop it.

Two SWAT officers in combat fatigues came jogging out from behind the stainless-steel escalator bank. Shoppers were still gliding up the stairs like ducks in a shooting gallery. One of the cops yelled '*Police! Freeze! Drop your weapons!*' although he could hardly make himself heard over the muzak.

Conor yelled, '*Everybody down! Get down on the floor!*'

Most of the shoppers couldn't understand what was happening, and continued to mill around the perfume counters in bewilderment.

Four or five more cops burst in through the store's main entrance. They were all wearing flak jackets and carrying M-16 assault rifles. Christ, thought Conor, what a way to deal with an armed robbery in a crowded Fifth Avenue store. He pulled his billfold out of his pocket and held it up, even though he didn't have a badge in it any more. 'Police officer! Don't shoot!'

'*Hit the floor!*' a police sergeant shouted at him.

But Conor called back, 'Don't shoot! Let these guys get out of here, OK? Let them get out!'

'*I said hit the fucking floor!*' the sergeant screamed, almost apoplectic. Conor recognized him: a big-bellied, thick-necked bully of an officer called Wexler, from the 21st Precinct.

'Let them out of here!' Conor insisted. 'Let them get clear!'

Sergeant Wexler squinted at him in disbelief. 'Captain O'Neil? I might have fucking known.'

'Use your head, Wexler. You can't have a firefight in here. Take it outside.'

'Oh, I see. You want me to walk out there in front of ten different TV stations and tell them that me and my SWAT team couldn't arrest two sad little store thieves?'

At that moment the Angel Gabriel glided right up behind Conor and clasped him tightly, almost amorously, around the waist. He pressed the Uzi's muzzle to the side of Conor's head and whispered in his ear, 'Move. I said *move*. If you don't get us out of here, I swear to God, I'll kill you.'

'You're not going to get away with this one,' Conor told him. 'These guys want nothing more than to see me caught in the crossfire.'

'Move,' the Angel Gabriel urged him. 'Come on, move.'

Conor said, 'Are you out of your mind? One

48

step and these cops are going to drop us.'

'*Move*, I said!' Gabriel insisted, and pushed him forward.

'Stay where you are!' Sergeant Wexler shouted. 'Stay where you are and lay your weapons down on the floor! This is your last warning!'

Conor tried to stop but the Angel Gabriel kept shoving him forward.

'Ray, come here,' the Angel Gabriel called to the black man, without turning around. 'Stay real close, Ray. And you, lardass, don't you stop pushing that trolley. That's my pension in there. That's my house in Acapulco.'

'You're out of your mind,' Conor told him.

'Test of strength,' said the Angel Gabriel, holding him so close that Conor could feel his breath on the back of his neck. 'Battle of wills!'

'That's far enough!' shouted Sergeant Wexler. 'You come one step closer and we'll open fire.'

They had reached the counter where Doris Fugazy was crouched. She looked up at Conor with her blotchy mascara and her bright red lipstick and she was shivering like a whippet. All around the perfume department, women were lying on the floor or crouching down behind pillars. Two or three of them were weeping, and one of them was babbling hysterically to her babysitter on her mobile phone. 'If anything happens to me, make sure that she gets her shots.'

Very slowly, the Angel Gabriel lifted his Uzi and pushed the muzzle under Conor's chin. The machine-gun was so close that Conor could smell the oil on it. 'If you bastards open fire,' Gabriel called out to Sergeant Wexler, 'you're going to see the top of this guy's head fly off.'

'Oh, really?' said Sergeant Wexler, as if he couldn't wait. He kept his weapon aimed unerringly at Conor's head.

'Hold it!' called Conor. 'Just give me a couple of minutes, will you, and we can work this out!'

'No – no,' said the Angel Gabriel. 'I'm not doing any deals.'

'So what *are* you going to do? Right now they're itching to off the both of us.'

The Angel Gabriel hesitated. He whistled tunelessly under his breath for a moment or two. Then, without warning, he shoved Conor with his left hand, right between the shoulder-blades. Conor staggered to one side, and struck his hip against the Chanel counter.

There was a belligerent clatter as the police lifted and aimed their assault rifles but Gabriel ducked to one side and snatched at Doris Fugazy's arm. She gasped, and tried to twist away, but he swung her around and lifted her right up onto her feet. He clutched her tight in front of him, his left arm around her throat.

Conor, off balance, made a wild attempt to snatch the Angel Gabriel's gun, but the Angel Gabriel backed away as smartly as a dance instructor. 'I don't want to kill you, man. I admire what you did. I like you. But I'll kill you if I have to. I'll kill anybody if I have to.'

Conor lifted both hands. 'OK – OK. Stay cool. Just don't hurt her, all right?'

'Put down your guns!' Sergeant Wexler shouted at

the Angel Gabriel. 'You're not going anyplace!'

'You don't think so? I'm prepared to shoot this lady's face off right in front of you. You want to see that happen? You want to be responsible for that? You want to explain on TV news tonight why you allowed this lady to die?'

The Angel Gabriel was so hyped up that he hadn't noticed that the escalators had stopped. But Conor suddenly realized that they were silent and when he turned around he saw why. Two police snipers were kneeling on the metal treads, just below ceiling level. The narrow red laser beams from their high-powered rifles were already criss-crossing the perfume department floor.

His hands still raised, Conor stepped back three or four paces, well away from their line of fire. He didn't want to give the snipers any excuses. 'How about some calm here?' he suggested. 'We can resolve this situation without anybody having to get hurt.'

'Sorry, O'Neil,' said Sergeant Wexler. 'You should know the tactical procedure better than anybody. *At all costs prevent a perpetrator from taking a hostage away from the scene of the alleged offense.*'

'I wrote that goddamned protocol and you know it.'

'Well, let's see how it works in practice, shall we?'

There was a glowing red spot of light hovering in the center of the Angel Gabriel's forehead, like an Indian ruby. Conor said, very quietly, 'They're going to kill you,' but the Angel Gabriel didn't reply, and pressed the muzzle of his Uzi even harder against Doris's head.

51

'Oh, God,' sobbed Doris. Instantly – as if Doris's words were the signal that they had been waiting for – the SWAT team fired, and there was a sharp crackle of high-powered rifle fire.

Conor dived behind the Chanel counter. Darrell dropped almost on top of him, wheezing with fright. The perfume department echoed with wails and cries.

Ray ducked his head. A high-velocity 7.62 mm bullet hit Salvatore just behind the left ear and burst out of his right cheek. He flung up one arm in what looked like a ridiculous ballet posture, and threw himself to the floor. Ray was finely spattered in blood and he stared down at his tunic, shocked. 'Shit, man.' Another rifle-bullet pinged off the marble pillar close beside him. He stumbled, turned and fired two heavy-caliber shots up toward the escalator. The bangs were ear-splitting.

'That's it!' shouted Sergeant Wexler. 'Let's go, let's go, let's go!'

'Stay back!' The Angel Gabriel dropped to his knees, dragging Doris down with him. He lifted his Uzi over his head and fired a five-second burst into the ceiling. The chandelier shattered and sparkling glass and plaster came down like a blizzard. Conor shouted, *'Drop it! Throw it down!'* but the Angel Gabriel grabbed Doris even more tightly around the neck and screamed out at Darrell, 'We're going for it! We're going for it! Come on!'

Darrell was crouched next to Conor with his eyes shut and his hands over his ears. The Angel Gabriel screamed at him again. *'Lardass! We're going for it! Move!'*

52

Furiously Darrell shook his head. '*Lardass!*' the Angel Gabriel insisted. '*Can you hear me, lardass! We're going for it!*'

Three or four more rifle shots echoed across the perfume department. Counters shattered, mirrors burst apart, display bottles of perfume exploded. A huge Lalique statue of a woman combing her hair blew up like a bomb, and scattered fragments everywhere.

'Hold fire!' yelled Conor. 'For God's sake, this is insane!'

Ray hunkered down next to them, still panting and still sweating. 'Holy shit, man, this is a massacre!'

Conor ducked between the counters. He came right up to the Angel Gabriel and said, 'Give this up! In the name of the Lord thy God, give up!'

'Come on, man,' said Ray. 'We don't have any goddamned choice!'

Doris mewled in terror and kicked her feet. The Angel Gabriel jabbed the Uzi's muzzle even harder into the side of her head and whispered, 'I'll kill her. I swear on the Holy Bible that I'll kill her.'

Ray was babbling, 'Save my ass, Jesus whatever you do, save my ass Virgin Mary, don't let me die here today.' Abruptly he stopped babbling and fell forward, his arm flopping across Conor's legs. As Conor turned, blood sprayed all over the side of the counter. Half of Ray's head was missing and a piece of skull like a coconut shell was rocking backward and forward on the floor.

The Angel Gabriel was screaming something at Sergeant Wexler. While his attention was distracted,

53

Conor pried open Ray's bloodied fingers and took his .44. He unfastened the bottom two buttons of his uniform shirt and shoved the gun into his belt. He paused for a moment to catch his breath. Then he shouted, 'Sergeant Wexler! Do you hear me, Sergeant Wexler?'

'I hear you.'

'I'm coming out! Do you hear me? Our friend here wants to make a deal.'

Gabriel hissed, '*Deal?* What the fuck are you talking about, *deal?* I'm not making any goddamned deal. Either they let me out of here, or the woman gets it. That's all.'

But Conor pressed his finger to his lips. 'Trust me, OK? I want to get you out of here as much as you want to leave.'

He cautiously stood up, with his hands half raised. 'Come on, then,' said Wexler, beckoning him forward.

Conor made his way between the counters. Sergeant Wexler holstered his gun as he approached and said, 'Get this straight. I'm not going to be making any concessions here, O'Neil.'

'You don't have to. I just want to take this firefight out of the store before any more civilians get hurt.'

'So what's the proposition?'

Conor leaned forward as if he were going to say something quietly; and Sergeant Wexler leaned forward too. Without warning, Conor seized him around the neck and dragged Ray's gun out of his waistband. He jammed the muzzle into Wexler's love-handles. The surrounding officers swung their rifles around and screamed out hysterically, '*Drop it!*'

but Conor kept so close behind Sergeant Wexler that none of them dared to shoot.

'What the hell do you think you're doing, O'Neil?' Wexler raged, in a strangled voice. 'I'll have your guts for this!'

'I'll be having your guts first. Tell your guys to back off.'

'The hell I will. You won't shoot me and you know it.'

'Try me. When did you ever know me to make a threat and not carry it out? I mean, *ever*?'

Sweat was glistening between the prickly folds of Sergeant Wexler's neck. He was panting as if he had just run up and down a fire escape.

'OK,' he said. 'But I swear on my mother's life that you're not going to get away with this.' He took a deep breath, and then ordered, 'Everybody lower your weapons and hold fire. Miskowtec – that means you, too!'

The officers reluctantly did what they were told. Conor recognized some of them – Kosherick, Caploe, Farbar and Murray. They used to think that he was some kind of god. Now they were looking at him all pouchy-mouthed as if they were summoning up enough saliva to spit on him.

Conor turned to the Angel Gabriel. 'Let's go! And make it quick!'

The Angel Gabriel dragged Doris onto her feet. He said to Darrell, 'You too, lardass. And the boxes, for Christ's sake! Don't leave the boxes behind!'

Conor waited until the Angel Gabriel and Doris and Darrell were assembled all around him. Then he started to edge his way toward the doors. He held

Sergeant Wexler so close that he could smell his Gillette deodorant.

They pushed their way through the swing doors and emerged into the heat and the glare of Fifth Avenue. The street had been cordoned off for two blocks in both directions, and there were squad cars and ambulances and TV trucks everywhere. Bright lights shone in their eyes and cables snaked across the sidewalk.

'Hold your fire!' shouted Sergeant Wexler. 'Everything's OK! Everything's under control!'

'*Drop your weapons!*' bellowed a distorted voice through a loud-hailer. Conor recognized it immediately, and thought: it just *had* to be, didn't it? Lieutenant Drew Slyman, suspected of being one of the three leading hit men of the Forty-Ninth Street Golf Club – the 'umpires', they called themselves. Lieutenant Slyman had been implicated in seven Golf Club executions, but Conor had never been able to gather enough evidence to bring him to court.

'*Drop your weapons!*' Lieutenant Slyman repeated. '*Hit the sidewalk! Now!*'

Darrell whimpered in fright, but Conor said, 'Ignore them. Just keep going.'

The Brinks-Mat truck was still parked at the curb, as well as a white Camaro. Conor could see that the police had deflated the Camaro's tires, presumably thinking that it was the getaway vehicle, but they hadn't disabled the security truck.

'*This is your last warning!*' said Lieutenant Slyman. But Conor kept on shuffling across the sidewalk until he reached the truck. The Angel Gabriel backed up to it, too, and let go of Doris for long enough to open

56

the side door. Doris looked wide-eyed at Conor as if she were thinking of making a run for it, but Conor frowned at her and shook his head and mouthed, '*Don't.*'

Puffing and sweating, Darrell loaded the safety deposit boxes into the truck. Then the Angel Gabriel opened the cab door and told him to get in.

'Me? What for?' Darrell protested.

'You're driving, that's what for.'

'But I can't!'

'Ray was going to drive. But Ray just bought the farm. Now, *you're* driving. Got it?'

Darrell climbed up into the cab and sat round-shouldered and miserable behind the wheel. Before the Angel Gabriel climbed in, he took two or three steps forward and yelled out, 'Listen up! If I see one police vehicle following us – if I see one vehicle that I even *think* is a police vehicle – if I see a police motorcycle or a helicopter – if I see a goddamned *horse* – the woman gets it in the head!'

He waited to make sure that his warning had sunk in. Then he climbed up into the cab, pulling Doris after him, hiking up her skirt to show her stocking top and dropping one of her shoes.

'If you hurt those people . . .' Conor cautioned him.

'You're a civilized man, Chief O'Neil,' said the Angel Gabriel, and actually grinned. 'No wonder you had to quit the police department.' Just before he slid the door shut, Conor heard him say to Darrell, 'Cut across to Eighth Avenue. Then head uptown. *Move!*'

Darrell started the engine. Several police officers

stood up from behind their cars and took aim with their rifles, but Lieutenant Slyman shouted, '*Hold fire! Hold fire!*' Conor could guess why: the Brinks-Mat truck was heavily armored and there was far too high a risk of ricochets. It pulled away and started to head downtown, leaving a black cloud of diesel exhaust.

'Satisfied, you piece of shit?' spat Sergeant Wexler.

5

Car doors slammed like a cannon volley as the police prepared to set off in hot pursuit, but Lieutenant Slyman called out, '*Hold it, hold it, hold it!*' and two senior officers stepped out into the street and waved at the squad cars to stay where they were. One siren gave a single mournful whoop and died away. Engines were switched off and doors were opened again. Above their heads, a police helicopter flackered around and around in deafening, frustrated circles.

'You're just going to let him go?' one officer was shouting.

'That's the decision. We'll keep track of him, OK?'

Conor kept his elbow around Sergeant Wexler's throat and the .44 pressed deep into his gut. 'You're choking me, you bastard,' Sergeant Wexler told him.

'Sorry, sergeant. It's all in a good cause.'

Conor quickly looked around. Several police officers were still pointing their guns at him, but shoppers started to pour out of Spurr's front entrance, some of them crowing and sobbing in hysteria. There was a tidal swirl of confusion. Police officers and press and paramedics started to mill around the sidewalk, and several people broke through the cordon at the end of the block.

Lieutenant Slyman ordered, '*Stay back! Everybody stay back! We still have a situation here!*'

Conor was trying to find a car: any car, so long as it wasn't a police vehicle. All he could see was a taxi at the intersection with West 48th Street and a black Lincoln limousine on the corner of East 47th, just behind the police cordon. The taxi had been abandoned and the driver had probably taken the keys; but the Lincoln's chauffeur was still sitting behind the wheel. Conor could see the sun shining off the peak of his cap.

'Come on,' Conor told Sergeant Wexler, 'let's get the hell out of here, on the double!'

Three or four police officers were already beginning to advance toward them, their weapons raised, but they were obviously still doubtful about what exactly was happening. Conor jostled Sergeant Wexler across the street, in between the tangle of parked squad cars. One of the police officers shouted, 'Hey! Stop them! Those two! Stop them!' but there was so much confusion that none of the cops around the cars really understood what was going on, particularly since Sergeant Wexler was in uniform and Conor's face was so familiar.

Conor dragged Sergeant Wexler under the police tape and around the front of the Lincoln limousine. The chauffeur was talking on his mobile phone and didn't see them at first. Conor pulled at the doorhandle but it was locked. The chauffeur looked up, startled, and Conor pointed the .44 at him.

'Open the goddamned door! Now!'

White-faced, the chauffeur sprang the central locking. Conor opened the door and said, 'Out!'

'What?'

Conor didn't have any time for discussion. He pushed Sergeant Wexler away and dragged the chauffeur out of his seat.

'Don't kill me, sir,' the chauffeur begged him. He was pink-faced, only in his twenties. 'My wife just had twins.'

'You want to stay alive, keep out of the way,' Conor warned him, climbing into the white leather driver's seat. 'There's going to be some strays flying.'

Sergeant Wexler turned back to his colleagues and hoarsely screamed, 'O'Neil's here! He's here! He's trying to make a break for it!'

He made a girlish and ineffectual effort to throw himself onto the Lincoln's hood, but Conor jammed his foot on the gas and the huge black limousine hurtled out of East 47th with its tires shrieking. The police officers had just reached the intersection and they crouched down and leveled their guns at him. He heard three distinct shots and one of the rear windows cracked. But then he was bouncing across Fifth Avenue, and speeding along West 47th, and all that he could see of Sergeant Wexler and his men were two puffs of smoke in his rear-view mirror and a stirred-up ants' nest of uniforms.

He sped westward across Sixth Avenue, Seventh Avenue and Broadway, flashing his lights and blaring his horn. At the intersection with Eighth Avenue he looked wildly left and right. At first he could see nothing but taxis and private cars and a huge tractor-trailer with a huge steaming bowl of chicken soup painted on the side, Momma Somekh's Finest. The traffic signals changed to green and a taxi driver behind him leaned on his horn, urging him to move, but he stayed where he was, even when another driver pulled up behind the taxi and started hooting at him, too.

The Lincoln's air conditioning was set to Nome, Alaska, and the sweat on the back of his shirt started to chill.

The signals changed back to red. At that moment the Brinks-Mat truck appeared two blocks to his left, turning out of West 45th Street and heading uptown. As it passed him, Conor could see the Angel Gabriel through the green armored glass, pale and intent; and Doris, too. The lights were still red, but he jammed his foot on the gas and the huge Lincoln fishtailed into Eighth Avenue in a cloud of blue tire smoke.

He swerved to avoid a Pony Express motorcycle messenger and bumped against a taxi, ripping off his nearside mirror. Horns blared all around him in a furious fanfare. With less than six inches to spare, he passed an elderly blue Datsun filled with nuns. Angrily they tooted their weak little hooter at him and shook their fists. 'Forgive me my trespasses, sisters,' he said, under his breath. He caught up with the Brinks-Mat truck and tucked the Lincoln in behind it, only inches away from its rear fender.

As it slowed up for Columbus Circle, on the south-west corner of Central Park, he nudged the Lincoln's front bumper into the back of it. Not too hard – he didn't want to damage the limousine too badly, but enough to give the Angel Gabriel an unpleasant jolt. He swerved to the left so that his car couldn't be seen in Gabriel's side mirror and then collided with the Brinks-Mat truck a second time.

Instantly, the Brinks-Mat truck accelerated and took a sharp right turn, almost tilting onto its side. It started to speed eastward on Central Park South, weaving in and out of the traffic and blasting its horn. Conor stamped his foot on the gas and went after it. The huge limousine dipped and bounced as he steered it around a mail van, a U-turning taxi and a slow-moving garbage truck. Its tires set up a hallelujah chorus, and Conor was followed all the way along the street by a barrage of angry car horns.

Darrell was having difficulty handling the security truck, especially at this speed. It weighed nearly four and a half tonnes, and its armor plating made it much more top-heavy than a regular truck. He crashed it into the side of a taxi, ripping off the rear fender and crumpling the doors. The taxi slewed away and mounted the pavement, colliding with a fire hydrant. Water fountained into the air and momentarily blurted on the roof of Conor's limousine.

Halfway along Central Park South, Darrell was confronted by a bus and two automobiles driving three abreast. He hovered behind them for a few seconds, swerving from side to side in an attempt to find a way through. But he must have seen in his mirror that Conor was overhauling him fast, because he suddenly rear-ended the middle car and forced it forward, its tires smoking on the blacktop.

The car driver lost control. His vehicle hit the side of the bus and then the car next to him. Pieces of broken plastic rattled against Conor's windshield and he instinctively ducked his head. The Brinks-Mat truck forced the automobile out of its path, and the automobile spun around 180 degrees and hit the car next to it head on. Both of their hoods flew up.

Conor could see that the gap between the bus and the two wrecked cars was scarcely wide enough for him to drive through, but he put his foot down even harder and rocketed toward it. There was a complicated crashing and squeaking as his second side mirror was torn off and the limousine's door panels crunched against the side of the bus. But he forced his way through the gap and used every ounce of the Lincoln's 210 horsepower to catch up with the Brinks-Mat truck as it neared the Grand Army Plaza, the intersection with Fifth Avenue.

As they reached the side entrance of the Plaza hotel, Conor managed to steer the Lincoln up alongside the Brinks-Mat truck so that they were bumping and grating against each other in a spectacular cascade of orange sparks. He twisted the wheel hard over to the left and the two vehicles, locked together, skidded diagonally across Central Park South and mounted the curb. They narrowly missed a horse-drawn carriage, and even above the grinding of metal Conor could hear the passengers scream. Pedestrians scattered as they bounced and jostled their way down the footpath into Central Park, tearing up railings and ripping up shrubs.

Conor's limousine hit a park bench and then a small maple and stopped. The driver's-side airbag burst out and punched him in the face. But the Brinks-Mat truck continued to career along the footpath until it tilted sideways down the grassy slope that led to the Pond. A mother dragged her two small children out of the way just before the truck launched itself off the sidewalk and hit the water in a massive clatter of spray.

Conor kicked open the limousine's door and hobbled down the slope, shouting, 'Police! Clear this area as fast as you can!'

He reached the water's edge. Up on Central Park South sirens were already wailing and red lights were flashing; and the police helicopter that had been hovering over them outside Spurr's suddenly reappeared, swooping low around Bergdorf Goodman.

The passenger door of the Brinks-Mat truck slid open. The Angel Gabriel appeared, holding up his Uzi by the barrel. Conor pointed the .44 at him double-handed and barked, 'Wade over here! Keep that weapon where I can see it! Bring it to the bank, then drop it like it's red hot!'

The Angel Gabriel climbed down from the truck until he was waist deep in water. He began to wade toward the edge of the Pond. Then Doris appeared, looking pale and shaken. Conor's relief was almost overwhelming.

'Doris? Are you OK? He didn't hurt you, did he?'

'I'm fine,' said Doris. 'But young Mr Bussman – he's hit his head. You'd better call for an ambulance.'

The Angel Gabriel heaved himself out of the Pond with water gushing from his pants. He laid the Uzi down on the asphalt and then – without being told to – spread himself face down on the grass. By now eight or nine police officers were running down the slope toward them, including Sergeant Wexler and Lieutenant Slyman. Two of them waded into the water to help Doris; a third went to see what he could do for Darrell.

Holding the butt between finger and thumb, Conor fastidiously laid the .44 on the ground next to the Uzi. Then he lay face down, too. He didn't want to give any trigger-happy officer the slightest excuse to open fire.

The Angel Gabriel looked at him through the blades of sunburned grass. 'You're a persistent bastard, aren't you? I should've known you wouldn't let me get away with it.'

'It's my job. It's only a job, but it's my job.'

Two officers yanked the Angel Gabriel's arms behind his back and handcuffed him. Lieutenant Slyman came up to Conor, casting a shadow across his face. Conor didn't look up but he recognized him by his Cerruti aftershave and his immaculately polished brogues.

'Well, well,' said Lieutenant Slyman. 'You've certainly done some spectacular damage today. How much do you reckon they cost, those stretch limos? Fifty K? More?'

He held out his hand to help Conor onto his feet. Conor ignored it. He stood up and brushed himself down and then said, 'I'll write you out a full statement, lieutenant, if it helps.'

Lieutenant Slyman shook his head in mock admiration. He was a thin man, with a very narrow head.

He had black slashed-back hair and bulbous but hooded eyes. His mouth was red lipped and bow shaped, almost like a woman's.

'Still the knight in shining armor, aren't you, O'Neil? One man struggling alone against the forces of darkness. You'll be even more of a hero after this.'

Sergeant Wexler was scarlet and sweating. 'What's this hero shit? He stuck a gun in my goddamned gut.'

'Oh, get real, sergeant. He apprehended an armed felon without killing any civilians and he recovered the very valuable property he was paid to protect. Nobody's going to make a fuss about a few wrecked vehicles.'

'He took me hostage, for Christ's sake.'

'He took steps to prevent you from making even more of an asshole of yourself than you already are. You were supposed to go in there to contain the situation, not re-enact the Battle of Antietam.'

Two paramedics had managed to lift Darrell out of the Brinks-Mat truck and were wheeling him on a gurney up to their waiting ambulance. He had suffered a deep gash on his forehead and his eyes were closed. His head was held in a bright red neckbrace and his nose and mouth were covered by an oxygen mask.

'How is he?' asked Conor.

One of the paramedics shrugged. 'Hard to tell with a head injury like this. Could be nothing more than a minor concussion. Could be a fracture.'

'Take him to Roosevelt-St Luke's. They have an emergency room there, don't they? His uncle owns most of Spurr's Fifth Avenue. I'll have somebody

call and work out the insurance details later.'

He watched as they wheeled Darrell away. Lieutenant Slyman came up and stood next to him and said, 'Answer me one thing, O'Neil. How could you be sure that guy wasn't going to shoot the hostage?'

'I wasn't. But you get a feeling about people, you know? You can always tell when somebody is really capable of killing, and when they're not. You can *smell* it.'

Lieutenant Slyman laid a long-fingered hand on his shoulder. 'I'll look forward to your report,' he said.

6

Before he went home he visited Salvatore's wife, Maria. The Morales lived in a second-story apartment on 104th Street, up in El Barrio, with window-boxes crammed with geraniums. The windows were wide open because of the heat and he could hear samba music and somebody laughing. He had been half hoping that Maria would have been watching television and would already know what had happened.

He paid off his cab and climbed the steps to the front door. A small boy with a runny nose was sitting against the railings, staging a fight between two identical Batman dolls. Conor recognized him from the photo on Salvatore's desk.

'Who's winning?' asked Conor, hunkering down beside him.

The boy stared at him as if he were a mental defective. 'Batman,' he said.

'I see. Ask a stupid question.'

The boy took pity on him. 'This Batman is good and this Batman is bad. The bad Batman is winning.'

Conor said, 'Maybe I should help the good

Batman, huh?' He reached into his coat pocket with his left hand. He kept it there for a moment, and then he brought it out again and popped his fingers, right in front of the bad Batman's face. A puff of smoke blew out of his fingertips, and Conor said, '*Bang!* Got you!'

The boy stared at him in amazement. 'How did you *do* that? That's so cool! Wait till I tell my dad!'

Conor stood up and scruffed the boy's hair. 'Sure,' he said, sadly.

He pressed the doorbell marked *S. Morales*, then stepped back. Maria Morales leaned out of her living-room window, a dark curly-haired woman in a bright red blouse, with a glittery rhinestone crucifix around her neck.

'Mr O'Neil? What are you doing here?'

He didn't reply. She hesitated for a moment and then she said tensely, '*Wait.*'

She came flying down the stairs with bare feet. He could see her red blouse through the frosted glass. She opened the door and there was a stricken look on her face.

'What's happened? Where's Sal?'

'Maria, I think we'd better go inside.'

'Is he hurt? Tell me! Is he in hospital?'

Conor took hold of both of her hands. He felt as if somebody had wedged an apple down his throat. 'I'm sorry, Maria. There was a robbery. He couldn't have known what hit him.'

Tears started to flow down Maria's cheeks and the boy on the step stopped playing with his Batman figures and stared at his mother in sympathetic awe.

He didn't arrive home until well after ten o'clock. He went straight to the icebox and took out a Bud. He pressed the freezing cold can against his forehead as if he wanted to numb his brain. Lacey stood beside him and didn't say anything.

After a while he opened the can, drank a mouthful, and looked at her.

'I'm so sorry,' she said, touching his cheek.

'He's dead. There's nothing anybody can do to bring him back. I just feel so bad about him. He resented me so much but he was always so polite.'

'How was Maria?'

'How do you think? Her sister came around, and she'll get a lot of help from the neighbors. But God . . . she has four school-age kids to take care of.'

He dragged out one of the yellow-painted kitchen chairs and sat down. The whole apartment smelled of fresh varnish and paint and she was still wearing her blue OshKosh dungarees with the yellow and white splashes on them. Since they had moved up to East 50th Street, five months ago, she had been turning a collection of stuffy, brownish 1950s rooms into a Swedish country cottage – with stenciled walls and bare sanded floorboards and decorative tiles.

'I saw you on TV,' she said. 'What you did . . . that was so brave. It was *amazing*.'

He shook his head. 'No it wasn't. It was arrogant. I should have let Slyman handle it.'

'But you caught the thief, didn't you? You got all of those safety deposit boxes back.'

'Oh sure. And Sal's in the morgue with a ticket on his toe.'

She stood close to him, one hand held out as if she wanted to touch him, but couldn't. She couldn't share what he was feeling, no matter how much she wanted to. He looked up at her and gave her a quick, wry smile.

'I'm sorry,' he said. 'It's just beginning to hit me, is all.'

'You must be exhausted. Do you want anything to eat?'

'Maybe later. It's so damned hot. Is that air conditioning still on the fritz?'

'The air-conditioning guy was supposed to call but his wife went into labor.'

Conor swallowed more beer. 'I thought when I took this job at Spurr's . . . well, I didn't think that I'd be visiting other men's widows any more.'

She sat beside him and ran her fingers through his thick black hair. 'Two gray ones,' she said, plucking them out. 'Maybe you should try something different.'

'Oh, yes? Like what? What else am I good for?'

'You could be a magician. Look at that David Copperfield. He makes a fortune.'

'I can just see two thousand people flocking to Carnegie Hall to see an ex-detective produce hard-cooked eggs out of his ears.'

She took hold of his chin and turned his face sideways until he was looking directly into her cornflower-blue eyes. 'Think about it. It could have been you that was shot today. Then it would have been Salvatore coming to tell me that I was a widow, and I'm not even married yet.'

'You always said you wanted to be a free spirit.'

'If it's a choice between losing you and keeping you, I'd rather not be free at all.'

'Well, that's just as well. We Irishmen expect our women to cook all of our meals and wash our shirts and blacklead our stoves, at the same time as bearing us twenty-three children and holding down a job at Grand Central Station, sweeping out the trains, to keep us in beer money. You won't have the *time* to be free.'

She was silent, stroking his hair. After a while he said, 'What?'

'I don't think this is the right moment to tell you.'

'Tell me, for Christ's sake. Don't keep me in suspense.'

'Well, I had a call today. I *could* get a job.'

He stared at her. 'Meaning?'

'Meaning nothing at all. Except that I *could* get a job.'

'A good job, you're talking about, like you had before? A full-time, well-paid job?'

She nodded. 'Frank Rossi wants me for a new late-night discussion show.'

'So you're going to take it?'

'I don't know. I wanted to discuss it with you first.'

'Why do you have to discuss it with me? It sounds like a wonderful offer. Take it.'

'It's just that if I *did* take it . . . well, you wouldn't have to work at that security job any more. You'd have time to look around for something that wasn't so dangerous.'

'Lisbeth, I used to be a police detective. As far as I'm concerned, this job doesn't even register on the Richter Scale as mildly risky.'

'How can you say that, when you could have been killed today?'

'A 747 could have fallen on my head, whether I was chief of security at Spurr's Fifth Avenue or not.'

'That's ridiculous. I could have been sitting here on my own this evening. And every other evening to come.'

Conor kissed her. 'Do you know what my grandfather used to say? He said that when a woman comes to live with a man, she brings two suitcases with her. One suitcase filled with pretty underwear and another suitcase filled with chains.'

Lacey went to change while Conor finished his beer. He glanced toward the bedroom door and he could see her reflection in the mirror. After his experience with Paula, he still found it extraordinary that he could love a woman so much. But he loved everything about her, right down to the way she scolded him for eating hamburgers, and the way she sang shrill, wildly off-key songs when she was decorating. Bob Seger would have wept to hear her sing 'Hollywood Nights'.

Her real name was Lisbeth Johannsen. She was very tall, with shoulders like a swimmer. She had blond flyaway hair, high Nordic cheekbones and a tip-tilted nose. Conor always said that she had pink satin pillows instead of lips.

She had started her working life as a researcher for NBC, eventually graduating to television reporter and then to early-evening anchor. But her career was mortally wounded by a disastrous two-and-a-half-year relationship with Larry Elgar, a failed producer who drank Stolichnaya for breakfast and regularly beat her. She couldn't turn up to present the six o'clock news with two black eyes and a plaster over the bridge of her nose, so she was forced to quit. Eventually, however, a gay friend called Sebastian Speed found her a part-time job at *American Interior* magazine, producing photographic features on elegant people's elegant homes.

Lacey first met Conor at one of the press conferences after the Forty-Ninth Street Golf Club trial, when she was filling in for NBC's regular trial reporter. They were literally pushed together by jostling and shouting pressmen, and he put his arm around her to protect her. She met him next at a formal cocktail party given by the Mayor at Gracie Mansion. That was after Conor's resignation, and hardly anybody would talk to him; not that he was ever an easy man to talk to. He looked sober and handsome that evening, in a snow-white shirt and a navy-blue suit. She wore a very low-cut dress of blue shot silk, with her hair pinned up. 'You remember me,' she introduced herself. 'You saved me from the baying mob.'

His only response was a smile. But Lacey persevered, even when he was silent, and the next day he called her up and asked her for dinner.

They explored each other that evening, talking for hours. She was fascinated by Conor's mixture of sly flirtatiousness and the unusual logic by which he lived his life. Every time she felt that she had opened up one door in his personality, there was another door, and another. He was romantic and occasionally sentimental, and he could take a joke, but she felt that beyond the very last door there was a man who was capable of making very hard decisions indeed.

For his part, he had never met a woman so outspoken, but he was alarmed by her disregard for her own emotional safety. He didn't know how she could have stayed with a sadistic creep like Larry Elgar for so long. And she still blamed herself for provoking him into hitting her. 'I should have known better. I was strong and he was weak.'

'Not too weak to crack two of your ribs.'

'So what? Physical strength, that doesn't count for anything.'

He fell in love with her because she was driven and unusual and beautiful. But he fell in love with her most of all because she was vulnerable and he wanted to protect her – just like, ultimately, he wanted to protect everybody. *To protect and serve* wasn't just a slogan.

She walked in wearing a plain white linen dress. 'Do you want another beer?'

'No thanks. I could use a shower.'

'You don't mind about the job?'

He shook his head. He *did* mind, but how could he tie her down? He had learned a long time ago that nobody owns anybody else.

While Conor was showering, Lacey sat on the edge of the bathtub and talked to him. He was very muscular, and she liked to watch the foamy water running down his chest. 'So tell me all the grisly details about the hearing.'

'There's not much more to tell you. I can get to see Fay whenever Paula thinks it's convenient.'

'So what does *that* mean? Convenient?'

'In practice it probably means that I'm allowed to act as babysitter whenever she and that oily broker friend of hers decide they want to spend a long weekend upstate.'

'What are you going to do? Can you appeal?'

'I don't know what I'm going to do. I'm beginning to think that it might be better if I turn my back on the whole situation.'

'I don't understand.'

Conor came out of the shower, looking as tired as a marathon swimmer, his chest hair spread in a dark wide fan. 'Meaning I may be prepared to wait to see Fay until she's old enough to come find me for herself.'

Lacey stood up and rubbed him with his towel. 'You've had a bad day. You don't want to make decisions like that, not until you've gotten over it.'

Naked, he held her close, and kissed her, and stroked her hair. She touched the star-shaped scar on his left cheekbone. It was kind of a code. It meant that she knew what hardships he had been through, and that she was prepared to share them.

The doorbell rang. 'I'll get it,' said Lacey. 'It's probably Gina, wanting to borrow some coffee.'

Conor continued to towel himself while Lacey opened the door. In the steamed-up mirror over the washbasin, he didn't look like himself at all. Older, tireder. A man who had lost his mission in life.

The bathroom door was slightly ajar. He heard Lacey saying, 'It's OK . . . I'll get him. Just hold on a minute.'

77

She came into the bathroom. 'It's Drew Slyman, and he's brought two uniforms with him.'

'Slyman? What the hell does he want?'

He wrapped the towel around his waist and went into the living room. Lieutenant Slyman was standing by the window. The pharmacy sign across the street made his face glow green. Two police officers stood beside the couch with matching Village People mustaches and self-satisfied looks on their faces.

'O'Neil . . .' said Lieutenant Slyman. 'Sorry to interrupt your ablutions.' He stepped away from the window, looking around the apartment and rubbing his hands together. 'This isn't quite what you're used to. But maybe, well . . . let's not beat around the bush. Maybe that was your motive.'

'Motive? What are you talking about? My motive for what?'

'Oh, come on, now. You didn't think we were that slow, did you? I don't exactly know yet what kind of a complicated stunt you've been trying to pull here, but believe me I very soon will.'

'I don't know what the hell you're talking about.'

'Hey,' said Lieutenant Slyman, spreading his arms to appeal to his officers. 'He doesn't know what the hell I'm talking about? What did you think I was going to do, once we'd taken those safety deposit boxes back to Spurr's? Say: "That's it, fine, case closed, ex-Chief O'Neil has stitched everything up, we can all go home early?"'

'Why not? None of the boxes was missing. I put them back into the strongroom myself. You saw me.'

Slyman came up close. His eyes were shining and

his mouth was even more Cupid-like than ever. 'Yes, I did. But you know me. I always like to be extra-specially thorough, cover my ass. I went through that list you gave me and I managed to contact nine of the fifteen lessees of those safety deposit boxes and tell them what had happened.'

'Thanks a lot. That'll be great for business.'

'I invited all nine of them to come to Spurr's and check that their boxes were still *virgo intacta*, so to speak. Only seven of them live in the midtown area and only four of them were able to drop into Spurr's, but those four were enough.'

'I still don't know what the hell you're talking about.'

'The boxes were *empty*, that's what I'm talking about.'

'*Empty?*'

'I'm still trying to work out how you did it. It's possible that you could have switched boxes, who knows – but there were no other boxes in that Brinks-Mat truck. My strongest suspicion is that they were empty even before those poor saps came in to steal them.'

'Meaning?'

'Meaning only one thing. That you had already cleaned out those boxes before your Brinks-Mat robbers got there.'

Conor shook his head in exasperation. 'This is ridiculous, Slyman, and you know it. I can't open the strongroom on my own. They give me only half the code and a senior member of Spurr's staff has the other half.'

Lieutenant Slyman took out his notebook and

flipped it open. 'That's right . . . this week it was Darrell Bussman. Well, Darrell Bussman's still in a coma, and so he can't speak for himself, but I'd sure like to talk to *you*.'

'Darrell wouldn't steal from Spurr's. Give him a couple of years he's going to inherit most of it.'

'Well, this wasn't exactly stealing from the store, was it? It was stealing from its customers. And from what your people have told me, the contents of those safety deposit boxes could have run into billions. Hard to resist, especially for a young man with a taste for Ferraris and women and betting on the track. And even harder to resist for an ex-cop on a third of his previous salary and a whole lot of legal bills to pay.'

'You're talking out of your ass.'

'Am I?' Lieutenant Slyman tucked his notebook back in his pocket and bared his teeth. 'You'd be surprised how often I've seen sons-and-heirs get too greedy and good cops turn rotten.'

'So what's supposed to be missing?' asked Conor, trying hard to suppress his temper.

'Hey, you're talking like you don't even *know*.'

'Of course I don't know. As far as I'm concerned, what people want to keep in their safety deposit boxes is their own business.'

'Well, *we* don't know either, not for sure. None of the four lessees would give me any specifics on what their boxes had contained, and only one of them said that he was covered by insurance. But you should have seen how worried they were. I mean they were practically filling their pants. It's my guess that those boxes contained some pretty compromising material, and it's my guess that they'd all pay a whole lot of money to get it back.'

'You're trying to suggest that I was going to blackmail them? Come on, Slyman, you're way off beam.'

'I don't think so, somehow. You know – you were my role model once. I really admired you. The way you broke the Baroccis, incredible. But you never knew what side you were on, did you, and you never knew when to stop. You had to go on to break the Forty-Ninth Street Golf Club, too, and the Golf Club were the only team of law-enforcement officers that ever put the fear of God into the goodfellas, ever.'

'They were extortionists and murderers, Slyman, and you know it.'

'Maybe they were. But they were *our* extortionists and murderers. All you had to do was to turn a blind eye.'

'Couldn't do that, Slyman.'

'I know. You were always such a saint. But even saints can fall off their pedestals, can't they? You're under arrest for the theft of personal property from four sample safety deposit boxes lodged in the strongroom at Spurr's Fifth Avenue. Do you want me to read you your rights?'

Conor said, 'You bet. And I want my attorney present. And I'm not moving out of this apartment until he's here.'

Lieutenant Slyman shook his head. 'I'm afraid you don't have the right to insist on that. You're charged with abducting a police officer, four counts of larceny, one count of grand theft auto, seven counts of dangerous driving and criminal damage. And more, do you want the whole list? You're under arrest, O'Neil. You're coming downtown and you don't have any choice in the matter.'

'He's a hero!' said Lacey, quaking with indignation. 'How can you arrest him when he's a hero?'

'Miss, in my book he was always a hero,' said Lieutenant Slyman. 'The trouble is, he wasn't always a hero for the right reasons.'

Conor said, 'I have to get dressed. Lacey – will you put a call in to Michael Baer – he's probably gone home now but you'll get him on his mobile. Tell him we've got some kind of ridiculous misunderstanding here.'

Lacey picked up the phone. Conor walked toward the bedroom and one of the officers swaggered after him. 'Back off,' Conor told him. The officer stopped, perplexed. Conor turned to Slyman and said, 'Next time I want to be followed into my bedroom by an adolescent walrus, I'll call the zoo.'

'Just making sure you don't try to abscond,' said Lieutenant Slyman.

'From seven floors up?'

'I don't know. You might try to commit suicide.'

'And you'd care about that? You'd push me, if you had the chance.'

'Just leave the bedroom door open, will you? That'll do.'

In the yellow-painted bedroom with its big pine bed, Conor pulled on a fresh pair of shorts, a blue polo shirt and a pair of Calvin Klein jeans. In the corner, out of sight of Slyman and his men, he crammed more clean clothes into a small nylon bag, as well as a toothbrush and a razor from the washbasin. He slung the bag over his shoulder.

Lacey came in. 'Michael's attending a B'nai B'rith dinner. He's going to meet us at the precinct just as soon as he can.'

He put his finger to his lips.

'What?' she said. Then she saw the bag.

'You can't *go*,' she whispered.

'I have to. I swear to God they'll kill me if I don't.'

'But how can they?'

'Are you kidding me? They have a dozen different ways of doing it, once you're in custody.'

'But how are you going to get out of here? It's so high up.'

'I'll go over the roof. I'll go to Sebastian's place.'

'But you can't take heights. You know you can't.'

He held her close, and he kissed her. She smelled of Calvin Klein perfume and that warm natural biscuity smell of blondes. 'I'll get in touch with you as soon as I can. Don't say anything to Slyman until Michael shows up. And I mean *anything*. Don't let these bastards bully you.'

'But you didn't do it, did you? You didn't steal anything out of those boxes?'

'That doesn't matter. They'll kill me, Lacey. If they don't kill me down at the precinct when they're questioning me, they'll make sure that I go to Attica, where they sent the rest of the Forty-Ninth Street Golf Club, and they'll kill me there for sure.'

'O'Neil!' called Slyman, just outside the door. 'Got your pants on yet? We don't have all night.'

'I have to go,' Conor whispered into Lacey's ear. 'I never wanted anything like this to happen to you

83

. . . but you'll be brave, won't you? I won't let them harm you, whatever happens.'

'Come on, O'Neil!'

Lacey gave Conor a smile that he would never forget. Then she positioned herself behind the half-open bedroom door so that her back was reflected in the cheval-mirror in the opposite corner of the room.

'*Trust me*,' she whispered. '*I love you*.' Then she reached behind her and tugged down the zipper of her dress, and let it fall open.

Looking in through the door, Lieutenant Slyman and his two officers must have been able to see her – if only a dim, angled reflection. They were silent, and they didn't shout out any more.

She slipped her sleeves off her shoulders and then wriggled her hips so that the dress dropped down to the floor. She stepped out of it, and now she was wearing nothing but a white bra and a white lacy thong.

Conor rolled quietly over the bed. He went to the window and eased it open. Fortunately their old air-conditioning unit was making such an irregular racket that he could have set off Chinese firecrackers and nobody would have heard. He could see that Lacey was reaching behind her to unfasten her bra but he didn't want to look, not directly, knowing that Lieutenant Slyman was watching her.

The window gave onto the narrow triangular airshaft. Conor cautiously put his head out and looked down to the rubbish-strewn area below. A wave of vertigo came over him and he felt as if it were almost physically lifting him up, like a wave in the ocean. What frightened him so much was the urge he felt to throw himself out, as if he *wanted* to kill himself. He swallowed, and clamped his hand to his sweaty forehead. He couldn't do it. He simply couldn't do it.

He glanced back and Lacey was dropping her bra on the floor, her big pale breasts swaying as she did so. He almost gave himself an excuse not to climb out of the window. How could he leave her, naked and unprotected with Drew Slyman and his men? But he knew what would happen if he didn't escape, and he knew that Lacey would never forgive him, every time she put flowers on his grave.

Quaking, he lifted his leg over the sill and found some purchase for his toes on the narrow ledge outside. Then he climbed right out, trying not to think how high up he was, and what would happen to him if he fell. Even though it was dark now, the heat was still overpowering. Sweat rolled down his forehead and stung his eyes. He gripped the windowsill with one hand and swung the window shut with the other. For a split second, he saw Lacey turn toward him, but then he looked away. He had to concentrate on where he was going, and that was all.

He edged his way along the ledge. The concrete was corroded by weather and traffic fumes, and after only two or three feet it began to crumble, so that he almost lost his footing. He managed to get a grip on a stubby overflow pipe, but there was a moment when he felt that he was going to fall backward. However, he managed to stretch out his right leg and find the next section of intact ledge.

Sweating, gasping, he turned his head and looked

downward. Seven stories below, the yard was cluttered with trashcans and broken beds and rusty sheets of corrugated iron. He was only four feet away from an old iron ladder which led up to the roof, but in between the ledge and the ladder was a large ventilation pipe, which he would have to climb around.

He reached out and gripped the drainpipe. The black paint was scaly and blistered, but the pipe seemed to be securely anchored. All he had to do was take hold of it in both hands and swing himself around until his feet found the ladder on the opposite side.

'Come on, Conor,' he told himself. 'You've done scarier things than this.' And then he said, 'No, you haven't. Who are you kidding?' He found himself whispering a prayer, *'Mary, Mother of God don't let me fall because if I do I'm going to be guillotined by rusty sheets of corrugated iron and I don't want to die like that.'*

He took three deep breaths. He was about to launch himself around the pipe when the bedroom window behind him suddenly racketed open. He looked back and saw one of the police officers waving his gun at him. *'Freeze!'* he shouted.

'I'm frozen already,' Conor told him, trying not to sound calm.

'Come back here. Make it slow and make it as easy as you like.'

'I can't come back. The ledge is broken.'

The officer leaned even further out of the window. He hesitated for a moment, and then he disappeared back into the bedroom.

Conor thought: this is it, this is my only chance. He grabbed the ventilation pipe with his other hand

and swung himself around it. He was wrong: it wasn't fixed securely. As he pulled on it with all his weight, one of the upper brackets was wrenched out of the brickwork with a high-pitched screech and the pipe tilted outward at nearly 45 degrees. He was showered with grit and fragments of mortar.

He hung onto the crazily leaning pipe, trying to locate the iron ladder with his right foot. But every time he tried to swing toward it, the pipe creaked and bent a few inches further outward. He stared at the brick wall in front of him. He didn't dare to look down.

Lacey had been teaching him to control his breathing; to concentrate his strength. But the ventilation pipe was making a steady tortured noise like '*ih – ih – ih – ih –*' and he knew that it was only a matter of seconds before it ripped away from the wall completely.

The police officer reappeared at the window. 'O'Neil!'

He didn't answer – couldn't. He had much more critical matters to take care of.

'O'Neil – you get your ass back in here or else I'm going to have to shoot!'

Conor closed his eyes for a moment. You would. You would shoot. That's your answer to everything, isn't it? If it frightens you, if you don't understand it, if it threatens your miniaturized view of the world, you shoot it. If Jesus showed up tomorrow morning, you'd probably shoot Him, too.

He thought: what the hell, I'm going to die anyhow. He swung his body to the left, and then to the right. He managed to touch the edge of the iron ladder with the tip of his right shoe, but he wasn't close enough to get his foot onto the rungs, and he swung away again. The ventilation pipe bent away from the wall even further, and its rusted paint ground even more deeply into the palms of his hands.

Conor heard Lieutenant Slyman's voice. 'O'Neil! You're resisting arrest! If you don't get back here, I'm going to open fire!'

Conor ignored him. He swung to the left for a second time, and then back to the right, trying to build up as much momentum as possible. He nearly managed to hook his right foot into the iron ladder, but his shoe slipped and he had to swing back again.

Lieutenant Slyman fired a warning shot. It ricocheted from one side of the triangular airwell to the other, and finally hit one of the corrugated-iron sheets with a bang like summer thunder.

'Next one's aimed for the head,' he called out.

'*Mary, Mother of God,*' Conor breathed. He swung himself to the left as forcefully as he could, and then threw himself off to the right, letting go of the ventilation pipe altogether. His foot found the ladder, and slipped, but he grabbed at it, too, and clung on. Lieutenant Slyman fired two more shots in quick succession. His first bullet hit the ventilation pipe and whined off into the darkness: his second broke a window on the opposite side of the airshaft.

Conor climbed the ladder as rapidly as he could, his whole body surging with adrenalin. He heard Lieutenant Slyman shout, 'Up on the roof! The bastard's gone up on the roof! Don't just fucking stand there! Go after him!'

Conor reached the flat, asphalt-covered roof. He ran across it and vaulted the low brick wall which separated it from the roof of the building next door. It was so hot and humid that he could hardly breathe, but he climbed another ladder to the building after that, which was three stories taller, and then down to the next building, which was two stories lower. He was greasy with sweat and his calf muscles were trembling, but he carried on running and jumping across parapets and pipes, dodging behind chimneys and ventilation shafts whenever he could. Eventually he reached the Dane & Bulziger Building, which stood thirty-four stories high, a towering cliff of silvery steel and shining glass, and there was no way round it. Conor could see himself reflected in its windows, hunched up, gasping, like a primitive caveman encountering his mirror-image for the first time.

He turned around. Above the thrumming and parping of the traffic on Third Avenue, he heard a persistent, echoing knock. Lieutenant Slyman's men were trying to break open the door to the roof.

He took a deep breath and leaned over the railings. He was standing on top of a 1950s office building with Manzi's Italian restaurant on the first floor: he recognized the red-and-green-striped awning and the bay trees on the sidewalk, seven stories below. He went across and tried the door to the stairs, furiously rattling the handle, but it was locked. He kicked it two or three times but it still wouldn't budge. He heard Lieutenant Slyman's men bursting out of their door and shouting out, 'Where is he? He can't have gotten far! You try that way!'

Quickly Conor looked around. There was an old neon sign on the roof, partly dismantled. There were rusty pipes and something that looked like a beehive. On the far side, he saw a window cleaner's cradle. It must have been abandoned, because its cables were all wound up around it, and its remote control had lost its innards. But at least it gave him a chance of escape. Ducking down low, so that Lieutenant Slyman's men couldn't see him, Conor ran across and picked up one of the cables in both hands. It was thick with dirty oil, but it had a heavy-duty clip on the end and it still seemed to be firmly attached to the cradle itself.

One of the officers had reached the top of the taller building behind him. 'I see him!' he shouted. 'Lieutenant, he's right over here!'

A shot cracked out, and then another. One of them hit the asphalt close to Conor's foot: the other starred a window in the Dane & Bulziger Building. Conor knew that it was time to go, no matter what.

Dragging the cable after him, he hurriedly hunched his way to the railings. Another shot, and chips of concrete spattered his cheek.

He climbed over the railings and wound the cable around them. He glanced down and saw tiny people walking up and down the street and miniature taxis drawing in to the front of the restaurant. The wave came again, and that sickening urge to throw himself into the street. He heard Lieutenant Slyman yell, 'Hold it, O'Neil! Hold it right there!' He wound the cable around his waist and fastened the clip to form a loop. He didn't even have time for a prayer: he just dropped down the side of the building, colliding with

90

windowsills and architraves. The cable made a furious zizzing noise against the railings as he fell. But he had only gone down three stories before it abruptly snagged. The jolt almost cut him in half, and he couldn't stop himself from letting out a shout of pain. He hung there, twisting around and around, winded, bruised, grazed and a dangling target for Lieutenant Slyman and his men.

But even Lieutenant Slyman couldn't justify shooting a man hanging helplessly suspended on the end of a cable. He shouted down, 'We're pulling you up! Do you hear me, O'Neil? We're pulling you back up!'

The cable had kinked itself into a knot. The two officers leaned over the railings and took hold of it, trying to take the strain of Conor's weight so that Lieutenant Slyman could ease the knot free.

Conor put out one foot and managed to stop himself from twisting around. Then he put out the other foot, and braced it flat against the building. Gripping the cable tight, he began to walk up the wall.

He wasn't as fit as he used to be, and he grunted with effort. But he managed to walk up six or seven steps, until he reached the fifth story. His hands kept sliding on the oily cable and its coarse wire strands sliced his skin. Blood ran down his wrists and dripped off his elbows.

'What are you trying to do?' called one of the officers. 'Keep still, will you, for Christ's sake – we'll haul you back up!'

Conor reached out with his left hand and pulled himself toward one of the fifth-story windows. He climbed unsteadily onto the narrow stone ledge, and clung there. 'OK, that's better,' said the officer, with relief, and the cable relaxed.

Conor craned his head right back so that he could see what Lieutenant Slyman was doing. The knot had caught tight between the cable and the railing, but Slyman was gradually forcing it off the pipe with a length of TV antenna he had found on the roof.

At last, he managed to release it. Conor saw him stand up, toss the length of metal aside, and say, 'That's it. Pull the bastard up.'

At that instant Conor jumped backward off the window ledge. It was marginally less horrifying than jumping forward, because he couldn't see where he was going. All the same, there was a heart-stopping millisecond of free fall when he was sure that he was going to die. But then the cable tightened with a crack and a boom and a twang. '*Shit!*' shouted one of the policemen. 'He's almost cut off my fucking fingers!' Lieutenant Slyman called out, 'Hold him! Hold him!' but they could only keep their grip on the cable a few moments longer before they both swore loudly and let go. Conor plunged downward again, kicking at the wall and dragging his feet on the brick-work to slow his helter-skelter rush toward the red-and-green awning below.

He had almost reached it when he was jolted to another violent stop, and swung from side to side like a human pendulum. Badly winded, he was breathing in high-pitched screams, but he was so close to the top of the awning that with every swing of the cable his shoes were actually scraping the canvas.

Conor looked up. He could see Lieutenant

Slyman's pale face staring down at him with malicious glee. He could also see what had stopped him from falling any further. As he fell, he had dragged the cradle clear across the roof, and it was now precariously tilted sideways against the railings.

'Hey! O'Neil!' Lieutenant Slyman shouted down to him. 'Don't you know it's against the law to hang around the streets?'

Conor didn't have the breath to answer. He gripped the cable in his left hand and tried to heave himself up. That last jolt had yanked the cable right up underneath his armpits and tightened it so much that he found it impossible to release the clip. Lieutenant Slyman and his men had already left the roof and it was only going to be minutes before they made their way down.

He looked up again. The window cleaner's cradle was lying on its side. The railings were very low, so there might be a chance he could pull it over. The only trouble was he would then be directly beneath it as it fell. It wasn't much more than a collection of planks and scaffolding guard-rails, but it would be quite enough to kill him.

All the same, he reckoned that pulling down that cradle would at least give him a chance of survival, which was more than Lieutenant Slyman would.

Seven or eight people had gathered on the sidewalk and were watching him. One of them called out, 'Hey, man, do you need some help? Are you advertising something, or what?'

He kicked at the wall two or three times and managed to stop himself from swinging. He could have used some help but he knew that he didn't

have the time to wait for somebody to bring him a
ladder. He braced his feet against the metal bracket
on top of the awning. Then he took hold of the
cable in his bloodied hands and yanked at it. By
now the skin on the palms of his hands was in
ribbons, and he blasphemed under his breath. But
he managed to pull himself up a few inches and
then let himself drop. He did it again, and again.
The cradle banged against the railings every time he
tugged it, but it didn't seem to show any signs of
budging.

Trembling, soaked in sweat, he heaved himself up
as far as he could manage. An even bigger crowd of
onlookers had gathered now, including the restaurant manager in a white shirt and a fancy red vest.

'Hey! You! What the hell do you think you're
doing up there? You damage my blind, you moron,
you're going to have to pay.'

Conor let himself go one more time, and this time
the window cleaner's cradle toppled right over the
railing. He heard a woman scream, and then he
dropped onto the awning and rolled to the edge. He
managed to swing himself over and jump down onto
the sidewalk, just as the cradle crashed and clattered
onto the canvas, ripping it away from its framework.
Scaffolding poles and planks bounced everywhere,
and the cable came snaking down like a bullwhip,
lashing the leaves off one of the bay trees.

'Looka my blind!' screamed the restaurant
manager. 'Looka my fucking tree!'

Conor shakily climbed to his feet. He loosened the
cable clip and freed himself.

'Who'sa going to pay for this?' the restaurant

manager demanded. 'You know what this is going to *cost*?'

Conor slapped him on the shoulder, leaving a greasy, bloody handprint on his crisp white shirt. 'Charge it to the NYPD,' he said. 'They'll be here in a couple of minutes. But meanwhile, sorry, I really have to run.'

7

He rang the bell twice and Sebastian quickly opened the door for him. 'Lacey called me,' he said, as he ushered Conor into the hallway. 'She told me you'd probably come over.' He glanced left and right and said, 'Nobody followed you, did they?'

Conor shook his head. 'I checked the street before I came in here. Trust me, I'm an expert.'

Sebastian closed and bolted the door. He was tall, willowy and black. His head was shaved and he was wearing a gold braided headband and dangly gold earrings in the shape of leopards. His features were Abyssinian: high cheekbones, hooked nose and heavily lidded eyes. He was wearing a flappy white silk shirt and pants that could have been pajamas. He flowed along the hallway as if he were modeling them.

'My God, Conor, you look like a vagrant. What's happened to your hands? Look, come into the bathroom and wash them. You're going to drip blood all over the carpet.'

The carpet was snowy white, so Conor could understand his anxiety. He went to the bathroom

96

basin and Sebastian ran the faucets for him. The bathroom was white, too, with gilded fittings, and a spray of gilded ostrich plumes in a mock-Etruscan vase. Matching white bathrobes hung from gilded hooks and there was a large print of a sulky Grecian athlete holding a discus where it mattered.

Conor looked at himself in the brightly lit mirror. His face was swollen and covered in big crimson bruises. He had split his lower lip so that he sported a little goatee beard of dried blood. One shirt-sleeve was torn and there were cross-cross streaks of grease all over his pants.

Sebastian held his head as if he were a child and washed his face with a large soft cloth. Then he gently took Conor's hands and sponged out as much of the dirt as he could. 'We'd better put some iodine on these. You don't want to get some disgusting infection.'

Conor said, 'Mother of God,' when Sebastian poured on the iodine. But he waited patiently while Sebastian wrapped his hands with surgical gauze.

'So . . . am I allowed to know how you ended up like this?' Sebastian asked.

'Of course. But I could use a drink first.'

Sebastian led him into the living room. He had completely remodeled it since Conor had last been here. The walls were painted in a faded, distressed pink and the limed-oak furniture looked as if it had come from an old French farmhouse. On one of the couches lolled a handsome bare-chested boy of 18 or 19 with golden curls and a dark blue sarong wrapped around his waist, reading a copy of *Variety*.

'Conor, this is Ric,' said Sebastian, flapping across and kissing the boy on the forehead. 'Ric's a dancer. Hugely talented. *Hugely*.'

'Sorry,' said Conor, holding up his bandages. 'Can't shake hands.'

Ric looked him up and down as if he were appraising a handsome but disheveled beast at a cattle market. 'Jesus,' he said. 'What happened to *you*?'

'What would you like to drink?' asked Sebastian. 'I have some Stag's Leap chardonnay that's positively *myumph*! Unless you'd prefer something stiffer.'

Ric let out a sardonic *pfff*! of amusement and Sebastian waved one of his sleeves at him in annoyance.

'A whiskey would be fine,' said Conor. 'Do you think I could use your phone to call Lacey?' He knew that Slyman wouldn't yet have had time to set up a wiretap.

'For sure.' Sebastian handed him a mobile phone in a quilted gold cover. Conor's legs were beginning to tremble and he sat down in one of the large cushioned armchairs. Sebastian went to the cocktail cabinet and filled up a huge cut-crystal goblet with ice.

The phone rang for a long time before Lacey answered.

'Hi. It's me. I just made it to Sebastian's place.'

'Sorry,' said Lacey, in a cold, abstract tone. 'He's not here right now.'

'Is Slyman still there?'

'All right, then. I'll tell him. Is everything OK?'

'I'm fine. A little knocked about, but nothing serious.'

'Good. I'll let him know you called.'

Conor switched the phone off. 'The police are still round there. I'll try calling again later.'

'Well, do,' said Sebastian. 'I'm simply itching to know what this is all about. Hang on, I must get another bottle of wine out of the icebox.'

While Sebastian went into the kitchen, Conor turned to Ric. 'So you're a dancer,' he said. 'Modern or classical?'

'Whatever I can get. Tap, mainly.'

'Have I seen you in anything?'

Sebastian swept back in. 'Ric was in *A Chorus Line*, weren't you, Ric?'

'Oh sure I was. In Buffalo. And what do you think the mathematical odds are that Conor ever saw *A Chorus Line* in Buffalo?'

'Stranger things have happened, sweet cheeks,' said Sebastian, handing Conor a huge Jack Daniel's. 'Besides, you were in *Vaudeville Days*, too, and that was on Broadway.'

'Oh, yes. I forgot that starring role. I held a hoop so that a chihuahua could jump through it.'

'Why do you always bring yourself *down*? How are you ever going to make any progress in show business if you're always so self-deprecating? Show business is all about *confidence*! Pizzazz!'

'God, you sound more like Deanna Durbin every day. Show business has nothing to do with confidence. Show business is all about freaky strokes of luck and kissing the right rear ends.'

'You'll have to forgive Ric,' said Sebastian. 'He's the victim of an excessively well-balanced childhood.' He sat down next to Conor and crossed his legs. He was wearing strappy gold sandals with little bells on them. 'Now why don't you tell us how you got into such a mess?'

Slowly, Conor did. He felt exhausted now, shattered, and the events of the day were all jumbled up in his mind. But Sebastian thought it was all enthralling, especially the Brinks-Mat truck crashing into the Pond.

'It *is* a mystery, though, isn't it?' he said. 'Those two people waiting outside your door. Do you think they had any connection with the robbery?'

'Hell, Sebastian, I don't know what to think. I haven't any idea what they were doing there or what they wanted. All I know is that I started to talk to them and I lost twenty-nine minutes out of my day.'

'That's so *weird*,' said Sebastian. 'Maybe they were aliens. You have to be so careful about aliens. They take you up to their spacecraft and perform all kinds of strange sexual experiments on you.'

'Oh, really?' said Ric. 'And how do *you* know? Has that ever happened to you?'

'Me? I should have such luck.'

'But wait a minute,' said Conor. 'Remember that Darrell Bussman met them, too, in another department, and he lost some time as well. Not as much as I did, but a few seconds maybe. One moment he was talking to them, then they were gone.'

'Can you remember what they said to you?' asked Sebastian.

Conor shook his head. 'The woman didn't speak

at all. The man just lifted up his hand and said, "Do you know me?" and that's all I remember. Maybe he said more. He must have done, but I couldn't tell you what it was.'

'Describe them,' said Ric.

'I can do better than that. I can draw them.'

Sebastian brought him a gold mechanical pencil and a sheet of white writing-paper. Quickly Conor repeated the sketches he had shown to Salvatore.

Ric took the sheet of paper and frowned at it. 'You were right, Sebastian. They *are* aliens.'

'I'm – uh – not exactly an artist,' Conor told him.

'No, no. Joking aside, you've pretty much caught them.'

'Caught them? You *know* them? You're putting me on.'

'Ric knows *everybody*,' said Sebastian, showing his claws. 'He gets around New York like a dose of the flu.'

Ric sat up straight, rewrapping his sarong. 'The woman's tall, right, about thirty-five years old, white face, totally black eyes like she's a zombie or something? The guy looks like he's Latino, sharp clothes, curly hair, Little Richard mustache?'

'Absolutely dead right. That's them. You don't happen to know what their names are?'

'Sure I do. Ramon Perez and Magda Slanic. He's Mexican and she's Romanian. Leastways, she always *said* that she was Romanian. She had a thick accent but as far as I'm concerned it could have been anything. Greek, Russian, who knows? They were a weird pair, didn't talk too much, and when they did you weren't too sure what they meant. I haven't seen

101

them for over a year, not since *Vaudeville Days* closed down.'

'They were involved in *Vaudeville Days*, too? They're entertainers?'

'That's right. Their stage names were Hypnos and Hetti.'

Conor pressed the heel of his hand against his forehead. He couldn't think why it hadn't occurred to him before. *Hypnotists*, for Christ's sake. They had simply put him into a mesmeric trance, and made him do whatever they wanted him to do. That's where his twenty-nine minutes had disappeared.

Ric said, 'They were amazing hypnotists, Hypnos and Hetti. But they weren't audience friendly, if you know what I mean? They used to make people do all these really humiliating things on stage, like wet their pants or swear at their wives or burst into tears because they thought they were kids and they'd lost their mommy at the market.

'I really had the feeling that they *hated* their audience, you know? They never knew when to draw the line. They once made a woman lick the soles of her husband's shoes.'

'They must have hypnotized Darrell, too,' said Conor. 'I only knew half the code to open the strongroom, but he knew the other half. Do you think they could have made him tell them what it was? I mean, just like that, snap, in the blinking of an eye?'

'You're joking, I hope. Those two could make you do anything, whether you wanted to do it or not. You know that myth about hypnotism – that you can never make anybody do anything against their will?

102

That's so much bullshit. We had a backstage party the night *Vaudeville Days* opened, and Ramon made this middle-aged make-up artist take off all of her clothes and dance on the table with a pink feather duster sticking out of her ass. I left. I mean, quite apart from the fact that I don't like women with no clothes on, it was *wrong*, you know? It was degrading. It was morally wrong.'

Sebastian brushed an invisible mote of dust from his knee. 'Ric's quite the religious fundamentalist, isn't he, when he gets going? Mind you, he's more interested in fundaments than he is in religion.'

Conor said, 'The Mexican guy – what was his name, Perez? – he was carrying a large bag. They must have hypnotized me into opening up the strongroom and emptied out all the safety deposit boxes they took a fancy to.'

'But how would they know which boxes to choose?' asked Sebastian.

'I don't know. We have a list of who rents which box. It's stored in the company's database, but it's strictly confidential and it's encrypted.'

'They might have gotten you to download it for them,' Ric suggested. 'After all, they had plenty of time.'

'I wouldn't have done anything like that, I'm sure, even if I was hypnotized. I *couldn't* have. It's so much against my training.'

'I told you, Conor: Hypnos and Hetti can make people do *anything*. They can even make people kill themselves, if they want to. Hypnos always used to boast that he hypnotized Sonny Bono into skiing into a tree.'

'Why the hell would he want to do a thing like that, even if he could?'

'Oh, there was supposed to be some mob connection. Bono trod on too many influential toes, and that was the cleanest way to get rid of him. Hypnos said there were others, too – really big names. And the beauty was that nobody could ever prove if he was lying or not.'

'All right, then,' said Conor. 'Supposing for the sake of argument that I *did* download the list for them . . . how come the other robbers had a list, too? And a list which sounds as if it was substantially the same as Hypnos and Hetti's list?'

'Maybe somebody hacked into your computer and sold it to them on the black market.'

'That's a possibility, I guess. But it doesn't explain why they were two separate attempts to rob Spurr's strongroom literally within hours of each other.'

'Coincidence,' Sebastian suggested. 'I was mugged twice on the same block once. Do you know what I said to the second mugger? "If you want my money it's no good threatening me. Go and chase after that scumbag down there."'

Conor said, 'I don't think it was a coincidence at all. I think there's a whole lot more to this than meets the eye.'

'Well, the two robberies couldn't have been connected. Why storm into a store to steal a whole lot of safety deposit boxes if you know that they're already empty?'

'Exactly. But none of this really makes any difference, not to the cops. They're convinced that *I* cleared out those boxes and I don't have any way of proving them wrong. My only witness is in a coma and he can't remember what Hypnos and Hetti did to him, either.'

'In other words, you're up your neck in very deep doodoo.'

'There's only one way out of this. I have to find Hypnos and Hetti – preferably with some of the stuff still in their possession.'

'So what kind of stuff are we talking about?'

'I don't have any idea. It could be emeralds, it could be dope, it could be title deeds. What customers keep in their safety deposit boxes is their own business.'

'Supposing they *don't* have the stuff on them? Or supposing they do, but you can't prove that it came from Spurr's? I mean, nobody's going to put up their hand and say, "Oh, yes – that three-pound package of Colombia's purest, that's mine!"'

'In that case, I'll have to find a way to make them confess.'

Ric smiled and shook his head. 'Ooh no, I don't think so. Not those two. They'd have you in a trance before you even got to the first question.'

'Beat them with rubber hoses, that's what I say,' put in Sebastian. 'How about another drink, Conor? You look terrible. You're going to have two gorgeous black eyes tomorrow.'

'Do you have any idea where Hypnos and Hetti might be?' Conor asked Ric.

'Not any more. They used to rent a loft in TriBeCa, but I don't think they live there any longer. I'll tell you what I could do, though. I could give you Eleanor Bronsky's number. Eleanor used to be their agent. Maybe she knows where they are.'

Conor couldn't have a shower that night because of his hands but Sebastian ran him a deep, hot bath and he sat in it for nearly twenty minutes, with his eyes closed.

He dreamed that he was walking along an empty, echoing corridor. Right at the very end stood two dark figures. He knew that he had every reason to be afraid of them, but he kept on walking toward them. He had almost reached them when he realized that they weren't two figures at all, but one, two people intertwined like a tree.

For some reason this filled him with dread, and he turned to run. As he did so, however, there was a deafening metallic clang and a huge door shut in front of him, blocking his escape.

He knocked and knocked, knowing that the two people that were one person was gradually approaching him. But no matter how hard he knocked, he couldn't make a sound any louder than a gentle tapping.

He opened his eyes. It was Sebastian, coyly tapping at the bathroom door.

'Didn't mean to disturb you. Would you like me to wash your back?'

8

That night, he dreamed one bad dream after another. He fell down elevator shafts, he ran down tunnels, he was trapped under suffocating heaps of blankets. In spite of the air conditioning, Sebastian's apartment was stifling, and he woke up again and again, smothered in sweat. Pretty little clocks were ticking and chiming everywhere, and he found it almost impossible to get back to sleep.

At six o'clock a huge dumpster parked outside and garbage collectors started to throw trashcans around. It sounded like the *1812 Overture*. As stiffly as a 70-year-old he climbed out of bed and hobbled to the kitchen where he made himself a cup of arabica coffee and listened to the portable television at very low volume, so that he wouldn't wake up Sebastian and Ric.

He turned to the early-morning news. After an item about a shootout at a grade school in the Bronx, Lieutenant Slyman appeared. He was standing beside the torn awning of Manzi's restaurant, his face made devilish by the red flashing lights of firetrucks and squad cars.

'. . . *Conor O'Neil was one of the most skilful and experienced officers in the New York Police Department . . . today he has also shown himself to be one hundred per cent ruthless and determined . . . he has successfully engineered a robbery which may have netted him over a billion dollars . . . if you have any knowledge of his whereabouts, don't try to approach him . . . Just call this number . . . I have already been told that the owners of the missing property are prepared to pay very substantial rewards for its return . . .*'

'Hey, maybe we ought to turn you in,' said Ric, who had been standing behind him in the kitchen doorway. 'Sebastian and I could use some extra cash.'

'Don't worry,' said Conor. 'If I can find this Hypnos and Hetti, I'll make sure that you get the credit for it.'

Ric came into the kitchen. He was wearing a short purple robe and a hairnet. He took a giant-sized guava juice out of the icebox and drank it straight out of the carton. 'Don't you worry about that. Sebastian and I will get our reward in Heaven.' He sat down and peered at Conor closely. 'My God,' he said. 'You *do* look a fright.'

Eleanor Bronsky's office was on the fourth floor of a narrow 1930s building on Broadway, a block and a half north of Times Square. Conor walked there, in spite of the heat and humidity, because he didn't want to risk being recognized by some smartass taxi driver who might have watched this morning's news. He knew from his police experience how closely taxi drivers scrutinize their fares. Scrutinize them and

108

instantly categorize them: out-of-towner, tourist, minor celebrity, Wall Street broker, crack addict, drunk, harmless lunatic, dangerous lunatic and worst of all, parsimonious tipper.

He crossed Times Square through a host of fluttering, hopping, scabrous pigeons. He was wearing only a white T-shirt and beige canvas pants, no socks, but the perspiration still dripped down his cheeks. Today's forecast was a high of 103. People had been collapsing in the streets.

He reached the narrow doorway and pressed the button marked BRONSKY THEATRICAL REPRESENTATION INC. A down-and-out in a filthy brown shirt was sitting on the step with a small, panting mongrel on the end of a string.

'Spare some change?' he asked. His eyes were crusted and he was missing most of his teeth.

Conor gave him a dollar bill. He pressed the bell again. There were two cops on the opposite side of Broadway, leaning against their squad car and talking casually to an ice-cream vendor. The sooner he got inside the building the better.

'You're in trouble, aintcha?' said the down-and-out. 'I can always smell a man in trouble.'

'Thanks for your consideration, but I'm fine.'

'They're after you, ain't they? They're on your heels.'

A ditsy little girl's voice came out of the intercom. '*Who whizzit?*'

'Jack Brown. I'm a friend of Ric Vetter. He called you before?'

'You want a word of advice?' said the down-and-out. His dog gave Conor the most hopeless look that he had ever seen from man or beast. Conor didn't answer.

'The word of advice is: two into one does go, and when they do, you'd better watch your ass.'

'What?' asked Conor, but then the door buzzer went, and he pushed his way into the gloomy hallway, leaving the down-and-out sitting outside. There was a strong smell of gas and mold inside the building. On the right was a battered row of disused mailboxes, their doors hanging open. On the left was a tiny elevator with a powder-blue-painted door. Up ahead rose a staircase covered in grim green linoleum with metal protective edges, but on the second-story landing shone a stained-glass window, pure art deco, of an airliner flying over the ocean, accompanied by seagulls. In a decrepit building like this, it was weirdly ritzy and romantic.

Conor took the elevator up to the fourth floor. It clanked as if it were being winched up by Quasimodo. There was a small, dim mirror at the back of the elevator and he took off his Ray-Bans so that he could look at himself. Both of his eyes were so swollen that they were almost closed, and his lips looked like two large slices of raw pig's liver.

The door marked BRONSKY THEATRICAL REP-RESENTATION INC. had been left open and Conor stepped directly into a cramped outer office. The ditsy girl was sitting at her desk, a redhead in a sleeveless purple T-shirt with purple lipstick to match. She rattled away at the keyboard of her word-processor and chewed gum at five times the average speed. 'Mr Brown?' she said, scarcely bothering to look up. 'Go ride on through.' Then, 'Shit!' as she mistyped something.

Conor said, 'Thanks,' and knocked on the inner door.

Eleanor Bronsky herself was sitting in a tilting chair, her feet crossed on top of a desk which was cluttered with contracts and gilded statuettes and framed telegrams, as well as an overflowing onyx ashtray. Behind her there was a grimy view of Broadway. Despite the efforts of an asthmatic air conditioner, the room was uncomfortably humid and hazy with her cigarette smoke. She was a handsome woman in her middle sixties, thin, etiolated by smoking and decades of late nights, with well-cut white hair and a face that, once, must have been striking. She still had fine cheekbones and large blue eyes, although the skin of her cheeks had softened and withered, and the blue of her eyes had faded, like cornflowers pressed in a bible.

She wore a cream silk dress and a gold chain belt. As Conor stepped in, she was talking on her hands-free telephone and lighting another Marlboro in an amber cigarette-holder. She waved her hand to indicate that he should sit down.

'No, David,' she was saying. 'I'm not going to risk Stella's reputation in a production like that. No, I don't believe it will. Not for a moment. It's a *terrible* idea.'

Conor looked around the office. The shelves were crammed with dogeared screenplays and theatrical scripts: the walls were cluttered with scores of photographs of Eleanor Bronsky with Shelley Winters, Eleanor Bronsky with Lee Strasberg,

111

Eleanor Bronsky with Tony Franciosa and Harry Guardino and Tennessee Williams. Late-night flash photographs of Eleanor Bronsky with drunkenly grinning producers taken at the tables of Sardi's and Downey's.

Eventually she said, '*Shalom*, David,' and switched off the phone. She blew out a cloud of smoke and said, 'Can you believe it? That was David Bramwell. He wants to make a musical based on the life of Hugh Hefner – *Centerfold*! Can you imagine it? *Centerfold*! Indeed! It won't be just the center that's folding, it'll be the whole goddamned ridiculous production.'

Conor held out his hand. 'Jack Brown. Pleased to meet you.'

Eleanor Bronsky's handshake was dry and surprisingly firm. The handshake of a woman who was used to dealing with powerful men. 'My God, Mr Brown, if you'll excuse my saying so, you look like you had an argument with Godzilla, and lost.'

'Minor auto accident, that's all. I'll get over it. Ric Vetter called you this morning.'

'Yes, he did. Darling, darling Ric. If he wasn't as queer as a three-dollar bill, I could fancy him myself. He brings out the Blanche Dubois in me. Excuse my smoke,' she said, flapping her hand. 'I've been trying to give it up since the opening night of *Wedding Feast*. Or was it *The Member of the Wedding*?'

Conor said, 'Did Ric tell you who I was looking for?'

'Uh-huh. Hypnos and Hetti. What a pair they were. I represented them for three and half years, right from the time they first came over here.'

'But you don't represent them now?'

She shook her head. 'They were incredibly good. They could hypnotize a dozen people standing in a bus line and make them gobble like turkeys. But I don't know . . . there was something I didn't like about them, something *unhealthy*. There was no *joy* in them, you know? And they didn't seem to be very interested in performing for the sake of performing, not like most artistes. They didn't want acknowledgement. They didn't want applause. Quite frankly I don't really know *what* they wanted.'

'When was the last time you saw them?'

Eleanor Bronsky sucked on her cigarette and peered at him narrowly. 'Are you a cop?' she asked.

'Of course not. I'm a theatrical producer.'

'Jack Brown? I've never heard of you, and I've heard of everybody.'

'I'm based in Toronto, that's why. Haven't you heard of *My Man's a Mountie*?'

'I'm sorry. I never did. But it sounds . . . well, I don't know what it sounds.'

'Ran for two and a half years at the York Theater. Now I'm interested in reviving *Vaudeville Days*.'

'You want my honest opinion, Jack? You've got more screws loose than David Bramwell. *Vaudeville Days* died a slow and terrible death. People have the Internet these days. They have pay-per-view. They're not going to make a special trip into town to sit through two hours of Wu Chin the Chinese juggler or Leila and her Performing Poodles.'

'Well, I don't agree with you. I think people still have a hankering for live entertainment. It's the new nostalgia, if you like. Anyhow, I have dozens of

113

new ideas for bringing the show up to date.'

Eleanor puffed, and waited, and puffed some more. 'And one of these ideas is to bring back Hypnos and Hetti?'

'That's right. Hypnotism is hot. Especially their kind of hypnotism. Audiences love to see people being humiliated.'

'Oh, if it's *humiliated* you want, Hypnos and Hetti are just what you're looking for. In fact a whole lot more than humiliated. They were sacked, you know, from *Vaudeville Days*. They hypnotized a man so that he ate a whiskey glass on stage. He cut half his tongue off, there was blood everywhere. It was lucky he didn't die, but so far as I know he was never able to talk again.

'I refused to represent them after that. I'm not saying that I'm such a moralist that I won't represent a drug addict or a bigamist or a man who beats his wife. If they can act, if they can sing, what business is it of mine? But there was something very, very unpleasant about Hypnos and Hetti. My late husband Ned used to say that they must have made a contract with Satan, or David Merrick at the very least.'

'So you really don't know where they are?'

Eleanor Bronsky shook her head. 'I could give you their last known address, but I doubt if it'll do you any good.' She paused, and crushed out her cigarette. 'You *are* a cop, aren't you?'

Conor hesitated, but then he raised both hands in surrender. 'OK, I admit it. But it's critical that I find them. It's a long story, but it's almost a case of them or me.'

114

'*My Man's a Mountie*, ha!' Eleanor Bronsky gave a fruity, tobacco-thickened laugh. 'For a second there, I almost believed you.'

She stood up and walked over to a battered wooden filing cabinet. She pulled out a drawer and started to leaf through it. 'You know something, you should have seen the office I had in the old days. I represented everyone who was anyone. I had tigerskin rugs and Louis XIV furniture and a cocktail cabinet the size of Grand Central Station. I had Jackson Pollock paintings. God, I hated those Jackson Pollock paintings, but they were so expensive. Still, they're gone now. And look at me. I never thought that the glory days would pass so quickly.'

She took out a file and said, 'Here it is. Ramon Perez and Magda Slanic, 981 Thomas. But I can almost guarantee that you won't find them there now. I sent them mail. I even sent them money, but it all came back.'

'Still, thanks, I'll check it out.'

'Did they do that to you?' asked Eleanor Bronsky, leaning against the filing cabinet. 'Beat up your face?'

'They didn't actually do it, but let's say they caused it.'

'Well, there's one more possibility you could try. Sidney Randall, if he's still alive.'

Conor made a face to show her that he didn't have any idea who Sidney Randall was.

'Sidney Randall,' she said. 'One of the greatest hypnotists in history. He had his own show in the 1950s, *When You Awake*. I represented him for three and a half years, and he made me a great deal of money. Sidney was fascinated by Hypnos and Hetti. He didn't care for them personally, not at all, but he thought their hypnotic technique was amazing. There's a chance that he might have kept in touch with them.'

'So where do I find this Sidney Randall?'

'The last I heard, he was broke and he was retired. As I say, there's no audience for that kind of act these days. That's why I'm quite relieved that you're a cop, Jack, and not some poor misguided producer.'

'Actually, I'm not a cop any longer and my name's not Jack. I'm Conor O'Neil.'

Eleanor Bronsky was right in the middle of lighting another cigarette. 'My God, so you are! I saw you on the news this morning! That doesn't say much for my memory for faces, does it? You're wanted, aren't you?' She paused, and blew smoke out of her nose. 'Would I get a reward for turning you in?'

'This may sound corny, but I'm innocent. That's why I need to find this Hypnos and Hetti . . . to *prove* that I'm innocent.'

'You're *innocent*, huh?'

Conor didn't say anything but sat and looked at her as she smoked.

Eventually, she said, 'You're the cop who cleaned up all that police corruption, aren't you?'

He nodded. 'The Forty-Ninth Street Golf Club. Don't know whether you remember that.'

'Of course I do. You were some kind of a hero, weren't you?'

'I made a lot of enemies, if that's what you mean. That's why they're looking for me now.'

116

'OK,' she said, at last. 'If you really *are* innocent, I'll call my friends at the Vaudeville Artistes' Benevolent Fund and see if I can find out where Sidney's living – that's if he is still living. If not there are one or two more people I can try. How can I get in touch with you?'

'Just leave a message with Ric. And, thanks. You don't know how grateful I am.'

She touched his cheek. 'You're a friend of Ric's. You're innocent. What else could I do? It's nice to know that after all these years I can still do *something* outrageous.'

9

'I can't tell you how frightened I was,' said Lacey. 'Lieutenant Slyman told me that he thought you were seriously hurt.'

She took hold of his hand between hers and kissed his fingertips. Conor said, 'Sorry. Pastrami flavor.'

It was 1:05. They were sitting at a table in back of Stars Deli on Lexington Avenue. It was hot and busy. The counter was crowded with office workers ordering turkey and liverwurst and salt beef sandwiches, so that they could eat their lunch on the benches and walls around the Citicorp Center. Signed photographs of movie and theater stars hung on every wall. Conor had bought himself pastrami on rye but Stars' sandwiches were three inches thick and it hurt him to open his jaws so wide. Apart from that, his appetite wasn't improved by the awareness that he could be whacked without warning, at any moment, by a cop, by one of his own kind. A bullet in the head, no witnesses, no questions asked. He was still police, whatever had happened. He had been born police. But now his family had cast him out, and all they wanted was his blood.

118

He knew the way they worked. If he were Lieutenant Slyman, he would have Lacey under twenty-four-hour surveillance. Not to mention phone taps and e-mail intercepts. That was why he had chosen Stars for them to meet. They used to lunch here regularly, in the days after the Golf Club trial, and it had taken only an untraceable copy-shop fax saying **1 (Stars, at 1) for Lacey to realize where he wanted to see her, and when. Stars was only three blocks south of the Lipstick Building, where Lacey worked, and the lunchtime crowd kept them well screened from the doorway and the street outside.

He couldn't see Lacey well because she was silhouetted against the light, but he thought she looked beautiful. All that blond flyaway hair. She was wearing a gauzy white cheesecloth blouse and tailored taupe slacks and lots of bangly jewelry. She was trying to act composed but there were dark shadows under her eyes because – like Conor – she had hardly slept.

'You made sure you weren't followed?'

'I stopped to look in a couple of shop windows. Then I went left on 53rd Street and went all the way around the block. Then I went into the Steinman Pharmacy and came out by the other door.'

'Good girl. Slyman hasn't been giving you a hard time, has he?'

'He never stops nagging me to tell him where you are. He says it's my public duty. He keeps saying that if you're innocent, why did you run away?'

'But he hasn't threatened you, or anything like that? He hasn't touched you?'

'If he tried anything like that, he'd regret it,

119

believe me. I *can* look after myself, you know.'

'What about my lawyers? You talked to Michael Baer?'

She nodded. 'Michael said the same thing as Slyman. He was even on television, saying it. If you're innocent, why are you running? He said you should give yourself up and let him defend you in a court of law. He told me that he couldn't protect you, otherwise.'

'He *can't* protect me. Not from Drew Slyman. Nobody can.'

'But Slyman can't just shoot you down in cold blood.'

'He can, sweetheart, and he's determined to, and I don't want to spend the rest of my life wondering when the bullet's going to hit me. What's that perfume you're wearing?'

'Issey.'

He gripped her hand and squeezed it. 'It makes me homesick. But I can't come back yet, sweetheart. I did nothing wrong here, and I have to prove it.'

She leaned across the table and kissed his cheek. 'I love you,' she said. 'I won't let these bastards hurt you, I promise.'

'Any news of Darrell Bussman?'

'The last time Slyman talked to me, Darrell was still in a coma.'

'Well, God take care of him, that's all I can say. Right now he's the only witness I've got.'

'There's something else,' said Lacey. 'After he appeared on TV, Michael said that he had calls from three attorneys representing some of Spurr's deposit-box customers. They were all offering to pay

120

large amounts of money to have their property back, no identities revealed, no questions asked.'

'That's unreal. When you say "large amounts of money", what are we talking about?'

'Millions, that's what Michael said. Eight, maybe nine, maybe more. He couldn't be specific.'

Conor couldn't help shaking his head in amusement. 'If only I *had* their property.'

Lacey brushed back her hair with her hand. 'It wouldn't matter, would it, if you had their property or not? So long as they *thought* you did. You could make a deal. Take their millions of dollars, and give them nothing in return. You and me, we could buy a big house in Florida, couldn't we, overlooking a golf course?'

'You know I couldn't do anything like that.'

'Yes,' she said. 'And that's why I love you. Because you will never do anything like that, even now, when you're not a real cop any more.'

'That's where you're wrong,' he told her. 'I'm always going to be a real cop. I can't help it, even though it's a curse. Could you stop being beautiful?'

'Don't try to flatter me. I'm not beautiful. But I love you, and I'm going to fight for you.'

He touched her hair. She closed her eyes while his fingertips traced her eyebrows, her cheekbones, her nose and her lips. He didn't usually like to display his affection for her in public, but he knew that he might not see her again for a long time, or maybe never.

'I'm asking you to be patient, that's all,' he told her. 'I'm going to sort out this mess and I'm going to stay alive. Don't talk to anybody else about me.

Don't ever say you saw me. I'll keep in touch.'

They held hands on either side of Conor's uneaten pastrami sandwich and that was all they could do. At the next table, a skinny old gent was sitting in a wheelchair with a cup of coffee and a donut. He gave them a white-whiskered smile, and then he leaned toward Conor and whispered, 'Excuse me, sir. But are you going to eat that sandwich?'

'Sure, you go right ahead,' said Conor, and passed it over to him. As he leaned across, he glimpsed a man waiting on the street corner outside the deli door. The man was wearing a flappy linen coat and a narrow-brimmed straw hat and there was something about the way in which he was standing that gave Conor the warning taste of salt in his mouth. Cops are like dancers or weightlifters: they give away their profession by the way in which they carry themselves. Conor couldn't be totally certain, but he would have put even money on this man being a plainclothes detective on surveillance.

'What's wrong?' asked Lacey.

'I'm not sure yet,' he said. He waited until the pedestrian crossing signs had changed from *Walk* to *Don't Walk* and back to *Walk*. The man stayed where he was, occasionally glancing to one side. A police patrol car drew up on the other side of the street, and then another. This was it.

'I have to get out of here,' Conor told Lacey.

She could tell by his eyes what was wrong. 'How did they manage to follow me? I took so much care.'

'It's not your fault. They're very experienced.'

He glanced quickly around the deli. There was no rear entrance, only the door to the washrooms, and if Slyman's men had half a brain cell between them they would already have covered that option.

He looked back toward the hot, glaring street. There was no question about it: the cops were waiting for him. They wouldn't come inside in case he was armed, and they couldn't risk bullets flying in a space as tightly crowded as this. But they would have him as soon as he stepped out of the door.

He said quietly to Lacey, '*Faint.*'

'What?'

'Faint. Go all woozy and fall over onto the floor.'

'I don't know what you mean.'

'Just do it, will you? It's the only way I'm going to be able to get out of here.'

'Well . . . OK,' she said. She stared at him for a moment longer, still holding his hands, then suddenly slid sideways and toppled off her chair. She did it so realistically that Conor almost believed that she really *had* fainted. There were cries of dismay all around them and Conor quickly scraped back his chair and knelt on the floor beside her.

'Air – please, give her some air!' he called out, and everybody shuffled back a few inches. He laid his hand on her forehead. 'Heat exhaustion . . . she's dehydrated. I need to get her to a hospital.'

'You want I should call 911?' asked the little Italian behind the counter.

'Sir – I have a cellphone right here,' offered a young businessman in yellow suspenders.

'No, no thanks. She's been having this trouble for weeks. I should take her directly to her specialist. If somebody could hail a taxi for me?'

'Sure thing.' The little Italian went to the door and let out a piercing whistle.

Lacey began to murmur and stir, but Conor bent over her and whispered, 'Stay floppy, OK?' He could see a yellow taxi draw up outside. The little Italian came back in and said, 'I got one. You want me to help you carry her?'

Conor turned to the skinny old man in the wheel-chair. The old man's mouth was still cramful of pastrami sandwich. 'Sir . . . do you mind if I borrow your chair . . . just to take her out to the taxi? I'll bring it right back to you.'

The old man said, '*Mmmmfff, mmmfff*,' unable to speak, but he waved his arm to show that he was agreeable. He let down his left-hand armrest and heaved himself onto the chair next to him.

'That's wonderful,' said Conor. He lifted Lacey up from the floor and sat her in the wheelchair. The skinny old man raised the armrest for her and gave her a reassuring pat on the arm.

'And, er, maybe your hat?' asked Conor. 'Just to keep the sun off her head.'

'*Mmmfff*,' said the man, and handed over the beaten-up old blue cotton hat that was resting on the table next to his coffee cup.

'You're a true gentleman,' said Conor.

'Did you see that?' said a woman by the counter. 'That's what I call differently abled.'

Conor pushed Lacey through the crowd of customers until he had almost reached the deli's front door. Then he leaned forward and said quietly in her ear, 'I want you to get out of the wheelchair and walk across to that taxi that's waiting by the curb. Get in, and ask the driver to take you back to the office. Whatever you do, don't look back.'

More customers were coming into the deli doorway, but they stood aside to let Conor and Lacey out. For a moment there was a minor flurry of jostling and pushing on the sidewalk outside.

'*Now*,' said Conor, and patted Lacey on the shoulder.

She climbed out of the wheelchair and elbowed her way through to the sidewalk. There were complaints of 'Hey!' and 'Pardon *me*!' Conor meanwhile took her place in the wheelchair. He tugged the old man's hat right down over his eyes, and heaved himself out of the door. He took a sharp left toward 51st Street and kept on going, wheeling himself through the lunchtime crowds as fast as he could. He found the wheelchair almost impossible to control and he collided with shopping bags being carried by a large black woman in a loud African-patterned dress. 'You one crazy driver,' she told him.

He had no way of telling if the waiting cops had realized who he was, and as he weaved his way toward the next intersection he expected at any second to hear a challenge or a gunshot. He didn't dare to turn around. But he reached 51st Street and nobody shouted out. He slewed the wheelchair to the left, and kept on pushing himself as hard as he could until he reached the wide, descending entrance ramp to an underground parking facility. He turned into it and gave his wheels a final heave. A car was coming up the ramp toward him with its headlights blazing. It gave an echoing blast on its horn but he couldn't stop himself. He pulled the

125

wheelchair to one side and deliberately tipped it over, rolling onto the concrete floor and colliding with the curb. The car pulled up only inches away from him, and the driver climbed out, open-mouthed in horror.

Conor climbed to his feet and limped down the ramp toward him. 'It's OK,' he said. 'There won't be any lawsuits.' The driver couldn't even speak; he watched in bewilderment as Conor hobbled to the elevators. As he did so, he heard a police car come howling down Lexington Avenue, closely followed by another.

Conor reached the elevator and pressed the button for the first floor. Just before the doors closed, two women joined him. Both wore wide-shouldered suits and their foundation was a concentrated shade of orange. They stared at him unblinkingly until the elevator chimed their arrival at the lobby and Conor was able to escape.

10

The following morning he met Eleanor Bronsky at the Staten Island ferry terminal. The weather was still hot, but a refreshing breeze was blowing across the Upper Bay and ruffling the water. Eleanor was wearing a flowing white pants suit with blue flowers on it, and a blue straw hat. Conor wore dark glasses and a baseball cap and a big floppy sweatshirt with St Francis College printed on the back.

He kissed Eleanor on the cheek and then said, 'How did you find him so quick? I should have had you on my team when I was chief of detectives.'

'It wasn't too difficult. The Vaudeville Artistes' Benevolent Fund didn't know where he was. In fact they thought he was dead. But they put me on to Renata Valli, who was part of a famous mind-reading act. She gave me this address on Staten Island.'

'And she thinks he's alive?'

'She *knows* he's alive – unless he's died since last Thursday. She had a letter from him dated August 5. He told her that he's writing the definitive book on hypnotism and mind-reading and clairvoyance, and he wanted to know how Renata and her husband worked their famous truth-and-consequences act.'

They shuffled on board the ferry in the middle of a chattering crowd of Japanese tourists.

Eleanor said, 'The Vallis' act was very clever. Renata would go into the audience and touch the shoulder of anybody who had recently lied to their partner; and her husband would tell them exactly what they had lied about. I don't know how they did it. Maybe they could read minds. Maybe they were nothing more than good judges of human nature.'

They walked across the ferry's deck and stood by the rail. 'I haven't done this since I was at school,' said Conor.

Eleanor took off her hat and let the breeze blow through her hair. 'I used to take the ferry two or three times a week. I had a lover who lived at Oakwood Beach. An artist. Rex, his name was. Somewhere in this world there's a very beautiful painting of me, lying on a couch wearing nothing but a pearl necklace.'

The ferry sailed out into the bay, past Governors Island and the Statue of Liberty. The water glittered like broken glass, and seagulls circled around them, keening and crying.

'Rex used to say that gulls sound so sad because they're the souls of people who have drowned at sea. All the people who went down on the *Titanic* and the *Lusitania*. All those poor merchant seamen who were torpedoed during the war. That's why he always brought crackers with him, to feed them.'

She took out a cigarette and inserted it into her cigarette-holder. 'Poor Rex. He was a very good artist, but he couldn't stay away from the booze.'

Conor looked back at the Battery and the shining towers of the World Trade Center. 'You're quiet,' said Eleanor, after a while.

'It's this robbery. It's driving me crazy.'

'Well, tell me what's bothering you about it. Maybe I can help.'

'It just doesn't make any sense. I mean, *two* gangs of thieves, both going after the identical safety deposit boxes, all within the space of a couple of hours? I believe in coincidences but I don't believe in miracles.'

'I suppose Ramon and Magda must have hypnotized you into giving them the combination to the strongroom.'

'Well, me and Darrell Bussman both. I knew half of the code but Darrell was the only person who knew the other half. Even my deputy Sal didn't know it.'

'And of course you don't have any way of proving that you're telling the truth?'

'I should have let the other two guys get away with the boxes, shouldn't I? Then everybody would have thought it was them, instead of me.'

Eleanor blew a stream of cigarette smoke into the wind. 'You were only doing what you thought was right, weren't you? Sometimes, when you do what's right, the consequences can be very unfair. Then all you can do is grin and bear it.'

Conor had the feeling that she wasn't talking only about the robbery. She turned her face away for a while, and he didn't say anything to interrupt her thoughts.

Eventually, though, she said, 'It's interesting, you

129

know, that both pairs of robbers went for exactly the same boxes. How do you think that happened?'

'The only feasible explanation is that they both had an identical list.'

'But where do you think they'd gotten that from?'

'Don't ask me. I guess there's a remote possibility that Ramon and Magda hypnotized me into downloading the list from my computer . . . but how those two other buttheads got a hold of it . . . who knows? Apart from Spurr's lawyers, the only people who had access to it were me and Sal – and Sal, well, he had his problems, poor bastard, but he was straight as they come.'

The ferry was passing the Military Ocean Terminal with its cranes and its containers and its railroad cars. Off to the south-east, past the Narrows, they could see the cat's cradle of the Verrazano suspension bridge. Beyond the bridge, in the Lower Bay, an opalescent haze hung over the ocean, and a white-painted ferry was sailing out of it like a ghost ship.

'There's another thing that's been bothering me,' said Conor. 'When those two thieves held us up in my office and told us to open the wall safe, the white guy went directly to the picture that it was hidden behind and took the picture down himself. Now, I'd be really interested to find out how he knew where it was.'

'It does sound more and more like an inside job, doesn't it?'

Conor shook his head. 'I don't know, Eleanor. None of this has any logic to it. I have this really strong hunch that something's going down here, something big, but I just can't get any kind of a handle on what it is, or how it's being done, or why.'

'That's why we've come to talk to Sidney, isn't it?'

'Listen,' said Conor. They were approaching the Staten Island pier. The ferry blew its whistle and children waved at them from the shore. 'The last thing I want to do is get you involved in any kind of trouble.'

'Trouble? My dear man, I've been in trouble most of my life. I can't get enough of it.'

Just as they docked, Eleanor's mobile phone rang. It was Lacey, speaking from a callbox outside the Rockefeller Center.

'Michael Baer called me about five minutes ago, from your lawyers. Almost all of the safe deposit box owners have doubled their offers to pay you a reward. They say they just want their property back as soon as possible, no questions asked.'

'They've *doubled* their offers? All of them?'

'Almost all of them. They told Michael that you called every one of their lawyers personally and that you insisted on it.'

'I'm pretty goddamn demanding, aren't I?'

'You sure are. But it looks like it's paid off. Michael says we could be looking at over seventy million dollars.'

'Holy Mother of God. Michael has to tell them that I've got nothing to do with this. Whoever's been calling them, it sure wasn't me.'

'He tried to tell them. They won't believe him. They thought he was just trying to screw the price up even more.'

131

'I'm really beginning to wish I *had* taken the stuff. Did I say anything about how I wanted the money paid over?'

'It seems like you're going to call everybody later and tell them exactly what to do. Where to drop the money, where to pick up their property.'

'How am I going to tell them all that when I don't even know it myself?'

'I guess the person who's pretending to be you will fill them in with everything they need to know.'

'Listen, Lacey, keep me up to date, huh? I need to know how the safety deposit box owners are going to hand over the money. The money-drop, that's where they're going to be really vulnerable.'

There was a pause, and then Lacey said, 'Are you OK, Conor? You don't know how much I miss you. I know it's stupid, but I've almost forgotten what you look like.'

'I miss you, too. But I'm OK. I'm making progress. I think so, anyhow.'

'I feel like we've lost each other for ever.'

'We haven't, believe me. Two or three days, tops, this will all be straightened out.'

'I can hear seagulls.'

'They're not seagulls, sweetheart. They're souls.'

Sidney Randall lived in a tall, three-story house on Seguine Road, right down on the southern tip of Staten Island by Wolfes Pond Park. The house was made of stained red wood, with cream-painted windows and elaborately carved woodwork along the veranda; and it was deeply shaded by elms. In the driveway a ginger tomcat slept away the morning

132

on the rusting gold roof of an elderly Chrysler New Yorker. The front yard was overgrown with wildflowers and creepers; and convolvulus had already started to embrace the house, as if it wanted to drag it down into the earth.

Conor and Eleanor climbed out of the taxi into the heat.

'You know this guy?' asked the taxi driver.

'He's a friend,' said Eleanor, sharply.

The taxi driver shrugged and said nothing, although he clearly implied that Sidney Randall was a well-known local fruitcake. 'You want to be rescued, call this number,' he said, and handed them a card.

'Funny,' said Eleanor. 'I never thought that I'd ever come back to Staten Island. Rex had a studio not far from here, on Sharrott Avenue.'

The front yard was busy with crickets. They climbed the steps and Conor pulled the doorbell, which had the cast-iron head of a snarling wolf. They waited a long time, listening for any response. Eleanor shaded her eyes with her hand and peered in through the diamond-shaped panes of yellow stained glass. 'I can't *see* anybody,' she said. 'But it looks like the back door is open, and I'm sure that I can hear music.'

'Let's try the rear,' said Conor.

They walked around the side of the house, negotiating a narrow path prickly with briars. The music grew more distinct: it was *Pavane pour une infante défunte* by Ravel – slow, melancholy piano music, in time with the heat and the chirruping of the crickets, and the treacly feeling that they had left the city behind and arrived in another world.

In the yard, in a hammock slung between two apple trees, a tall bony old man was sleeping, with a white linen hat over his face. He wore a blue-striped shirt with a white collar, and voluminous white pants. A butterfly was perched on his bare big toe.

'God, he's aged,' said Eleanor.

She approached him through the knee-length grass. The butterfly flickered away. She stood beside him for a while, just looking at him. Then she slowly lifted his hat.

He opened his eyes. He had an angular, sculptured face, with a prominent nose and a straggly gray beard. He looked like one of those characters standing third from the left in a Civil War photograph, while Sherman sits in front of him at a small folding table.

'Saints alive, I'm dreaming,' he said.

'No, you're not,' said Eleanor. 'It's really, really me.'

He sat up and peered at her. 'By God, Bipsy, you've grown older.'

'It's been a long time, that's why.'

'Oh, don't get me wrong. You're just as beautiful as you ever were.'

'Too late,' said Eleanor, in mock-petulance. 'You've said it now.'

'But it's true! Did I ever lie to you? Did I ever lie to you once?'

'Oh, stop all the sentimental nonsense. I'd like you to meet a new friend of mine, Conor O'Neil.'

Sidney swung awkwardly out of his hammock. He came forward and laid his hand on Conor's shoulder. 'Glad to know you, Mr O'Neil. I won't shake hands with you, it's just a little problem I have. But you're welcome all the same. How about some iced tea? Or maybe a glass of wine? It's damned hot, isn't it?'

'The Vaudeville Artistes' Fund said you were dead, Sidney,' Eleanor told him. 'You'd better call them up and tell them that the rumors are exaggerated.'

'Hell, no. I told them that I was dead to stop them pestering me. They kept calling me and asking me to come to charity cookouts and old folks' gettogethers. I never worked for nothing before I retired and sure as hell I'm not going to work for nothing now. Just because I'm a senior they think they can take advantage.'

He led them inside the house. It was much cooler here, even though he didn't have air conditioning. He had left the doors open so that the heat could flow through and six or seven windchimes jangled in chorus.

The floors were bare-boarded and varnished, with a scattering of threadbare rugs. The furniture looked as if it had been ordered from a Sears catalog at the turn of the century. Heavy quarter-sawed-oak chairs with leathercloth upholstery; sideboards that whole families could have lived in; Roman couches and china cabinets. In the hallway there were scores of framed posters advertising 'Sidney Randall, Mesmerist Extraordinary' with photographs of a much younger Sidney with his eyes bulging and his fingers extended in the archetypal pose of the stage hypnotist.

135

'Never thought that I'd ever clap eyes on you again, Bipsy,' said Sidney. He led them through to a high-ceilinged living room with a tigerskin rug and two bronze statuettes of naked Native American girls with feathers in their hair. The blinds were drawn but it was so sunny outside that the whole room was suffused with light. 'Sit down . . . what'll you have to drink?'

'You don't remember?'

Sidney touched two fingertips to his forehead and then he said, 'Sure I do. White Witch. Not sure if I have any Cointreau.'

He padded off on his bare feet to fix Eleanor's drink. While he did so, Conor leaned forward in his chair and said, '*Bipsy*? You and he were—?'

'Close,' Eleanor nodded. 'Very, *very* close. But Sidney's trouble is that he has to go off from time to time and commune with nature. He'll wake up one morning and say, "That's it, I'm gone," and he'll pack his bag and fly to New Mexico and spend the next six months living with the Zuñi Indians. He loved me, you know, in his way. But he never really understood what devotion meant. Well – not the kind of devotion that *I* needed.'

Sidney came back with a White Witch for Eleanor, complete with sugar-dusted mint leaves, and a large glass of cold white wine for Conor. He sat down and said, 'You didn't come over just to say hello. Not that I'm complaining.'

'Conor needs your help,' said Eleanor.

'This is nothing to do with hypnotism, I hope? I don't get involved with hypnotism any more, except to write about it.'

136

'Well . . . it is in a way,' said Conor, and explained what had happened at Spurr's Fifth Avenue. Sidney shook his head from side to side like a pendulum. 'That's a bad business. That's a real bad business. But I can't help you there. I had a tragic experience with hypnotism six or seven years ago and I swore that I'd never get involved in it again.'

'You don't have to get involved with hypnotism again,' said Eleanor. 'All that Conor needs to know is how he can find Hypnos and Hetti.'

'I wish I could help, Bipsy. I really do. But I haven't heard a word from Ramon in a coon's age. I thought he'd gone back to Tijuana or wherever. Even if you could find them, what could you do? They'd shake your hand, and the next thing you knew you'd be waking up five hours later wondering what the hell had hit you.'

'That's what Ramon did to me,' said Conor. 'He shook my hand. He shook my hand and said, "Do you know me?"'

'Standard hypnotic induction,' Sidney nodded. 'That's why I won't shake hands with people. And that's why you can't go looking for Hypnos and Hetti without knowing about hypnosis, and what powers it can give you, and how you can resist it; and that's why I can't help you, because I won't have anything to do with it. Not any more.'

'What happened?' asked Conor.

'Well . . . I'm sure you don't want to hear another sad story. You've got problems enough of your own.'

Conor said, 'I'm desperate, Sidney. And I'm so damned frustrated. If I can't find Hypnos and Hetti then I'm going to spend the rest of my life as a

137

fugitive. Nobody can go on running for ever; and one day I'm going to be crossing the street or stepping out of some market and smack! that's going to be it.'

Sidney stood up and walked across to the fireplace. Over the fireplace hung a huge romanticized oil painting of a Native American struggling with a bear.

'A young girl came to me,' he said, with his back turned. 'Her name was Vanessa. She was anorexic, and she wanted to learn how to hypnotize herself so that she wouldn't think that she was overweight. I refused at first, because she didn't seem to be stable, you know? She was prone to mood swings, outbursts of weeping, that kind of thing. But she was persistent, and her parents gave me their blessing. So I taught her how to put herself into a mild hypnotic trance. I taught her how to convince herself that she was light as a feather.'

'And did it work?' asked Eleanor.

'Oh, yes. It worked only too well. Vanessa believed that she was so light that she could fly. One day she went to the top of the building where she lived and stepped right off the edge, thinking that the wind would carry her.'

He paused, and licked his lips, and then he said, 'She fell eighteen stories, right through a glassed-in conservatory. She was decapitated.'

'How do you know it wasn't suicide?'

'Oh, there was a witness. One of her friends. Vanessa said, "Look at me . . . I'm as light as a dandelion-clock!" and over she went. That's when I gave up hypnotism for good.'

'Couldn't you make one last exception?' said Eleanor.

138

Sidney gave her a world-weary smile. 'I was always making exceptions for you, wasn't I, Bipsy?'

'Wasn't I worth it?'

'Oh for sure. I'm just sorry that you and me ended up the way we did. I hurt you, didn't I?'

'Come on. You were young. You had other things to think of.'

'I guess.' Sidney's pain was self-evident.

Eleanor stood up and took hold of Sidney's hands. 'You can't go on regretting the past, Sidney.'

'Why not? I'm seventy-eight now. I don't have much of a future.'

'Neither will Conor if you don't help him. Come on, Stanley. Please. Pretty please.'

She gave him a look that was almost ridiculously coquettish. Sidney looked away, looked back, and then burst out laughing.

'I can't believe you! You're damn well flirting with me, aren't you, just like you always did!'

'Don't tell me you don't like it.'

'All right,' he said. 'I like it. And – all right, I'll see what I can do to help you out.'

'You're an angel,' said Eleanor, and kissed him twice.

11

Sidney took them to a local restaurant called the Richmond Inn, a cozy colonial building with red checkered tablecloths and decoy ducks over the fireplace. They sat outside on the veranda overlooking a small paved garden. Conor ordered ham hock and peas, while Eleanor chose a smoked chicken salad. Sidney said that he wasn't hungry and contented himself with repeated handfuls of salted pecan nuts.

There was no wind here, absolutely none, and the garden was so hot that it looked as if they were seeing it through polished glass.

Sidney ordered a bottle of dry white wine. Before the waiter could open it, Conor lifted it out of its earthenware cooler. 'Here,' he said, showing it to Eleanor and Sidney. 'A perfectly ordinary bottle of wine. But watch.'

He wrapped the bottle in his napkin so that only the neck protruded. Then he nicked the foil cap with his knife, peeled it back and folded it so quickly that neither Eleanor nor Sidney could see what he was doing. He banged the bottom of the bottle on the table, so that the cutlery jumped. There was a second's pause, and then the cork dropped onto Eleanor's place-mat, with a tiny man sitting astride it, fashioned out of foil.

Sidney couldn't help laughing. 'That's about the fanciest way of opening a bottle of wine I've ever seen.'

'You should have been in vaudeville, too,' said Eleanor.

Conor shook his head. 'It's only a trick my Uncle Dermot taught me. He said that stage magic was a good lesson in life. People will believe what they want to believe, even when you prove them wrong.'

'Very much like hypnotism,' said Sidney.

As they ate, he explained the difference between clinical hypnotism and stage hypnotism. He had a curiously soft, droning voice that reminded Conor of a bee going from flower to flower. 'Before I went on the stage, I was a clinical hypnotherapist. Studied eight years at Temple University in Philadelphia under Milton Erickson. I took up public performing more to make a point than to make a living – although I *did* make a living, and a very good one. I simply wasn't impressed by any of the stage hypnotists, even the famous ones. They were all so clumsy . . . and some of them were positively dangerous. I mean, gosh, it was like handing a loaded revolver to a three-year-old.

'Most of the time they were putting their subjects into trances that were far deeper than they needed to be. In the Forties and Fifties I used to go see guys like Ralph Slater or Franz Polgar, "the World's Fastest Hypnotist". But they couldn't hold a candle

141

to clinical hypnotherapists like Erickson.

'Somebody like Erickson could hypnotize you without even talking to you. I had breakfast with him once, and although he never put me into what you might call a formal trance, he kept making this repetitive little movement with his hand and before I knew what I was doing I had reached out spontaneously and picked up the pot of coffee on the table. He had given me a nonverbal request that he wanted another cup.

'A good hypnotist doesn't have to swing a pendant in front of your eyes, or say any of that stuff like "sleep . . . sleep . . . your eyes are getting heavy". He can use a whole variety of nonverbal techniques to induce catalepsy – and he can have you in a trance before you know it. That's what Ramon Perez and Magda Slanic were especially good at. I'm pretty convinced that at least one of them must be a clinically trained hypnotherapist. I talked to Perez a few times when Hypnos and Hetti were performing in cabaret off Seventh Avenue, but Perez wouldn't answer any questions about his act, or where he learned it. He used to say that his talent was *"una maldición"* – a curse – but whether he meant it was a curse to him or a curse to other people, I never found out. It was certainly a curse to *you*, Conor.'

Conor said, 'I always thought that I was too darn suspicious for anybody to hypnotize me – too wary. You know, I'm a cop. I'm actually *trained* to be suspicious. But I'll tell you one thing for sure: I'm never going to let it happen again.'

Sidney nodded sympathetically and Conor found

himself watching him nod. His eyes were unfocused as if he were staring not at Conor's face but at the creeper-covered wall just behind Conor's chair.

'You *thought* you were too suspicious. You *thought* you were too wary. But you forget that it's very comfortable, going into a trance, and it doesn't take long for you to feel that you don't care whether or not you are going into a trance or not, you recognize that your suspicions and your hostility are quite unfounded.

'Of course you know you will never let anybody put you into a deep trance again but a light trance is very comfortable. You can allow yourself to be taken into a light trance while still staying alert

'And

'Doing your job properly

'And

'After all a light trance is very, very comfortable. In fact it's unbelievable how comfortable it is, how restful. You don't have to move or talk or let anything bother you.'

Conor couldn't take his eyes off Sidney's nodding head. He knew where he was. He knew that he was here, sitting at the lunch table with Sidney and Eleanor, and yet he wasn't.

'You don't want to go into another trance, do you?' said Sidney. 'You know that you would much prefer to be doing something else

'And

'While you're thinking about that, there's something else, isn't there? So why don't you look at it?'

Conor felt strangely light-headed. He turned toward the restaurant door and there was Lacey in

143

the kitchen. The table was covered in newspaper and she was mixing paint.

'Lacey?' he said. She turned and smiled at him, and brushed a wispy hair away from her face with the back of her hand. 'Did you paint the bedroom door yet?'

She shook her head. Conor could hear music in the background, and traffic.

Sidney said, 'Lacey . . . that's your girlfriend?'

'That's right. She's been painting the bedroom.'

'Where is she now, Conor?'

'There . . . in the kitchen. She's mixing paints.'

'Maybe she needs some help. Why don't you take her that paintbrush?'

Sidney pointed to the large paintbrush on the table in front of him. Conor picked it up, pushed back his chair, and walked across to the restaurant door and right inside. He laid the paintbrush on the kitchen table and then he leaned forward and gave Lacey a kiss on the forehead.

'Conor, you're awake now,' said Sidney.

Conor said, 'Of course I'm awake.' And then suddenly he looked around and found himself standing inside the restaurant next to a table where an elderly couple were staring up at him in alarm.

'Excuse me, I'm sorry,' he told them. He turned to Sidney, who was leaning back in his chair and smiling. 'I guess I, um – I guess I thought you were somebody else.'

He went back outside, but as he did so the elderly man called after him, 'Pardon me, sir. But I think you've forgotten something!'

He was holding out the large wooden salad spoon which Conor had put down in the middle of his corned-beef hash.

'You hypnotized me,' said Conor. 'I was alert. I was aware. I didn't want to be hypnotized. So how the hell did you do it?'

'It wasn't difficult. You've been under a whole lot of stress lately, mental and physical. I simply suggested that you would find it relaxing and comfortable to go into a very light trance, and that's what you did. There are so many people like you who think that nobody can ever hypnotize them, but I'd say that ninety per cent of the population are susceptible to hypnotic induction.'

'So what did I do? Why did I put that spoon in that poor old guy's lunch?'

'You imagined it was something else – a paintbrush. You were taking it to your girlfriend Lacey. You saw her in the kitchen, mixing paint.'

Conor shook his head. 'I don't remember thinking that it was a paintbrush. I don't remember anything.'

He was impressed. He couldn't help being impressed. But he was annoyed, too, because Sidney had been able to manipulate him so easily and because he had made a fool out of him, however gently he had done it. The elderly couple were eating peach-and-vanilla ice cream now and watching everything he did with deep suspicion.

Eleanor took hold of his hand and gave it a reassuring squeeze. 'Sidney would never do anything to harm you, believe me. He's just *showing* you.'

Conor said, 'The difference is, Sidney, you *talked* to me. You talked me into that trace. But Ramon Perez only shook me by the hand and said, "Do you know me?"'

Sidney clapped another handful of nuts into his mouth and vigorously chewed. 'That's right. That was a textbook handshake induction. It's very effective indeed. What you do is, you begin by shaking hands with your subject in the normal way. "Oh, hi, how do you do?" You can do it to anybody. But it's the way you *let loose* that's important. You draw your hand away with a gentle touch of your thumb, a kind of trailing sensation with your little finger, a touch of your middle finger, too. This feeling is enough to distract your subject's attention. It makes him uncertain, and at the same time it gives him or her a feeling of expectancy, that something important is going to happen.

'At this point, you lift your subject's wrist – but very, very gently, so that it doesn't even feel like an upward push. Then you give a downward touch. The subject's hand is left in midair – not going up and not going down. They can't move it unless you tell them to.

'That's when you say something confusing like "Didn't I see you in Memphis last year?" – which makes your subject turn inward. He's looking for an answer, some kind of orientation, and you're encouraging him to go into a trance by asking him questions which make him look inside of himself. The whole nature of hypnotic trance is *inner direction* and *searching*. Your subject is so preoccupied with rummaging around inside of his mind that he

146

experiences anesthesia, or a temporary lapse in vision or hearing, or a feeling of *déjà vu*.

'The thing of it is that some level of light trance isn't at all unusual, even in everyday life. Think of all the times when you've been hungry or thirsty or tired but you've put those feelings aside because you've had a job to do – some case to solve. Your inner search has taken priority over your physical demands.'

'I still don't see how Ramon Perez could have hypnotized me so quickly.'

'OK. You want quick? Give me your hand.'

'I'm not sure I want to do this.'

'It'll be fine. Trust me, I'm a hypnotist.'

Conor reached out across the table and Sidney took hold of his hand. His fingers were dry and gentle and caressing. He said, 'Something's happened to your hand. It's numb. You can't lift it.'

Conor tried to raise his arm but it wouldn't move. It didn't feel heavy, but it felt anesthetized, as if he could have stuck needles into it without feeling any pain at all. He tried to wriggle his fingers but they wouldn't respond.

'Now you're going to lift up your arm . . . that's it, higher, higher, higher.' Sidney touched Conor's knuckles to prevent him from taking it up any further. 'Good . . . now you're going to lower it. You're all right now. All of your feeling is starting to return. Feels a bit sore, doesn't it? Feels like you've broken out with some kind of a rash.'

He was right: Conor felt a burning sensation, as if he had brushed up against poison ivy. 'How do you *do* that?' he said.

147

'It takes training, but fundamentally it isn't difficult. You have to care about people, that's all; and learn to recognize what their anxieties are. Most people have the answers to their own problems right there, right inside of themselves. They want to confront them but they daren't. All a hypnotherapist does is to reassure them that they can cope with them, that everything's going to be manageable. Oh, and by the way, your rash has cleared up.'

The burning faded. Conor turned his arm this way and that, but there was no sign of any redness whatsoever.

'Could you train me to do that?' he asked.

'For sure. You seem to have the right kind of demeanor for it. You speak quietly. You give off a strong sense of inner authority. You're experienced in dealing with people – particularly people with problems.'

'And that would help me to handle Hypnos and Hetti? Always supposing I can find them, of course.'

Sidney nodded. 'I could show you most of their induction techniques, and how to be resistant to them. You'd just have to bear in mind that they're two of the best hypnotists ever.'

'How long would it take?'

'It depends what level of competence you want to reach. I could teach you basic trance induction in a matter of days.'

'And would you?'

Sidney hesitated, but Eleanor said, 'Come on, Sidney . . . Conor and I could stay here for a long weekend. It would be just like old times.'

'Well . . . all right,' Sidney agreed.

Eleanor leaned over and kissed him. 'I missed you so much when you left me,' she said.

'I wish I never had. I really do.'

They were still talking about old times when Conor noticed two men walk into the front of the restaurant and approach the desk. Both of them wore amber-lensed sunglasses and had short, cropped hair. In spite of the heat, they wore sport coats. One of them spoke to the manageress, and she pointed to the garden.

He nodded, and then started to make his way swiftly toward them, while his companion remained by the door. That aroused Conor's suspicions instantly. If they had come here to eat, why weren't they coming to the garden together?

No – this was your classic hit situation. One man to whack the victim and the other to keep him covered. As he came weaving between the tables, Conor could already see the man's hand reaching inside his coat.

Without hesitation he picked up his half-finished plateful of food and hurled it through the restaurant door. The man tried to dodge it, but it caught him on the shoulder and splattered peas and gravy all over his coat.

The gun came out. Conor tipped their table over, smashing their plates, glasses and water-jug. Cutlery jangled on the patio floor like alarm bells. He dragged Eleanor off her chair and onto the paving, so that the table acted as a shield. He shouted, '*Down!*' to Sidney, seizing the leg of his pants and pulling him off his chair, too. There was a sharp whistling crack from inside the restaurant and a bullet banged into the oak-plank tabletop.

Eleanor, with her hands clapped over her ears, crouched down as low as she could and stared at Conor open-mouthed and fearful. There was another crack, and splinters of wood flew off the rim of the table and showered them. Inside the restaurant people were screaming and Conor could hear chairs being knocked over.

Normally, a gunman would have allowed himself only a few seconds to finish them off so that he could make his getaway. But if this gunman was a cop himself – which Conor suspected he was – there was every likelihood that the Richmond County police would make their way here by the scenic route.

Through a chink in the tabletop he saw the gunman cautiously approaching them. He couldn't see his face, but *you are a cop*, he thought. *I can tell by the way you move.*

'Has he gone?' whispered Eleanor.

Conor shook his head.

'Then what are you going to do?' asked Sidney.

Conor waited until the gunman was less than fifteen feet away. But there was only one thing he *could* do. He couldn't risk Eleanor or Sidney getting hurt, or anybody else in the Richmond Inn, for that matter. He called, 'Don't shoot, I'm coming out!' then stood up in full view of the gunman with his hands lifted.

'Don't try anything cute,' the gunman told him. 'I don't care whether you wind up dead or alive, but I get more money if you're alive.'

150

'Are you a cop?' asked Conor.

'What's it to you?'

'I know a cop when I see one, that's all.'

The gunman held his automatic two-handed, steady as a rock. 'I used to be a cop. Just like you.'

'You *used* to be a cop? So what are you now?'

'Security adviser, just like you.'

'Oh, yes? So who sent you here?'

'Certain interested parties.'

'Name one.'

'I don't have to name one. I just want everything back. All of it.'

'You want *what* back? I don't know what the hell you're talking about.'

The gunman was growing agitated. His partner, by the restaurant door, gave him a sharp whistle, which obviously meant that time was running out. If his partner had a gun, he wasn't showing it, but he was standing right in the aisle so that none of the customers could leave. The customers had stopped screaming, and now they were beginning to show signs of irritation and bravado. *Very explosive situation*, thought Conor. The last thing he wanted was for some white-haired senior to start playing the hero.

'OK,' he told the gunman. 'But none of it's here. We'll have to go back to Manhattan to get it.'

'You'd better not be jerking me around.'

'Come on, man,' urged his partner. 'We're running out of time.'

'Listen,' said Conor. 'Stay cool. You can take me back to Manhattan and I'll hand the stuff over.'

'You'd better not be jerking me around. I mean it.'

151

'You're a barbarian,' said the elderly man in whose corned-beef hash Conor had laid his salad server.

'I'm a what? I'm a fucking what?'

'A barbarian. A throwback. That's all. You're nothing without that gun.'

'Are you talking to me?' said the gunman. 'Are you talking to *me*?' Then, without hesitation, he pressed the muzzle of his silencer up against the old man's right kneecap and fired. The old man collapsed onto the floor, his knee spraying out blood. His wife let out a cry like an injured bird and knelt on the floor beside him.

'For Christ's sake!' raged Conor. 'What the hell did you have to do that for? He was wrong: you're not a barbarian! You're a goddamned animal!'

The gunman came right up to Conor and pointed his gun between his eyes, so close that Conor had to squint. The gunman's cheeks were sandblasted with acne and his close-cropped hair was thick with dandruff. He was breathing very hard.

'This is your last chance. We want the fucking stuff, all of it, and we want it now.'

'OK,' said Conor, trying to control himself. 'Just don't hurt any more people, OK?'

'Come on, then,' the gunman told him. 'The quicker we get out of here the quicker we get out of here.' He turned to the elderly woman on her knees on the floor, sobbing as she tried to bind her husband's knee with gingham napkins. 'Ma'am . . . will you do me a terrific favor and shut the fuck up?'

From years of experience, Conor could quickly sense when criminals were losing control. It

152

happened in crime after crime, especially in armed robbery. The most important thing to do was to try to keep them calm, and well below the critical point where fear and excitement would lead them to start shooting anybody and everybody, no matter whether they presented any real threat or not. 'Red mist', they called it.

Conor came out from behind the table. But, as he did so, Sidney stood up, calmly brushing his pants with his hand. The gunman swung his gun round, pointed it at him and barked, 'You stay right there, grandad. And don't even think about moving.'

'I wouldn't dream of moving,' said Sidney. 'Don't you know who I am?'

'I'm not interested in who you are.'

'I know. But I'm the one who can sort out all of your problems for you.'

'What are you – what are you babbling about? What problems? What?'

Sidney's voice droned, settled, gathered its nectar and then went droning on. 'You don't know what's wrong with you. Many people don't know. They need to be guided to find their inner capacities. I know you've difficulties but we can deal with those difficulties.'

'What the hell's the matter with you? I'm not listening to this!'

'But you're interested, aren't you? You're interested in dealing with your problems. You don't have to do anything. You don't have to talk or move or make any kind of effort. You don't even have to listen to me because your unconscious will go on listening to me and feed you all the information you need. You're so tense but you don't need to be tense. It's much more comfortable for you to be relaxed. You don't have to go into a trance but it would make you feel much more able to cope

'And

'Much less stressed because you've been so stressed lately, haven't you, worrying about money

'And

'All those other things that irritate you, especially since your life doesn't seem to be going so well at the moment. But it's temporary, it's only a bad patch which you and I can sort out between us

'And

'Help you to find stability again, security, and comfort

'And

'Comfort

'And

'Sleep.'

The gunman was staring at Sidney as if he had been hit on the head by a falling brick. His eyes were unfocused, his breathing shallow.

His partner by the front door was panicking. 'Jed! Jed! What's going on, man? We gotta get out of here!'

Sidney said, 'You can't hear anybody, Jed, except for me.'

'Jed! For Christ's sake! What's happening?'

Jed stayed where he was, still staring. 'You are going far away now, Jed,' said Sidney. 'You are going far, far away.'

At last, desperate, Jed's partner left the front door and came hurrying through the restaurant, wrenching a huge nickel-plated Magnum out of his shoulder-holster. He was bigger than Jed, black-haired with a puglike nose and a large gold earring.

'Jed? What's happening, man? Come on, Jed! Move!'

'He can't,' said Conor.

'What are you talking about, he can't? What the hell have you done to him? Jed! For Christ's sake, man, get it together!' He shook Jed's shoulders. Then he slapped his face, hard, but Jed didn't even flinch.

'I want to know what the fuck's happening here,' his partner insisted. He pointed his gun at Conor and said, 'You've got a price on your head, man, dead or alive, so don't think that I'm spoiled for choice.'

'Jed,' said Sidney, in the same persistent, flower-pollinating tone of voice. 'A wild bear has come into the restaurant, and he's threatening to kill you. He's standing right next to you. Can you see him?'

'Yes,' Jed replied. 'I can see him.'

'I think it would be a wise move for you to protect yourself, don't you, Jed? Lift your gun and point it at the wild bear's head.'

'Now, hold up a damned minute here,' Jed's partner protested. 'What's this bear shit?'

Jed raised his right arm and pointed his gun straight at his partner's forehead. His partner looked horrified and mystified at the same time. 'Jed, man, what are you doing? Jed, man, this is me. This is Yapko.' But Jed's gun arm didn't waver.

Jed's partner was still pointing his Magnum at Conor but his resolve was beginning to waver.

'Mexican standoff,' said Conor. 'If you shoot me,

155

Jed's going to shoot you. Why don't you put down the gun and admit when you're licked?'

There was a long-drawn-out moment of extreme tension. The sweat dripped off Yapko's upper lip and he nervously licked it. Eleanor tried to stand up, but Sidney laid a hand on her shoulder to prevent her. The crickets sang in the hot, glutinous garden.

'He really thinks I'm a bear?' asked Yapko.

Sidney nodded. 'He really thinks you're a bear. An angry, man-eating grizzly.'

'Come on,' said Conor. 'Let's end this thing peacefully, shall we?'

Yapko sniffed and lowered his head slightly and that was when Conor knew that everything had gone wrong. Yapko swung his gun around to point it at Jed, and at that instant Sidney said, 'Fire!'

The two explosions were almost simultaneous. Jed's face was blasted apart in a horrifying blizzard of scarlet flesh, baring his teeth in a terrible grin. Yapko's head ballooned for a second, and then his scalp flapped open at the back – spurting out a short, sharp torrent of brains and blood and fragments of bone.

The men dropped into each other's arms like clowns and tumbled noisily onto the floor. A cloud of acrid smoke dawdled over them for a while, then gradually edged away.

Eleanor stood up, trembling. The manageress started to scream, a high-pitched scream that was more like a whistle.

12

Conor said, 'Out – before the cops get here. Don't catch anybody's eye. Don't hesitate.' They walked quickly through the pandemonium and out of the restaurant's front door. They were already two blocks away and around the next corner before they heard sirens and the sliding of tires.

'Stop—' said Eleanor. 'I have to stop for a moment.' She was breathless and her face was ashy gray. 'Angina . . . I'm not supposed to do anything too strenuous.'

'Don't you have medication?'

'Left it at home. Don't worry. I'll be all right. Just let me get my breath back.'

She leaned against a bookstore doorway with her hand over her heart. While they waited, Conor said to Sidney, 'That was pretty quick thinking back there.'

'I didn't have any choice, did I?'

'I guess you didn't. But all the same.'

Sidney looked away. 'Now you know why I gave up hypnotism. It always gets you into situations where you don't have choices.'

'I'm OK now,' Eleanor volunteered. 'Just so long as we don't have to go too fast.'

They made their way slowly back toward Sidney's house, Indian-file, following a network of alleys and back lots and unkempt pathways. It was stunningly hot, and they were all still shocked by what had happened at the Richmond Inn. None of them spoke. Conor had seen people shot before; but even he had never witnessed a double shooting, and at such close range. There was a fan-shaped spray of blood halfway up his left sleeve.

They emerged on Seguine Road by the side of a green-painted clapboard house. Conor said, 'Wait,' and edged forward alongside the fence to check that the street was clear.

At first it appeared to be deserted, except for six or seven empty cars with heat rippling off their hoods, and a brindled dog asleep on somebody's front porch. But then, off to his right-hand side, deep beneath the shadow of a giant elm, Conor saw the silhouette of a black Ford Taurus. As far as he could make out, two men were sitting in it, one of them smoking.

'Everything OK?' asked Sidney, anxiously.

Conor shook his head. 'They're waiting for us. I'm sorry, but they obviously know where you live.'

'You're trying to tell me we can't go back there?'

'Not just yet, no.'

'"Not just yet"?'

'Not until I've managed to find Hypnos and Hetti. Not until I've managed to get this whole mess sorted out.'

'But for Pete's sake, that could take days, couldn't it? Or weeks, even?'

'I know, Sidney, and I'm truly sorry. If I'd had any idea that they were going to be able to track us down, I wouldn't have come here, believe me.'

'But they don't want anything from *me*, surely!'

'They'll want to know where I am; and they'll want to know who Eleanor is, and how much she knows.'

'You don't seriously think that I'd tell them anything?'

'I seriously think that you would. These are the kind of guys who wouldn't think twice about squeezing your head in a vise.'

'Oh, Sidney,' said Eleanor. 'I didn't mean to bring you so much trouble. It seems like I never bring you anything else.'

Sidney closed his eyes for a moment. He looked as if he were praying for God to keep him from losing his temper. Forgive us our tantrums, and lead us not into exasperation, amen. But then he opened his eyes again and said, 'Never mind. Don't go blaming yourself, Bipsy. Maybe this was meant to be.'

'I don't understand.'

'Well, maybe I needed something like this to shake me up a bit. It's all very well lying in a hammock day after day listening to music. But what am I doing, really, except filling in time while I'm waiting to die?'

One of the men waiting in the Taurus tossed his cigarette butt onto the sidewalk and immediately lit another. He was obviously prepared for a very long wait. 'First we have to get off Staten Island,' said

159

Conor. 'It's going to be too risky to try taking the ferry back. The best thing we can do is take a taxi into Jersey. We can change taxis at Perth Amboy and take another one to Elizabeth. Then we can get back into Manhattan through the Holland Tunnel.'

'And where are we all going to stay?' asked Sidney.

'With some friends of my girlfriend's, Sebastian Speed and Ric Vetter. They have a huge apartment on 47th Street.'

'All right, then,' said Sidney. 'I guess the sooner we get out of here, the better. I'll show you the best place to find a taxi.'

'What about your cat?' Eleanor asked him.

'Mesmer? He'll be OK. He'll go round to my neighbor when he's hungry. She'll take him in.'

'Sidney – I didn't mean to turn your whole life upside-down.'

'Well, better to be upside-down than six feet under.'

When Conor arrived on his doorstep with Eleanor and Sidney, Sebastian puckered his lips to show that he was less than delighted. He was having an early-evening cocktail party for some of his friends in the theater, and he was wearing a calf-length purple silk caftan and gold slave bands around his ankles.

The hallway was pungent with the smell of cannabis and there was high, hysterical laughter coming from the living room.

Conor said, 'Sebastian, I need a favor. I know it's an imposition, but I have two more people here who need someplace to stay.'

Sebastian threw open the door. 'Honestly, Conor,

you know you're terribly welcome, but this isn't the Chelsea.'

'Listen, I'm sorry. But I couldn't think of anyplace else to go. Besides, come on, let me make some introductions here. This, since you obviously don't recognize her, is Eleanor Bronsky.'

There was a moment's pause while Sebastian drew in a long, hyperventilating breath. Then he screamed out, 'Eleanor Bronsky! You're Eleanor *Bronsky*! My God, you're a legend! Conor, what a *coup de théâtre*! Eleanor Bronsky, at *my* cocktail party!'

Eleanor was tired and suffering from the heat, but she managed to shake Sebastian's hand and tell him, 'I'm flattered.'

'Oh, no! My God! Don't be! I'm the one who should be flattered! Ric will be over the moon!' He turned to Sidney and held out his hand. 'This must be your husband, yes? What a lucky man!'

'I'm afraid my husband's passed on. Emphysema. All those Cuban cigars.'

'How awful! I'm sorry! How crass I am! But you only have to look at Fidel Castro to see what effect those cigars can have on you! And he's a doctor, too!'

'This is Sidney Randall,' said Conor. 'The greatest hypnotist in the history of – well, hypnotism.'

'Well, it takes all sorts,' said Sebastian. He led them through to the living room, where twenty or thirty guests were gathered, some of them men and some of them men, even though they wore short skirts and high-heeled shoes and flapping false eyelashes. Calexico was playing on the CD, far-out Tex-Mex steel guitar music with marimba and

161

trumpets. Ric was standing in the far corner, wearing a floppy white see-through shirt, tight black pants and brown Errol Flynn boots. He had his arm around a pale, white-haired creature with enormous brown eyes and a short white muslin dress, like a stick insect that had never seen the light of day.

'*Eleanor!*' crowed Ric. 'I can't *believe* it!' He and Eleanor kissed and embraced, while the stick insect clung to its elbows and let out testy, impatient sighs and rolled its eyes up into its head.

'So you're a hypnotist?' Sebastian asked Sidney. 'I don't think I ever met a hypnotist before.'

'I used to be a hypnotherapist,' Sidney told him. 'I don't practice any more.'

'Well, that's such a pity! I have this insatiable craving for Reece's Pieces, but they play havoc with my figure.'

'Do you live here?'

Sebastian looked perplexed. 'Yes. I live here, yes.'

'Do you work in interior design?'

'Yes.'

'Is today Thursday?'

'Yes.'

'Is it five forty-five p.m.?'

'Yes.'

'Do you wish to stop eating Reece's Pieces?'

'Yes.'

'If I could put you into a trance to stop you from eating Reece's Pieces, would you want me to do it?'

Sebastian stared at Sidney and said nothing. Sidney looked across at Conor and gave him a tired, amused smile.

'This is what we call the "yes set",' he said. 'Your

162

subject has a comparatively short span of attention so he goes into a trance simply to escape the boredom of giving the same answer to the same obvious questions.'

'He's in a trance? Already? Just like that?'

'I told you: it's easy. He's a very receptive subject and he wants something from me.'

He turned back to Sebastian and said, 'You hate Reece's Pieces. Next time you eat one of them, you will feel sick to your stomach. You will awake when I count to five and you will forget everything that happened. One – two – three – four – five—'

Sebastian looked around him and shivered. 'Do you know something? I had the strangest feeling, like a goose just walked over my grave.'

'Maybe you shouldn't have the air conditioning so cold,' said Conor.

'You're right. Maybe I shouldn't. Maybe a sheen of sweat would make me look more Afro-American. What do you think?'

The party broke up around eight. There were giggles and screams and kisses and endless goodbyes, but at last there was silence and Conor and Sidney and Eleanor were able to go to bed. Conor shared the main guest room with Sidney, and Eleanor was put up in the small, prettily wallpapered 'writing room' which contained an antique desk and a single bed where either Sebastian or Ric could sleep if they had a tiff.

After she had showered, Eleanor put on a long, flowing creation in shimmering turquoise which Sebastian had lent her as a nightdress. She came to

163

Conor's door and knocked. 'I just wanted to tell you that the bathroom's free.'

'Thanks, Eleanor.'

'There's something else . . . I wanted to say that you shouldn't blame yourself for everything that's happened.'

'Well, that's generous of you to say so, but if I hadn't come to you for help—'

Eleanor firmly shook her head. 'You didn't oblige us to help, Conor. In my experience there are some powerful currents running through life, and sometimes we get swept along with them, whether we want to or not.'

Sidney was sitting on the end of the bed, incongruously dressed in a Dolce e Gabbana T-shirt and a pair of silk shorts that looked as if they had once belonged to Muhammad Ali. 'I think you're right, Bipsy. Whatever this current is that we're caught up in now, it was strong enough to bring you back to me, after all these years, wasn't it?'

Sidney and Eleanor were looking into each other's eyes so meltingly that Conor had to change the subject. 'That was incredible, Sidney – the way you hypnotized those taxi drivers so that they would never remember that they picked us up.'

'Nonsense. That was nothing but a party trick. Easier than the way you opened that wine bottle. I'll teach you to do it yourself.'

'Thanks. But what I have to do next is talk to some of the people whose safe deposit boxes have been rifled. I need to talk to their lawyers, too. I want to know exactly what I'm supposed to have said to them, and how I've managed to double the money they're prepared to pay to get their property back. There's no case that doesn't have clues.'

'So what's your plan of action?' asked Sidney.

'Well . . . I know for sure that one of those stolen safe deposit boxes belonged to Davina Gambit, who used to be married to Jack Gambit, the property tycoon. I'm going to see if I can fix up a meeting with her and her lawyer.'

'Don't you think that's kind of *chancy*?' asked Eleanor. 'They may call the police.'

'I don't think they will. This is the beauty of this particular heist. Nobody wants the cops to know what was taken . . . or the IRS, or US Customs, or the Justice Department. Besides, I'm going to arrange it so that we can't be followed. I'm going to arrange it in a location where Slyman and his cronies won't dare to whack us.'

'I still don't see exactly what you have in mind.'

'Listen . . . I don't think there's any question that Davina Gambit's lawyer will have been approached by Hypnos and Hetti offering to sell her private papers back. The Gambit divorce settlement was like the collapse of the Holy Roman Empire. The alimony payments ran into tens of millions, and Jack Gambit was really sore about it. But supposing for instance that Davina Gambit has been hiding evidence that she committed adultery, or that she shifted some of Jack Gambit's funds out of the country without him knowing, or who knows what else? Jack Gambit's worth so much he doesn't know how much he's worth, but if he finds out that somebody's been ripping him off . . . well, let's put it this way: he may be rich but he's not forgiving. That's how he got rich in the first place.'

'So how is this going to lead us to Hypnos and Hetti?'

'I don't know. But that's what detective work is all about. Gathering bits and pieces, putting them together. Most of the time, even your star witnesses don't realize the value of their own evidence.'

The phone rang. It was Lacey, calling from the payphone in back of Gristede's market on Third Avenue. 'Conor? Are you OK? I'm going to have to make this quick.'

'Fine, I'm fine. How about you?'

'I miss you so much. The place seems so empty.'

'Don't worry, I think we're making progress. I've got some good people here to help me.'

'All I'm going to say is – watch the news tonight. Somebody did it again.'

'What?'

At that moment, she put down the phone. She must have been worried that somebody was watching her. Conor looked at the receiver for a moment as if he expected it to speak to him, and then hung up.

'That was Lacey. She says there's something on the news.'

The top headline of the day was that FBI agents had raided a house on East 86th Street on a tip-off that a suspected terrorist, Dennis Evelyn Branch, had been sighted in New York. Then there was the President's 'emphatic' denial that he had slept with a Cuban transvestite called Jola Ramada.

'At the midtown law offices of Goldman, Farbar

166

and Scheier today, police were trying to solve the mystery of how more than a hundred confidential files have disappeared. According to informed sources, all of these files relate to the personal lives and business dealings of some of their most eminent clients.

'The files were discovered to be missing from thirty-fourth-floor offices in the GE Building shortly after noon. No intruders were seen, no force was used, and video surveillance tapes are said to show that several trusted members of Goldman, Farbar and Scheier's staff seem to have taken the files out of the firm's security room and handed them voluntarily to a third party. All however strongly deny that they can remember doing it.'

A detective with a shock of white hair and a pastrami-colored face appeared on the screen. 'So far we're keeping a very open mind. Either we're dealing with a conspiracy here, amongst more than a dozen previously loyal staff; or else it's a case of mass memory loss. Either way, it's straight out of Ripley's *Believe It Or Not.*'

Eleanor said, 'Surely your Lieutenant Slyman is going to put two and two together after *this.*'

'I don't know,' said Conor. 'There's no hard evidence that it was Hypnos and Hetti, and I think that Drew Slyman only believes what he wants to believe – and more than that, he wants to see me dead, or at the very least indicted.'

'Hypnotically speaking, what Hypnos and Hetti are doing is *very* interesting,' Sidney remarked, in that flat, world-of-his-own voice. 'It's not so uncommon, either. There was a whole rash of

167

hypnotic robberies in South-East Asia a couple of years ago. I've written a chapter about them in my book.'

'So what happened?'

'Much the same as what's been happening here. Same kind of hypnotic induction – distracting people – confusing them – putting them into a trance. For instance there was one case in September 1966, where two men came up to a grandmother in a bus station in Singapore. They started chatting to her, nice and relaxed. Then they showed her a piece of foil with Arabic characters on it. They placed the foil in her hand – and gently touched her hand while they did it. Then they asked her to say a prayer and to perform some special ceremony by cutting a lemon with a razor blade.

'I mean, it was all nonsense, but that was the point. It was deliberately intended to confuse her. The woman says she can't remember what happened next . . . but what *did* happen was that she took off her gold bracelet and her necklace and handed them over. The two men disappeared with her jewelry and the woman didn't fully come out of her trance until four days later.'

'Four *days*?' asked Eleanor, in disbelief.

'There was nobody around to snap her out of it. I know that doctors don't believe it, but trances can continue for a week. The evidence is indisputable. There was a sixty-year-old woman from west Java who had a conversation with three men on a bus. She gave them all the jewelry she was wearing. Then she took them back to her house and gave them all the rest of her jewelry and cash. She didn't regain consciousness for almost ninety-six hours.

'Then – in 1991, in Italy – there was a gang of two men and one woman who stole over nine hundred and fifty thousand dollars. They hypnotized their victims by repeating the letter "I" to them, over and over, in a special way . . . the same way that I hypnotized your friend Sebastian by using a "yes set". This gang went up and down the main street of Novara, going from store to store and hypnotizing the storekeepers into handing over all of their money. The trance was very light and it didn't last long, no more than a couple of hours, but that was all the time they needed.

'There were plenty of eyewitness descriptions of them, and it didn't take long before the Italian police tracked them down to a hotel in Turin, and arrested them. They had Pakistani passports even though they obviously weren't Pakistani. The police had everything they needed for a prosecution – forensic evidence, stolen goods, positive identifications. But the very next day they released all three of them. Nobody could explain why, except to say that it was some kind of "administrative error". Nobody could remember what the error was, or who had made it. But Turin's chief prosecutor Flavia Nasi is on record as saying that they probably hypnotized the police into letting them go.'

Conor said, 'Before I met Ramon Perez and Magda Slanic – and before I met you – I wouldn't have believed it.'

'Well, no. Most people don't. They don't want to think that somebody could take control of them, as easy as holding their hand. But heck, it's

169

true. You've seen it for yourself. And you can do it, too.'

He paused, and then said, 'By the way . . . from the descriptions issued by the Turin police, two of the members of that gang were Hypnos and Hetti. Latin-looking man, tall dark woman. The third man was a bald-headed character whose body was found two or three months later floating in the River Po.'

'Sobering thought,' said Conor. 'Maybe we'd better sleep on it.'

'I'm not sure that I *can* sleep,' said Eleanor.

Sidney said, 'I could help you to sleep, Bipsy. No problems.'

'Oh, come on, now, Sidney. I won't have you putting me into one of your trances. I'm not in the mood.'

'That's all right. Would you prefer to sleep now or in a few minutes?'

'I think I'd prefer to go to bed first.'

'Would you like to sleep sitting up or lying down?'

'I don't really care, so long as I sleep.'

'Do you want to go into a deep sleep or just a light sleep?'

'A light sleep, Sidney. A light sleep will do.'

'When you fall asleep, your hands will begin to feel as if they don't weigh anything, as if they're floating in the air. Which hand do you think will begin to feel light first? Or maybe they'll both feel light at the same time?'

'I really don't know, Sidney.'

'You don't have to fall asleep as a person but you can fall asleep as a body.'

'So what does that mean?'

170

'It means you have a choice . . . you can fall asleep in any way you like

'And

'You will.'

Eleanor was still sitting up but her eyes were closed and she was breathing deep and slow. Sidney turned to Conor and said, 'You couldn't carry her to bed, could you? There was a time when I could do it. But not now.'

Conor lifted Eleanor out of the chair. She seemed to weigh almost nothing, all skin and bones, like a starved bird. But she was still beautiful, in her way, and for the first time in his life Conor realized how age never erases beauty, but simply shows us what it was made of.

As he carried her to the door, Sidney kissed his fingertips and touched them to her forehead, and there were tears twinkling in his eyes.

Not long after midnight, they heard Sebastian gagging and retching in the bathroom.

'Oh, God,' he was moaning. 'Never again. Never!'

Sidney listened for a while and then turned over in bed. 'Reece's Pieces,' he said, in satisfaction. 'I said that I could cure him.'

13

On their way uptown, Sidney said to Conor, 'I want you to try a little exercise now. When you give the taxi driver his money, stroke the inside of his wrist with your middle finger, and say, "Haven't you taken me here before?"

'Look into his eyes, but focus on a point about three feet behind him. Then say, "You must be very comfortable in this taxi. Very relaxed. You're so comfortable you don't care about anything. You don't even care that I'm not going to give you a tip."'

'I'm not sure I can do that,' said Conor.

'You don't know unless you try.'

The taxi pulled up outside the side entrance to Temple Emanu-El, the vast Turkish-Italianate synagogue on East 65th Street. 'This is it, gents,' said the taxi driver, in a voice thick with phlegm. He was a squat little hunchbacked man with heavy-rimmed glasses and a prickly gray mustache. His license said his name was Chaim Reeven Weintrop. Conor reached forward and handed him a $10 bill. As he did so, he lightly touched the man's wrist and the palm of his hand.

'Haven't you taken me here before?'

'Say what?'

'I said, haven't you taken me here before?'

'Maybe I did. Who knows?'

'You look very comfortable in this taxi. Very comfortable.'

'Comfortable? Are you kidding me? The seat adjuster's broke. I have to sit up straight all the time just to see over the dash. You know what a coccyx is? Yeah? Well, you wouldn't want to trade coccyxes with me, I can tell you.'

'So you're not comfortable?'

'Am I hell comfortable. I'm driving around here like a frog sitting down the bottom of a well.'

Conor turned to Sidney for help; but all Sidney could so was smile and shake his head and say, 'Don't forget to tip him.'

They climbed out of the taxi into the roasting mid-morning heat. 'So what did I do wrong?' asked Conor.

'You lost confidence in what you were doing because he didn't immediately give you the answers you were looking for. You let him steer the conversation whereas it should have been you who was doing the steering. You should have surprised him, distracted him. It doesn't matter how.'

They climbed the steps between the synagogue's limestone pillars. 'So what would you have done?' asked Conor.

'Well . . . since he wasn't comfortable in his taxi, I would have put him in mind of someplace where he usually *was* comfortable. I would have said, "I bet you can't wait to go home . . . I bet you have a comfortable chair at home where you can ease your back . . . how would you like to go home sooner and sit in that comfortable chair?"'

'I don't know. I don't think I've got what it takes to do that kind of thing just yet.'

'It takes confidence, Conor, and you've got plenty of that. All you have to do is keep on practicing, every opportunity you get.'

They walked into the huge, vaulted synagogue. There was a rustling hush in here, as tourists wandered around, their sneakers squeaking on the floors, and men knelt and mumbled prayers, their heads covered with *talysim*. The light was dim, and diffused, with dust twinkling in the air, and the limestone walls gave the synagogue a coolness and a feeling of spiritual refreshment. Even though Conor was a Catholic he felt that God was here. Temple Emanu-El was the largest Reform Jewish place of worship in North America. Two and a half thousand people could come here to pray, although Conor and Sidney had come here looking for another kind of salvation.

They couldn't miss Davina Gambit. She was standing in the far left-hand corner in a bright yellow suit and a hat that looked like a monstrous daffodil. She was a tall woman, a tanned, gleaming blonde of 48, with a pouting red mouth and eyes that had the wind-tunnel look of somebody who has had all their wrinkles erased by cosmetic surgery; and probably more than once.

Next to her was her lawyer, David Dempsky, a small man with thick black curly hair and a face like an unhappy lemur, with dark-ringed eyes and a

174

pointy nose. He was wearing a dark three-piece suit and a black yarmulke.

Conor approached them cautiously, looking right and left, with Sidney following close behind. He made a quick check of the tourists and worshipers in the immediate vicinity, but it looked as if all of them were genuine.

'Ms Gambit?' he said, holding out his hand. 'I'm Conor O'Neil.'

Davina Gambit held out a yellow-gloved hand. Conor didn't try the handshake induction on her. He didn't dare.

'Who's this character?' asked David Dempsky, nodding tersely toward Sidney.

'He's a friend, that's all. He's totally neutral. You don't have to know who he is.'

'So why did you want to meet here, of all places?'

'Because it's the house of God, that's why, and I wanted to make sure that you honored your word. No wires, that's what you promised. No cops, no nasty surprises.'

David Dempsky looked around, as if he half expected to see God watching him from one of the balconies. 'You stole my client's property and you're talking about honor?'

'I didn't steal your client's property.'

'Are you trying to be funny here? You sent me copies of three of her private letters.'

'Not me, Mr Dempsky.'

'Not you? What do you mean, not you? What are you trying to do, screw her for even more money? She's given you two and a half million, for God's sake—' He ducked his head down and said, 'Forgive

175

me, Lord.' Then, 'She just can't afford any more.'

'If you were trying to bankrupt me, Mr O'Neil,' said Davina, in a strong Estonian accent, 'then believe me, you have succeeded.'

'You've already sent me the money?' asked Conor, in bewilderment.

'Transferred it yesterday afternoon, as per your lawyer's instructions. I hope you're satisfied.'

'Ms Gambit, I didn't take your money, and if my lawyer accepted it then he was certainly acting without my authority. I didn't take your letters, even though the police and the media are convinced that I did. However, I have some idea who *might* have taken them, and the reason I asked you to meet me here today was to see if you could help me to locate them.'

David Dempsky shook his head from side to side. 'I don't know about this. What can I say? I talked to Lieutenant Slyman just yesterday afternoon and he said that he's one hundred per cent convinced that you're the perpetrator.'

Davina Gambit said, 'If it wasn't you who took my papers, Mr O'Neil, then who was it? Please, I beg you! I have to get those letters back, or else I really *will* be ruined! My reputation, my alimony payments, everything!'

'Davina – will you please try to keep your mouth closed?' David Dempsky demanded. 'We still don't have any evidence that Mr O'Neil here isn't playing some kind of double bluff.'

'But he has such an honest face!'

'An honest face? John Gotti has an honest face!'

'It's ridiculous!' Davina Gambit suddenly sobbed,

with tears glittering in her eyes. 'They are only love letters!'

'Love letters, and that's all?' Conor asked her.

'Maybe a little more than love letters. Some of them contain other things . . . wild things, fanciful things. Things I should never have done. Things I should never have written about, anyway.'

'Davina, for God's sake will you shut your trap?' David Dempsky protested. Then, 'Forgive me, Lord.'

Conor said, 'When the perpetrator called you up and made his demand, did you tape-record that conversation?'

'The perpetrator? What the hell are you talking about? *You* were the perpetrator!'

'Mr Dempsky, I was not. And I really need to know if you made a tape recording.'

David Dempsky sniffed and twitched. 'Tape? No, no tape.'

'You mean to say you don't normally record conversations with your callers?'

'Not in this case, no.'

'But you're a very good lawyer, aren't you?' Sidney put in.

'Yes, I like to think so.'

'And you work for Litwak & Dempsky?'

'Yes.'

'And you represent Ms Davina Gambit personally?'

'Yes.'

'And you always make sure that you protect her best interests?'

'Yes.'

'Which makes you feel quite comfortable?'

'Yes.'

'In fact it makes you very comfortable. Very comfortable indeed. You don't have to worry about anything I'm saying because you're still in control of everything that matters. You're very comfortably in control. Your mind will act as your secretary, taking care of all the minor details.'

'Yes.'

'So after the man called, asking for money for Ms Gambit's letters, where did you put the tape? Did you file it? Did you put it in your desk? Did you give it to one of your assistants?'

'What's going on here?' asked Davina Gambit, in a forced whisper. 'What are you doing to him?'

'Ssh,' said Conor. 'Let him finish.'

'I put the tape into my deshk drawer,' said David Dempsky. His voice was wet and blurry, as if he had just had a local anesthetic at the dentist. 'My middle deshk drawer, and locked it.'

'You locked it?'

'Yesh.'

'Is it still there?'

'Yesh.'

'In that case I want you to go back to your office with Ms Gambit and take the tape out of your drawer. I want you to give it to Ms Gambit, that's all you have to do. Then I want you to sit at your desk and stay there and write out "Some say the world will end in fire . . . some say in ice", over and over. After a while the phone will ring and you will hear my voice. I will count to five and you will then be fully awake. You will remember nothing about the tape whatsoever. You will remember nothing about coming here to the synagogue.'

'Are you *hypnotizing* him?' asked Davina Gambit. 'My God!'

Sidney smiled. 'We're just encouraging him to be a little more co-operative, that's all.'

'Ms Gambit, will you go back to his office with him and collect the tape?' asked Conor. He took hold of her hand, grasping it firmly at first and then slowly and provocatively letting go, in the way that Sidney had shown him. 'Meet us in the entrance lobby, by the news-stand.'

He looked into her eyes, except that he focused on the pillar just behind her. 'You know that this is the best thing to do. You can trust us completely.'

Davina Gambit frowned at him. 'All right,' she said. Then, with much less confidence, 'All right.'

She kept on blinking as if she couldn't decide where she was or what she was doing. She took hold of David Dempsky's hand and the two of them walked off together toward the temple's Fifth Avenue entrance. Her yellow high heels clicked and clattered on the floor like a young filly trying to negotiate a slippery ramp up to the horsebox.

Sidney took off his glasses and held them up to the light. 'I really must clean these. Thumbprints. You had her in a trance. A light trance, admittedly, but she was extremely receptive. She was looking for somebody to tell her what to do next; with any luck she'll do what you suggested. Now – let's get down to Litwak & Dempsky and see if that luck holds out.'

★   ★   ★

179

They loitered around the lobby of the American Legal Building for over twenty minutes, trying not to look conspicuous. This wasn't easy, because the lobby was a vast marble-clad atrium that went up three floors, with over a third of an acre of floorspace, and splashing fountains and elevators continually sliding up and down its sides.

Two security guards in brown uniforms came out of the elevators and walked around the atrium for a while. Conor recognized one of them as John Shaughnessy, a detective who had been retired from Conor's squad after a shooting incident, and lifted his newspaper higher in case he recognized him.

The elevator doors opened again and Davina Gambit emerged, her high heels clickety-clacking. She came straight over to Conor and thrust a tape cassette at him as if she were returning it to the store because it was faulty. 'Here,' she said, her accent thick, very back-of-the-throat.

'Thank you, Ms Gambit, you don't know much I appreciate this.'

'I don't care whether you appreciate it or not. You just make sure that you get my letters back.'

'I'll do what I can. But listen . . . whatever you do, don't pay out any more money to anybody until you hear from me.'

'And supposing they threaten to send my letters to my ex-husband? Or the media, even? What do I do then?'

'Call this number. Talk to my girlfriend. She knows how to get in touch with me.'

'You really think I can trust you?'

'Oh, yes,' said Conor. 'You can trust me.'

'You give me a strange feeling, you know, like I've known you for a long time.'

Maybe it was the lighting in the atrium but Conor suddenly saw her in a different way. Underneath all the foundation and the blusher, she had a strong, plain, well-structured face. He saw her for what she was: an Eastern European woman of no particular background who had determined to make herself into a wealthy New York socialite.

Conor said, 'You won't remember that you gave me this tape.'

'Oh, yes I will. You think that you can hypnotize me, too? Well – maybe you can – but not in the way that your friend can do it. A different way.'

They went back to Sebastian's apartment and played the cassette on his elegant Bang and Olufsen tape deck. The voice of the blackmailer was very indistinct: he had obviously covered the telephone mouthpiece with a scarf or a handkerchief. There was no question that he was trying to sound like Conor: his voice had the same thoughtful pacing and the same resonant timbre, and there were one or two attempts to use the kind of Irishisms that Conor might have used – 'You'll not be wanting to keep me waiting, will you?'

But they all agreed that it wasn't Conor. 'It could be Ramon Perez,' said Sidney. 'It's a long time since I talked to him, but there's kind of a Spanish lisp to it, don't you think?'

181

'Sounds more like a Southerner to me,' said Ric. 'And a gay Southerner, at that.'

Conor said, 'That doesn't help us much. And the only contact address he gives is my own lawyer, Michael Baer.'

'Did you manage to talk to him yet? Your lawyer?'

'He's in court for the rest of the day. But I left him a message.'

'Play the tape again,' said Ric.

'We've heard it a hundred times already,' Sebastian protested. 'God, I thought *Cats* was boring.'

All the same, Conor played the tape again.

'There!' said Ric.

'Where? What? What are you talking about?'

'*There*, in the background. Don't listen to the voice. Listen to the background.'

Sure enough, when they strained their ears, they could faintly hear music playing, and an extraordinary *whumping* noise. *Whump* and *whump* and shuffle and *whump*.

'That's a rehearsal,' said Ric. 'Whoever made that call was making it from a theater, someplace backstage. Listen, play it again, that is definitely dancing. Very ragged dancing, too. A pretty big ensemble, maybe twenty or thirty people, and a lot of them are out of sync.'

'So he must have called from a theater where a musical's being rehearsed?'

'That's right. They're rehearsing a musical. And a big musical, too, if they have that many dancers. And a *new* musical, if they're that much out of step. What do you think, Sebastian?'

Sebastian gave an airy wave of his hand. 'I think you missed your vocation. You should have been a detective, instead of a dancer. Ric the Dick.'

Ric played the cassette again, and then again, keeping his ear pressed to one of the speakers. 'I'm sure I know this number. I've heard it before. One of my friends played it to me, about three or four months ago. It came from some show he was hoping to audition for.'

'Can you remember anything about it?'

'No . . . but I can call him.'

They waited while Ric sat crosslegged on the floor with the telephone in his lap and punched out his friend's number. Conor said to Sidney, 'Sebastian's right . . . I should let Ric solve this whole case on his own. He has contacts in places where I didn't even know there were places.'

Ric's friend answered. 'Tyne! It's Ric. Yes. Wonderful. *Won-der-ful.* Well, terrible, if you really want to know the truth. Tyne, listen, heart, you remember that musical you were going for – yes, that's it, the one at the Rialto. What was it called?'

'*Franklin*,' he told Conor, with his hand over the receiver. 'A musical based on the life of Benjamin Franklin, God help us.'

'Yes, I know about that,' Eleanor put in. 'George Kranz, with a book by Felix Steinberger. One of my juveniles has a part in it.'

'Tyne – what was that song you sang? That's right – the lightning one.' He listened for a while, nodding, and then he covered the receiver again and said, 'That's it . . . I was right,' and haltingly he started to sing along with his friend on the phone.

'There's a storm brewing between us
Lightning and thunder they're threatnin' to crack
  us apart
But I'll fly my kite
Up into the night
Carryin' the key to your heart.'

Conor nodded. 'It's the same melody. The same as the tune on the tape.'

'Isn't it just awful?' said Eleanor. 'If it doesn't close in three days, I'll give up smoking. If it doesn't close in ten days, I'll give up breathing.'

'That doesn't matter,' said Conor. 'What matters is that Ramon Perez made his call from the Rialto; so that's where we're likely to find him. It's logical when you think about it. Where does a vaudeville act go to hide? No better place than the theater district. That's where their friends are. That's where they can move around backstage without attracting attention.'

Sidney said, 'What are you going to do? You can't go after them unprepared. They'll put you into a trance as soon as you look at them, and then God knows what they'll make you do.'

'Well, I'm ready, Sidney,' said Conor. 'If I need to be prepared, prepare me.'

'It's going to take at least two days to make you capable of even the minimum amount of hypnotic resistance.'

'Then what are we waiting for?'

14

At 7:09 p.m. Conor managed to get through to his lawyer, Michael Baer, in the Oak Bar at the Plaza. He reckoned it was highly unlikely that Slyman had thought of setting up a wiretap there. In the background he could hear the tinkle of cocktail glasses and the deafening sound of egos colliding.

'Michael, what's happening?'

'People are sending me money, that's what's happening. Over sixty-five million dollars at last count.'

'For Christ's sake, Michael, sixty-five million dollars? We can't accept sixty-five million dollars. We can't accept *any* of it.'

'Conor, we can't *not* accept it. These people want their private papers and their property back and they don't want anybody else involved, especially not the police.'

'But this makes us part of a conspiracy to blackmail.'

'You think I don't know that? But let's worry about that when somebody makes a complaint. Meantime we're dealing with people who are

185

prepared to pay sixty-five million dollars for their personal privacy, and I can tell you something for nothing: I'm a whole lot more frightened of them than I am of the law. I'm not ready to trade in my Gucci loafers for cement boots, not just yet.'

'Christ,' said Conor, and pressed his hand to his forehead.

'There's only one problem – two or three people are insisting that you show them samples of their property in person. You can't blame them. They've been asked to hand over anything up to five million dollars, and they don't want to find that they've been hoaxed.'

'How can I do that? I don't *have* their property.'

'I don't know. I'm ignoring them for now. I don't know what else to do.'

'What are we supposed to do with all of this money?'

'Well, I had two calls from our friends yesterday afternoon, just to make sure that the deal's in shape.'

'Did they give you any indication who they were?'

'Not a clue. The guy didn't try to disguise his voice, though. I'd say southern. Alabama, Louisiana, something like that.'

'How about a contact number?'

'Unh-hunh. As soon as I receive all of the payments, I'm supposed to make an electronic transfer into their bank account.'

'Which is where?'

'Oslo.'

'Oslo, Minnesota?'

'Unh-hunh. Oslo, Norway.'

'Oslo, *Norway*?'

'It's supposed to be sent to the Fjords Finanskompaniet, Karl Johansgate, into a business account registered in the name of J.A.S.'

'Michael, this is insanity.'

'All right, it's insanity. But if you've been telling me the truth, this scam is absolutely nothing to do with you. As your lawyer, my advice to you is to stay well out of it. Let the ransom money be paid: let the property be given back. Then you can start to prove that you weren't involved.'

'It's not as easy as that. I have to prove it, for sure. But I have to prove it so publicly and so convincingly that Slyman won't dare to come near me any more. Either that, or—'

'Either that or what?'

'Either that or I do unto him what he's been trying to do unto me, and make sure that I do it first.'

'Conor, you're Irish. You should know better than anybody else that violence never solved anything.'

'Sitting on your duff waiting for the sky to fall in, that never solved anything either.'

Conor and Sidney spent the next forty-eight hours closeted together in one of Sebastian's bedrooms, with the shades pulled down. Sidney put Conor in and out of trances so often that he didn't know whether he was sleeping or waking. Time seemed to flicker past like a landscape seen from a train, with frequent plunges into the blackest of tunnels.

Sidney taught him how to induce hypnosis in other people – how to speak more softly when he wanted to engage the listener's closer attention, how to speak more slowly when he wanted a listener to think more carefully.

He taught him how to use subtle cues to make his subjects behave the way he wanted them to – how to move his head to the left when he talked about livelier things; and how to move his head to the right when he talked about sleep, and comfort, and trance – so that after a while his subject would automatically learn to relax when he inclined his head to the right, and perk up when he inclined to the left.

'For most people, going into a trance is a pleasant surprise. They think that they direct their own associative processes, like a bus driver directs a bus. But most mental activity is autonomous, and when you persuade people really to relax – not to talk, not to move, not to make any sort of effort – not even to listen to you talking if they don't want to – they're totally amazed to discover that their mental processes go on flowing all by themselves. This is what trance is.'

From time to time, Ric or Eleanor would come in with mineral water or fruit juice. Sidney wouldn't allow coffee because it was too stimulating. They ate nothing but sandwiches which Eleanor and Ric made for them. Ham, cheese, salad and plenty of apples and bananas.

There were no clocks in the room, and they would take a break whenever they felt like it.

Toward evening, at the end of the second day, Conor was trying to persuade Sidney to relax when Sidney suddenly said, 'You've got it. You can do it.'

'What do you mean?'

'I mean that you can hypnotize almost anyone.'

'How do you know?'

'Because – just now – you almost managed to hypnotize me. You're a very good student.'

'I'm flattered.'

'You don't have time to be flattered. You can induce a hypnotic trance, yes. But now you have to learn how to be resistant yourself. You have to learn what a hypnotist is trying to do to you, and make sure that you deflect him. You remember that taxi driver? You think of him. Whatever you said, he didn't directly contradict, but he kept steering the conversation the way he wanted it to go. If you believe that somebody is trying to hypnotize you, you can resist them by externalizing your thoughts. Don't try to think about it as an inner struggle, or a mental wrestling match, because the moment you concentrate on what's going on inside of your mind you've already lost.

'Don't pay any attention to what the hypnotist is saying to you. Don't answer yes or no, no matter how harmless his questions appear to be. If you do have to answer, say that you don't understand the question and ask him to explain what he means. Put him on the defensive. Break up the pattern of his induction. And keep changing the subject. If he asks you what you enjoy doing, what makes you feel happy and relaxed, tell him instead about things that upset and irritate you and make you angry.

'Interrupt him. Ask him irrelevant questions. "Where did you buy that sport coat?" "What time is it?" "Have you ever been to Delaware?" Don't give him time to set up a trance-inducing rhythm of speech.

189

'Beware of the double bind. You remember that I said to Eleanor, "Do you want to fall asleep now or later?" That question presupposed that, whatever happened, she would fall asleep. Your answer to a question like that should be, "I'm not going to fall asleep at all." Not, "I don't want to fall asleep," or, "I wasn't planning on falling asleep." Don't even consider sleep as an option.

'Keep up a high level of physical activity. Take quick, shallow breaths. Walk about. Sit down, and then immediately stand up again. Walk out of the room, if that's possible, and walk back in again. Move close to the hypnotist and then quickly move away again, so that he has to keep refocusing his eyes. Turn your head away from him, look some-place else. Go round behind him.

'Watch for any distracting touches or repetitive movements. Don't shake hands, whatever you do. In fact don't allow him to touch you in any way – a hand on the shoulder, anything.

'Most of all, don't ever try to resist a skilled hyp-notist on his own terms. Don't try to out-think him, because to do that you have to keep still and concen-trate and that's just what he wants you to do. Now . . . let's try that in practice.'

Shortly after 11 p.m., Sidney said, 'I could use a drink. How about you?'

'You mean we're finished?'

'For now. You've got a good handle on the theory. All you have to do now is keep practicing.'

'Who should I practice *on*?'

'Anybody you like. Passers-by. Store assistants.

Bank tellers. Friends. Enemies. You'll soon get to the point when you can put people into a trance in the middle of an ordinary conversation. I was at a mental health convention in San Diego once, and I saw a clinical hypnotherapist put a consultant pyschiatrist fellow diner into a trance during dinner. He ate all the best pieces of steak off the fellow's plate and then he said, "You're feeling so full . . . you really enjoyed that steak," and then he woke him up.'

They stood up and stretched. Conor put his hand on the doorknob but before he turned it he said, 'I don't know how I'm going to thank you for this, Sidney. I wish there was something I could give you in return.'

'You already have,' said Sidney. 'You brought my Eleanor back to me. Just go find Hypnos and Hetti and then we can have a chance to make up for some of the time we missed.'

Lacey called him from her friend Trina's loft in the Village. 'That Lieutenant Slyman came around to see me again this evening.'

'Oh, yes. What the hell did *he* want?'

'He said he had a proposition to make to you. He said maybe you could find a way to get in touch with him.'

'Did he give you any idea what kind of proposition?'

'No . . . but he said you would be very foolish not to consider it. He said it would be a way out for you and a way out for him.'

'Oh, yes? I wouldn't trust Drew Slyman to hold his breath underwater.'

191

There was a pause, and then Lacey said, 'I'm missing you, Conor. I'm really missing you. If you can please find some way of working this out.'

'I'm trying, you know that.'

'But it's taking so *long*. I wish I could see you. I'd do anything just to touch you again.'

'Maybe you can. Let me ask Sebastian about it. If you can make sure that you get here without being followed . . .'

'Oh, Conor – please – if I only could. I won't let them follow me this time, I promise.'

Sebastian was sitting opposite him, frowning at some intricate needlework. 'You want to know if Lacey can come over,' he said, without looking up.

'Do you mind? I'll make sure that nobody follows her.'

'Lacey was a friend of mine long before you were, dear heart. Of course she can come over.'

'You know there might be some risk?'

'Getting up in the morning is a risk. You should know that more than most people.'

She arrived shortly after midnight, wearing a gray linen coat that she had borrowed from Conor's closet and a pair of stone-colored slacks. All her hair was tucked up into a black golfing cap, and she also wore heavy tortoiseshell glasses. She was breathless as Sebastian let her into the hallway.

'I did everything you told me . . . I got into a taxi and out of the other side . . . I doubled back on myself. And guess what I did – I even went into the men's room at the Inter-Continental.'

'Yes, I've been there,' said Sebastian. Lacey gave

him a long, affectionate hug. Then she turned to Conor. She took off her cap and shook her hair free. 'Well,' she said.

There was a moment when Conor felt as awkward as if they were strangers. 'It seems like forever,' he said, and he came forward and took her in his arms and held her tight.

'Your bruises are beginning to fade,' she said, touching his cheeks.

'Still pretty colorful.'

'*Colorful*,' mocked Sebastian. 'That's an understatement. You look as if you've been made up by Henri Matisse.'

'I've brought your mail,' said Lacey. 'And Paula's lawyers called to say that they've taken out a formal injunction to prevent you from seeing Fay until further notice.'

'Jesus. As if I'm going to take her to the zoo while Slyman's trying to hunt me down. Any news about Darrell? Did you manage to call the hospital?'

Lacey nodded. 'He's still unconscious. I wasn't family so they wouldn't give me any kind of prognosis.'

Conor led her through to the living room. Eleanor had already gone to bed, but Sidney was still up, playing a last game of chess with Ric.

'Sidney – Ric – this is Lacey.'

'Pleased to make your acquaintance,' said Sidney, holding out his hand.

'You watch that handshake,' Conor warned her. 'Sidney is a world-class hypnotist.'

'I think he's been hypnotizing me while we've been playing this game,' Ric complained. 'I keep putting myself in such ridiculous positions. Not like me at all.'

'Oh, I wouldn't say that,' said Sebastian.

Ric got up from the couch, took Lacey's hand and kissed it. Then – still holding her hand – he stared into her eyes and said, 'You're an Aries, aren't you?'

Lacey shook her head in disbelief. 'How did you know that?'

'I only had to look at you. Strong, wilful, determined, passionate, but inclined to sentimentality, too. Besides, we were talking about star signs the other night and Conor told me you were.'

Sebastian opened a bottle of his latest favorite wine, a 1996 August Sebastiani Zinfandel. He liked it because it tasted of watermelons and flowers, but most of all because it had the same name as him. They sat around and drank and talked until well past 1:30.

Lacey had no more news about Lieutenant Slyman's proposition, but she still believed that Conor ought to hear what it was, at the very least. Conor, on the other hand, had seen what Slyman was capable of. He had seen the awkward, bloodstained bodies of a senior mafioso's wife and six-year-old daughter, shot dead while they were out on a picnic. He had investigated the murder of another *capo*, garrotted with a flexible saw while he was sitting by his dying father's bed in the New York University Medical Center. There had been at least six or seven more 'birdies' – that was what the Golf Club called them – but no witnesses who were willing to put the finger on Slyman in open court and insufficient forensic evidence to carry a conviction without them. The Golf Club had friends in the medical examiner's department, too.

'At least the Mafia have honor,' said Conor. 'Drew Slyman doesn't know the meaning of the word. The only proposition I'm interested in is if he admits that I'm innocent.'

They went to Conor's bedroom and closed the door. Lacey took off her coat and then sat on the end of the bed to take off her shoes and socks. The room was lit by a single pink-shaded lamp on the nightstand. It made Lacey's hair shine and it sparkled in her eyes. She took off her pants and then she was standing in front of Conor wearing nothing but one of his white shirts.

He took her in his arms and kissed her. 'You're shivering,' he said.

'I'm just nervous, I guess. This whole thing has frightened me so much.'

'We'll work it out, believe me. We're going to try to find Hypnos and Hetti tomorrow – and once we've done that, all our problems will be solved.'

He loosened her necktie and unbuttoned the top of her shirt. 'I'm not so good at this. I never undressed a man before.' She reached up and took hold of his wrist, and cupped her hand over her breast. She wasn't wearing a bra and he could feel the stiffness of her nipple through the thin white cotton. 'I've missed you so much,' he breathed.

She kissed him back. She gave him little quick gasping kisses at first, but then they became much greedier. She opened her mouth wide and pushed her tongue in between his teeth. Their tongues

195

fought while they stared at each other with intense, wide-open eyes.

They didn't speak. There wasn't any need. She pulled open the last few buttons of her shirt and pushed it back over her shoulders, so that it dropped onto the floor. She was wearing nothing underneath but a tiny white lace thong. Her breasts were disproportionately large and heavy for a girl so slim, with wide areolas the color of faded pink rose petals.

They toppled sideways onto the bed. Conor pulled off his clothes, kicking his pants away from his ankles. Lacey moaned and kissed him more urgently. He squeezed and fondled both of her breasts but that wasn't enough for her. She cupped her breasts in her hands and squeezed them until they bulged through her fingers, rubbing her nipples through the dark fur on his chest.

'I want you,' she mumbled. 'I want you, I want you, I want you.'

She ran her hands down between his legs. She pumped his penis lustfully up and down. Then she rolled over and knelt beside him on the patchwork comforter and took him into her mouth. Conor couldn't stop himself from letting out a deep groan of pleasure. Through the flying tangle of her hair, he could just about make out her pink lips encircling his purple glans and her tongue licking and swirling and circling until his penis glistened with her saliva. She bent down even further and took his balls into her mouth, gently tugging and sucking them. Conor was so tense that his chest and stomach muscles were as hard as fists and his toes were tightly curled.

Just when he felt that he wasn't going to be able to hold himself back any longer, Lacey stopped sucking him and sat up, her eyes dreamy and her mouth half open in pleasure. She sat astride him, bending forward to kiss him so that her breasts swung against his chest. Then she sat up straight again, and tugged aside her thong, revealing her blond-haired vulva with its moist coral-pink lips. It was plain from her wetness that she was already highly excited, even though Conor normally found that she was very slow to be aroused.

She took his penis in her hand and guided it between her legs. Then, with a long lascivious shudder she sat down on it, until it was sunk as deep inside her as it possibly could be. She rode up and down it, rhythmically and elegantly, her head flung back, her hair flying, her eyes closed, her breasts performing a swaying, complicated dance of their own.

She went on and on. Conor had never known her to make love with such eloquence.

But suddenly, when he was close to climaxing, she stopped, and let her head drop forward like a broken marionette.

He reached out and touched her shoulder. 'What's the matter?' he panted.

She pulled her tangled hair aside and looked at him and shook her head. 'I can't do it . . . I can't get there . . . I keep getting right to the edge and then I can't.'

'Do you want me to help you?'

'I don't understand.'

'Stanley taught me hypnosis. I can help you.'

'You're kidding me, aren't you?'

'No, I'm not kidding. Just say the word.'

She was silent for a long, long time, just looking at him. Then she nodded, and eased herself up a little, and down again, and up.

'You remember that time in Albany?' he asked her. 'The time you came to that police convention? We were supposed to go to that memorial dinner but we spent the whole evening in bed?'

She nodded again, still easing herself up and down.

'You remember how good that felt? That felt good, didn't it? You can feel that way again. In fact, you're beginning to feel that way now.'

'I am?' Lacey murmured. Then, 'I *am*.'

'You're feeling more pleasure than you thought was ever possible. You feel as if your skin is tingling . . . as if every inch of your body is being stroked . . . your forehead, your lips, your shoulders. Your breasts are being stroked, too, and you have a sensation in your nipples unlike anything you've ever felt before.

'Fingers are trailing down your back and around your hips. They're so light that you can barely feel them but they're very, very exciting. Someone's stroking your thighs, all around your knees and then up between your legs . . .

'And

'Every part of your being . . . is concentrating itself . . . tighter and tighter . . . darker and darker . . .'

As Conor murmured on and on, his voice seemed to caress her just like the fingertips that he was describing. She closed her eyes and her head

198

gradually tilted back. Sweat beaded her forehead and slid between her breasts. She moved up and down on Conor as if she were weightless, her internal muscles going through the most complicated spasms. Conor was so close to a climax himself that he found it difficult to speak coherently, but he managed to continue in a series of gasps.

'And now you've reached that point . . . that ultimate point where you can't reduce your being any more . . .

'And

'*You're going to explode.*'

There was an instant when Lacey stopped. She stayed frozen, her head still tilted back. Then she let out a soft cry and her body began to shake. She shook more and more violently, clawing at the comforter with both hands.

Conor climaxed too. For a split second he felt as if the whole world had gone black, like a camera shutter. The pleasure was so intense that he said something, but he didn't know what it was.

Lacey went on shaking and shaking until she finally fell forward and he held her in his arms. They lay like that until the clocks started to chime three. Conor said softly in Lacey's ear, 'It's OK. You're awake now.'

She opened one eye and looked at him for a while. Then she said, 'No, I'm not. I'm asleep.'

Conor didn't wake up until 9:15. The sun was lying in bars across the bed. Lacey was still asleep, her arm resting awkwardly on his hip.

Carefully he climbed out of bed and opened the

drawer that Sebastian had given him to keep his clothes in. Ric had done the laundry yesterday and everything was neat and pressed and folded. He remembered watching *The Fugitive* and wondering what Dr Richard Kimble had done for clean shorts.

He dressed and went through to the kitchen. Sidney and Eleanor were already there, drinking coffee with Sebastian and Ric.

'Sleep well?' asked Sebastian archly.

'Pretty good, thanks.'

'Eleanor's been regaling us with all kinds of fascinating gossip, haven't you, Eleanor?'

'She should write her autobiography,' put in Ric. 'She knows more dirt about Broadway than anyone I ever met.'

Sebastian poured Conor a mug of coffee. 'Well . . . today's the day you're going to go looking for Hypnos and Hetti, yes?'

'That's right.'

'Ric and I were talking about it last night and we think we ought to come with you.'

'I don't think so, Sebastian. This could turn out to be very dangerous.'

'Believe me, you won't get backstage at the Rialto without us, especially when they're rehearsing. They're *very* strict about their security.'

'Well, I don't know. I think that I've disrupted your lives quite enough, don't you?'

'Conor, sweetheart. The sooner you find these people the sooner we can all get back to our normal humdrum lives, and the sooner Lacey can stop worrying that you might get killed at any moment.'

At that moment Lacey came in, buttoning up her

shirt. 'That sounds good to me.' She came up to Conor and put her arm around him. Conor turned to Sidney. 'What's your opinion?'

'I guess there's no harm in it,' Sidney shrugged. 'It could help to put Hypnos and Hetti off balance, too. It's pretty difficult to hypnotize four people simultaneously, even if you're as good as they are.'

'OK, then. But listen here, Sebastian: I'm going to be calling the shots, you got it? If I tell you to get the hell out, then I expect you to get the hell out, no questions asked.'

'You're so *masterful*,' said Sebastian.

They finished their coffee and Lacey brushed her hair up and put on her coat and her shirt and tie. She took hold of Conor's hand and kissed him. 'I don't have to tell you to take care, do I?'

'Don't worry . . . I'm not going to do anything stupid. And this time *I've* got the jump on *them*.'

'What do you think?' asked Ric. 'The emerald-green pants with the sapphire shirt or the white calico pants with the daffodil polo?'

15

They asked the doorman to hail them a taxi and waited inside the lobby until he managed to flag one down. Conor kissed Lacey and said, 'I'll call you later. Don't worry . . . everything's going to work out fine.'

She didn't say anything, but she didn't have to. She pushed her way out through the revolving door and walked off in the direction of Fifth Avenue without looking back. Not for the first time, Conor found himself thinking that she deserved better than him – a younger man, with his career ahead of him. Somebody who really knew who he was, and where he fitted into the world.

The doorman let out a piercing whistle and beckoned to them. 'Our carriage awaits,' said Ric, and they hurried across the sidewalk and climbed into the taxi.

The humidity was even more oppressive than the day before. Crowded together in the back of the taxi they were soon sweltering and sticking to the black vinyl seats. The cab driver had run an old vacuum-cleaner hose from the front air-conditioning vents

202

into the back, but all it did was pour out a stream of tepid, second-hand air.

All the way, the cab driver kept up an endless complaint that religion was to blame for everything that was wrong with the world. 'The Methodists hate the Catholics and the Catholics hate the Jews and everybody hates the Muslims. If you ask me, that Branch guy's got it right.'

'What Branch guy?' asked Ric.

'That *Branch* guy. That terrorist. He says that everybody oughtta be the same religion.'

'Oh, *him*,' said Sebastian. 'They had something about him on the news this morning. He's raving. He's the kind of guy who gives lunatics a bad name.'

They reached the side entrance to the Rialto Theater on West 45th. Conor climbed out of the taxi and mopped his forehead and his neck with his balled-up handkerchief. He checked the street while Sebastian paid the fare. There was a hot dog stand at the intersection of 45th and Broadway, but the hot dog seller was hugely fat, with a pink Hawaiian shirt and Coke-bottle glasses, and Conor didn't think it was likely that he was an undercover cop.

Sidney laid a hand on his shoulder. 'Try to clear your mind of everything except your principal objective. Keep your attention locked onto it at all times, and don't let anybody or anything distract you or confuse you. You are going into this theater to find Hypnos and Hetti. That's it.'

Conor said, 'All right, then. Let's do it.'

Ric rang the doorbell. They waited for over a minute and nobody answered so he rang it a second time. Conor could feel the perspiration sliding down his back and he had to mop his forehead again. At last the door opened and an elderly black man with grizzled gray hair looked around it. He blinked at Ric in astonishment.

'Well how about that?' he cackled, and gave Ric a leathery high five. 'Mr Ric Vetter, how about that? I haven't seen you since *Bus Stop*. And your friend here, Mr Sebastian Speed, how are you, sir?'

'Ex-quiz-seet as always, thank you, Sammy.'

'Anything I can do for you gentlemen? We're smack in the middle of rehoisal right now, most everybody's kind of tied up.'

Behind Sammy, inside the theater, Conor could faintly hear music playing and the random thunder of dancers' feet. Ric said, 'We were looking for some old friends of ours, as a matter of fact. Lost their address. Somebody told me they were hanging out someplace here.'

'There's all kinds of people come and go. What's their names, these old friends of yours?'

'There's two of them. Ramon Perez, he's a real dapper little guy, Cuban. Then there's Magda Slanic, she's tall, almost six feet. Black eyes like coalholes. They used to do a stage hypnotism act called Hypnos and Hetti.'

Sammy slowly shook his head. 'There's nobody like that hanging out here. I would've seen them if they was. I'm here for most of the day and it's one of my jobs to lock the place up when they finish their rehoisals.'

'Maybe you made a mistake about what musical it was,' Conor suggested to Ric.

'No, no. It was *Franklin*, I'm sure of it.'

'That's what they're rehoising now,' Sammy nodded. '*Franklin.* Not my kind of music. Gives me the deep-down dyspepsha.'

Sidney stepped forward and held out his hand. 'Sammy . . . you don't mind if I call you Sammy?'

'Why should I mind? That's what my name is.'

'Well, Sammy, my name's Sidney and I was wondering if you ever saw me before.'

Sammy frowned. 'Can't say that I have.'

'Never mind. You don't have to remember me even if you do.'

'Say what?'

'I'm just thinking about something that may be on the very extreme edge of your vision, Sammy – something that you can only see if you turn your eyes as far sideways as they can possibly go.'

Sammy was still frowning but he turned his eyes as if he were trying to see inside of his own head. Sidney said, in his calm, dry voice, 'It's possible that you've seen something but somebody's told you to forget it.'

'I don't think so. I don't understand how that could be.'

'Two people, Sammy. A man and a very tall woman. They talked to you the same way that I'm talking to you now. You have a better memory of them than you know about.'

'I don't know . . . I kind of think that maybe I did see them, yes.'

'Think about something that puzzled you when they talked to you. Something about the way they looked.'

'The man . . . the man, he was wearing *gloves.* I

205

thought it was pretty strange that he was wearing gloves.'

'I want you to take hold of that man's hand. Do you remember taking hold of that man's hand?'

'Yes, I do. I remember.'

'I want you to look around you . . . I want you to tell me where you're standing.'

'I'm standing in dressing-room eleven.'

'And what can you see, when you look around you?'

'A dressing-table . . . a chair . . . a television set . . . a coupla valises . . . some clothes hanging up. An ironing board. All the dressing-rooms got ironing boards.'

'Is there anybody else in the dressing-room with you?'

Sammy nodded, his eyes distant. 'For sure . . . there's a woman sitting on the bed.'

'There's a bed in dressing-room eleven?'

'That's right. They use it when there's a matinée. Get some sleep in between shows. Or maybe later, to screw some stagedoor groupie, you know?'

'The woman on the bed . . . describe her.'

'She's wearing this kind of black corset. Pinches her waist in like a Coke bottle. She's rolling down her stocking, you know, and she's looking at me and she's smiling this real strange smile. I can't tell you why but she reminds me of a spider and I'm like a fly that's caught in her web.'

'Is the man talking to you?'

'Yes, sir.'

'Tell me what he's saying.'

'He's saying that I'm going to wake up, and that

when I wake up I won't remember that he was here, and I won't remember that the woman was here either, and I won't even remember that dressing-room eleven even exists. When I see the door with eleven on it, I won't see no door, all I'll see is a plain blank wall.'

Sebastian was simultaneously blowing his nose and shaking his head in amazement. 'This is just *incredible*, isn't it?'

Sidney said, 'Sammy . . . when I count to five you're going to wake up and you're going to remember all of this conversation quite clearly.'

'Yes, sir. I understand, sir.'

'One, two, three, four, five. You're awake.'

Sammy stared at all of them with a suspicious look on his face, as if he had just missed the point of a joke. 'What?' he demanded.

'Nothing,' said Ric. 'We're just pleased that we've found our friends.'

'You have?'

'Sure . . . the people in dressing-room eleven. Ramon Perez and Magda Slanic.'

'Oh, yes! That's right! They came last week! Hypnos and Hetti! I used to know them from way back! Did you ever see that act they did when they made this woman think that she was in love with a codfish? I mean, they used to be something!'

'Are they here now?' asked Conor.

'Hetti is, for sure. I don't know where Hypnos went.'

'OK if we go in and talk to her?'

'Why not? I'll show you the way.'

He opened the door wider and let them all in. As

Sidney passed him by, he said, 'I know you, don't I? I'm sure I know you.'

'You do now,' smiled Sidney, and gave him a pat on the shoulder.

He led them past his office with its coffee percolator and its untidy heaps of programs and its signed photographs of dozens of toothily grinning stars. '*For Sammy . . . you're an ace . . . Gene Wilder*', '*From one Sammy to another . . . all the best . . . Sammy Davis Jr*'. They climbed a flight of concrete steps and then walked along a corridor that took them behind the stage.

Conor thought: every profession has its smell, and the theater is no exception. Dust, sweat, emulsion paint, overheating lamps. The stage itself was brightly lit in pinks and blues and some of the company of *Franklin* were standing around in leotards, stretching their ankles and arching their backs and striking poses. A slim girl in a black T-shirt and black leggings was standing stage right and singing.

> '*For want of a nail*
> *The horse lost his shoe . . .*
> *For want of a forgiving heart, what did I do?*
> *I lost you . . .*'

'What do you think?' asked Sammy, standing close beside Conor and nodding at the girl. 'Not exactly Rodgers and Hart, is it?'

Conor listened for a moment longer and then he said, 'I don't know . . . I'm not sure about turning

Poor Richard's Almanac into a song, but the music's catchy.'

'Ten dollars it closes on the first night. I've never been wrong.'

'Come on,' said Sebastian, 'let's get going. This song is making my bicuspids ache.'

They crossed the back of the stage and Sammy took them up another flight of stairs to the dressing-rooms. Most of them were empty. In one, a young woman in jeans and a white powdered wig was staring at herself in a make-up mirror, pulling down the plum-colored bags under her eyes with the tips of her fingers.

'Not another hangover, Carla?' Sammy remarked, as he passed her by.

'Couldn't sleep, Sammy. I had that dream again, the one where I'm drowning in molasses.'

They reached the end of the corridor and there, facing them, was the green-painted door for dressing-room eleven. It was about an inch ajar and Conor could smell Balkan cigarette smoke and hear the intermittent blurting of laughter from a television comedy show. This was one moment when he badly missed his gun.

Sammy lifted his fist to knock on the door but Conor caught his arm. 'We want this to be a surprise, OK?'

'A surprise? OK by me.'

'What's the plan?' asked Sidney.

'The plan is, there is no plan. I'll push open the door and roll into the room. You stay well clear until I've made sure that neither of them is armed. Then, in you go, and grab them.'

209

Sammy said, 'Here, here, here! Wait up a cotton-pickin' minute! *Armed*? What's this armed?'

Conor laid a reassuring arm around his shoulders. 'It's nothing for you to worry about, Sammy. I want you to keep out of the way, that's all, in case Ramon loses his sense of humor.'

'You said he was your friend.'

'Well, he is and he isn't. You know how friendships can be. One day you're best buddies, the next day you want to rip each other's heads off.'

'What's really going down here?' asked Sammy. 'Come on, folks, this is my theater. I'm responsible. I want to know the truth.'

Sidney came up to him. 'Relax. You're completely relaxed. Absolutely nothing is wrong. You have a strong urge to go to your office and make yourself a cup of coffee.'

'Sure. I'll just go make myself a cup of coffee.'

Sammy turned and walked off and Sidney said, 'There. Let's get on with it, shall we?'

'I still don't know how you do that so easy,' said Conor.

Sidney shrugged. 'You'll learn.'

Conor stepped up to the door and prepared to shoulder it open. Sebastian and Ric stood close behind him.

'You ready for this?' asked Conor. Both of them nodded.

But at that moment the door opened and Magda Slanic appeared, with a sparkling black scarf wound around her head like a turban and a long black satin robe. She looked even taller than Conor remembered her, as tall as he was, so that she was staring him directly in the eye; and her face was as white as the moon on a winter's night. A black-papered cigarette dangled from her lip and a sparkling diamond cross hung in her cleavage.

'Well, well,' she said. 'Chief Conor O'Neil. How quickly you have found us.'

Conor thought: *don't let her distract you. Don't let her confuse you. There's only one issue here, and that's to nail Hypnos and Hetti and retrieve the contents of those safety deposit boxes.*

'Ramon not here?' asked Conor, peering into the dressing-room behind her. It was catastrophically untidy. The bed was unmade and clothes were heaped all over the couch – dress-shirts, Armani coats, filmy black lace bras, bias-cut evening gowns. Bottles of cosmetics littered the dressing-table, as well as lipsticks and eyeliner brushes. Empty bottles of Smirnoff Black Label and discarded Entenmann's cake cartons showed that Hypnos and Hetti had actually been living here.

'Ramon went out. He had business to take care of. Who are your friends?' She looked at Sebastian and Ric and Sidney and she didn't say it out loud but her expression said, 'Weird.'

Conor said, 'This isn't a social call, Ms Slanic. I want all that stuff back from the safety deposit boxes at Spurr's.'

'You think *we* took it? What makes you think *we* took it?'

'Careful, Conor,' said Sidney; and Conor realized that he was alerting him to Hetti's induction technique. Ask a confusing question: make the subject turn his attention inward. Catch him off balance.

211

'I know you have it,' said Conor, flatly. 'I'm here to give you a chance: hand it all over and I'll give you and Ramon twenty-four hours to get the hell out of New York City before I sic the cops on you.'

'You only *think* we have it. You don't have any way of knowing for sure.'

'Oh, no? If it isn't you, then who else could possibly have it?'

'Who else had access to your safety deposit boxes?'

Shit, thought Conor. *She's good. She's making me think. She's putting me off track.*

Sidney could tell what was happening. 'You're tense,' he told Hetti. 'You're trying to pretend that you're relaxed but you're totally wired. Why don't you try to calm down and see if we can deal with this situation like grown-up people.'

'Do I *know* you?' Hetti demanded.

'Yes, you do. It was a long time ago, wasn't it?'

'Step into the light.'

'I don't have to, Magda. You remember me. Think of those *Vaudeville Days*.'

Hetti peered into the triangular shadow which fell across Sidney's face. There was a long moment of hesitation, and then she said, '*Ce?* It can't be. Sidney Randall? I heard you were dead.'

'I *was* dead, in a way, Magda, but now I'm alive again.'

'I heard you were suffering from terminal cancer.'

'Not cancer, Magda, but almost the same thing. Remorse.'

'And now you're trying to mesmerize me? *Me*, Hetti, from Hypnos and Hetti? You must be crazy.

212

This is all crazy. What are you doing here, Sidney, with this policeman? That was never like you.'

Conor said, 'I have to tell you, Ms Slanic, you don't know what you've gotten yourself into. The sooner you give me that stolen property back, the easier it's going to be. We're not dealing with idiots here. We're dealing with people who own half of Manhattan. Personally, I'm asking you to hand over whatever it is you've taken. These people won't even ask you. They'll have you tortured until you tell them where it is, and then they'll kill you. And the cops won't help you, either.'

Hetti half closed her eyes and looked at Conor from beneath lids that were shadowed dark purple, like two gleaming beetles. In spite of the whiteness of her face and the eccentricity of her dress, he could see now that she was actually very beautiful. She had bone structure that made Greta Garbo look like her less attractive sister, and her mouth was an indecent promise made flesh.

'You think this is all about robbery and black-mail?' she said, in a husky, barely audible voice. 'You think so *small*.'

'Maybe you'd like to tell me what it *is* about?'

'Do you really want to hear it?'

'Yes.'

'It's a long story but you like long stories, don't you?'

'Yes.'

'Conor,' Sidney cautioned him.

Conor quickly and deliberately turned his head away, breaking the pattern of Hetti's 'yes set' and cutting off her visual communication. Hetti glanced at him and the expression on her face was almost murderous.

'Oh, I get it! I see! Sidney teaches you a little bit of hypnotic jiggery-pokery and you think that you're resistant? You think that you can take on a professional like me?'

'No harm in trying.'

'Well, you're ridiculous. I won't admit to anything. Look around you. Do you see any papers, any bonds, any jewelry?'

'You'll tell us, given time.'

'You think so? You're all mad! You wait till Ramon gets back. He'll have you filleted, all of you.'

'Well, we're not going to wait until Ramon gets back,' said Conor. 'We're going to take you with us; and when Ramon comes back he's going to find out that you're gone; and he's also going to find out that he won't get you back until he tells me where you've hidden your loot.'

Hetti stared at Conor unblinkingly and her eyes were so black and unfocused that he felt drawn toward them, as if he were diving from the edge of a cliff into a black and bottomless pool, plunging deeply into space and time, another existence altogether, where there was nothing to run from, no problems of any kind, no stress, no terror.

And then Sebastian laid a hand on his shoulder and he took a grip on himself and remembered where he was and what he was doing.

'Get dressed,' he told her.

'What?'

'You heard me. We're leaving.'

'I'm not going with you. I refuse. I don't give a damn what you think. We didn't steal your stupid stuff. We didn't steal anything.'

Conor approached her, very close. She was breathing hard, so that her nostrils flared. He lifted the diamond cross that was hanging around her neck and held it up in front of her face.

'You didn't steal anything, hunh?' he asked her. 'This cross belongs to Mrs Nils Stannard the Second. Her late husband gave it to her after he'd been to Lourdes. It was deposited at Spurr's Fifth Avenue less than a week after I was appointed chief of security and she made a point of showing it to me. If you have *this*, Ms Slanic, then I think the logical conclusion has to be that you have everything else.'

Sebastian excitedly clapped his hands. 'There! That's detective work for you! My God! Isn't he a *genius*?'

'You still can't prove anything,' breathed Hetti. Her nose was no more than six inches away from Conor's and he could smell her perfume and the tobacco on her breath. 'I could have bought this necklace from a pawnshop; from a friend; from anyplace at all.'

'You hypnotized me once,' Conor told her. 'You're never going to do that again.'

The silence between them seemed to go on forever. Then she tilted back her head a little and said, 'I can do it any time I like.' And with that, she let her black satin robe slide off her onto the floor, with a soft swooping sound, and stood in front of them in a black basque and sheer black stockings.

Conor didn't allow himself to take his eyes away

215

from her face. 'Get dressed, Ms Slanic. We have some talking to do.'

She hesitated for a few moments longer. Then she turned and picked up a long black dress that had been hanging over the back of the chair. She lifted it over her head and slid into it. Then she came back to Conor and said, 'Zipper, please, Chief O'Neil.'

Conor took hold of the zipper at the back of her dress and tugged it upward. Although her skin was so white it was very warm. There was a small pattern of moles on her left shoulder-blade in the shape of the constellation Hydra, the water-snake. Sidney was watching Conor closely.

She put on a pair of strappy black sandals. 'So where are you taking me?' she demanded. 'I hope you realize that this is kidnap, and what the penalty is.'

'And you're going to complain to the cops?' asked Conor. 'I don't think so, Ms Slanic.'

Hetti picked up her purse and closed the dressing-room door. Conor took hold of her right arm and Sidney stayed close to her other side. Sebastian and Ric went on ahead. The dance music from *Franklin* was still blaring, and the cast were still going *whump – shuffle – whump* on the brightly lit stage. 'No!' they heard the director screaming at them. 'You're supposed to be bolts of lightning! Crackling, dazzling, bursting with voltage! For Christ's sake, you look like *cows*!'

They hurried along the landing that led to the stagedoor stairs. They had almost reached the end of it when they heard the door bang open. A square of sunlight suddenly jumped up the pale green wall, a square of sunlight with flickering shadows in it. They heard voices, and somebody coughing.

'*Tengo mucha prisa.*'

'OK, OK. *Comprendo.*'

'Who's that?' said Conor, gripping Hetti's arm more tightly.

Ric peered over the railings. 'I can only see their legs. There's three of them. No – that must be Ramon in the middle. I'd recognize those Cuban shoes anywhere.'

'What are we going to *do?*' hissed Sebastian.

'Rush them,' said Conor. 'Straight down the stairs as fast as you can, grab hold of Perez and go for the street. Shout a lot. Surprise them. Standard SWAT technique.'

Hetti tried to twist herself away from him. 'Ramon!' she called out. 'Watch out, Ramon! O'Neil's here!'

'Sebastian! Ric! Go for it!' Conor shouted.

'What the hell?' came from downstairs. But then Sebastian and Ric hurtled down the stairs, three and four at a time. They screamed at the tops of their voices, as Conor had told them, but they were so shrill and high pitched that they sounded like ululating Tuareg women. *Eee-ee-ee-eee-eee!* They collided emphatically with Ramon and his cronies, and Conor could hear nothing but scuffling and swearing and windows cracking in Sammy's office.

'Get oudah heah!' Sammy was shouting. 'Get oudah heah, all of youse!'

'Come on!' Conor told Hetti, pulling her arm.

'Let go of me, you bastard!' she spat at him. 'You don't even know what you're doing!'

She deliberately dropped to the floor, wriggling around, her sandals slapping against the wall. Conor wrenched her back onto her feet again and slapped her face, hard. She staggered back, one cheek flaming, her eyes wide with shock.

'You think I have any sympathy for you?' Conor yelled at her. 'You think I have any goddamn sympathy for you? You've ruined my life, you've ruined my girlfriend's life, you've almost gotten me killed! Now get down these goddamn stairs and don't you even think about getting away from me!'

Sidney said, 'Let's just get out of here, shall we?'

Conor was furious now. He pulled Hetti down the stairs, heaving her upright when she tripped. Right outside Sammy's office, Sebastian and Ric were fighting with two heavily built men, both of them bearded. They were silhouetted against the brilliant sunshine from the street outside, their arms swinging like windmills. Sparkling specks of dust flew into the air. Ramon Perez was keeping well back, one yellow-gloved hand lifted in front of his face as if he found all of this mayhem too offensive even to look at.

Sammy was standing in his office, his fists clenched, his mouth opening and closing, powerless to do anything at all.

'*Magda!*' said Ramon, as Conor dragged her downstairs.

'I want both of you!' Conor raged. 'Because of you, innocent people died, and you're not going to get away with it, either of you!' He felt so full of righteous anger, almost like Christ in the temple throwing out the money-changers. He felt that he could tear down the walls of the theater, if that was

218

what it would take to bring Hypnos and Hetti to confess what they had done to him.

Again, Hetti attempted to wrench herself away, but Conor shoved her against the wall and said, 'Don't even think about it. You understand me?'

The fight between Sebastian and Ric and Ramon's bodyguards grew fiercer and quicker and bloodier. Both of the bodyguards wore jeans and T-shirts – one man was crop-headed, the other had long greasy black hair combed in a high, exaggerated quiff. They were big: but Sebastian and Ric were lightning quick on their feet. Sebastian was ducking and weaving and spinning around, kicking his opponent in the arm, in the chest, in the hip, in the side of the head. Ric couldn't kick, but he was so nimble that every time the bodyguard in the green polo T-shirt tried to swing at him, he simply wasn't there.

Sebastian cornered the greasy-haired bodyguard and hit his face with a flurry of blows, so fast that they were almost invisible. There was a blur of noise like *thwickety-thwackety-thwickety-thwack!* The bodyguard's nose spouted a fountain of blood and he staggered and dropped to the floor.

Sebastian then turned to the other bodyguard. He leaped from the floor with all the grace of a ballet dancer – his face contorting, his long legs extended, every muscle concentrating on a devastating dropkick. But the bodyguard saw him a split second too soon, and swayed away sideways. Sebastian missed him and landed against the half-open stage door with a loud slamming sound.

The bodyguard twisted around, his fist clenched, his arm cocked up like a pistol hammer. But Conor tapped him on the shoulder, said, 'Hey! You've forgotten something, haven't you?' and punched him in the stomach, very hard; and then gave him an uppercut which pitched him backward into the doorway of Sammy's office.

Sebastian climbed to his feet, clutching the back of his head. Ric dusted off his polo shirt.

'Beginners,' sneered Sebastian. 'I've been learning karate for seventeen years. I could have been a second Bruce Lee.'

'Gypsy Rose Lee, more like,' put in Ric.

'Never mind about that,' said Conor. 'Let's get going. Sammy?'

Sammy nodded, his eyes still wide and his mouth still hanging open.

'How about hailing us a couple of taxis? Could you do that for us?'

'Taxis? Fuh shaw. *Two* taxis, is that what you want?'

Hetti went over and stood next to Ramon: Hypnos and Hetti, the double act, close together again.

'So what is this all about, Chief O'Neil?' asked Hypnos. He was trying to sound controlled but his voice was quivering.

'It's what we call the end of the line, Mr Perez. You stole the contents of my customers' safety deposit boxes. Now I want them back.'

'Or else?'

'Or else Lieutenant Slyman finds you sitting on his doorstep with enough *prima facie* evidence to send you to the slammer for a very long time. Conspiracy, theft, blackmail . . . extortion.'

'You'll have to prove all of that.'

'Oh, I will, believe me. I'll prove it to the point where you and Ms Slanic don't have any conceivable chance of release. How does fifteen years' prison sound to you? Think how old you're going to be, the day they let you out.'

'Fuck you,' said Ramon.

'I see,' said Conor, laying a hand on his shoulder. 'Never lost for words.'

Hypnos reached into his coat pocket and took out a small folded packet of aluminum foil. 'Mind if I take a snort?' he asked Conor. 'All this aggression . . . it's totally stressed me out.'

'What is that?'

'What do you think? Just a little recreational talcum powder.'

Conor noticed that Hetti was half smiling, in spite of her fiery cheek. He thought: *something's wrong here . . . Why are they both so cool about this?*

Ramon unfolded the foil. Inside was less than half a teaspoonful of brownish-white powder.

'See? No surprises. Just a little nose candy.'

'Let me take a look at that.' Conor held out his hand and Ramon gave him the foil. With some hesitation, Conor sniffed at the powder. But with no hesitation at all, Ramon Perez stepped up and blew it into his face, and then at Sebastian and Ric and Sidney.

Conor said, '*Shit!* What the hell are you—!'

The walls revolved sideways. The floor tilted onto its end. And then the whole theater silently collapsed inside of his head.

★   ★   ★

221

He was dreaming, he was floating, he was spinning around in circles. He was high in the air, up above a circus tent. He was sleeping in his own childhood bed, with the crucifix hanging on the wall above it, the crucifix that always frightened him so much. He was horrified by Christ's emaciated body, but at the same time he felt such pity for Him, such compassion, that he used to kneel on his pillow and touch His wounds, and promise to save Him, no matter what. He even brought Him food, tiny crumbly pieces of cookie or pound cake, and tried to feed them into the statue's mouth, so that at least He wouldn't die of starvation.

'I'm sorry, Jesus,' he used to say, and he was saying the same thing when he opened his eyes. 'I'm sorry. I'm truly, truly sorry.'

'You're *sorry*?' said a sarcastic voice.

He blinked. The light was so strong that it was difficult for him to see who was talking to him. But gradually the fuzziness came into focus, all the images collected themselves together.

He was sitting on a hard wooden chair in a plain yellow-painted room. In front of him stood a tall white-haired man in a black three-piece suit, wearing tiny sunglasses with sapphire-blue lenses.

The man leaned forward and peered directly into Conor's eyes. 'Y'all awake?' he asked, in an echoing voice. 'Good, you're awake. I was worried for a while there. Thought you might sleep for the rest of your natural life.'

16

Conor looked around in mystification. There was nothing in the room to indicate where he might be. It was sunny outside and he could hear traffic in the street below but a parchment-colored blind had been drawn down over the window. There were no pictures on the walls but darker rectangles on the wallpaper showed where pictures had once hung. In the far corner stood two other men, also dressed in black suits and black turtlenecks, one of them thin and ascetic looking, the other crewcut and ruddy cheeked. On a small canvas chair sat another man, heavily built, with a head like a knuckle of pork. His legs were crossed and he was waggling one immaculately polished black Oxford in time to his relentless gum-chewing.

The man in the blue sunglasses walked around in a circle. Then he sat down in a minimalist steel-and-canvas chair, his fingers steepled, and stared at Conor with an expression that was half contemptuous, half amused.

'What's happened?' asked Conor. He had a raging sore throat. 'What am I doing here?'

223

'You are here, sir, so that I can take a good look at you,' the man told him, in a throaty Missouri accent. He was strikingly handsome. He had a high, broad forehead and a long straight nose and a sharp movie actor's jawline. His skin, however, was dead white, and as dry and flaky as filo pastry. Although he was so handsome, his head was disproportionately large for his body. He was both fascinating and repelling, like the beautiful woman whom Conor had once met whose arms and legs had been horribly scarred by fire.

'Who are you? I thought I was—'

'You thought you were in the Rialto Theater. Yes, sir, you were. But you took a leap, my friend. A quantum leap from there to here; and here you are.'

Conor didn't know what to say. The man in the blue sunglasses continued to smile at him and the two men standing in the corner murmured like gossiping monks and the man with the head like a pork knuckle continued to chew gum and waggle his foot.

At last, the man in the blue sunglasses said, 'You really don't know who I am, do you? That just goes to show that publicity isn't worth squat. I'll bet they could have put up a poster of me, a hundred feet high, right in the middle of Times Square, and you still wouldn't know who I am.'

'I guess that you're something to do with Ramon Perez and Magda Slanic.'

The man let out an operatic '*ha!*' of total contempt. 'Hypnos and Hetti? Those two? I rescued those two from destitution. They were down as low as a man and woman can go, before I picked them

224

up, and showed them that they still had a part to play in God's great purpose.'

'Who *are* you?' Conor repeated.

'You seriously don't recognize me?' said the man, pointing to his own face. 'You and I have been on the same TV news reports. Maybe I look better on the small screen.'

The man's face suddenly fitted into place. 'I know you now. You're that religious terrorist. Branch.'

'The Reverend Dennis Evelyn Branch to you, sir. And "religious terrorist" isn't exactly the lifestyle description I'd choose. You might just as well call Moses a religious terrorist.'

'Moses didn't plant bombs in public buildings, as far as I remember.'

'Moses did worse! Moses brought down floods, and locusts. Moses brought down the angel of death. Moses didn't need no *bombs*.'

'So what's going on here, Reverend Branch? How did I get here?'

'Oh, Hypnos worked one of those little tricks of his. And as for what's going on . . . you don't need to know that, Mr O'Neil. All you have to know is that fate has involved *you* – you personally – in the single mightiest crusade that this world has ever known.'

'Crusade? I don't know what you're talking about.'

Dennis Evelyn Branch scratched the back of his hand, loosening a dry fragment of white skin. He lifted his hand to his mouth and tore it off with his teeth, and distastefully chewed it. 'The day will come when you and I can stand hand in hand in a world of in-*finite* harmony. A world where no man ever raises his fist to his brother.'

'Listen, I'm sorry, but I don't want to stand hand in hand with you *anywhere*.'

'Well, I'm sorry, too, because you don't have any choice no more. The Lord has picked you out, in His mysterious way, and you know what happens to those who show reluctance to serve the Lord.'

Conor stood up; but Pork Knuckle immediately stood up, too, and gave that aggressive forward shrug of his suit-shoulders that bouncers always do when they're getting ready to hit you.

'Please, Mr O'Neil,' said Dennis Evelyn Branch. 'I'd consider it a favor if you sat down. I don't have a whole lot of time. As you probably saw, the FBI have discovered that I'm here in New York and me and most of my people have to leave before five o'clock if we're going to catch the flight to where we're going. I don't relish spending the rest of my life locked up in maximum security with some tedious obsessive like the Unabomber.'

Conor remained standing. 'I don't understand what you want from me,' he said. 'I don't have any of the contents of those safety deposit boxes. I got caught up in this robbery by accident and all I'm trying to do is get the cops off my back.'

'Well, I'm aware of that,' said Dennis Evelyn Branch, scratching deep inside his left sleeve. But the whole point is that you *did* get caught up in it. You shouldn't have been so conscientious, should you? I guess you forgot that you weren't a boney-fidey policeman any more, that's what happened. You

226

kind of got intoxicated by the thrill of the chase, didn't you?

'If you'd have let that Gary Motson get away, you wouldn't be up to your neck in this situation now.'

'Gary Motson, that was his name?' Conor still pictured him as the Angel Gabriel.

'Gary Motson, that's right. Well, he's not anybody in particular. He's just some coach-class hood that your partner knew. An inveterate sticker-upper of liquor marts and corner convenience stores. Exactly the kind of fall guy we were looking for . . . until *you* came along, of course, and gave us a fall guy of real quality . . . someone the police were absolutely salivating to get their hands on.

'*Sal-i-vating*,' he repeated, picking a piece of skin from between his teeth.

Conor slowly sat down. 'My *partner* knew him? My partner Salvatore Morales?'

'That's the man. Very helpful. Very courteous. I was sorry to hear what happened to him.'

'I don't get this. Salvatore knew this Gary Motson *before* the robbery?'

'Of course,' said Dennis Evelyn Branch, with obvious pleasure. 'We needed somebody to take the blame for the missing safety deposit boxes, didn't we? It's what you call laying a false trail.'

'I don't believe that Salvatore would have gotten involved with anything like this,' said Conor.

'You don't? Then you don't know how weak people can be. That's one of the things I'm crusading for, Mr O'Neil, to make us all strong again. Your partner had a gambling habit, I'll bet you didn't know, and he was into the bookmakers for more

227

than you can imagine. Not only that, his mother had cancer of the tongue and he owed the hospital tens of thousands of dollars. There was something else, too: he hated Spurr's for giving you the job that he believed was rightfully his, and there is no man easier to suborn than a man who is poisoned with jealousy.'

Conor lowered his head. It all fitted into place now. How else had Gary Motson acquired a list of safety deposit boxes? How else had he known where the wall-safe was?

Dennis Evelyn Branch said, 'We got to hear of your partner through one of our disciples, who does a little money-lending on the side. We put a proposition to your partner and he accepted it. He told us how to get into the strongroom, and in return we were going to give him a very healthy retirement plan. Pity he'll never collect it.'

'What about this Gary Motson character?'

'That was your partner's idea. A second robbery, to distract attention from the first. He offered Gary Motson a third share in whatever he and that black individual could steal from Spurr's safety deposit boxes. He even volunteered to act as a hostage to help them get out of there safely; and to make it look less like an inside job. Gary Motson loved that touch, poor sap. He didn't know those safety deposit boxes were empty, any more than you did. He wouldn't have made any money out of that raid, but at least he would have got away. He and that black individual were supposed to go to Canada for a spell – and they would have done, if you hadn't been so – *phewff!* what can I call it? – all-fired hot on the job.'

He paused, and lifted one white, almost-invisible eyebrow. 'Still, we mustn't gainsay the ways of the Lord, must we? As it turns out, everybody thinks that *you* committed this robbery, and all of the owners of those safety deposit boxes have come to you to get their goodies back. And it's all been working very well, thanks to that very co-operative lawyer of yours.'

He burrowed into his cuff with his teeth and pulled off another strip of translucent skin.

Conor glanced at Pork Knuckle and said, 'What's to stop me from going to the police and telling them all this?'

'Three reasons – apart from the fact that I could kill you here and now. Of course I don't want to do that, because who's going to pay blackmail money to a dead man? Number one, the police would drop you the second you walked in through the precinct door – or, if not, they would make sure that you accidentally suffocated in your cell. Number two, even if you survived, nobody would believe you. Hypnotists came in and made you open the strongroom? *Hypnotists?* I don't think so! Not only that, you have money problems of your own, don't you? What with your divorce, and your new apartment, and your pretty new girlfriend to take care of. Just think of the way that a jury might look at it. Your partner was prepared to betray his trust to straighten out his debts. Who's to say that you weren't prepared to do the same? I don't know what your partner said to Gary Motson, but I gather from what I hear on the news that Motson's going to testify that you were involved in the conspiracy, too. I know you weren't.

But I'm not going to testify on your behalf, am I? And you only have one witness to your hypnotism story, Darrell Bussman, and he's in hospital in a coma and unlikely to recover.'

Conor cleared his throat. 'So . . . what do you want me to do?' he asked, hoarsely.

'Well, there's one thing in particular,' said Dennis Evelyn Branch. 'Several owners of those safety deposit boxes have been kind of wary about handing over so much money until they see you in person. We already have most of the money we need, but we're talking about an extra fifteen to twenty million dollars, and I'd hate to lose out on those funds if we have the means to lay our hands on them.'

'And you want me to *help* you? Forget it.'

'Oh, you *will* help. No question about it.'

'And what if I refuse?'

'You won't refuse.'

'I'm refusing now. It's going to be difficult enough to prove that I didn't have anything to do with this robbery, without actively extorting money on the strength of it. Do you know what it's like, walking around the city knowing that you could be shot on sight at any second, and never know what hit you?'

'Well, that's pitiful. It is. But you should think of yourself as a martyr. We're all martyrs to something, Mr O'Neil. I've been a martyr to eczema all of my life. But I think of my eczema as a constant reminder from God that – even though He's empowered me to carry out His will – I shall never be perfect, as He is. It's all for the greater good, Mr O'Neil. I may be asking you to make a small sacrifice, Mr O'Neil, but what's that, when it's going to help to bring about the greatest crusade since the beginning of Christianity.'

'I don't know what the hell you're talking about, Reverend Branch, but the answer is no, I'm not going to help you. No way. What do you want the money for, anyhow? More bombs? Do you think I could live with myself if I helped you to kill some innocent women and children?'

'In this case, Mr O'Neil, I don't think you have a choice.'

The two black-suited men in the corner stopped murmuring and looked toward Branch expectantly. Pork Knuckle rose from his seat and came to stand close to Conor's shoulder.

After a calculated pause, Dennis Evelyn Branch stood up too. He reached up and slowly took off his blue sunglasses. Underneath, his eyes were bright pink, as pink as a rabbit's, with only the tiniest dots for pupils.

'I was chosen by the Lord for a special mission in this life,' he told Conor. 'The Lord spoke in my ear and gave me a personal dispensation to do whatever I deemed necessary in order to build for Him the greatest temple that the world has ever seen.'

He came closer, and touched his forehead with his fingertip. 'Not a temple of brick, or stone, not at first, although there will be one, when my crusade is over. I'm talking about a temple in the mind – a temple to which the whole world belongs. And I'm telling you, Mr O'Neil, that temple is going to be built, and I'm going to be the builder of it, and you will do whatever I say until that day comes about, because the Lord wills it.'

231

Conor said, 'Why don't you kiss my ass?'

Dennis Evelyn Branch gave him a wavering smile. 'Not to my taste, I'm afraid. But I think I have something to *your* taste. You must be hungry.'

'I'm fine, thanks.'

'No, no. I insist. No guest of the Reverend Dennis Evelyn Branch can possibly leave without being offered some refreshment. And maybe, once you've eaten, you'll find that you have a different view of things. Less *self-centered*, know what I mean? Some people have to be *taught* to devote themselves to God.'

He popped his fingers and at once the tall, ascetic-looking man went across the living room and pushed open a squeaky swing door that led to a brightly sunlit kitchen. Dennis Evelyn Branch said nothing while they waited, but continued to stare at Conor with his bright pink eyes, not blinking once.

'I'd better warn you,' said Conor. 'There's nothing that you can do to me that's going to make me change my mind.'

'Well, we'll see,' said Branch.

He beckoned to Pork Knuckle. The man came up behind Conor and, without warning, seized his arms. Conor tried to twist around and throw himself sideways, but Dennis Evelyn Branch swung his arm back and slapped his face, hard, in a shower of dead skin. Pork Knuckle wrenched Conor's arms around the back of the chair and fastened them together with handcuffs.

'Don't you go riling me, Mr O'Neil,' trembled Dennis Evelyn Branch, raising a single cautioning finger. 'The Lord has a terrible temper when He's

232

riled, and I'm the Lord's own instrument.'

'That's a pretty good catch-all excuse for behaving like a sociopath,' Conor retorted. He could still feel the awful scaliness of Branch's palm against his cheek.

Pork Knuckle knelt down beside the chair and lashed Conor's ankles together with wide black Advance industrial tape. At the same time, the tall, ascetic man came out of the kitchen holding at arm's length a tall glass screwtop jar, with a label for kosher dill pickles still on it.

'Did you ever read Leviticus?' asked Dennis Evelyn Branch. '*Yet these may you eat among all the winged insects: those which have above their feet jointed legs with which to jump on the earth. But all other winged insects are detestable to you.*'

He held the jar up in front of Conor's face. 'What do you think?' he said. 'Do you think these are detestable enough?'

Inside was a crawling, jerking confusion of shiny brown cockroaches, scores of them, their antennae waving, their legs sliding uselessly up against the glass.

'Lunch,' said Dennis Evelyn Branch.

233

17

Conor struggled wildly, rocking his chair from side to side in an effort to wrench himself free. But Pork Knuckle gripped his shoulders and he couldn't even tip the chair over.

'Let me loose, you freak!' Conor demanded.

'I can't do that. Not until I have your solemn promise that you'll assist us, in any way we ask you.'

Conor hadn't often felt helpless. Once, he had been caught by three suspicious mafiosi who had tied him up in a garage in Queens and doused him in gasoline. He felt the same kind of desperation now: the same kind of breathless panic.

'I'm not agreeing to anything. Two people died because of you.'

'Oh, yes. A treacherous security officer and a low-life thief. You should be glad for them. Anybody who dies to help my crusade will find his place in Heaven.'

'You're crazy.'

'You think so? You really think so? That's what they said about Jesus, isn't it? He's crazy, that's what they said. But they don't say that now, do they? And they don't accuse *Him* of being a murderer, in spite of all of the millions of people who have died in His name.

'It's quite possible that many more will die before my crusade is complete. Many, many more. But you don't have to be one of them.'

'Go to hell.'

Dennis Evelyn Branch unscrewed the lid of the jar full of struggling cockroaches and said, 'Unpleasant little suckers, aren't they? *Periplaneta americana*, introduced from Africa, in spite of their name.'

'You can skip the natural history lesson. You're wasting your time.'

'They have a particularly nauseating smell of their own, don't they?' said Dennis Evelyn Branch, wafting the jar under Conor's nose. Conor caught the oily, brownish odor of cockroaches, and twisted his head away.

Branch nodded to Pork Knuckle. Pork Knuckle seized Conor's hair and pulled it back so hard that he felt his scalp crackle, and a fiery pain all over his head. Then, with his other hand, Pork Knuckle gripped the sides of Conor's jaw, pressing the nerves so that he couldn't help but open his mouth.

'My friend here used to be a psychiatric nurse,' smiled Dennis Evelyn Branch. 'He has the knack of feeding your reluctant eater.'

'*Ggahh!*' Conor gargled, trying to clench his teeth shut.

But the tall, ascetic man came up to him with a plastic funnel in his hand, and held it over his wide-open mouth.

'I'll bet you're thinking to yourself, "He's not going to do this . . . he's just trying to scare me some." But, you know, I'm not even going to give you the chance to change your mind, because you've had your chance. You've had three chances, and just like Peter you've denied your Lord every time.'

He said, 'Carry on, Tyrone,' and the tall, ascetic man forced the plastic funnel into Conor's mouth, knocking it hard against his teeth and scratching his tongue. As it scraped the back of his throat, he gave a dry, agonizing heave, and then another, and another.

Conor tried to bite at the funnel but Pork Knuckle was still pressing the nerves at the side of his jaw and he was almost completely paralyzed. He tried to thrash his ankles but the industrial tape was stuck too tight.

'Maybe I ought to say a few words,' said Dennis Evelyn Branch. 'After all, these are God's creatures, too, however much we revile them, and now that they're going to meet their Maker, we shouldn't let them go unmourned.'

'*Nggguhhh* . . .' choked Conor. He gagged and gagged and his stomach let out a deep groan of sheer revulsion.

Dennis Evelyn Branch shook his head and said, 'Mmm,' in satisfaction. 'This is such an effective form of persuasion. The Klan used to use it to discourage liberal-minded newspaper editors, but don't let that put you off. It works in ninety-nine per cent of cases; and the other one per cent who manage to tough it out can easily be made to change their minds when you mention the magic words "cockroach enema". Great idea, isn't it? Cheap, practical, and *organic*, too.'

'*Aggh! Ggahh!*'

'Here,' said Dennis Evelyn Branch. He lifted the jar so that Conor could clearly see the cockroaches trying to climb up the side of the glass, their leathery forewings flaring every now and then, their antennae desperately waving. Conor closed his eyes, and tried to close his throat, too. But he heard Dennis Evelyn Branch shake the jar over the funnel, and he distinctly heard a few of the cockroaches rattle against the plastic. *Oh, God, no!* They dropped helter-skelter into his throat, their legs and their wings tickling his esophagus. He heaved, and bile gushed out of the sides of his mouth, but he couldn't stop himself from swallowing at least six or seven cockroaches, and another one was caught frantically flailing its legs in his windpipe.

'*Aaagggh!*' he shouted, cackling for breath.

Dennis Evelyn Branch peered at him from only three or four inches away – so close that Conor could see the dry flaky skin inside his nostrils. He tried to think of the stories that Father O'Faoghlin had taught him, all about tortured saints. Saints who had plunged their hands into burning braziers, rather than recant their beliefs. Saints who had been hoisted aloft on spears, still proclaiming their love of God while the pointed steel penetrated their entrails. It had been Father O'Faoghlin more than anybody else who had taught him the meaning of justice, and why justice was worth suffering for.

'You're the stubborn one, aren't you?' said Dennis Evelyn Branch. 'Stubborn like all of your faith. You

237

wait until my great crusade. You wait until the cloak of death sweeps over you all! Then we'll see how stubborn you are.'

His pink eyes wide with evangelical glee, he shook the jar a second time, much harder, so that dozens of cockroaches dropped into the funnel. They thrashed and struggled and clung together, but Dennis Evelyn Branch flicked the side of the funnel with his finger to dislodge them. They dropped into Conor's throat in a wriggling mass. He didn't want to swallow. His neck muscles ached from the effort of not swallowing – but then Pork Knuckle suddenly released his grip, and his first reaction was to take the whole throatful down into his stomach.

His eyes bulged and he arched his back. Dennis Evelyn Branch stepped away, circling the jar. 'You *still* refuse?' he crowed, at the top of his voice. 'Look at him here, everybody! Did you ever see such stubbornness? Are you still going to refuse me, Mr O'Neil? Or are you going to help me to fulfil the Lord's great plan?'

Conor shook his head wildly from side to side.

'What does that mean?' insisted Dennis Evelyn Branch. 'Is that a no, you're not going to refuse me? Or is that a no, you're not going to help me?'

Conor's head was bursting and he couldn't even think. He was whining for breath and his stomach muscles were churning so fiercely that he felt as if a truck were rolling over him, backward and forward. He shook his head again, and the tall, ascetic man took the funnel out of his mouth.

'You give in?' asked Dennis Evelyn Branch. 'Is

that what you're telling me? You're going to help us out?'

Conor tried to speak but then he spewed a fountain of coffee and bile and cockroaches all over himself. Most of the cockroaches were still alive and they scuttled across his knees and dropped onto the wooden floor. He coughed and coughed, and spat, and coughed again, and at last he managed to dislodge the last cockroach out of his windpipe. He sat with his head lowered, sweating, shivering, and still trying to spit out the taste of cockroach.

Dennis Evelyn Branch replaced his blue sunglasses with the same slow-motion flourish with which he had taken them off.

'You want *seconds*, Mr O'Neil? There's a few left here in the jar. It seems a shame to let them go to waste.'

Conor shook his head. He wasn't going to be able to stand any more of this. He had to think of another way to deal with Dennis Evelyn Branch. Like so many sociopaths, he thrived on outright defiance: it excited him, it empowered him, and God alone knew what he was going to make Conor swallow next.

'Well, well. Praise the Lord. You don't know how glad I am that you've seen reason.' Dennis Evelyn Branch shook the rest of the cockroaches onto the floor and stepped on them, a little crunching tap-dance. 'As I said before, it isn't much I'm asking you to do. Just meet a few people, do a little business, and keep yourself alive and out of the clutches of the law until we're all done here in New York, and the money's all been transferred.'

Conor nodded.

239

'You give me your solemnest word on that, so help you God?'

Conor nodded again.

'Well, you don't really have to give me your word because I've arranged for a little security.'

'I'll give you my word, OK? Isn't that enough?'

'Al-most, but not quite. You're a fugitive from the law, after all. Your word, quite frankly, doesn't count for too much.'

'So what do you want? I don't have anything else to give you.'

'Don't you go worrying yourself . . . I've already made the arrangements.'

'What arrangements? What are you talking about?'

'Your girlfriend has decided to change her address for a while. She's staying across town with some friends of mine.'

'Lacey? You mean *Lacey?*'

Dennis Evelyn Branch nodded and smiled.

'You bastard! If you hurt her – if you so much as—'

'I know, I know. I've read the script. "If I so much as touch one hair on her head, etcetera, etcetera." But you see my problem, don't you? I need to let you out while I finish fixing this deal up; but I can't have you misbehaving yourself. It's an incentive, too, to get it all concluded as soon as possible. Trust me. So long as you keep your part of the bargain, she's safe.'

Pork Knuckle unlocked the handcuffs and cut off the tape with a craft knife. Dennis Evelyn Branch said, 'You can go now. You'll be hearing from a man called Victor Labrea later today. Don't try to come back here . . . we'll be gone.'

Conor shakily stood up. He didn't know what to say so he didn't say anything at all. He left the apartment and slowly made his way down the bare-boarded stairs to the street. As soon as he opened the front door and the heat hit him, his stomach clenched and he was sick. A man in a filthy undervest watched him with pity.

'The end of the world is next Wednesday,' he kept repeating. 'The end of the world is next Wednesday. Three-fifteen.'

Conor returned to Sebastian's apartment by a devious route, taxi-hopping and changing buses and doubling back on himself five or six times, so that a six-block journey took him almost thirty-five minutes. By the time he reached Sebastian's door the perspiration was stinging his eyes and his shirt was glued to his back.

Sebastian quickly opened the front door, wearing turquoise silk pajamas and looking tense.

'Conor! My *dear!* We thought we'd lost you for ever*!*'

'I don't know what happened – one minute we were fighting with Hypnos and Hetti in the theater, the next thing I knew I was sitting in some strange apartment with all of these strange people standing around me.'

He walked through to the living room. Sidney and Eleanor were sitting on the couch. Sidney was pale and obviously shaken and Eleanor had her arm around his shoulders.

'Ric isn't feeling too good . . . he's gone to bed for a sleep.'

'I think Sidney should see a doctor,' said Eleanor.

'No, no, please, I'll be all right,' said Sidney. 'This isn't any worse than your regular three-martini hangover.'

'What happened to you, Conor?' asked Eleanor. 'You look positively *gray*.'

Conor sat down and Sebastian brought him a glass of water. He told them all about the Reverend Dennis Evelyn Branch and the cockroaches and Eleanor wrinkled up her nose in disgust. 'The upshot is, the Reverend Dennis Evelyn Branch wants me to help him extort a few more millions, and just to make sure I do what I'm told, he's holding Lacey as security.'

Sebastian jumped up like a jack-in-the-box. 'He's got Lacey? The bastard! I'll *kill* him! If he so much as—'

'I know,' said Conor. 'If he so much as touches one hair on her head.'

'What are you going to do?'

'What *can* I do? The guy's a complete fruitcake and I have no idea where to find him.'

'There must be *some* way.'

Conor licked his lips and he was sure he could still taste cockroach. He went over and sat down next to Sidney. 'You feeling OK?'

'Sure, sure, I'm feeling OK. A little woozy, that's all.'

'What happened to us, Sidney? I thought that even Ramon Perez couldn't hypnotize four people simultaneously. I mean, you trained me to be resistant, but it was like *whoofff!* and there I was, some-where on East 29th Street without the faintest idea of how the hell I got there.'

'Ramon blew some powder at us, remember that?'

'Sure. But he didn't touch me, or shake my hand, or say anything. Not so far as I can remember.'

'We're not just dealing with ordinary trance induction here. That powder was almost certainly burundanga.'

'Burundanga? What the hell's that?'

'Zombie dust, that's what they call it in Haiti. It's a powder made from very powerful tranquilizers. Ativan, usually, which is a strong barbiturate, and scopolamine, which is sometimes called hyoscine. They use scopolamine in hospitals as a sedative and as a pre-medication before anesthesia. I've occasion-ally used a mild dose to make it easier for me to induce a hypnotic state in very resistant patients.'

'But a strong dose?'

'A strong dose can cause hallucinations, loss of memory, disorientation and great suggestibility. Robbers in Colombia have been using burundanga for the past forty years. They induce a state of suggestibility in their victims by spiking their drinks with it or blowing it into their faces, the same way that Ramon Perez did to us.'

'Sidney and Sebastian and Ric found themselves sitting on a bench at the Rockefeller Center,' Eleanor put in. 'They couldn't remember how they got there, not for the life of them.'

Conor said, 'This is all to do with some great religious crusade. Dennis Evelyn Branch kept on and on about it. But God alone knows why he needs so much money.'

'The first thing we have to do is find Lacey,' said Sidney.

'Oh, yes?' said Sebastian. 'And how do you propose we do that? Hypnos and Hetti have gone. I called Sammy at the Rialto. He was in a trance for over an hour, too. When he woke up, Hypnos and Hetti had skedaddled, with all their belongings, too.'

'So we've lost them again,' said Conor. 'It's back to square one.'

'How about some tea?' asked Sebastian. 'I have these wonderful little madeleines. I'm sure they'll make us *all* feel better.'

18

A corner of Sebastian's living room had been made into a tiny office,with an antique mahogany desk and a fax machine and a Hewlett-Packard PC connected to the Net.

Conor pulled out the chair and said, 'Let's do a little surfing, shall we, and see what we can find out about our friend Dennis Evelyn Branch.' He set down a tumbler of Irish whiskey next to the computer. Sebastian instantly picked it up and slipped a silver coaster under it.

It didn't take Conor long to find a website devoted to *Branch, Dennis Evelyn/ Global Message Movement.* The Global Message Movement was an evangelical church based in Lubbock, Texas, and Dennis Evelyn Branch was its 'Leader and Divine Inspiration'. The Movement's declared mission was to 'bring the true message of God's holy will into the hearts and minds of all people of all cultures throughout the world'. It organized mass prayer meetings, hymn festivals, charity telethons and 'outdoor training activities'. Founded in 1987, it was now said to have a membership of more than two and a half million devotees and subscribers. The website showed a list of Global Message Movement churches in eleven major US cities, most of them Southern, such as Atlanta and Birmingham, but including Minneapolis/St Paul, Philadelphia and New York – 1441 West 19th Street.

There were dozens of news cuttings, as well as features from *Time* and *Newsweek* and even media releases from the Global Message Movement themselves.

Dennis Evelyn Branch was the seventh son of Wayne Branch, a Baptist minister from Wichita Falls, Texas, and his wife Noreen (née Tuttle). He was born in 1956 or 1957 – 'no birth registration appears to exist'. Wayne Branch had been one of the most influential of early TV evangelists, and his fifteen-minute show *The Message* had been a fixture of Sunday morning television in the Wichita Falls area for over seventeen years. It was devoted to 'the defeat of Satan in whatever guise he might contrive to appear, and the cleansing of all earthly sin – nothing more, nothing less'.

Dennis Evelyn Branch had appeared on his father's show at the age of nine, and a black-and-white picture showed a thin, serious-looking young boy with shining white hair. He had been credited with 'a gift of healing, by finding the demons that live within us, and exorcizing them'. He had shown signs of a precocious intelligence, and he graduated from high school in Wichita Falls a year early, with exceptional grades in science and Bible studies. He went on to the University of Texas Health Science Center and took a doctorate in microbiology, while at the same time studying at Dallas Bible College. In 1979 he found a well-paid research post with Texas Bio-Systems in Houston, where he was responsible for 'an original and highly creative' method of dealing with potential outbreaks of smallpox – a hugely significant medical advance since the United States possesses only seven million shots of smallpox vaccine for a population of nearly two hundred and sixty million.

Dennis Evelyn Branch's achievements might have been fêted in the specialist press, but it was plain that he wasn't widely liked by his colleagues at Texas Bio-Systems. His company personnel report described him as 'sociopathic, devious, deeply involved with fundamentalist religion and white supremacy'. On the other hand, he was 'highly motivated in his work to the point of obsession, and unquestionably a considerable asset to our research department'.

A research assistant described him to *Time*'s reporter as 'a ghost, with attitude'.

He seemed to have no close friends, and his albinism and eczema had evidently made it difficult for him to form relationships with women, so he spent most of his spare time organizing evangelical meetings for his father's ministry.

Three years in Houston came to an end when Dennis Evelyn Branch was arrested after a minor explosion in the PX at Fort Sam Houston, head-quarters of the US Fifth Army, in which two servicewomen were slightly injured. Military police were unable to work out how a white-haired pink-eyed evangelist had managed to penetrate base security, and Dennis Evelyn Branch refused to enlighten them. He told the court that it was a protest against America's close diplomatic ties with Islamic countries such as Saudi Arabia and Iran, and that he was sorry.

Prosecuting attorney: You're sorry? You could have killed someone.
Dennis Evelyn Branch: Of course. But I failed to kill someone. That is why I am sorry.

Dennis Evelyn Branch was sentenced to ten years' imprisonment, but was released without any official explanation after only eleven months. No official explanation was really needed: his name next appeared on a roster of scientists employed at the US Army medical facility at Moab, Utah.

According to a press release from the Pentagon, the scientists were working on ways to counteract the threat posed by Biopreparat, the Soviet Union's germ warfare program. But in 1986 there was an emergency at the medical plant which was officially described as 'a minor compromise of sterile containment' but which led to half of Moab being evacuated for over a week. The *Washington Post* was prompted to ask: 'Are we finding ways of defending ourselves against germ warfare or are we secretly and illegally developing our own biological weapons?'

In November 1989, Dennis Evelyn Branch failed to report for work. An immediate search of his house gave no clues to where he might have gone. The FBI investigated the possibility that he might have been kidnaped by Soviet agents in retaliation for the

248

recent defection to the west of the Soviet micro-
biologist Vladimir Pesechnik – whose claim to fame
was that he had found a way of turning the Black
Death into a practicable biological weapon.

Some reports said that Dennis Evelyn Branch had
been murdered by rival white supremacists. Others
suggested that he had accidentally contracted a
virulent disease and had gone to the woods to die so
that he wouldn't infect his fellow workers.
('Unlikely, given his character,' noted the FBI agent
in charge, dryly.)

During the investigation that followed the
bombing of New York's World Trade Center in
1993, Dennis Evelyn Branch was named as a
possible suspect, along with several other religious
extremists, although it was later established that an
Islamic terror group had been responsible. His name
was also connected with plots to bomb the Midtown
and Holland Tunnels.

From time to time, there were unsubstantiated
sightings of Dennis Evelyn Branch in Canada, South
Africa and the Irish Republic. A CIA agent claimed
to have seen him in Chile. But it was not until 1995
that he dramatically reappeared, with a full-page
advertisement in the *International Herald-Tribune*
and several Arab-language newspapers, declaring
the formation of his Global Message Movement, 'the
object of which is to convince all unbelievers
throughout the world that there is only one true way
to God'.

In August 1996 Dennis Evelyn Branch sent a
rambling letter to NBC News, claiming responsibility for the bombing of the Municipal Center in

Omaha, Nebraska, in which one secretary was killed and three other office workers seriously hurt. He said that he was dedicated to the cause of 'wresting the human race from the grip of atheists and blasphemers and backsliders, to re-establish God's holy law throughout the world, and to convert all those who follow false and deluded religions to true Christianity'.

He said, 'Our churches must be filled again. We must learn to sing our sacred hymns again. The light of the Lord must shine everywhere, from the greatest cathedrals to the humblest dwellings in the slums. I swear that I will root out every single Muslim, Mormon, Catholic, Jew and all other devotees of false religions. If they cannot be converted by persuasion, then they will have to be converted by the fear of God.'

He was prepared to sacrifice the lives of 'every man, woman and child on the face of the Earth' if that was what it took for his mission to succeed. His message was: *be saved or die, for not to be saved is a hundred times worse than death.*

After that, the Global Message Movement was officially repudiated by the Southern Baptist Conference, who said that Dennis Evelyn Branch was 'an agent of Satan'.

A blurry black-and-white photograph of a man reputed to be Dennis Evelyn Branch was displayed on the screen. It showed a thin, white-faced man with very short hair and sunglasses. The camera had caught him just as he was climbing into a Toyota Landcruiser. He was staring in the direction of the camera with a look of hair-raising menace, quite unlike the small boy standing next to his father in church.

Conor stared back at him for a while, then switched off the PC and sat with his head bowed.

'Well?' asked Sebastian. 'Got what you wanted?'

Conor shook his head. 'I still don't know why he needs all this money. But I can guess he's planning something pretty damned terrible.'

They talked late into the evening. Apart from Eleanor, they were all hungover with burundanga poisoning, and from time to time Conor felt strange hallucinatory waves. When he looked out of the window, he thought he saw his mother in the street below, returning from the market with her shopping. She looked up at him and her face was blurred against the summer sunshine. She waved, and he waved back. He thought he saw his father, exhausted after a night shift, sitting with his head bent, as if it was his fault that innocent people had been mugged and robbed and stabbed in the subway.

Most of all, though, he felt the persistent ache of fear. The fear of what Dennis Evelyn Branch and his men might do to Lacey. It gripped his mind like a cold-cast engineering vise and it wouldn't let go.

Eleanor must have sensed what he was feeling because she reached her hand across and stroked the back of his knuckles. 'You always have to believe that things are going to work out right,' she told him. 'They did for me.'

'But, for you, look how long it took. How many years.'

'The years don't matter, Conor. You'll learn that, when you get older. Five minutes of bliss is worth fifty years of loneliness.'

By ten or eleven o'clock their minds began to clear. They ordered Korean take-out – stuffed cuttlefish, vermicelli with beef and cucumber, and the cabbage and mung bean pancakes known as *bindae duk.*

Conor slept fitfully that night. He kept trying to think of ways in which he could find out where Dennis Evelyn Branch was keeping Lacey; and how to track down Ramon Perez and Magda Slanic. When he was captain of detectives, he had a whole force to help him, and a computer database that could tell him at any one time which officer was where. Now he felt as if he were stumbling around in a blindfold.

All the same, there were still plenty of routine inquiries he could follow up. He could go back to the Rialto Theater tomorrow to see if anybody in the cast of *Franklin* had any idea where Hypnos and Hetti might be hiding out. He would also ask Eleanor to call up every theatrical agent she knew to see if they might still be on somebody's talent list. And Ric, when he recovered, might be able to help with more contacts in the cabaret business.

He closed his eyes and said a prayer that his mother had taught him, asking the Blessed Virgin for guidance and strength.

At 6:30 in the morning, Sebastian's mobile phone rang. After a moment's conversation, he came into Conor's room and gently shook his shoulder.

'Are you awake? It's for you.'

Conor frowzily sat up. On the other side of the room, buried under a blanket, Sidney whuffled and turned over like an old dog in his basket.

'Mr O'Neil? This is Victor Labrea speaking. I think that the Reverend Branch may have mentioned my name.'

'That's right. What do you want?'

'There's a little errand that I want you to run for me this morning. A certain gentleman wants sight of certain letters.'

Conor said nothing but, 'Go on.'

'I've arranged for him to meet you by the entrance to the Children's Zoo in Central Park at 11:35 precisely. He'll be wearing a Panama hat with a red headband and he'll be carrying a copy of this week's edition of *New York* magazine.'

'I see. Are you going to tell me what his name is?'

'No need for that. All you have to do is introduce yourself and give him two sample letters. Then walk away.'

'How do I know it's safe?'

'Easy. We have the rest of the letters and this gentleman would rather cut off his own dick with a pair of blunt scissors than have those letters made public.'

'Is that all I have to do?'

'That's all. If you go down to Mr Speed's mailbox you'll find the letters waiting for you there.'

'How did you know I was here?'

'You don't think Magda recognized your friend Ric Vetter? Come on, Mr O'Neil, you used to be a detective. Anyhow – *ciao* for now.'

253

'Don't hang up! Before I do this, I need to know that Lacey's safe.'

'She's safe, take my word for it.'

'You haven't hurt her, have you?'

'Of course not.'

'If she's safe, then let me talk to her.'

'Oh, I don't think so.'

'Listen, Labrea—'

'Listen, yourself, Mr O'Neil. Your girlfriend's fine. But before you start getting funny ideas, just bear in mind that she's being taken care of by a couple of friends of mine who are training as plastic surgeons. They'd just love to have the opportunity to work on somebody as lovely as Lacey. A nip here, a tuck there. Maybe a breast reduction.'

'I'll find you, I mean it, and I'll kill you.'

'You won't find me and even if you did you wouldn't kill me. You're a fine upstanding Catholic, O'Neil. You wouldn't murder anybody in cold blood, even me.'

'You'd be worth going to Purgatory for, believe me.'

Victor Labrea gave a hissing little laugh. 'Purgatory! Don't you just love it!'

Conor took a deep breath. 'Listen, I won't meet this guy at the zoo today until I've had the chance to talk to Lacey.'

Victor Labrea was silent for a while. Conor thought that he could hear him licking his lips, or maybe it was his dentures clicking. 'All right,' he said, eventually. 'I'll have her call you in five minutes. But keep it short, OK? And – you know – keep it clean.'

'You bastard.'

Victor Labrea hung up and Conor waited and waited for Lacey to call. Even though he was expecting it, when the phone rang he jumped.

'Hello? Lacey?'

There were a few blurred, crunching moments while the phone was handed over. Then Conor heard Lacey say, 'Conor? Is that you?' in a voice like ice-crackled milk.

'It's me, baby. Are you OK? They haven't hurt you, have they?'

'They just smashed their way in, Conor. I didn't know what was happening. I tried to call you but I couldn't.'

'But they haven't hurt you? Touched you, or anything?'

'No, they haven't. But they've been threatening all kinds of things. Please, Conor, you have to do what they say.'

'Where are you? Do you have any idea? Just say yes or no.'

'No.'

'Is it an apartment?'

'Yes.'

'An old building or a new building? Say first or second.'

'First.'

'Is it quiet or noisy? Say red for quiet or white for noisy.'

'Mostly red.'

'Are there any unusual sounds that you can hear? Like helicopters, or river traffic? Say hungry or thirsty.'

255

'Hungry. Every few minutes.'

The phone went dead. Conor looked at it for a moment and then dropped it on the bed.

He sat for a long while with his head in his hands. He felt like his father. Yet there was something in the back of his mind. A vision, or an instantaneous flash of a vision. The blink of an eye. *The door opened and Magda Slanic stepped out, confronting him.* He made an effort not to look at her, in case she hypnotized him. He took Sidney's advice and *looked beyond her*, into the dressing-room, and he saw crumpled silk blouses and filmy black bras and discarded black thongs. And they distracted him. They *had* distracted him. Sexually, he was ashamed to admit. But he had seen the room in greater detail than that. His mind like a camera had seen all of the room, everything in it, and it was all still there.

He shook Sidney awake. 'Sidney . . . there's something you have to do for me.'

'What time is it?'

'Seven. Well, six fifty-four.'

'I never open my eyes until nine. I'm retired, remember.'

'Sidney, I really need your help.'

At last, with his hair sticking up at the back, and his eyes as glutinous as two freshly opened clams, Sidney sat up. 'What is it, for Pete's sake?'

Conor sat down on the bed beside him. 'We're looking for Hypnos and Hetti, right?'

'That's right.'

'They won't be going back to the Rialto Theater, so what we have to do is track them down.'

'You're the detective, Conor. *You* track them

256

down. I'm nothing but a hypnotist; and a retired hypnotist at that.'

He pulled the blanket over his head and started to breathe with exaggerated harshness.

Conor waited for a few moments, and then he said, 'I have this feeling . . . are you listening, Sidney? I have this feeling that I *saw* something. A clue. Maybe not even a clue. An indication, I don't know.'

Sidney sat up again. 'What indication?'

'When Magda Slanic opened the door of dressing-room eleven . . . I didn't want to catch her eyes because I was afraid that she was going to hypnotize me . . . but I saw the whole dressing-room, in intense detail, and I really have this feeling that—'

'I know. You really have this feeling that if I could hypnotize you, then you'd remember it all. Am I right?'

'You're right,' Conor admitted. 'How did you know that?'

'Because I've had people coming to me for thirty years trying to remember stuff that they've lost. "It's there someplace, I put it right down" – "It's on the tip of my tongue" – and they've paid me to hypnotize them to find out what they've forgotten. Sometimes it works out good. You help them to locate a wedding ring, or a piece of jewelry. Then it's all kisses and free champagne.'

'Sidney, hypnotize me. Take me back to yesterday afternoon, when we went to the Rialto. Take me back to the moment when Hetti opened the door.'

'I don't think so, Conor. You've already had your cerebral cortex messed up by burundanga. It's not going to do you any good, especially in your state of mind.'

'I don't have a choice, do I?'

Sidney dragged his blanket aside and stood up. He was wearing a long pink T-shirt with a red stencil of the Golden Gate Bridge on it. His toes were as dry and hairy as tree roots. 'OK . . . if that's what you want. Sit quiet. Sit still. Breathe deeply. Try to relax.'

'I'm relaxed,' Conor told him.

'Oh, no you're not. In fact you're very tense. But that isn't a problem. You need to learn negative things as well as positive things. You need to learn that you can forget things even more easily than you can remember them. Do you know what Erickson used to say to me? In teaching students at medical school, you can tell them, most impressively, "The exam will be held on Thursday in room seventeen in building C and it will begin at two p.m." And as you turn to leave the classroom you can see the students leaning toward each other and saying "What day?" "What room?" "What building?" "What time?" They heard what you said, but they immediately forgot it.

'The information is there, though, and it's still possible to retrieve it. You simply have to relax and go back to the most memorable moment immediately preceding the incident that you want to remember.'

'I tried to hypnotize the cab driver,' said Conor. 'It didn't work so I tipped him and climbed out of

258

the cab. Ric went to the stage door and rang the bell.'

Sidney sat beside him. 'Then what happened?' he asked. With the tip of one finger he stroked the knuckles of Conor's right hand. The feeling was soothing and disturbing at the same time: men didn't normally touch each other like this.

Sammy opened the door – Conor could see him nodding his head and moving his lips, but he couldn't hear what he was saying. Now they were following Sammy into the theater. Conor was quite aware of Sebastian's apartment all around him, quite aware of Sidney's presence, but he was walking along the theater corridor, too, as clearly as if he were actually there.

'You reach the dressing-room door,' said Sidney. 'You hesitate for a while. Then the door opens and Magda Slanic appears.'

I see her. She's all dressed in black.

'She's trying to hold your attention. But forget about her. Move past her into the room and take a look around. Do it slow. Take all the time you need.'

Conor went into the dressing-room. On the back of the couch was the cascade of clothes that he had seen before. On the dressing-table was a jumbled array of foundation creams and lip glosses and eyeliners. He found that if he scrutinized them very carefully, he could even read the brand names on them. Revlon, Christian Dior, Oil of Olay.

'*I see clothing. I see cosmetics.*'

'What else do you see? Do you see any letters, any tickets, any pieces of paper?'

Three empty vodka bottles. An ashtray. A crumpled pack of Marlboro. A half-eaten chocolate fudge cake in an Entenmann's carton. Something else. A bottle of tablets. He leaned forward and peered at the label. Ms Magda Slanic. Phenelzine. Kaufman Pharmacy, Lexington Avenue and 50th Street, NY 10022. Telephone 755 2266.

He blinked and he was out of his trance. 'Give me that pen,' he told Sidney. 'I have to write this down before I forget it. Phenelzine.'

At that moment there was a soft knock at the door and Eleanor put her head in. 'I heard you talking . . . I couldn't sleep.'

'Come on in,' said Conor. He passed her the slip of paper on which he had written the name of Magda Slanic's prescription. 'Do you have any idea what this is?'

'Monoamine oxidase inhibitor,' she nodded. 'It's a fairly common type of antidepressant. My sister used to take it after her husband left her. The creep.'

'So Hetti's depressed,' said Sidney. 'Who wouldn't be, the kind of life she's living?'

'That's not the point,' said Conor. 'Depression is a long-term condition, right? From what I saw of that bottle, there were only a few capsules remaining. That means that Hetti may soon be going back to the Kaufman Pharmacy for more.'

'You're not suggesting we stake it out?' asked Sidney, although there was a hint of excitement in his voice.

'Are you kidding? The Kaufman Pharmacy is open twenty-four hours a day, seven days a week. No, I can do better than that. I know most of the guys that work there. When I was on undercover work, I was always in and out for coffee and a sandwich. All I'm going to do is ask them to call me the next time Magda Slanic makes an appearance.'

'It sounds like kind of a long shot to me,' said Eleanor.

'It is. But long shots are the only kind of shots I've got.'

19

He was early for his appointment in Central Park. It was crowded outside the entrance to the Children's Zoo: a party of schoolkids had arrived, and they were chasing each other around and screaming and laughing. Conor stayed up against the wall and kept his eyes open for the man in the Panama hat.

Two cops walked slowly past him, and one of them eyed him up and down suspiciously. He almost felt like saying, you don't have to worry about me, officer. I'm not a pedophile, I'm just a garden-variety fugitive.

At 11:35 precisely, a slightly built fiftyish man in a white short-sleeved shirt and sunglasses appeared. He was wearing a Panama hat with a red headband and carrying a magazine under his arm. He stopped in the middle of the chaos of children, and looked around nervously.

Conor didn't step out and introduce himself right away. He checked the surroundings for anybody who looked as if they might be a plainclothes cop or a bodyguard or even a hit man. But all he could see were nannies with grizzling children and harassed teachers and a cleaner with a Walkman doing a balletic rap dance while he collected up cigarette butts.

Eventually, Conor left the shadow of the wall and weaved his way through the scuffling children, knocking sharply against the man's elbow. The man swung around and said, 'Hey—!' but he instantly recognized Conor and took an unsteady step back.

Conor held up a large yellow envelope. He didn't have any idea who the man was or what his papers contained, but he was twitchy and clearly exhausted, and his anxiety was pitched like a dog-whistle, undetectable to anybody but him, but keeping his nerve endings constantly on edge.

'When the money's gone through, I get everything back? That's the deal, right?'

Conor said nothing. He simply didn't know what to say. He handed over the envelope and the man tore it open and peered inside. 'Shit,' he said. Then he looked up at Conor and shook his head. 'I used to think you were some kind of a hero. That's rich, isn't it?'

Conor said, 'Just organize the payment, OK? The sooner this is all over, the better.'

'You goddamned crook,' the man snarled at him.

Conor would have given anything to be able to tell him the truth. But all he could do was turn and walk away, leaving the man standing amidst the children with his envelope clutched in his hands. Conor thought: I may seem like a crook, but God alone knows what sins are revealed in those papers, that you're prepared to pay $5 million to get them back.

He was walking toward the 64th Street entrance

263

when suddenly he heard a child's voice cry out, *'Daddy!'*

Every daddy in the English-speaking world is called Daddy, so he kept on walking. But then he heard pattering footsteps coming up behind him. He turned, and it was Fay. Dark haired, wide eyed, in a pink summer dress, all arms and legs and tooth-braces.

'Hey, I can't believe it! It's the sugar plum fairy!' He picked her up and swung her around and held her tight.

'Daddy, what are you doing here? Mommy said you were locked up in prison!'

'Prison? Me? Phooey! Only criminals get locked up in prison!'

'I saw you on the news. They said the cops were looking for you.'

He squinched up his nose. 'Complete mix-up. You know how stupid the cops are. I should know. I used to be one.' He narrowed his eyes against the bright sunlight and looked around. 'Where's your mother? You're not on your own, are you?'

'Her mother's right here, as a matter of fact,' said a flat voice, right behind him. And there she was, with her dark hair tied back in a severe ponytail, looking even more Audrey Hepburn than usual. She was wearing a silk Hermès blouse in crimson and dark blue, and an off-white skirt that reached just above her knees. He had always thought that she dressed too old and conservative for her age.

'Paula . . . you're looking good. Lost a little weight. Suits you.'

'Can you put my daughter down, please?'

Conor gave Fay a squeeze and said, 'What do you think, sugar plum fairy? Think I ought to put her daughter down?'

Fay covered her eyes with the back of her hand. She always did that when Conor and Paula started to fence. Conor put his hand into his pocket and tugged out a white handkerchief. He twisted it around, pulled it twice with his teeth, and it took on the shape of a rabbit with big floppy ears.

'Why don't we ask Mr Rabbitinski what he thinks?'

Fay peered out through her fingers. 'I'm too old for Mr Rabbitinski.'

'Come on, Conor,' Paula repeated. 'Put her down.'

'You may be too old for Mr Rabbitinski but Mr Rabbitinski still misses you. Come to that, I do, too.'

Fay wriggled and slipped down from his grasp. Paula reached out and took hold of her hand and pulled her away. Conor made Mr Rabbitinski flop over in sadness and disappointment.

'I thought they would have caught you by now,' said Paula.

'I didn't do anything, Paula. It's a misunderstanding, that's all.'

'Of course it is. You've always been so upright and honest, haven't you, Conor? Always done the right thing, no matter how much it hurts everybody around you. You betrayed your fellow officers, you betrayed me, you betrayed your daughter. All for the sake of your precious principles! And now look at you. Wanted for robbery. What price your principles now?'

'Paula, I really didn't do this. I swear it on my life. I swear it on Fay's life.'

Paula looked at him with such hatred that he felt a physical chill. 'Don't you ever swear anything on my daughter's life. She doesn't have a father now, because of you. Didn't it occur to you once what it would do to you, breaking the Forty-Ninth Street Golf Club, and what it would do to your family? Who were they hurting? Nobody but the Mafia, the scum of the earth! Why in the name of God didn't you turn a blind eye?'

Conor looked down and realized that he was still holding Mr Rabbitinski in the crook of his elbow. A grown man with a handkerchief rabbit.

He didn't know what to say to Paula. He had broken the Forty-Ninth Street Golf Club 'because it was wrong'? That sounded so naïve. Yet that was why he had done it.

Paula said, 'If you're really innocent, why don't you turn yourself in, and prove it?'

'It isn't as simple as that.'

'Yes it is. Look, let me show you how it's done.'

With that, she lifted her arm and shouted out, 'Officer! Officer! Over here, officer!'

'Paula, what the hell are you doing?' Conor demanded.

But Paula dodged out of his way and continued to wave her arm. 'Officer! There's a wanted man here! Hurry!'

Conor snatched hold of her arm and stared right into her face. 'You're hurting me,' she said, with a triumphant smile. 'But that's what you're good at, isn't it? Hurting people?'

'*Daddy!*' shrilled Fay. 'Daddy, the cops are coming!'

For a split second, Conor could see in Paula's face the woman that he had once fallen in love with. She was still there, but she was inaccessible to him now. If only there was something he could say to bring her back. One word. But then he heard one of the cops shout, 'Freeze, mister! Hold it right there!'

'*Daddy!*'

He didn't turn around. He ducked past Paula and started to run through the thick of the crowd – deliberately barging his way through school parties and groups of tourists and even a covey of nuns. The cop yelled out, '*Hold it! Stop or I'll shoot!*' but Conor knew that he wouldn't risk hitting a child.

He ran past the seal pool and the merry-go-round, and then dodged out of the park by the 64th Street entrance. He ran across Fifth Avenue through the middle of the traffic, almost vaulting over the hood of a taxi; and by the time the cops had come puffing into view, he was turning the corner into 63rd Street and he was gone.

20

Eleanor spent all morning on the phone, talking to every theatrical agent she could think of, trying to pick up the slightest hint of Hypnos and Hetti's possible whereabouts.

It took a long time. Most of the agents were delighted that she had called them, and wanted to spend hours reminiscing about the old days on Broadway, about Lee Strasberg and Ben Gazzara and Christine White and Harry Guardino and Jay Julien. Every conversation brightened Eleanor more and more, in spite of the urgency of what she was doing, and Sidney sat smiling at her as she laughed and talked.

'What a woman,' he said, in quiet admiration, as Conor came into the room.

After his escape from Central Park, Conor had walked across to the Rialto Theater and talked to Sammy the doorman again and some of the cast of *Franklin*. Hypnos and Hetti must have used their hypnotic influence with enormous skill, because hardly anybody could remember them being there.

One young girl from the chorus line said, 'I remember seeing a man and a woman in the corridor . . . but I always had the feeling that I shouldn't look at them.'

A male dancer said, 'I saw people who weren't there. I really began to think that the theater was *haunted*, you know? By *ghosts*.'

Conor returned to Sebastian's apartment at 1:56 p.m. hot and tired, with no new information at all. 'Has Eleanor had any luck?' he asked Sidney.

'Not so far. Everybody remembers Hypnos and Hetti. Who wouldn't? But nobody has any idea where they are now.'

'How about a glass of chilled Chab-lee?' asked Ric, pirouetting into the room in black Versace jeans and a white silk blouse. 'And maybe you'd like me to mop your fevered whatever.'

It was then that Sebastian's mobile phone rang. Ric picked it up and said, *'Ye-e-e-ess?'* Then he frowned and passed it to Conor. 'It's for you. Somebody called Morrie Teitelbaum.'

Conor said, 'Morrie? What's happening?' Then he put his hand over the phone and said, 'It's Morrie, from Kaufman.'

'Conor! That broad you wanted us to keep a weather eye out for . . . she came into the drugstore two or three minutes ago . . . Jimmy did like you told us and told her we were all backed up in filling prescriptions . . . she's coming back here in ten minutes.'

'Morrie, there's a place waiting for you in Heaven.'

'Forget Heaven. A couple dozen White Owls will do.'

Conor switched off the phone. 'That's it. We've found her. Sidney – Ric – Sebastian – do you want to come with me?'

'What about that burundanga shit?' said Ric. 'Supposing they blow that all over us again? I mean, God knows what they could make us do next.'

'Take a scarf,' Sidney suggested. 'If Perez tries to pull that stunt again, hold it over your nose and mouth.'

Ric brought out four brightly colored scarves and handed them around. 'Dear me – we look like the Three Musketeers and D'Artagnan.' They collected their wallets and their keys and prepared to leave. As they did so, however, Eleanor lifted her hand and said, 'Sidney! Conor! Wait up a second!'

'What is it, Bipsy?' Sidney asked her. She was still on the phone.

'I'm talking to Norman Frisch. You remember Norman? He did all the stage sets for *April in Augusta*. He saw Hypnos and Hetti less than a week ago in the Shark Bar on Amsterdam Avenue.'

'Oh, yes?'

'He recognized the guy that they were talking to. He was that nutty Southern Baptist millionaire who tried to close down *Evangelists* at the Lyceum, on account of it was blasphemous.'

'Oh, sure. I remember that. But I don't recall what his name was.'

'Victor Labrea,' said Eleanor.

'Victor Labrea?' said Conor. 'That's the same guy who's working for Dennis Evelyn Branch. He's the one who's holding Lacey.'

'Well,' said Sidney, gravely, 'if we can find Hetti,

270

then we've got a good chance of finding *him*. And if we can find *him*, we've got a good chance of finding your Lacey.'

'Let's go,' said Conor. 'But for God's sake, let's take it easy. These freaks are capable of anything.'

They took a taxi to Lexington and 49th, one block south of the Kaufman Pharmacy. It was a sweltering morning, over 93 degrees with 92 per cent humidity, but unlike previous days the sky was curiously brown, like weathered bronze. As he stepped out of the taxi, Conor thought that he could hear the distant indigestive rumbling of thunder.

He posted Sidney outside the Hallmark gift store, directly opposite Kaufman. Sebastian he positioned at the east intersection of Lexington and 51st, in case Hetti left the pharmacy and started to head north. Ric stood point on the east side of Lexington at 49th. Conor himself went inside.

The pharmacy was coldly air-conditioned and brightly lit. Conor took a quick look around the shelves of hairsprays and cut-price perfumes to make sure that Hetti wasn't here already. When Conor had first graduated from the Police Academy, there had been a long counter at Kaufman with pound cake under domed glass covers and a narrow kitchen at the back from which they served up meatloaf and mashed potato and chicken with stringbeans and gravy. All that was gone, but Morrie was still here and so were three or four others who remembered Conor coming in hungry and exhausted at eleven o'clock at night.

'She ain't back yet.' Morrie was barely visible

271

over the top of the counter. A freckled bald head, thick 1970s sideburns and heavy-rimmed glasses.

Conor checked the Dexatrim clock on the wall. 'You told her ten minutes?'

'She'll be back,' said a tall, gingery pharmacist from the back of the dispensary. 'She comes in regular. Very strange woman. Gives me the heebie-jeebies.'

Morrie said, 'How're things going, Conor? I heard about that robbery business down at Spurr's. They still trying to nail you for that?'

Conor nodded. 'Drew Slyman's on my tail. He's the kind of guy who believes you're guilty even after you've been proven innocent.'

'Drew Slyman? I never took to that guy. A *gonef.*'

They were still talking when Morrie gave an upward jerk of his head and said, 'Hey . . . that's her coming now. You want to step back in here?'

He opened the side door and Conor stepped into the dispensary, keeping himself out of sight against a row of shelves. He heard the door open, a momentary blare of traffic noise, and then he heard Hetti's stiletto heels approaching the counter. He could see her reflected in a curved make-up mirror on display on one of the opposite shelves. She was wearing a black straw wide-brimmed hat and a short black dress with a sparkling silver brooch. She looked as if she were going to a funeral in Beverly Hills.

'Sorry about the delay,' said Morrie, and handed over her pills. 'The usual warning . . . don't take this in conjunction with alcohol or any other prescription drugs, especially phenylpropanolamine.'

Hetti put the pills in her purse. Then she lifted her

head and said, 'You're agitated about something. What's wrong?'

'Excuse me? Agitated?'

'Yes . . . I can sense it. Something's not quite right.'

'Hey, everything's fine. My wife's put her back out. One of my sons got caught for drunk driving. The cat's sick and my mother-in-law's coming to stay the weekend. Why should I be agitated?'

Hetti paused for a long, long time. Conor stayed rigidly still, his head pressed back against boxes of dextromoramide. If he could see *her* in the make-up mirror, then all she would have to do was look toward it and she would be able to see *him*. But she kept her eyes on Morrie, saying nothing, her eyes as dead as black beetles.

'Hmmm . . .' she said at last, and turned to go.

Conor was about to move when she stopped, and turned around again. 'There's something . . . I don't know what it is. You should let me give you some hypnotherapy some time.'

'Sure. Sure thing. Pleasure to see you. Have a nice day.'

Hetti walked out of the store. Morrie waited for a moment, peering out into the street. Then he touched Conor's arm and said, 'OK, that's it. She's crossing 50th, she's headed downtown. Good luck, that's all I can say.'

'Thanks, Morrie. *Mazel tov.*'

Conor pushed his way out of the pharmacy into the street. It was like walking into a steam laundry. Sidney had already seen Hetti and was walking down the opposite side of Lexington Avenue, eighty or

273

ninety feet behind her. Ric had seen her, too, and had detached himself from the corner of 49th Street to walk three-quarters of a block ahead of her.

Conor looked back and Sebastian was there, too. They had her boxed in, whichever direction she decided to go.

Hetti stopped at 49th Street. She crossed over Lexington Avenue and continued to head west, up the slope of 49th Street toward Park Avenue. Conor whistled and waved to Ric that he should head in the same direction on 48th, and hurry, so that he came out onto Park ahead of her.

The sky grew increasingly somber. Large, widely separated drops of rain began to measle the sidewalk. As Hetti reached Park Avenue a dazzling stroke of lightning struck the top of the PanAm building, followed by a bellow of thunder. The rain began to quicken, and by the time Conor and Sidney had got to Park Avenue, it was coming down in torrents.

'Where is she?' said Sidney, frantically looking around. 'Don't tell me we've lost her.'

'No – there she is,' said Conor. And there she was – entering the revolving doors in the front of the Waldorf-Astoria.

They splashed across the street, into the shelter of the hotel's canopy. Conor cautiously looked through the doors. He could see Hetti in the vast, glossy 1930s-style lobby. She was standing beside a banquette, talking to a florid-faced man in a yellow flannel sport coat. He had a heavy black mustache and cropped black hair. Hetti was nodding, and making a circling gesture with her right hand. The man was leaning forward slightly so that he could

274

hear her better, but by the expression on his face he didn't look very impressed with what she was saying.

Sidney recognized him immediately. 'That's your man,' he said. 'There was an article about him in last month's *Theater*. How religious pressure groups are threatening freedom of expression.'

Ric joined them, shaking his hair like a wet dog, then Sebastian. 'Look at this silk shirt. It's supposed to be dry clean only!' There was another crackle of lightning, and another avalanche of thunder. Beside them, the Waldorf-Astoria's doorman lofted a huge umbrella and crossed the sidewalk to greet the arrival of a white stretch Cadillac. Out of the front of the car climbed the greasy-looking bodyguard who had accompanied Hypnos to the Rialto Theater. He was wearing a smart gray suit now, although his cheek still bore two maroon bruises from Sebastian's kicking and there was a band aid across the bridge of his nose.

They pulled up their collars so that the bodyguard wouldn't recognize them, and half shielded their faces with their hands, but they needn't have worried. There were too many wet people clustering in the hotel's entrance for them to be noticed. Besides, the bodyguard was preoccupied with taking care of his charge: a blond fortyish woman in a short white Valentino dress who was climbing out of the softly lit white-leather interior of the Cadillac's back seat.

The bodyguard ushered the woman into the hotel, while a miserable-looking bellhop scurried out and collected shopping bags and packages from Bergdorf

Goodman, Norma Kamali, Charles Jourdan and Galeries Lafayette.

The blond woman went directly toward Hetti and Victor Labrea. She bent over and kissed Victor Labrea's cheek and he took hold of her hand. Conor saw heavy gold rings on all of his fingers, and a gold chain around his wrist that could have been used to bring up an anchor.

The woman picked an invisible hair from the man's shoulder with long, purple-painted nails, and every now and then she patted him or stroked him. She ignored Hetti; and from the way she was standing and the way that she was gesturing, Conor could see she didn't like Hetti being there at all. At one point, it looked as if they were arguing.

Suddenly, the conversation broke up. Victor Labrea stood up and began to walk toward the elevators, with everybody else promptly following him.

'This is it,' said Conor. 'Let's find out what room they're in.'

'And then what?' Sebastian demanded.

'We go in and rescue Lacey and take back the stuff from the safety deposit boxes, that's all.'

'We just "go in"? We just "rescue Lacey"? We just "take back the stuff"?'

'Do you have any other suggestions?'

Sebastian flared his nostrils and perched his hands on his hips. 'Other suggestions?' He hesitated for five or ten seconds, then he said, 'No, I guess I don't.'

'Let's do it, then, before it's too late.'

They crossed the Waldorf-Astoria's lobby with its chandeliers and its gleaming pillars and its art deco

276

statues. The thunder and lightning and the mid-morning darkness gave it a heightened sense of imminent apocalypse. Expensively dressed men and women milled around the reception desk, confused and irritated and not a little alarmed that the storm had washed out their shopping expeditions to Bloomingdale's and their lunch dates at the Quilted Giraffe.

In spite of the blandly tinkling piano music, it had something of the atmosphere of *The Poseidon Adventure*: the world turned upside down.

Conor walked quickly to the concierge's desk. The blond woman's bags and packages were propped up on a trolley, ready to be taken up to her room. The concierge himself was talking on the phone – a smooth, bald character with steel-framed eyeglasses.

'May I help you, sir?' he asked, covering the telephone mouthpiece with his hand.

'Don't you know who I am?'

'I'm sorry, sir?'

'Don't you know what my name is?'

'Sir – I regret—'

'You can't remember who I am but you're here to help me. You're still trying to think of my name but it won't matter if you do what I ask. You'll be able to relax. You want to relax, don't you?'

'Sir – I—'

'*Relax.* You don't have to worry about what I'm saying to you. I'm going to ask you some questions and all you have to do is let your unconscious mind answer.'

'Yes.'

277

'There are some packages here. Do you know who they belong to?'

'Mrs Labrea, sir. She asked for them to be taken up to her room.'

'What's Mrs Labrea's room number?'

'Seven one one, sir.'

'That's very good. You see how easy it is, how relaxed you feel? Now I'm going to take these packages up to Mrs Labrea's room right away and Mrs Labrea will be very pleased with you because you've done your job so promptly.'

'Yes, sir. Very good, sir.'

Cautiously, Conor picked up the blond woman's shopping. He handed two of the bags to Sebastian, including the Charles Jourdan shoes. Sebastian took one of them out – a strappy purple evening number – and said, 'Look at *these*! They're gorgeous! I wonder if they do them in my size?'

Sidney touched his finger to his lips. He had been watching Conor carefully and he could tell that the trance which Conor had been able to induce was very superficial. One noisy distraction and the concierge would wake up and catch them in the act.

'In exactly one minute from now you're going to come out of your trance,' Conor told the concierge. 'You won't remember that I took Mrs Labrea's shopping. The bellboy did it. You'll feel happy and satisfied and not at all anxious.'

Carrying the shopping, they walked toward the elevators. Conor glanced back but the concierge had returned to his phone call and seemed to be completely unconcerned. They stood back while a small gaggle of women in Armani and Chanel came

278

out of the elevator, leaving behind them an atmosphere so heavily laden with designer perfume that it was almost visible, like a heat haze.

'You all have your scarves?' asked Sidney. 'Good. Any sign of Hypnos blowing that burundanga at us, cover your nose and your mouth with your hand, and then pull up your scarf. Stay calm. Don't allow Hypnos or Hetti to distract you. You're going in there for one reason only: to rescue Lacey. Also, if possible, to retrieve the papers that were stolen from Spurr's deposit boxes. Any other consideration: ignore it.'

The elevator pinged to a stop at the seventh floor.

'Seven-eleven's to the left,' said Conor. 'Trust Hypnos and Hetti to pick a room that sounds like a convenience store.'

They hurried along the silent, chilly corridor until they reached the room marked 711. There was a room-service tray on the floor outside, with the congealed remains of fried chicken, shoestring potatoes and a Russian salad.

'So how do we get in?' asked Sebastian. 'I'm good, but I'm not good enough to kick a door down.'

'We knock,' said Conor. He approached the door and gave three sharp raps. Then he indicated to Sebastian that he should hold up Mrs Labrea's shopping in front of the spyhole.

There was no answer for a very long time. At last a voice demanded, 'Who is it? Whaddya want?'

'Concierge. I brought up your packages.'

'I can't see your face.'

'What?'

'Put down the bags. I can't see your face.'

279

'Look – I'm very sorry, sir, but I'm extremely busy here – and I'm just about to drop all these packages – so if you don't mind—'

Conor heard a woman's voice snap, 'Charlie? Is that my shopping? Open the door for goodness' sake.'

The door unlatched. Conor waited until he heard the chain slide away, and then he kicked the door inward with all the strength he could muster.

'*Go-go-go-go-go!*' he roared, and shoved the man standing behind the door with both hands. The man stumbled, hit his head against the wall and flopped heavily onto the carpet.

'Charlie!' screamed the woman's voice.

Conor strode into the sitting room, with Sidney, Sebastian and Ric following close behind. The room was large and gloomy, furnished with expensive reproduction antiques. Hetti was sitting on a chair with her shoes off. Hypnos was standing by the mini-bar on the opposite side of the room, a miniature tequila bottle poised in one hand. Mrs Labrea was half rising from the couch.

'Who are you?' she demanded. 'How *dare* yew-all burst in here like this? Ramon – take a look at Charlie, make sure he's OK.'

'Ramon, stay where you are,' Conor warned him. 'Brought your shopping,' he said to Mrs Labrea. He took the bags from Sebastian and tossed them onto the floor.

'Ramon – call security,' snapped Mrs Labrea.

Ramon took a step toward the phone but Conor waved his finger at him in a 'no-no' gesture.

'What is this, a robbery?' asked Mrs Labrea. 'What

do you want, cash? I have plenty of cash.'

'Where's Lacey?' Conor demanded.

'Lacey? Who's Lacey?'

'Don't play dumb with me. Where are you keeping her?' He walked across to the bedroom, opened the door, and looked inside. The bedroom was empty, except for a peach-colored négligé spread across the bed.

'Come on, Ramon, where is she?'

'Not here, Mr O'Neil. Sorry about that.'

'Then where?'

'You don't think that the Reverend Branch would be quite so obvious as to keep her here, do you?' smiled Magda. 'His mind is not so simple, like yours.'

'Who is this yahoo?' Mrs Labrea wanted to know.

Ramon put down the tequila bottle and stepped smoothly forward. A real stage professional, thought Conor. 'Let me introduce you, Mrs Labrea. This is Conor O'Neil, one-time captain of detectives, New York Police Department, one-time security chief at Spurr's Fifth Avenue.'

'I see,' said Mrs Labrea. She wasn't beautiful. Her eyes were bulbous and her nose was slightly hooked, but she was so expensively groomed that she had a compelling aura about her: an aura of power and wealth and always getting her own way. A titanium magnolia. 'So this is the man who everybody is blaming for stealing the safety deposit boxes?'

'This is the very man. How did you find us, Mr O'Neil? Clever bit of detective work.'

'I think you'd better leave, don't you?' said Mrs Labrea, picking up the telephone. But Ric came

281

around and snatched the receiver out of her hand. 'Excuse *me*,' she said, but Ric tossed it from one hand to the other and wouldn't let her have it.

'Give that here, you *faggot!*' she shouted, losing her temper.

'Where's Lacey?' Conor repeated. 'If you've done anything to hurt her, I swear to God I'll hunt all of you down until I find you, no matter how long it takes, and I will personally dismember you.'

'Hey – that doesn't sound like the self-styled arbiter of justice to me,' said Ramon.

'Just tell me where Lacey is.'

Ramon shook his head. 'It's not possible, Mr O'Neil. This whole thing is much bigger than you know. Best not to make a fuss. Best to go along with it. Do what the Reverend Branch wants you to do, and then we'll let your Lacey go.'

Conor pushed his way around the couch and seized hold of Ramon's purple silk necktie.

'Tell me where she is, or so help me—'

'So help you what?' asked Ramon. 'What are you going to do? Hit me?'

'Conor—' Sidney warned him.

Magda snapped open her small black crocodile purse. Sidney turned to see what she was doing and she ostentatiously produced a lipstick. As soon as he turned away again, she dropped the lipstick and took out a small foil package.

'*Watch her!*' Sebastian shrieked.

He lunged across the room and seized her wrist, shaking the package onto the floor. Ramon saw it and made a grab for it, but Conor punched him hard in the side of the jaw, a cracking right-hander, and he hurtled back against an occasional table, knocking over a large brass lamp.

Mrs Labrea stood up and screamed, 'Stop! Stop! I *order* you to stop!'

Conor took hold of Ramon's fawn cashmere coat and hauled him onto his feet. Then he twisted his arm behind his back in a fierce half-nelson.

'Tell me where Lacey is or I swear to God I'll pull your arm off.'

'What's the use? Why can't you accept the fact that you're totally fucked?'

Without warning, the bedroom door flew open and Victor Labrea appeared, still wet, with a large white bath towel wrapped around his middle.

'You – hold it right there!' shouted Conor, but without saying a word Victor Labrea slammed the door shut again.

'Sebastian – Ric – go drag him out here,' said Conor.

Sebastian skirted the couch and approached the bedroom door. He rattled the handle. 'He's locked it. We'll have to kick it in.'

'You can't do this,' Mrs Labrea insisted. 'This is against the law.'

'I *am* the law,' Conor retorted; the way he always used to, when he was captain of detectives, and although Mrs Labrea probably hadn't understood what he meant, he immediately wished that he hadn't.

Sebastian knocked at the bedroom door. 'You'd better come on out, sir. I don't want to lose my temper. You haven't seen me when I lose my temper.'

There was no answer, so Sebastian carried on knocking, even more furiously. 'You'd better come out, I'm warning you!' Victor Labrea opened the door, stiffly pointing a Beretta 9 mm pistol with a silencer. He shot Sebastian straight through the upper arm, *ffwhutt!* and a piece of bright red muscle slapped against the dado. Sebastian collapsed onto the carpet, shuddering like a run-over stag.

Ric howled, '*Sebastian!*' and vaulted over the couch. Victor Labrea fired again, hitting him in the shin. Ric rolled over with a feminine cry of pain.

Conor held Ramon in front of him and held up his hand. 'Labrea! Drop the weapon! Drop it on the floor *now!*'

Victor Labrea said nothing. There was an expression on his face of swollen contempt. He had watery blue eyes, a sweeping-brush mustache, and cheeks that were blotchy with broken veins. Still wearing his bath towel, he stepped over Sebastian and put his arm around his wife's shoulders, ushering her back toward the bedroom.

'Come on, Labrea, we need a doctor here! Do you know who I am?'

Victor Labrea took two or three deep breaths, and then wheezed, 'Sure I do. I know exactly who you are. You're one of the lowest creatures on God's good earth. You're a blasphemer and an adulterer. What gives you the right to break into my private hotel room and terrorize my friends and my wife?' He glanced toward his bodyguard, still lying by the door. 'Charlie?' he called. Charlie groaned and tried to lift his head, but Conor had obviously concussed him.

Ric, behind the couch, was weeping from pain. Sebastian was suffering in agonized silence.

Conor said, 'I'm going to call for the paramedics.'

'You're going to stay where you are and do nothing until the rest of my people get here.'

'Or what?'

'Or else I'll shoot you, too.'

'Right through Ramon?'

'If that's the way it has to be.'

'Well, *muchas gracias*,' said Ramon.

Sidney stepped forward. 'Can't we come to some arrangement here?'

Victor Labrea gave him a poisonous glare. 'What are you-all talking about – "arrangement"?'

'Think about it, Mr Labrea. You're in a real bind here. You've just shot two unarmed men.'

'This is my hotel room. I'm entitled under the law to defend myself.'

'Well, sir, to be frank, what you've done here goes way beyond the bounds of self-defense, even in New York. Surely you want to resolve this matter without any more unpleasantness.'

'So? So? What do you suggest?'

'I want you to calm down, that's all. Right now you're very excited and you don't enjoy being excited. It makes your heart beat faster but you want your heart to beat slower . . . and slower . . . and slower. You want to relax.'

'Don't listen to this guy, Mr Labrea,' Ramon interrupted. 'He's one of the best hypnotists in America. Don't you realize what he's trying to do to you?'

Conor forced Ramon's arm so far up that his

285

fingers touched the back of his hair. Ramon said, 'Shit, O'Neil, that hurts!' Victor Labrea pointed his gun at them, and then at Sidney.

'You think you can hypnotize me, old man?'

Sidney shook his head. 'I was trying to defuse the situation, that's all. I wanted you to relax, so that you wouldn't do anything you might regret.'

'You think you can make a fool of me, is that it?'

'My only intention, Mr Labrea, is to pour oil on troubled waters. I want you to think of one of those times in your life when you felt most at peace. Think back, tell me about it.'

Victor Labrea was silent for a moment. His eyes were quite blank and gave nothing away. His tongue was running around inside his mouth as if he were trying to dislodge food particles left over from lunch. Then he shot Sidney in the chest, twice. The impact forced Sidney to take two or three steps backward. He turned to Conor, looking vaguely baffled. The front of his shirt was suddenly flooded with scarlet.

'He's killed me,' he said. He dropped onto his knees. Then he toppled sideways, hitting his head against an armchair.

Conor's vision was blotted out with rage. He forced Ramon across the room in front of him and collided with Victor Labrea so violently that Labrea was thrown against the opposite wall. He rolled over, losing his bath towel as he did so. That split second of vulnerability was enough: Conor pushed Ramon down on top of Victor Labrea and made a grab for his gun. He managed to grasp Labrea's hand but couldn't pry his fingers apart. A shot hit the ceiling, and another shot ricocheted off the radiator. Ramon tried to struggle free but Conor gripped his thick, greasy hair and banged his forehead against Labrea's forehead, as hard as he could.

Grunting, cursing, Labrea tried to twist the Beretta around so that it was pointing at Conor's head, but the length of the silencer made it almost impossible. For almost a minute, all three men were locked motionless, straining against each other's muscles like a classical sculpture of Greek wrestlers. Then Victor Labrea forced his hand down and fired – just as Conor pulled Ramon's head up. The bullet went straight into Ramon's mouth, shattering his teeth and blowing up his tongue like a plum tomato. It exited out of the back of his head, missing Conor's hand by less than a quarter of an inch.

Conor snatched the gun out of Victor Labrea's grip and pressed it hard against his left temple. Labrea's eyeballs rolled up like a frightened dog, but he didn't speak. He didn't beg for mercy.

Conor heaved Ramon's body onto the carpet and stood up, still pointing the gun at Victor Labrea's head, his chest rising and falling with effort and emotion.

Mrs Labrea stood in the open doorway of the bedroom, the palms of her hands pressed together as if she were praying. Hetti had retreated right back against the brown velvet drapes, her face as white as an oriental mask.

'I ought to execute you here and now,' said Conor. He was so shaken and brimming with rage that he didn't even recognize the sound of his own voice.

'Don't kill him,' said Mrs Labrea. 'Please. You can have anything you want. Money, is that what you want? Anything.'

Conor went over to Ric, who had stopped sobbing now and was stroking Sebastian's forehead. Conor had never seen Sebastian look so white. 'Don't worry, Ric . . . I'll get the paramedics to take care of the both of you.'

'I won't dance again, will I?' whispered Ric. His face, usually so angelic, was ashy and haggard.

Conor gripped his shoulder to reassure him. 'You'll be OK. Before you know it, you'll be back in Buffalo, dancing *A Chorus Line*. And this time I'll come to see you.'

Conor picked up the phone and dialed 911. 'That's right. There's been a shooting. Three people down, one dead. Room seven-eleven, Waldorf-Astoria.'

He went back to Victor Labrea. He was still lying in the same position, his torso sprayed with Ramon's blood. He was still naked and he made no attempt to cover himself.

'I want to know where my girlfriend is being held and I want to know what you've done with all of the property that was stolen from Spurr's safety deposit boxes.'

'I'm not going to tell you,' said Victor Labrea. 'What you're trying to interfere with here, it's bigger'n you, and it's bigger'n me. It's paving the way for the Second Coming, and whether you kill me or not, well, that won't make a ounce of difference.'

'If you don't tell me right now, God help me, I'll blow your head off.'

'Tell him Victor,' Mrs Labrea pleaded. 'I don't want you to die.'

'No,' said Victor Labrea. 'I don't believe this fellow is up to killing me in cold blood, and if he is, and this is the moment that I'm going to meet my Maker, well, that's the will of the Lord, and who am I to argue with that?'

21

He returned to Sebastian's apartment with such reluctance and dread that he stood in front of the door for almost a minute before pressing the bell.

Eleanor answered almost immediately. 'Who is it?'

'Conor. Can you let me in?'

The door opened and Eleanor saw at once that Conor was alone.

'Something's happened, hasn't it?' she said, her hand rising to touch her throat.

Conor nodded. He entered the apartment and closed the door behind him. He had promised himself that he wouldn't cry but he couldn't help it. He had brought Eleanor and Sidney back together again after all these years; and now he was responsible for Sidney's death. It was almost more than he could bear.

'Conor, tell me,' said Eleanor. She reached out and held his hands, both of them, and the look on her face reminded Conor of a picture which used to hang in his grandmother's hall, of the Blessed Virgin taking Christ down from the cross. *O clemens, o pia, o dulcis Virgo Maria.*

'It all went wrong. Victor Labrea had a gun. Sebastian and Ric have both been wounded.'

'And Sidney? What's happened to Sidney?'

'I'm sorry, Eleanor. He was shot at point-blank range, for no sane reason at all.'

'I see,' said Eleanor. She slowly released his hands in the way that Sidney might have released them if he had been trying to induce a hypnotic trance. She turned away from him and walked slowly along the white-carpeted corridor to the living room. Conor stayed by the door and watched her. He thought how thin she looked, especially the back of her neck, as vulnerable as a child's. When she reached the living room she stood for a moment against the brightly reflected sunshine and it seemed to melt her outline, as if she were fading away altogether, going to the light.

Conor came up to her and held her in his arms. He didn't know how long they stayed like that, clutching each other, the two survivors. He could feel her bones; he could smell her cigarettes and her perfume; he could almost hear all her glory days. Applause, all faded away now.

'It was my fault,' he said. 'I shouldn't have rushed in there like that. It was totally unprofessional.'

She looked up at him. 'No. It wasn't your fault. Do you know what Sidney said to me? Better to die doing something exciting than gradually vanish doing nothing at all. He said he could imagine himself in that hammock, becoming more and more transparent every day; until one day the hammock would be swinging with nobody in it.'

291

'He shouldn't have died, Eleanor.'

Eleanor went across the room, opened her purse, and took out her cigarette-holder and a pack of cigarettes. 'Do you need a drink?' she asked him. 'I need a drink.'

They sat together in the sunlit living room and he told her everything that had happened.

'In the end, I had to get out of there quick. The paramedics were coming, and the cops, too. I only just missed them. But before I left, there was one moment when I could have shot that Victor Labrea right between the eyes.'

Eleanor reached across with her veiny, wrinkly hands and stroked the back of Conor's wrist. She wore three diamond rings, all of them very Forties and Fifties in their styling. 'Maybe you should have done. Shot him, I mean. I think there are times when you have to fight fire with fire.'

She reached over for the bottle and poured him another treble measure of Wyborowa. 'You feel vengeful, don't you? Well, so do I. So why don't you stop worrying about your Catholic conscience and go out and get your revenge? You're not in the police department any more. Maybe it's time you forgot about the rules.'

'I don't know. I come from a long line of very upright people.'

'I know that. But being upright, where has it got you today? Let me tell you something, Conor O'Neil, times have changed. Decency died a long time ago. You should see some of the scripts that writers send me. They're full of filthy language. Can

292

you imagine Willie Loman talking like that in *Death of a Salesman* in 1949? The audience would have walked out. But it's not like that any more, and it's getting worse. And it's no use people like you and me shutting our eyes and jamming our fingers in our ears and hoping it's going to get better, because it's not.

'So what we have to do – what we *have* to do – is beat the bastards at their own game.'

'You're drunk,' said Conor.

'No, I'm not. I'm hurting. And so are you. And you still have Lacey to worry about. You're caught between a rock and a hard place, Conor. And there's only one way you're going to get out of it. Beat them. Beat the bastards. You're not captain of detectives. You're not chief of security. You're Conor O'Neil. Nobody can tell you what to do, and you can do whatever it takes.'

Conor stood up, and walked to the window. It was covered by a thin handmade muslin blind, which he pulled up with a string. Below him was 47th Street, with cars and taxis crawling along it, and people teeming amongst them. He saw a girl in a red dress and he thought: you don't even know that I'm looking at you, do you? And I'll never see you again, not for the rest of my life.

He turned back to Eleanor. Her cheeks were glistening with tears. 'You're right,' he said. 'It's not going to get any better.'

The reply to his phone call was muffled and cautious. 'Who is this?'

'Conor O'Neil. Mr Guttuso knows me.'

293

'Mr Guttuso? Nobody by that name here.'

'Mr Guttuso gave me this number personally. Mr Guttuso said that if ever I wanted a favor of any kind, I was to call this number and say who I was. Mr Guttuso said that when I did that, his staff would immediately connect me to his private line, so that I could speak to him. Or didn't I hear him right?'

'What did you say your name was? Conoronil?'

Luigi Guttuso came on the phone and his voice was the same as always: like somebody pouring best-quality virgin olive oil over the shingle used in tropical fish-tanks.

'Conor . . . so good of you to call. I thought maybe something was wrong. Socially, you know. I sent you that invitation to my niece's wedding and you never answered. I was perplexed, you know? After all you did for the families. You were justice itself, you know? Can I compliment you for that? I won't embarrass you? You were justice itself. It's not often you see justice like that.'

'I'm sorry about the wedding,' said Conor. 'I guess I was busy.'

'Well I heard you was busy. I heard you was busy heisting safe deposit boxes from Spurr's Fifth Avenue. That's some switch, huh?'

'I didn't do it, Luigi. That's the reason I'm calling you now.'

'You didn't do it? Conor, you disappoint me. When I saw that report about you on the TV news, do you know what I said to Angela? I said, "There's a man with real talent." That's what I said. "He resigns from the police department, so what does he do? Does he open some orgiastic foodstore? Does he sell leg insurance? No – he stays in the business he knows about – crime.'''

'Thanks for the compliment, Luigi, but the fact remains that I didn't do it.'

'You're right. You're right to deny it, even to me. That's what I always say. "Your Honor, regardless of the fact that I have three sets of books for my business and my brother was stopped on Lower Matecumbe Key with fifteen keys of smack in the trunk of his car and two girls from my club offered an undercover police officer two hours in full bondage for two hundred and fifty bucks plus tax all major cards accepted – I deny it."'

Conor said, 'You know what you said after the trial. If I needed a favor?'

'You didn't think I meant it, did you? You pulled a face like an asshole after a hot chili supper. Well, I did mean it. You were justice itself. You want a favor? Name it.'

'Maybe we could meet.'

He hadn't expected Luigi Guttuso to meet him at Umberto's Clam House or one of those restaurants in Little Italy with red checkered tablecloths and the theme from *The Godfather* playing in the background. But he had at least expected some high-class Italian eatery like Contrapunto or Elaine's. Instead, Guttuso suggested the second floor of F.A.O. Schwarz, the huge expensive toy store at 767 Fifth Avenue.

He climbed up the curving staircase and made his way between the doll houses and the displays of Nintendo and Lego and Barbie surfboards. Children were running everywhere, and the screaming and howling were unexpectedly distressing. The last time Conor had come to F.A.O. Schwarz was to buy a Surfing Barbie for Fay.

Guttuso was leaning over one of the display tables, his eyes alight, a remote control unit in his hand, directing a large plastic police car with flashing lights and warbling siren. As always, he was dressed in a silvery silk three-piece suit, and his silver hair was combed straight back from his bony forehead. He was handsome in a dried-up, skull-in-the-desert way, with deeply set eyes and a fine, multi-faceted nose, and Conor could almost have liked him if he didn't know how merciless he was; and how corrupt.

Not far away from Guttuso stood two respectable-looking young men with short haircuts and very white shirts and well-cut suits, their hands neatly clasped in front of their genitals. They didn't show the slightest interest in any of the buzzing, hopping and beeping toys. Their eyes sieved the room from one side to the other, searching for anybody who looked like trouble.

'Conor!' said Guttuso, steering the police car between a tugboat and a huge green tottering Godzilla. 'Sorry to drag you up here: I gotta buy a gift for my grandson's birthday. You should try this squad car. It'll bring back memories.'

'Some memories I could do without,' said Conor.

Guttuso made the police car swerve so that it collided with a white fluffy cymbal-banging rabbit. It overturned and spun around on its roof, its siren still plaintively wailing. 'There,' he said. 'That satisfy you?'

296

Conor said, 'I'm not going to make any bones about this, Luigi. I wouldn't have come to you if there was anybody else.'

Guttuso hung a bony arm around Conor's shoulder. 'Listen, I understand that. I've lived a different life from you. Whenever I've seen an opportunity, I've taken it, regardless of whether it was legal or not. But I got respect for you. Deep respect. What you do, it takes self-denial, and that's something I've never had.'

Slowly, Conor and Guttuso walked around the store together. Every now and then Guttuso stopped and picked up a Star Trek action figure or a Mark McGwire baseball bat or a remote-controlled Dodge Viper and peered at it closely, but Conor knew that he was listening. He told him all about Dennis Evelyn Branch and the Global Message Movement; and how Branch had taken Lacey. 'I have to get her back, Luigi. If I was still in the police department, I would have all the manpower, all the facilities. But now I don't. That's why I'm asking you to do me this one favor.'

'You want manpower? I got manpower. I got facilities, too. Computers, all that crap. Windows, laplands. Wide world webs.'

'From what I've been able to work out so far, Lacey's being held someplace close to a heliport . . . she hears helicopters every few minutes. My guess is that she's close to either West 30th Street or East 34th heliport.'

'Well, I guess that narrows it. What do you suggest?'

'If you can get a couple of your guys to put a tail

on this Victor Labrea . . . and to see if he goes anyplace within the vicinity of either of those two locations.'

'No problem.'

Conor said, 'There's something else – I'm going to need someplace safe to stay for a couple of days. These Global Message people know where I live . . . and there was a shooting earlier today. The guys I've been staying with, both of them were wounded. The cops are bound to check out their apartment.'

'Conor . . . we're brothers. You don't have to explain yourself. My house is your house. We have a real nice apartment on Bleecker Street, top floor. You can use it for as long as you want.'

'There's one thing more. I could use a gun. Nothing too heavy. A Browning, maybe.'

Guttuso nodded. 'Leave it to me.'

'If you can get your men on to Victor Labrea's tail as soon as possible . . . I'm not sure how much patience the Global Message Movement has left.'

'So what do my people do if they find out where your lady friend is being hid?'

'Call me, that's all.'

Luigi Guttuso was silent for a while. Then he said, 'You know what I wish? I wish that crime wasn't against the law. Because I like you, you know. And if crime wasn't against the law, you and me, we would have been pretty good friends, wouldn't we?'

'I don't know, Luigi. All I know is that some religious maniac's holding my girlfriend and I want her back. This is where we forget ethics and start talking about survival.'

'You know something? My father told me something like that, a long, long time ago, when I was just about ten years old. He sat me on his lap and gave me a sip of Corvo Rosso and talked to me quiet and soft, I could hardly hear him, grown-up stuff, things that I didn't really understand. But that's what he meant. Taking care of your family, taking care of the people you love, that's more important than anything. More important than the Constitution. More important than anything.'

They shook hands next to a large display of Barbie dolls. Conor had never shaken hands with anybody like Luigi Guttuso before, not in a pact of friendship, and he felt as if he were committing an irredeemable heresy, as if the floor of F.A.O. Schwarz would crack open and he would drop down into Hell. Guttuso gripped his elbow and gave him a confidential wink which made him feel even worse. But then Guttuso nodded his head toward Barbie and said, 'If she was twenty times taller, and I was twenty years younger . . . even the second Mrs Guttuso wasn't arrayed like one of those.'

It was the lead story on the early evening news: FATAL SHOOTING AT WALDORF. There were bloody pictures of Ramon Perez lying on the floor of Victor Labrea's hotel room, and of Sidney and Sebastian and Ric being carried away by paramedics. It was almost more than Conor could bring himself to look at. In the glaring television lights, their faces looked even more damaged, their blood looked even bloodier.

But with huge relief he realized that Sidney – although badly hurt – was not yet dead.

CNN anchorman Walt Edridge announced, 'One man died and three others were injured, one of them seriously, in a mystery shootout at the swanky Waldorf-Astoria Hotel today.

'Police are hunting former NYPD captain of detectives Conor O'Neil, who was identified by witnesses as having been at the scene of the shootout, but who escaped before they arrived, apparently without injury. O'Neil is already wanted in connection with a multimillion-dollar robbery of safe deposit boxes from Spurr's Fifth Avenue.

'The fatality was thirty-six-year-old stage hypnotist Ramon Perez. Paramedics pronounced him dead at the scene of the shooting, room 711.

'Another stage hypnotist, seventy-eight-year-old Sidney Randall, was shot twice in the chest and remains in a critical condition at New York University Medical Center. Sebastian Speed, thirty-three, an interior designer, and nineteen-year-old Ric Vetter, a dancer, both sustained gunshot wounds and were taken to the New York Hospital, where their condition was said to be "comfortable".

'Police questioned the occupant of room 711, forty-six-year-old Victor Labrea, who describes himself as an international investment banker. They questioned him for over four hours before releasing him without charge. According to Mr Duke Johnson, Mr Labrea's lawyer, Mr Labrea was forced to open fire to defend himself and his wife against a "violent and threatening intrusion" by Conor O'Neil and his associates.

'He was unable to say why Mr O'Neil should have attacked him.

300

'Mr Labrea came to public attention in New York last year for his fight to close down the Bengers and Gench musical, *Evangelists*. A fervent supporter of the Global Message Movement, which espouses the cause of worldwide conversion to strict Baptist principles, he attempted to prevent the staging of *Evangelists* on the grounds that it was "blasphemous, and a gross insult to all Godfearing people".

'Police tonight appealed for anybody who sees Conor O'Neil to contact them on the following number. You are warned not to approach him as he is likely to be armed and dangerous.'

Joint anchorman Larry Hoffman turned to Edridge and asked, 'Do we have any idea what O'Neil was doing in the company of two stage hypnotists?'

'Not so far, Larry. It's certainly a mesmerizing case.'

Conor flicked over to another channel. *Star Trek Voyager.* He flicked again. *The Simpsons.* He flicked it off. Eleanor said, 'Maybe I should call the hospital to see how Sidney's doing.'

'Give it a little time,' said Conor. He stood up and took hold of both of her hands. 'The best thing we can do for him right now is pray.'

'I don't know if prayer ever does any good.'

'My mother did. She even used to pray for her soufflés to rise.'

'And you?'

'I'm a good Catholic, Eleanor. Good Catholics believe in the power of prayer.'

It was 6:17 p.m. As soon as Conor had returned from his meeting with Luigi Guttuso at F.A.O.

301

Schwarz, he and Eleanor had gathered up their clothes and their belongings from Sebastian's apartment and taken a taxi downtown. Now they were here on Bleecker Street, in the Village, on the top floor of a large Federal brownstone. Conor could only guess that Guttuso used the apartment for visiting friends. The floors were polished teak, with colorful handwoven rugs, and the living room was furnished with off-white leather couches and chairs and spindly Italian lamps. The walls were hung with large abstract oil paintings in vivid crimsons and aquamarines. A vast skylight filled the room with gilded early-evening sunshine.

It was almost eerily quiet up here, isolated from the street below.

'Do you want a coffee? A drink?' asked Conor.

'I'm fine for now,' Eleanor told him, although her voice was watery and she was looking extremely tired. Conor was hardly surprised, considering that she had believed this afternoon that she had lost Sidney for good.

On the table, Sebastian's mobile phone rang. Conor immediately picked it up.

'Mr O'Neil!' said an arch, over-familiar voice. 'And how are you this evening?'

'Who is this?'

'Don't you recognize me? This is your friend Victor Labrea speaking.'

'Labrea? Are you kidding me? You don't seriously think I've got anything to say to you, after what happened today?'

'Oh, come on now, Mr O'Neil, you have to take most of the blame for that yourself, now don't you?

That was a very rash and ill-considered thing you did, busting in on us that way. It could have turned out a whole lot worse.'

'Ramon's dead; Sidney's critical. I can't imagine how.'

'Well, you could have shot *me*, couldn't you, and if that had happened – I very much doubt that your little Lacey would still be livin' and breathin'. The Reverend Branch isn't normally a vengeful man, but he and I go back a long, long way. We're more than friends, if you understand what I mean. We're *soulmates*.'

'Is Lacey all right?'

'For the time being, yes, she's in the best of health. But if you try to pull any more stunts like you pulled today . . . well, I wouldn't like to give you any guarantees about her future sex appeal.'

'What the hell do you want me to do now?'

'I want you to have patience, that's what. Most of the money has been wired to Norway already, but we do need two more personal appearances like you did today, just to reach our target figure.'

'You don't seriously expect me to go out and raise more money for you?'

'Has to be done, ol' buddy. Crusades don't come cheap.'

'I'm not doing it unless you let me speak to Lacey again.'

'Well . . . I can do that, but not just yet. I'm still at the Waldorf, waiting for my baggage to be taken up to my new suite. Couldn't stay in the old one, could I, on account of all of that blood sprayed around.'

'You make sure that you call me. Otherwise, next time, I won't hesitate to pull the trigger. Not for one instant.'

'Don't get yourself all hot and bothered, Mr O'Neil. I'll call you in twenty minutes to give you your next assignment. You can talk to her then.'

Victor Labrea broke the connection. Immediately, Conor called Luigi Guttuso.

'Who is this?' asked the same slow, suspicious voice.

'Conor O'Neil. I need to speak to Mr Guttuso right now.'

'Nobody of that name here.'

'For Christ's sake it's Conor O'Neil. I was talking to him only a couple of hours ago.'

'Oh, right. Mr. Guttuso mentioned your name. Wait up a moment, OK?'

Conor sat on the couch with his head bowed, waiting for Guttuso to answer. Eleanor came and sat next to him, and took hold of his hand. 'Don't let this get to you. Be strong.'

Luigi Guttuso answered the phone. 'Conor? How's it going? How do you like the apartment?'

'It's great, Luigi. It's much more than I could have asked for.'

'Hey – you screwed the Forty-Ninth Street Golf Club. You don't have to ask for nothing.'

'Listen, Luigi. I think that Victor Labrea is just about to leave the Waldorf-Astoria and I think he's headed for the place where he's holding Lacey hostage.'

'We've got half a dozen soldiers outside of the

Waldorf, don't worry. Wherever Victor Labrea goes, we're going to be right on his tail.'

'Don't forget to call me when you find out where she is. Please. Don't do anything until I get there.'

'Didn't I promise you that already? What do you think I am?'

Conor didn't know what to say. Murderer, extortionist, loan shark, drug dealer, pimp?

'Just don't forget to call me,' he said.

22

He fell asleep while he waited for Victor Labrea to call back. He had a dream that Dennis Evelyn Branch was standing in the half-open doorway, watching him. Then he heard a whispery voice saying, 'Two into one *do* go, and when they do, you'd better watch your ass.'

A bandaged, filth-crusted hand was held up in front of him, jingling a persistent little bell. '*Unclean,*' whispered the voice. '*Unclean.*'

Another filthy hand reached out toward him and he shouted, '*Don't touch me!*' and sat up with a jolt. He found himself back on the bed, next to Eleanor. It was 8:15 p.m. and the phone was persistently ringing in the living room.

'Mr O'Neil? It's Victor Labrea. You got a pen ready? I'll tell you who you're going to meet tomorrow.'

'OK. But let me talk to Lacey first.'

'Sure,' said Victor Labrea, and handed over the phone.

'Lacey? How are you, sweetheart?'

'I'm all right. I'm all right.' She sounded close to

tears. 'But please get me out of here, Conor. Please.'

'Listen, try to stay calm. Everything's going to be fine, I promise you. If you can hold out for another hour or so, this whole thing's going to be over.'

'Just get me out of here, Conor, please.'

Victor Labrea took the phone back. 'You heard the lovely Lacey, Mr O'Neil. Just make those two meetings tomorrow, and we'll all be happy.'

He had only just hung up when the phone rang again.

'Conor? It's Luigi. We found your friend's little nest for you. It's a hotel on West 29th Street, half a block away from the heliport – some dump called the Madison Square Marquis. Labrea's checked into room 525 under the name of Mr and Mrs Tapatio. The desk clerk said that "Mrs Tapatio" was blond and tall and good-looking. His actual words were extremely complimentary but I wouldn't say them in front of my mother, God bless her, if only I could.'

'I know the Marquis,' said Conor. 'Tell your guys to stay where they are and I'll come right over.'

'Glad to be of assistance. And – you know – may God be with you.'

Two shiny black Buicks with darkly tinted windows were parked opposite the Madison Square Marquis, with two men in each of them. The evening was insufferably hot. Conor approached one of the cars and tapped on the window. The window slid down and released the chilly air-conditioned aroma of Cerruti aftershave. A smooth-looking young man

307

appeared, with black slicked-back hair and a lime-green A. Sulka shirt.

'Good evening, Mr O'Neil. How are you doing?'

Conor recognized him: Tony Luca, one of Luigi Guttuso's cousins and a particularly vicious enforcer of the Guttuso family's protection rackets. Luca had been arrested two or three years ago for stabbing a Chinaman in the eye, but the case had been dropped for the lack of any witnesses rash enough to testify against him.

'Labrea still in there?' asked Conor.

Luca nodded. 'From what the manager said, there's another two dudes up there, too. He didn't know what the hell they were all doing. He thought it was an orgy maybe.'

'You want to help me ride to the rescue?'

'That's what we're here for.'

Luca climbed out of the car and a thin, beaky man in his early forties climbed out of the driver's seat. John Convertino, another snappy dresser with perfectly sculpted scimitar-shaped sideburns and a record of extortion, drug dealing, arson, malicious wounding and suspected (but unproven) vehicular homicide.

'Pleasure to see you again, Captain O'Neil,' he said, although his face was expressionless and his eyes were like two steel nailheads. 'It's been a while, hah?'

They were joined on the sidewalk by the two Guttuso soldiers from the other car. Conor only recognized one of them: Frank Garibaldi, a dim but amiable palooka who usually worked as a doorman at one of Luigi Guttuso's nightclubs. He looked like

Jay Leno in a woolly black wig. The other man was huge, with a flattened boxer's face and a tight blue suit from Harry Rothman, who specialized in large, tall and unusual sizes. Conor had never seen him before, but he had a strong psychopathic aura about him, as if he were capable of pulling a chihuahua's legs off and seeing how far it could run.

'So, what's the plan, captain?' asked John Convertino. 'Mr Guttuso said these guys was holding the love of your life in there.'

'We can't be confrontational, otherwise there could be shooting. That means we can't go charging into their room. We have to confuse them.'

'OK,' said Luca, 'and how are we going to do that? You got CS gas? Shock grenades? Barry Manilow records?'

Conor said, 'Follow me,' and the five of them crossed the street to the Madison Square Marquis. The hotel was even further away from Madison Square than Madison Square Garden. It had been built in the mid-1950s and it had a decrepit, diseased look, with rusting metal window-frames and water-stained concrete. Its entrance was squarish and ill-proportioned, with rough-cast concrete pillars, and there was grit beneath the revolving doors so that they made a grating noise when they pushed their way through them.

Inside the flatly lit lobby, a young spotty man in a shiny maroon coat and a grubby white shirt was standing behind a reception desk that was upholstered in tan padded vinyl, cigarette-burned and ripped in places to expose the leprous yellow latex foam beneath. A television on the wall was tuned to *Scooby Doo*. The young man was watching the television and talking on the phone and laughing a silly, high-pitched laugh.

'No – you're putting me on! No – you're putting me on! You're putting me on! No! Really? You're putting me on!'

'Did you ever hear such an excellent grasp of the English language?' remarked John Convertino, and pinged the bell right under the desk clerk's nose. 'Hey, kid – how about some attention here, please?'

'OK, OK – just a minute. You're putting me on! You – are – *putting* – me – on!'

John Convertino took the receiver out of the young man's hand and gently replaced it on its cradle. The young man stared at him in alarm. Then he looked at Tony Luca and Frank Garibaldi and the man with the flattened boxer's face, as well as Conor with all of his bruises, and he opened and closed his mouth two or three times.

'I'm sorry, gentlemen. What can I do?'

'You can stay there and keep your trap shut and don't say nothing to nobody. There is nothing wrong with your life. We control the vertical and the horizontal. In other words, you want to stay vertical, you do what you're told. You want to be horizontal, you just try giving me shit.'

'Whatever,' the young man told them.

'Nice to know we have an understanding. Now, what are we going to do, Captain O'Neil?'

'We're going to go up to 525. Where's the fire alarm on that floor?'

'Right at the end of the corridor,' said the young

man, sweating and visibly shaking. 'Next to the ice-making machine.'

'OK . . . you'll hear the alarm go off, but there won't be any fire. You understand me? You don't have to evacuate rooms, you don't have to panic. All you have to do is call the fire department and tell them that you're experiencing a false alarm. Some drunken guest, something like that.'

'I got it. Whatever you say.'

John Convertino added, 'You won't try to call the cops. In fact, you won't call nobody. You'll stay here and act as normal as you can, which by the look of you isn't very normal.'

The young man dumbly and violently nodded his head.

'Let's go,' said Conor. 'Frank – can you stay down here and watch the door. That's what you're good at. Anybody tries to get in here, delay them, OK?'

'You got it, Captain O'Neil.'

As they walked toward the elevator, Conor thought how incongruous it was, not only to be walking in the company of wise guys, but to be addressed by his former rank in the police department, not sarcastically, in the way that Drew Slyman did it, but with respect.

They crowded into the elevator and waited while it chugged up to the fifth floor. The light-bulb was on the fritz and it flickered like a strobe. 'So what's this all about?' asked Tony Luca. 'How come these guys are holding your old lady?'

'It's a long story. But believe me, they're going to pay for it.'

'You know what, Luigi used to have a contract out

on you once, captain. Quarter of a million bucks. Just think about it, if I'd whacked you, I could be in Florida now, sitting on the beach, instead of doing this?'

'You'd hate Florida. You try getting a decent *maccheroncini alla saffi* in Fort Lauderdale.'

The elevator arrived at the fifth floor. The corridor was narrow and dimly lit and drab, with a patterned olive-green carpet that looked as if it had been salvaged from a fire-damage sale. There were framed prints all the way along the walls like the Stations of the Cross, except that these were photographs of various heavyweight boxing matches at Madison Square Garden, Primo Carnera and Joe Louis and Rocky Marciano, mountainous men in voluminous boxing shorts. Most of the photographs were blotched with damp.

They reached 525. 'Quiet now,' Conor cautioned. 'They're not expecting us. I don't want them getting jumpy.'

Without a word, Tony Luca and John Convertino took out their guns. They were so huge that Conor couldn't think how they had kept them concealed: a .357 Magnum revolver and a .44 automatic. The corridor smelled of mold and gun oil and danger. Conor reached around and pulled out the Browning that Luigi had left on the kitchen table at Bleecker Street. He had also left a note: 'Go out into the darkness and put your hand into the Hand of God. That shall be better to you than light and safer than a known way.' Deep man, Luigi Guttuso, Conor had thought, as he checked that the automatic's clip was full.

He took Sebastian's mobile phone out of his shirt pocket and pressed out the number for the Madison Square Marquis. After a few moments the spotty young man answered and Conor said, in a whining voice, 'Put me through to five two five, will you?'

There was a crackling pause. Then Conor heard Victor Labrea's voice on the phone.

'Yeah, what is it?' Labrea demanded, as if he had his attention on something else altogether.

Conor kept up the whining voice. 'I don't wish to alarm you, sir, but we have a small fire emergency in the hotel and I must ask you to vacate your room immediately and make your way to the stairway which you will find situated at the end of the corridor on your right-hand side.'

'What did you say?'

'I said, the hotel is on fire, sir, and you must leave your room at once. Make your way to the fire escape at the end of the corridor on—'

'Who is this?' Labrea demanded, suspiciously.

'Desk clerk, sir.'

'Desk clerk, hunh? And you're trying to tell me this hotel is on fire?'

'That's right, sir. It's on the third floor, directly beneath you. We have to evacuate the entire hotel immediately.'

There was silence. Conor could almost hear Labrea thinking. 'Sir—' he began. But then the door to room 525 opened up, and he and Luigi Guttuso's men flattened themselves against the wall. It opened only on the security chain, however, and was held open, and it was obvious that whoever had opened it was listening, and listening, and then Conor heard two or three deep sniffs, too. A few more seconds passed, and then the door was closed.

'Sir—' Conor repeated.

'I don't hear nobody else leaving their rooms,' said Labrea. 'I don't hear no fire alarm and I don't smell no smoke.'

'Well, sir, it's only a small fire. But we're concerned that it might get out of control.'

'You've called 911?'

'Sure. They should be here any minute.'

'I don't hear no sirens.'

'You're sure you don't hear sirens?' said Conor, in a flat, expressionless tone.

'What the hell are you talking about? Of course I don't.'

'You're sure you don't smell smoke? Remember all those times when you've smelled smoke before. All those burned-out buildings.'

Labrea sounded baffled. 'I know what smoke smells like, for Christ's sake.'

'Yes – and you can smell it now, can't you? You can smell smoke and you're worried that the hotel is on fire. You have an overwhelming urge to leave the room.'

'I can smell smoke. You're right. I *can* smell smoke.'

There was a critical moment when Conor thought that he almost had him. But then he heard somebody else in the room say, 'Mr Labrea? What's the matter with you? What are you talking about? There isn't any smoke!'

Labrea hesitated; and then he said to Conor, 'I don't know what kind of a stunt you're trying to pull,

314

Mr Desk Clerk or whoever you are, but me and my friends are staying put.'

'Sir – I have to warn you—' Conor said, but Labrea hung up.

'What was that all about?' asked John Convertino.

'I was trying to hypnotize him into believing that the place was on fire.'

'*Hypnotize him,* for crying out loud?'

'Say what you like, it nearly worked. The trouble was, one of his pals interrupted me and broke his trance. That's why it's difficult to induce hypnosis over the telephone. You don't have any control over anybody else – only the person you're talking to.'

'So what now?'

'Plan B, and quick. We make him believe there's a fire by starting a fire. Tony – do you want to get me that chair from the end of the corridor. And your big friend here – what's his name?'

'Bruno,' said the man with the flattened face, obviously irritated that Conor had asked Tony Luca instead of him.

'I'm sorry, Bruno. But here's what I want you to do. You see that fire alarm down there? When I give you the signal I want you to break the glass and set it off.'

'Fine by me,' said Bruno.

Tony Luca brought the chair back and Conor set it right outside the door to 525. It was a plain black metal-tube chair with a red padded vinyl seat. Without being asked, John Convertino took out a butane lighter and handed it over. Conor struck it and turned the flame up full. Then he played the flame along the edge of the seat, and underneath it, too.

The vinyl shrank like burning skin. Beneath it was gray foam rubber, which flared up almost immediately, and began to pour out thick black choking smoke. Like all the furniture and fittings in the Madison Square Marquis, it had probably been made long before fire regulations insisted on flame-resistant plastics.

As soon as the chair-seat was blazing, Conor gave Bruno a thumbs-up signal and Bruno smashed his elbow into the glass of the fire-alarm box. Instantly, the corridor was filled with a harsh shrilling, and Frank Garibaldi clamped his hands over his ears. The alarm didn't seem to disturb any of the hotel's other guests, however, if there were any. Neither did the rapidly thickening smoke. No doors opened, no anxious faces looked out.

'Jesus,' shouted Conor. 'If this was a real fire—'

'They're out of it,' John Convertino shouted back. 'They're on the nod. Crack or smack or Thunderbird Red. If this was a real fire, they'd all be burned alive.'

Tony Luca leaned close to him and said, 'You remember the Dauphin Hotel in Chelsea? Seventeen adults cremated, two babies. The Dauphin – that was one of the reasons that Luigi gave up torching hotels.'

Conor stared at him. Three of his detectives had worked with fire department special investigators for seven months to find out who had set fire to the Dauphin Hotel, and no arrests had been made. Yet here was John Convertino calmly admitting that it was Luigi Guttuso who had ordered it.

A terrible truth struck him. John Convertino and Tony Luca and Frank Garibaldi and Bruno with the flattened face were quite unworried about discussing their criminal activities with him because they now regarded him as one of them.

Tony Luca said, 'Jesus, look at this smoke. This Labrea guy's going to *have* to believe us now.'

Conor coughed and held his hand over his face. 'Don't breathe too much of this stuff. Hydrochloric cyanide. Kills more people than the fire itself.' The chair-seat was still burning and globs of flaming plastic were dropping onto the brown nylon carpet below. That began to smolder, too, much more quickly than Conor would have expected.

He could see the smoke being sucked under the door of room 525. The alarm bell was still clamoring, so loudly that it began to take on waves and patterns in Conor's ears. But the door remained shut, and when Conor tried to call Labrea again he didn't pick up.

'I can't believe it,' said Tony Luca. 'If I was in there, I wouldn't be in there. I'd be running for the fire exit by now.'

'Don't underestimate this man,' said Conor. 'I put a gun to his head and he didn't even flinch.'

Tony Luca wrapped a silk handkerchief around the lower part of his face. Over the noise of the alarm, Frank Garibaldi shouted, 'Hey, Tony! You look like a bank robber!' which wasn't especially funny because it was true.

The carpet began to char more fiercely, glittering with tiny orange sparks and shedding dense black

317

smoke. 'Bruno,' said Conor. 'You'd better bring us that fire extinguisher before this gets out of hand.'

'Yeah, sure thing,' said Bruno, and went shambling off along the corridor again, coughing.

Conor and Tony Luca and John Convertino waited tensely for the door to open. Conor said, 'Let them all rush out – all of them. Don't give any one of them the chance to duck back in the room.'

John Convertino nodded, his eyes reddened and watering over his handkerchief.

Somewhere, an elevator door was opened, and a sudden rush of air came along the corridor. It wasn't very much, but it provided enough oxygen for the carpet to flare up. Its glue backing acted as an accelerator, and flames began to sprout all along the wall, like flowers blooming in a speeded-up nature documentary.

Conor beckoned Bruno to hurry up with the fire extinguisher. He pulled the safety pin, unhooked the hose, pointed it down at the base of the fire, and squeezed. Two or three drips of water fell onto the floor.

'Terrific,' said John Convertino. 'Now what do we do? Stay here and choke to death?'

'Yeah, I mean this was a really good plan, man,' Tony Luca told Conor. 'You set fire to the whole goddamned hotel and what happens? Labrea doesn't come out, a hundred people get burned to death, you don't get your girlfriend back, and the only person who benefits out of this is probably the owner, because he's been dying to burn it down for years.'

Further along the corridor, a single door opened, and a thin, bewildered-looking young man with scarecrow hair came staggering out. He looked left, then he looked right. He was swaying so wildly that Conor thought he might fall over. The air from his room fanned the flames even higher. He blinked, breathed in a lungful of smoke, coughed, and then he went back inside, colliding with the door-frame as he did so.

'Hey!' Conor called. 'There's a fire! You need to get yourself out of here!'

The scarecrow teetered out again and stared at him, trying to focus through the smoke, trying to work out who was shouting at him and what they had said. Then he staggered back into his room again and slammed the door.

'I'm going to have to call the fire department,' said Conor. 'This is out of control.'

'In that case, we're going to have to get the hell out of here,' said John Convertino, urgently. 'I'm not being collared for torching a tenth-rate firetrap like this, especially since I didn't even do it.'

Conor couldn't believe how rapidly the fire was taking hold. He had attended fire department training sessions and he knew just how voracious fire could be. But he had reckoned without the highly inflammable materials which lined the corridors of the Madison Square Marquis – the carpet adhesives and the wax polishes and the varnish on the plywood wall-cladding. The styrofoam ceiling tiles which could give off gases that were deadlier than Zyklon-B. One lungful and you were history.

He beat on the door of room 525. 'Fire! You have to get out of there now!'

Still there was no reply. Tony Luca and John

Convertino were growing increasingly twitchy, their guns pointing at the door but their eyes darting nervously along the corridor.

'Come on, man, this isn't going to work,' said Tony Luca. 'The cops and the fire department are going to be here at any minute.'

'*Fire!*' roared Conor. And as he did so – as if he had commanded it – the flames in the corridor leaped up to the ceiling and came rolling toward them, right above their heads. Bruno was nearest to it, and even though he covered his head with both hands, his hair caught alight. Tony Luca slapped it out, and then shouted, 'That's it! We're out of here!'

Just as he was holstering his gun, the door to room 525 burst open. A young man in a black turtleneck and black pants came hurtling out, followed by another. Lacey was next, with Victor Labrea gripping her arm. The smoke in the corridor was so thick that they didn't realize at first that Conor and Luigi Guttuso's men were there; or who they were. Other doors were opening now, and people were stumbling out, coughing and retching and shouting in bewilderment.

Tony Luca slammed the first young man against the wall, frisked him, and tugged a revolver out of his belt. John Convertino did the same to the second man. Conor pointed his Browning directly at Victor Labrea's forehead.

'Lacey – are you OK?'

Lacey looked dazed and there was a huge crimson bruise on the side of her mouth. Her hair, usually so fine, was greasy and stuck to her scalp. 'I'm OK,' she

320

told him, in a high, panicky whisper, as if she were frightened to speak.

'Well, how about that,' coughed Victor Labrea, spitting onto the floor. The flames had subsided a little now, but they still flickered fitfully through the smoke and lit up one side of his face. 'You're even more goddamned crazy than I gave you credit for.'

'Let her go, Labrea,' Conor ordered him.

Labrea said, 'You're making life very difficult for me, Mr O'Neil. I'm a very dedicated man, very driven. What I put my mind to, I like to see it through, right to the bitter end. That's why I don't like people making life difficult for me.'

There was another breathy roar, and flames came rippling along the floor of the corridor like a shallow tide.

Conor said, 'Let her go, that's all you have to do, and get the hell out of here.'

Not far away now, they could hear the wailing and blaring of approaching firetrucks. 'Come on, Captain O'Neil,' Tony Luca urged him. 'We can make it out of the back way.'

'If we don't go now, we won't stand a chance,' put in John Convertino.

'That's right, men,' said a sharp, sarcastic voice. 'You won't stand a chance.'

Conor turned. Walking steadily toward them through the smoke was Drew Slyman, holding up a gun in both hands.

'Hi, there, O'Neil. Surprised to see me? You shouldn't be. Didn't you always tell me that the best way to hunt anybody down wasn't by keeping a watch on their friends, but on their enemies? Sooner or later they always show up to get their revenge.'

He came closer, keeping his gun pointed directly at Conor's head. 'I've had a tail on Mr Labrea here ever since we released him this afternoon. And lo and behold, who should come looking for him, but New York's most wanted, Conor O'Neil.'

He nodded his head toward Luigi Guttuso's men. 'Friends of yours?'

'That's right. Friends.'

'Look like wise guys to me. Isn't that John Convertino you've got there? How're you doing, John?'

'Been better, lieutenant. And it's Mr Convertino to you.'

Slyman said, 'Put down your weapon, O'Neil. You're under arrest.'

But John Convertino lifted his gun and pointed it at Slyman, and said, 'I don't think so, lieutenant. Not this time. Captain O'Neil happens to be here under the personal protection of Mr Guttuso.'

'Oh, really? And what will you do if I drop him, right here on the spot?'

'I'll drop *you*.'

'And *I'll* drop you, too,' said Tony Luca, bringing out his gun again.

'You don't have the guts,' Slyman sneered at them, without taking his gun away from Conor's head. 'You know what kind of a sentence you'd be looking at, for killing a cop?'

Conor said, 'Let's forget all this Mexican standoff stuff. I want Lacey out of here, Drew. That's all I came here to do.'

From behind Lacey's back, Victor Labrea

produced a .38 revolver. 'Sorry to disappoint you-all. The girl comes with me. And Mr O'Neil comes with me, too. We've got some unfinished business.'

'Drop the weapon, dickhead,' Slyman ordered him.

'I don't think I'm going to do that, sir,' Victor Labrea replied, quite matter-of-factly.

'Jesus, we got a double-triple Mexican standoff here,' coughed Tony Luca. 'Everybody's going to shoot everybody else, and even if they don't, everybody's going to fucking burn to death.'

Victor Labrea said, 'This is the way it's going to happen, gentlemen. Everybody is going to put down their guns, and then me and this lovely lady are going to leave, with Mr O'Neil following right behind us. Nobody is going to move until we're out through that door, got it?'

Conor cocked his automatic and stiffened his arms. His hair prickled at the back of his neck. His rage was so intense that even John Convertino gave him an alarmed, sidewise look, and said, 'Take it easy, captain. One false move and suddenly everything's blue.'

But then – without warning – chaos intervened. Five or six more people came bursting out of the smoke. A large Filipino woman was screaming in the same key as the fire alarm and waving her arms around. Two hollow-eyed men dodged past them like basketball players, carrying bottles of whiskey in both hands.

'Save us!' screamed the Filipino woman, seizing Tony Luca's arm. 'Mother of God, save us! We're all going to die!'

Her husband came careering out of the smoke, an even fatter man in a green flowery shirt, basted in sweat and whining in terror. He stumbled over the burned-out chair and fell heavily against Bruno's back. Bruno lost his balance and staggered into Victor Labrea and Lacey. Victor Labrea tipped backward, Lacey threw herself sideways. Conor dropped to the floor and rolled over, firing up at Victor Labrea twice. He hit him once in the shoulder and once in the neck. Blood flew everywhere, and Labrea collapsed against the corridor wall.

Conor twisted around to shoot up at Drew Slyman, but Slyman had seized hold of Lacey as she threw herself away from Victor Labrea. He clamped his left arm tight around her waist and jammed his gun against her right temple. Lacey's eyes were squeezed shut in terror.

'*Drop the weapon!*' Slyman screamed at Conor. '*Drop the fucking weapon!*'

The Filipino woman screamed even more shrilly. '*Save us! Save us! Everybody here is going to die!*'

Slyman thumbed back the hammer of his automatic and his eyes were bulging. Conor dropped his gun onto the floor and slowly stood up, his hands half raised.

'I was going to make you a proposition,' said Slyman. 'I was going to make you a proposition and you were so goddamned righteous you didn't even call me.'

'Let her go, Drew. You can take me now, if you want me. But she's done nothing to you. Nothing.'

'When I realized how much fucking money you were going to be making out of this deal . . .' said

Slyman. 'When I realized that you were going to be making *millions* . . . Why do you think I sent those two guys after you on Staten Island?'

Conor said nothing, but kept his hands cautiously raised. He glanced sideways. John Convertino still had his gun pointed at Slyman's head. The Filipino woman had blundered away now, and was screaming at the fat man in the flowery shirt.

'You blew them out, those two guys. Jed Ferris and Martin Yapko. Good cops, both of them. Well, not good enough, obviously. So I thought to myself, if I can't cut myself into this little moneymaker by force of arms . . . maybe I can make a proposition. A ten per cent share in return for your immunity. But what happened? You didn't even call me.'

The smoke rolled thickly between them, and Slyman coughed. 'The proposition still stands, if you're interested. Think about it, O'Neil. No more running and hiding. No more price on your head. Ten per cent, that's all I'm asking.'

Conor said, 'I don't have any of the money, Drew. It's not even in the country any more. I was used, that's all. Can't you believe that? I'm innocent.'

Slyman slowly shook his head. 'I don't believe you, O'Neil. And I'm going to make you an ultimatum, right here and now. Ten per cent, or Lacey gets it. And I won't even kill her. One downward shot to the pelvis should do the job. Instant hysterectomy, just to make sure that the world isn't plagued by any more O'Neils.'

He took the gun away from Lacey's head and pressed it against her back. 'Come on, then. What's it to be? I'll give you five. One – two – three—'

325

At that instant, a huge gout of flame burst out of the corridor. Victor Labrea sat up and screamed like a banshee. The heat blew over all of them, and Drew Slyman lifted his gun-hand to shield his face.

John Convertino shot him in the upper back, and then again, in the body. Slyman dropped to the floor on his hands and knees and Conor immediately snatched up his gun and pointed it at him.

Tony Luca reached out his hand and pulled Lacey away. *'Conor – don't!'* she begged. *'Conor, leave him, let's just go!'*

Slyman began to crawl away down the corridor, dragging his gun along the floor. The smoke was so dense now that Conor had to crouch down to see him. 'Let go of the weapon, Drew! There's no place to go!'

Slyman sat back against the wall, right next to Victor Labrea, couching his automatic loosely in his lap. Victor Labrea's head was slumped and his hair was singed but he was still breathing.

'Put the weapon down, Drew. I don't want to have to shoot you again.'

Slyman twisted himself around and managed to climb onto his feet. He took a step backward, and then another. There was an extraordinary look on his face, almost beatific, as if he expected to be sanctified. The smoke billowed all around him and through the smoke Conor could see biblical tongues of flame.

'Come on, Drew. It's over.'

'Forget him,' urged John Convertino. 'We have to get out of here, like *now*.'

Slyman retreated further and further into the

smoke, until all that Conor could see of him was a blurred, shadowy shape. Conor went after him, step by step, holding his gun rigidly in front of him, his eyes streaming from the smoke, his upper lip stained with a soot mustache. The heat in the corridor was almost unbearable, and the flames kept doing nervous little jumps, as if they were practicing a leap for the ceiling.

'Come on, man,' John Convertino repeated, and took hold of Conor's arm.

'Take Lacey and go. I've got to finish this.'

John Convertino hesitated a moment longer, and then he said, 'Your funeral, captain,' and turned away. The Filipino woman and her husband had disappeared; and the two men who had been guarding Lacey had escaped. Bruno and Tony Luca were halfway down the corridor already, hurrying Lacey toward the stairs.

Conor and Slyman remained in hell, facing each other, although they were almost invisible in the smoke.

'It's all over, Slyman. Come on out before this whole place goes up.'

'You think it's *over*? Hah! Not for you, O'Neil. It's never going to be over for you. If you won't give me the money then I'll take what I was after in the first place – you, with your brains blown out.'

He paused, and coughed. Conor couldn't even see him now. He remained crouched down to try to get beneath the smoke, keeping his gun raised in case Slyman tried to surprise him.

Slyman coughed again, and said, 'Anyhow . . . you didn't seriously think that I was going to let you live, did you, even if I *did* get the money? This is a blood score, O'Neil. This is something I'm going to settle before I die, I swear to God.'

'Come on out, Drew. If you don't come on out of there, you're going to choke to death. This smoke's lethal.'

'Screw you, O'Neil.'

Slyman coughed, and coughed and couldn't stop. Keeping his hand pressed over his nose and mouth, Conor cautiously stepped forward into the gloom. He was tempted to cough himself, but he suppressed it. The heat in the corridor was well over 120 degrees and the smoke had the throat-searing taste of burned varnish. He knew that he had already stayed here too long, and that he was risking his lungs and even his life.

'Come on, Drew. This is your last chance.'

But Slyman didn't even get the chance to say no. With an extraordinary scream that was almost human, the flames at the end of the corridor made a sudden jump for the ceiling, and the whole corridor exploded in a dark orange fireball.

Conor didn't hesitate. He ducked down and ran. He could feel a huge blast of heat chasing him down the corridor like a blazing rhinoceros. His hair was scorched and he clamped both hands on top of his head to stop it from catching alight.

Gasping, choking, he made it to the emergency stairs and almost fell through the door. John Convertino was waiting for him. The others had gone. Convertino quickly patted his hair and his shoulders to extinguish the sparks, like a fussy mother sending her son off for his first job interview.

'Slyman?' he asked.

Conor coughed and shook his head. Then he bent forward and painfully retched, and spat out a chestful of soot-colored phlegm.

'You go on,' he told John Convertino. 'The cops'll be here any second.'

'No, you're coming with me.'

'Forget it,' Conor protested, but that was all he could manage to say. John Convertino took hold of his arm and led him down the echoing concrete stairs.

'I know this dump. We can get out of the back. The fire department will be coming in the front. And they won't let the cops in till they've cleared out all of the rooms.'

They reached the ground floor. They hurried along a narrow corridor and through a heavy gray-painted fire door. Suddenly they were out in the open air. Conor took two or three enormous breaths, and then retched up even more soot.

'Come on,' John Convertino urged him. 'You can cough your lungs up later.'

They crossed a small shadowy yard stacked with packing-cases and overgrown with horseweed. Then up a rusting metal fire escape, across the roof of what appeared to be a laundry, with a puffing aluminum steam vent, and down another fire escape which dropped them onto the sidewalk on West 26th Street right outside S. Levitz Discount Carpets.

They started walking. Several passers-by stopped and stared at Conor as he hobbled past. His face was blacked up, his eyes were red-rimmed and his shirt was scorched. The backs of his hands were burned scarlet where he had tried to protect his head, and they were beginning to hurt badly.

From West 25th Street they heard more fire sirens honking and wailing, and over the rooftops, illuminated by criss-crossing fire department searchlights, a brownish haze of smoke was rising.

'Some plan, hunh?' remarked John Convertino. 'Next time I want to flush somebody out of some hotel room, I'll do it in the time-honored way, you know? Kick the damn door down and go in shooting.'

'I didn't want Lacey to get hurt, that's all.'

'Sure you didn't. But sometimes, you know, you can't afford to be sentimental. You got to follow your what's-its-name.'

He hurried Conor across the street, taking his Motorola mobile phone out of his back pants pocket as he did so. 'Tony? You got O'Neil's girl with you? OK, that's terrific. Meet us on Ninth at twenty-fourth Street.'

He put the phone away, and said, 'Tony says your girlfriend's fine.'

Conor nodded in relief. 'I guess I have to say thank you.'

'Not to me, you don't. I know what it cost you, that Golf Club thing. Putting those other cops away.'

'I still wanted to put you away, too.'

'Sure you did. But, you know, no hard feelings. If Mr Guttuso says you're one of us, that's good enough for me. Hell, you should ask him for a job. *He* may have chickened out of torching hotels, but *you* – I mean, you're *good* at it.'

They crossed West 25th and Conor glanced down

330

at the gathering of firetrucks and ambulances outside the Madison Square Marquis. Red lights flashed and hoses were uncoiled everywhere across the glistening street: Conor was reminded of a snakepit.

One of the black Buicks was waiting for them on the corner of the next block. John Convertino opened the door for him and Conor climbed in. Lacey was sitting there with Bruno. She didn't say a word, just put out her arms and clung to him, and kept on clinging to him all the way to Bleecker Street.

23

He was up early watching the news when Lacey came into the living room. She stood next to the window wearing one of his shirts, her hair still greasy and tangled from yesterday's ordeal.

'You want some coffee?' he asked her.

She shook her head and continued to look out of the window.

'The fire was on the news. It looks like the fire department managed to confine it to the fifth floor. Not too much damage.'

'And Slyman?'

'I don't know. I don't see how he could have gotten out of there but there were no reports of anybody found dead. Victor Labrea's critical – gunshot wounds and second-degree burns.'

There was silence between them. He watched her but he had the feeling that she didn't want to be approached. She had slept badly, and there were plum-colored circles under her eyes. After all of the trauma of being kidnaped by Victor Labrea and his associates, she had come back to Bleecker Street to learn that Sebastian and Ric were both hurt, and that Sidney was still fighting for his life.

'How are your hands?' she asked him.

He lifted them up. They were bandaged with gauze and adhesive tape. 'Still sore, but that ointment helped.'

'You could have been killed. We all could have been killed.'

'The fire got out of hand, that's all. If I could have hypnotized him—'

Lacey wrapped her arms around herself. 'I don't know, Conor. This is more than I can take.'

'You're safe now. Nobody can touch you here.'

'I don't want to be here. I want to go home. I want our life to go back to normal, the way it was before.'

'It can't, sweetheart. Not at the moment. Even if Slyman's dead, I'm still wanted for extortion, and the cops are still going to want to talk to me about what happened at the Waldorf-Astoria.'

'But so much damage, Conor! So many people hurt! It's like you're self-destructing, and you're bringing everybody else down with you.'

'So what do you suggest I do? Give myself up? I wouldn't last an hour in police custody, and you know it.'

She turned to him and there were tears sliding down her cheeks. 'It's too much, Conor. It's all too much. I don't think I can bear it any more.'

He stood up and walked across to her, but he didn't touch her, partly because of his bandaged hands and partly because he knew that she wouldn't want him to. 'So what are you going to do?' he asked her, his voice hoarse from smoke inhalation and emotion.

'I don't know what else I *can* do. I'm going to go back to Minnesota for a while to stay with my uncle and aunt. At least, in Minneapolis, I won't be in any danger of being kidnapped.'

'But, sweetheart, I told you. You're safe now.'

'Safe? Hiding in somebody else's apartment? A gangster's apartment? A man you spent years trying to put behind bars? What's *happened* to you, Conor?'

He lowered his head. 'I don't know. Another of my conjuring tricks, I guess.'

Without turning around, Lacey said, 'I'm going to have to leave you, Conor. There doesn't seem to be any way out of this. How can you prove you're innocent if you won't give yourself up? And the longer you keep on running, the more people seem to get hurt.'

At that moment Eleanor came into the room. She had her hair clipped back with diamanté barrettes and she was wearing a simple Indian dress of purple linen with gold-blocked patterns on it. She said, quite crisply, 'You know what would happen if Conor gave himself up.'

Lacey turned and stared at him. The hurt in her eyes was almost more than he could bear. He said, 'I'm sorry. I don't know what else to tell you. I can't stop you going if that's what you feel you really have to do. But if you could stay here . . . I need your love, Lacey. I need your support.'

Lacey wiped her eyes with her fingers. 'I'm sorry, too. I really am. But I'm exhausted, Conor. I'm frightened. You don't know what it was like, shut up in that hotel room with those awful men. The things they said to me. I thought they were going to rape

334

me; and then kill me; and they told me all kinds of ways in which they could get rid of bodies, so that nobody would ever find them.'

She took a deep, trembling breath. 'And then the smoke, and the fire. And everybody panicking. And then coming back here and finding out what's happened to Sebastian and Ric and Sidney. It's all too much, Conor. Nobody can live their life like this.'

Eleanor said, 'I just heard from the hospital. Sidney's stable. He may be out of intensive care sometime tomorrow, if he continues to make good progress.'

'Well, thank God for that,' said Conor, but he could tell that it wasn't going to change Lacey's mind.

'Is it OK to make calls from here?' asked Lacey. 'I need to call my uncle. Then I'm going to book a flight.'

Conor reached up with one gauze-wrapped hand and touched her hair. He suddenly realized that he had already forgotten the tiny mole on the right side of her chin. How quickly was he going to forget the rest of her? You think you're going to remember people for ever, exactly as they were, but once they've gone they flow away like water, and all you're left with is glimpses, and occasional disconnected moments, and photographs.

'I – Goddamnit, Lacey. It doesn't have to be like this.'

She said nothing. She waited. It was plain that her mind was made up. He stepped back, and said, 'Go on . . . you can use the phone.'

Eleanor came over and stood beside him as Lacey went through to the kitchen to make a call. Her chin was slightly tilted up and she was holding her right wrist with her left hand, proudly, a little demurely.

'Don't say a word,' Conor warned her.

'I wasn't going to. If I were her, I'd probably do exactly the same thing. She's young. She has a life to look forward to. She doesn't want to get involved with death and killing. Not real death. Not *real* killing. You and I are used to losing the people we love. She's not.'

They stood in silence for a while. Then Eleanor said, 'You *are* going to find the people who robbed those safety deposit boxes, aren't you? You *are* going to prove your innocence?'

Conor sat down. He felt as if ten sacks of sugar beets had been loaded onto his back, one after the other. Crushed, exhausted, unable to carry on. In the kitchen, he could hear Lacey saying, 'Uncle Jurgen? Uncle Jurgen? This is me, Lisbeth! Yes, from New York!'

When she had finished, Lacey came out of the kitchen and gave Conor a challenging look, but there was nothing he could say to her. He waited until she had gone to the bathroom and then he picked up the phone himself. As he punched out the number, Eleanor watched him with a mixture of sympathy and caution.

Michael Baer was at his gym. He must have been running on the treadmill because his voice came in breathless jiggles.

'Michael?' Conor asked him. 'That money . . . did you send it to Oslo yet?'

336

'Ninety per cent of it, yes. Where are you?'

'That doesn't matter. If anybody asks you, tell them I called you from the Yukon.'

'The Yukon? What the hell are you supposed to be doing in the Yukon? Digging for gold?'

'Something like that.'

'He put down the phone. 'What now?' asked Eleanor.

'What else? Oslo, here I come.'

Lacey left just after ten o'clock. She was booked to fly out of La Guardia that afternoon. Her uncle had paid for the flight in the name of Bengtsson.

Conor took her to the door. 'What can I do to change your mind?'

She brushed her freshly washed hair away from her forehead. 'Do you know what I thought? I thought that when you and I met, we could both make a totally clean break with the past. But nobody can shake the past off, can they? You can't pretend that it never happened. And the past has destroyed our present; and our future, too.'

'Lacey, nobody can make a clean break with the past. It isn't possible.'

'Well, I know that now.'

'If you know it, why are you running off to Minnesota?'

She looked up at him and her face was beautiful, but defiant, too. 'Because I'm scared, Conor, that's why. Because I'm very, very scared.'

On the lunchtime news, CNN reported that fire investigators had discovered the seriously burned body of a man crammed into a service closet on the fifth floor of the Madison Square Marquis Hotel. A police service revolver had been found not far away, every shell discharged because of the intense heat. Medical examiners had taken the corpse away for examination, but it was clearly going to take some time before it could be positively identified.

It was quickly confirmed, however, that the revolver belonged to an experienced robbery detective, Lieutenant Drew Slyman, but there was no confirmation from the NYPD that the body was his. Dental checks would have to be carried out, because the corpse – not to put too fine a point on it – was 'charcoal'.

Conor switched off the television. He closed his eyes and prayed for Drew Slyman's soul. He had wished many things, but he had never wished Drew Slyman dead. Maybe Lacey was right. He was fatally damaged below the waterline, and now he was sinking like the *Titanic*, dragging everybody down with him indiscriminately, both enemies and friends.

He came back to Luigi's apartment early in the afternoon and it was so bright that it looked like an ante-room to Heaven. There were dazzling reflections everywhere – from mirrors, from chrome-plated chair legs, from doorknobs, from picture frames. There was an array of white lilies in the center of the living room and the crystal vase in which they were standing was filled with sunlight, like a 200-watt light-bulb.

Eleanor was leaning over the kitchen table writing in the small notepad which was kept by the phone.

She had just poured herself a long-stemmed glass of cold white wine. That shone, too, and so did her silver hair.

'Well?' she asked him. 'How did it go?'

Conor poured himself a glass of wine and swallowed a large mouthful. 'Throat's still dry,' he explained, when Eleanor raised an eyebrow. 'What are you writing?'

'A diary, if you must know. A diary of everything that's happened since you first walked into my office. I reckon I could make a play out of it, given the right cast. A tragedy in three acts. But how did you get *on*? Did you manage to book your ticket?'

'Unh-hunh. Everything was fine until I came to pay for it. They've blocked all of my credit cards. Amex, Visa, Mastercard, everything.'

'Who has?'

'The police. It's standard practice. Stops fugitives from running too far.'

'Don't you have any money in the bank?'

'It's going to be the same story. They'll have frozen my accounts. Do you think you can manage to pay for them?'

Eleanor shook her head. 'Things haven't been going too well lately. I'm maxed out on all my credit cards.'

'This is going to be a problem,' said Conor. 'I mean, the airfare is only twelve hundred and fifty dollars coach. But who knows how long I'm going to have to stay there. And from what I've heard about it, Oslo isn't exactly the cheapest city in the world.'

'What about your friend Mr Guttuso? Can't you touch him for some money? After all, he is your brurrther,' she added, mimicking Luigi Guttuso's accent.

'Come on, Eleanor. It's bad enough my using his apartment, without asking him for air tickets and spending money. He'd give it to me, for sure. But supposing I manage to clear my name and get back to work in the security business? I'll always have that skeleton in my closet, won't I, that I took money from the wise guys.'

'You need an angel, that's what you need,' said Eleanor. 'An investor, just like we have on Broadway.'

'Jesus, I'm not much of an investment.'

'But think about it, you could be. I mean, why do you want to go to Oslo? Because all of the blackmail money was sent there. And if you manage to track down the people who framed you for the safe deposit robbery, you'll track down the money, too.'

'Of course,' said Conor. 'And with any luck at all, I'll be able to give it back to the people it was extorted from.'

'Davina Gambit,' they said, almost in unison.

'Mr O'Neil! I'm sorry I'm so late. I had a charity lunch at the Macklowe. Estonian orphans.'

Davina Gambit was dressed today in a scarlet silk moiré suit with a deeply *décolleté* top and pants that looked like wildly exaggerated jodhpurs. Around her neck she wore a gold-and-diamond star. She sat down at their table and ordered herself a mineral water with a twist of lime. 'I could kill a vodka.'

Conor had arranged to meet her at IBM Garden Plaza on Madison Avenue at 56th Street, under the sprouting bamboo trees. It was airy and cool in here, and it clattered with the sound of conversation and footsteps and coffee cups. Over in the far corner, a four-piece jazz band in Derby hats and humbug-striped vests played 'Pasadena'. Conor had brought Eleanor with him, partly because she was feeling claustrophobic after two days in Luigi Guttuso's apartment; and partly because – accompanied by an elderly woman – Conor looked much less like a dangerous fugitive.

'Ms Gambit, this is Eleanor Bronsky, the theatrical agent. She's been giving me a whole lot of help to sort this situation out.'

'Well, I don't know. It's a mess, isn't it? I don't understand it at all. But I got all my papers back, all my letters, all my photographs. There was nothing missing.'

'Nothing except four and a half million dollars, which you had to pay to get them back.'

'What else could I do? If Jack had seen them . . . I would have been left with nothing, nothing at all, except for the one pink dress I wore when I first arrived in America. I still keep it, you know. It reminds me.'

Conor said, 'Believe me, I did everything I could to get your papers back. But I'm sorry, I ran out of time, and there's much more than blackmail going on here. These people wanted your money, yes. But they didn't want it simply to make themselves rich.'

'How do you know?'

'Because the guy co-ordinating the robberies is a character called Victor Labrea, and Victor Labrea is an agent for the Reverend Dennis Evelyn Branch.'

Davina Gambit shook her head. 'I never heard this name.'

'He's a religious terrorist – the leader of an extreme evangelical movement calling itself the Global Message. He daren't stay too long on American soil because he's wanted by the FBI in connection with a number of bombings. So Victor Labrea does all his dirty work for him. Or *did*. He's hospitalized now.'

'But why should this Dennis Evelyn Branch want so much money? We must be talking about hundreds of millions!'

'He's talking about a worldwide crusade, and for that he needs funds. A war chest, I guess you'd call it. After all, he says he's committed to nothing less than the wholesale conversion of every man, woman and child on this planet to his own particular brand of fundamentalism.'

'How could he do that? You mean *everybody* – Catholics and Muslims and Hindu people, too? It's impossible!'

'Dennis Evelyn Branch doesn't seem to think so. I don't know what he's planning to do, but if he succeeds, he's going to start the biggest religious war in history.'

'He sounds like a mad person.'

'I don't know. He wasn't so mad that he couldn't organize one of the most original extortion operations this city has ever seen, and get away with it.'

'You said on the phone that you could get my money back.'

'I'm going to try, sure. I *have* to try. My whole reputation depends on it. My life depends on it.'

'Then how much do you need to go to Oslo?'

'I don't know. Oslo's pretty pricey, and I don't know how long this is going to take me.'

'If I give you twenty-five thousand dollars?'

'I guess that should cover it. Well, to begin with, anyhow.'

Davina Gambit turned to Eleanor. 'I've heard of you, haven't I? You're a very famous woman. Very respected.'

'I *was*,' Eleanor corrected her.

'To me, you still are. Do you think I can trust this man?'

'Conor? Yes. I trust him, and I'm a pretty good judge of character. It's my job, after all, characters.'

'Then do something for me. You go to Norway with him. Look after him. Make sure that he doesn't do anything too ridiculous. I know men like him. They're always their own worst enemy.'

'You want Eleanor to be my *nursemaid*?' Conor protested.

'Absolutely. All men need a nursemaid. Somebody to remind them that they're only men. That was why I was good for Jack. And look at him now. All those bimbos on his arm, making a fool of himself.'

Conor said, 'This could be very, very dangerous. We're dealing with fanatics here. We're dealing with people who are beyond fanatics.'

'All the more reason you need somebody like Eleanor with you.'

'What do you think, Eleanor? Wouldn't you rather stay here with Sidney?'

Eleanor shook her head. 'There's nothing much I

343

can do for him, not just yet. It's going to be months before he's fully recovered. What happens after that . . . well, that depends on all sorts of different things, like how much nursing he's going to need, and whether he wants us to get back together and whether *I* want us to.

'I'm not getting any younger, Conor. I wasted four years of my life loving Sidney before. I'm not so sure that I can allow that to happen again.'

Conor reached across the table and took hold of her hand. Davina Gambit laid her hand on top of both of them, so that they looked like the Three Musketeers. 'You'll have your money in the morning. Give me your number and I'll call you tomorrow morning at nine.'

24

Conor was pouring himself a second cup of coffee when the phone rang. He picked it up and said, 'Good morning, Ms Gambit. You're right on time.'

'Right on time for what?' replied a woman's voice. It certainly wasn't Davina Gambit.

'Who is this?' Conor demanded.

'Conor – what's the matter?' asked Eleanor, through a wreath of cigarette smoke.

The woman said, 'Your little friend at the Kaufman Pharmacy gave me your number. Don't blame him. He didn't do it voluntarily. I induced him.'

'*Hetti*,' said Conor.

'I'd prefer it if you called me Magda. Especially now that Ramon is gone. No more Hypnos: no more Hetti.'

'I'm sorry about Ramon, no matter what he did.'

'Don't be too sorry. Ramon was a fool. Bombastic. Thought so much of himself. I was always a better hypnotist than him. I don't know why I worked with him. I don't know why I loved him. It's crazy, isn't it, the things you do in spite of your better judgment?' She pronounced it 'yoodjment'.

'I guess we all make mistakes like that,' said Conor. 'What do you want?'

'I want to meet with you, talk with you. I can tell you everything I know about the Spurr's Fifth Avenue robbery – about *all* of the robberies.'

'And why would you want to do that?'

'They want to kill me, that's why. I need your protection.'

'Who wants to kill you?'

'You know who they are. Dennis Evelyn Branch and all of his people. Those men with their black suits and their crucifixes. They're looking for me, to make sure that I don't say anything.'

Conor said, 'All right, then, let's meet.'

'Tomorrow?'

'No, today. As soon as possible.' He didn't tell her why: that he was leaving for Norway in less than nine hours.

'Where are you?' asked Magda. 'Wherever you are, I can come to see you as soon as you like.'

'I don't think so. You want to meet me, I'll tell you where to meet me. John's Pizzeria on Bleecker at Seventh Avenue.' He checked his watch. 'Ten o'clock, precisely.'

'Very well. Anyplace at all. This is a bad thing that has happened, Mr O'Neil. But I think that there is something worse to come.'

'I don't doubt it, Ms Slanic.'

'Magda, please.'

'OK – Magda.'

Eleanor gave him a long, old-fashioned look. 'Are you sure this is wise?'

'Maybe not. But we don't have anything to lose, do we?'

At 10:05 a dour bald man in sunglasses and a bright pink polo shirt arrived, and handed Conor a large brown paper postal bag. 'Open it,' he said; and when Conor looked inside he saw that it contained bundles of $100 and $50 bills, all of them used.

'Twenty-five grand,' the man told him. 'You don't need to count it.'

'You want me to sign for it?' asked Conor.

The bald man said, 'I wouldn't bother. You lose this, your life's worth shit anyway.'

Magda Slanic was already waiting for him at a corner table in John's Pizzeria when he arrived. The atmosphere was sweaty, noisy, with music bumping and lines of lunchtime office workers waiting for take-out, so many that they had to form a crocodile into the street. The temperature was edging its way over ninety degrees, and the street was already distorted with heat.

Magda looked as striking as usual, with her white deadpan face and her startling eyes and her mouth that was almost invisible. Her jet-black hair was pinned up with a variety of silver stars, and her hands were clustered with silver rings. She wore a long black skirt and black high-heeled ankle-boots that were fastened by elaborate spiderwebs of thin leather laces.

'You hungry?' asked Conor, as a waiter approached them with his pad at the ready.

Magda whispered, 'No. But coffee maybe. Black. Strong.'

'Two large espresso,' said Conor. The waiter kept his pen raised as if he expected them to order a pizza, but Conor said, 'That's it. Two large espresso.'

Magda looked around her nervously. 'You're sure we're safe here?'

'It depends on your definition of safe.'

'I never thought that they were going to kill us,' said Magda. 'Victor Labrea was always so friendly, you know? Right from the very beginning he was always giving us money and treating us to meals.' She gave him a thin, quirky smile. 'He called me the Romanian Raven because I always dress in black.'

'How did you get to meet a scumbag like him?'

'It was April. The first of April, stupid fools' day, I should have realized! But it was a very bad time. Ramon and I hadn't had any serious work in over two years and we had no money. Ramon was wanted for crack dealing and for stealing food from grocery stores. But how else could we live? We were living in a horrible apartment near the Bowery. In the winter it was enough to freeze your bones and there was damp running down the walls.

'Being so broke, it hit Ramon very hard, even more hard than me. He came from a very poor family in Tijuana. To think that after all that fame and all that money he would have to go back to such a life . . .

'Then Victor appeared on our doorstep. I never knew how he managed to locate us. He told us that he needed our help and that he was prepared to pay us very well for it. Thousands of dollars, if we did good.'

'Did he tell you what you were supposed to do?'

'He said it was charity work.'

'So he didn't ask you outright if you were prepared to steal safety deposit boxes and confidential legal records, and extort money from their owners to get them back?'

Magda shook her head. 'He didn't say it was anything like that. He said that he belonged to a religious movement that wanted to launch a worldwide crusade. The Global Message Movement. He said they had no money left because they had been persecuted by the government and the Southern Baptist Conference. All of their assets had been taken by the FBI, and none of the TV stations would carry their fund-raising broadcasts. But he said they weren't criminals, they were people who believed in God and believed in the Bible, that's all.'

'Maybe. But it's a little difficult to see how he reconciled that with stealing other people's private property.'

'He said that God had given him a sign.'

'A sign, huh? What kind of a sign?'

'It was like, what do you call it, a *vision*. He said he drove past a field and saw ears of wheat all waving the same way, and he suddenly realized that God wanted the world to be the same as that field of wheat. He wanted everybody on the planet to pray the same prayers together, and cherish the same beliefs, and only then would there be universal peace and goodness, for ever. He said that God gave him the authority to take money from sinners so that he could spread His word. God said that it was only right to make sinners pay for their sins, especially

349

when they had hidden their sins away and had never been punished for them. "Be sure your sin will find you out," that's what he said.'

Conor sat back. Magda's eyes were so black that they looked like pools of oil, and they were quite unreadable. *What does she want?* he asked himself. *Why the hell has she come to me?*

'So you and Ramon thought that Dennis Evelyn Branch's sign from God – like, what *did* you think? Don't tell me you *believed* it? A sign from God? Ears of wheat, all blowing the same way? That was sufficient justification for robbery and blackmail and murder?'

'Mr O'Neil – you forget that I didn't have enough money in my purse for a single hot dog, and when you are like that, you are ready to accept almost any justification that anybody offers you.'

Their espressos arrived. 'You're one hundred per cent sure you're not eating?' asked the waiter, snippily. Conor gave him a look that – given two or three centuries – could have worn down granite. 'Well,' said the waiter, unnerved. 'If you change your mind.'

Magda tinkled her spoon in her cup. 'Victor Labrea saved us. That's what we thought, anyhow. And it wasn't only the money. It was the chance to practice hypnotism again, to control other people. It was the power.'

'You're telling me that hypnotism is all about *power?*'

'Of course. The power to heal. The power to hurt. The power to make people look ridiculous. A hypnotist can turn your whole life upside down.'

'So what about ethics? What about morality?'

'Nobody has ethics any more, Mr O'Neil. Nobody has morality. Who knows . . . perhaps that's what Dennis Evelyn Branch is trying to bring back, with his crusade.'

'So how did you plan the Spurr's robbery?'

'The same way we planned all of the other robberies. We called up, we made enquiries about safety deposit box facilities and then we made an appointment to meet your deputy Salvatore Morales.'

'And? What are you trying to say to me? He offered to help you steal all those safety deposit boxes?'

'At first, no. We put him into a trance to find out what kind of material we might expect to find in the boxes and what your security measures were. Easy.'

'Easy?'

'Oh, yes. In some of the law offices we visited, it was very difficult to find out about their confidential files. The staff were defensive, loyal and resistant to hypnosis. But with Salvatore, it was easy. He had a passion to get his revenge on Spurr's; and once he was out of the trance he helped us of his own free will. He hated you, by the way. He thought that you had ruined his whole career. He said you were *imperioso*.'

'I'm sorry to hear that. I didn't mean to be.'

'I don't know. It's sad that he died. Did you hear me say "sad"? I don't say "sad" very often because I'm not a person who believes in sadness. But he gave us all the information we needed and he even helped us to empty those boxes.'

'Would you be prepared to testify to this in court?'

Magda looked horrified. 'In court? No, no. What

are you asking me? You're mad! If I testify against the Global Message Movement, they'll kill me for sure.'

'The fact remains, Magda, that apart from Darrell Bussman, who's still in a coma, you're the only person in New York who can prove my innocence.'

'I understand that. I'm sorry. I know. But I don't want to die.'

Conor finished his coffee. 'You've come to me asking for my protection. What are you going to give me in return?'

'I can help you. I can use my gift. Also . . . I think I know what Dennis Evelyn Branch is planning to do.'

'Oh, yes?'

'I don't know very much. Victor used to talk on the phone to him almost every morning. Always in the morning. Sometimes he left his bedroom door a little way open so that I could hear bits and pieces of what he was saying. It was strange, though. It didn't sound as if they were talking about religion at all. More like – I don't know – *science*.'

'Science? What kind of science?'

'Victor kept saying something about "keeping it isolated, at any price". I don't really remember much more. Oh – he used the word "biohazard" a lot.'

'Is there anything else you remember?'

'There was one thing . . . in every conversation he kept mentioning "*she*", like they were discussing somebody else who was involved in what they were talking about. Like, "I don't know what she's going to think if we don't get this work finished up by the end of October." Or – I remember once – "How is she today? Not too much fire and brimstone, I hope".'

'Anything else?'

Magda dabbed her mouth with her napkin, leaving a pale coffee-colored kiss on it. 'Victor said once, "I want to know that Mrs Labrea and me are going to be safe. I want your assurance". Then there was a pause, you see, like somebody is talking on the other end of the phone. After that, Victor said, "You're telling me that millions of people are going to die. I'm just making one hundred per cent certain that one of those millions isn't me".'

'You're sure he said that?'

'I'm sure. You want to hypnotize me? You want to hear those conversations right out of my brain? I don't mind. I won't resist you, Mr O'Neil. I'll let you in.'

She took hold of his hand. 'You trust me, don't you?'

'I'm not sure yet. What else do you know about Dennis Evelyn Branch?'

'I know where he is. I have his address in Norway.'

'You're kidding me.'

'Of course not. He called Victor one morning and Mrs Labrea answered the phone. She didn't realize that I was using her bathroom, so that I could overhear everything that she was saying. She asked him what the weather was like, and how he liked his new apartment. She asked for his address and she wrote it down. She went off to find Victor – I sneaked out of the bathroom – and I memorized Dennis Evelyn Branch's address as I went past the phone.'

'Are you going to give it to me?'

'Are you going to protect me?'

'I'm not so sure that I can. You have to remember that *I'm* being hunted as well, no thanks to you.'

Magda passed a Post-It note across the table. *Hammerfestgata 17, Rodelokka, Oslo.*

'I think he's very serious. I think he's going to kill a lot of people. I think that what he's trying to do will make Jonestown or Waco seem like nothing at all.'

Magda looked away. There were tears brimming in her eyes. 'I wish that I had never helped them now. It would have been better to stay in that horrible apartment. It would have been better to starve. I am so shocked. How can I tell you how shocked I am? Ramon – I can't forgive myself for what happened to Ramon. Such a fool. Strut, strut, strut. And yet I loved him so much.'

Conor watched her for a while. The tears sliding down her cheek. He didn't feel sorry for her. If it hadn't been for her, he wouldn't be a fugitive, and he wouldn't have lost Lacey, and Sidney wouldn't be fighting for his life. All the same, he understood how she felt. He knew what it was like to open Pandora's box. He knew how impossible it was to close it.

'Listen,' he said, 'I've already arranged to fly to Oslo tonight.'

Magda stared at him. 'You're crazy. You're going to *go after* these people?'

'Why not? I spent my whole life tracking down criminals, mafiosi especially. And let me tell you: the safest thing to do is to find them first, before they find you.'

'They'll kill you. I never saw such heartless men, even in Romania.'

'Magda – for my own sake, it's something I have to do. If you want my protection, you're going to have to come with me. If you want to help me, you have to come with me. I can't force you to come, but what's your choice? Either you face these people down, or else you spend the rest of your life running from them.'

Magda stared at him. 'You would trust me?'

'No, I wouldn't. But right now I need all the help I can get.'

'You can trust me, I promise. After all, you find me attractive, don't you?'

'What?'

'You find me attractive. You wonder what I'm wearing beneath this long black skirt. Maybe I'm wearing nothing at all. Maybe some kind of underwear that you could never imagine, designed to arouse anyone who wears it. Black, with laces and chains.'

'Magda—'

'Look at me. Look at my eyes. Where are you going when you look at my eyes?'

'I don't know. Where am I going?'

'You are going into my soul, that's where you're going. Deeper and deeper. It's dark there. It's totally silent. You can't see anything and you can't hear anything and you can't feel anything. Nothing at all. You don't even know which way is up and which way is down.

'And you feel very happy now that I'm coming along with you. Very relaxed

'And

'You want to make love to me, but you don't want to say it just yet. That's a goodie to save for later.'

Conor was aware of the chatter and the bustle all around him. He was aware that Magda was trying to hypnotize him. He felt strong, he felt controlled, but he knew that he couldn't move until Magda told him to. Even Sidney's trances hadn't been as irresistible as this. He felt that if she had told him to stop breathing, he would have done that, too.

'I'll come with you,' she said. 'We can find Dennis Evelyn Branch and you can take your revenge on him for what he did to your friends; and I can take revenge on him for what he did to Ramon, and to me, too.

'You'll do that, won't you? You'll hunt him down; and when the moment comes, you won't have any pity. When you get your chance, Conor O'Neil, you'll kill him.'

She paused for a moment, still holding his hand. Then she said, 'You're awake. You remember everything we said. You're full of anger. You want to find Dennis Evelyn Branch and destroy him because of what he's done to you.'

Conor stared at her and said, 'You hypnotized me. I was trying to resist you. You hypnotized me! How did you do that?'

'It's not so hard, with a little practice. Sometimes you can use a person's resistance to hypnotize them more quickly. They're so busy locking horns with you that they don't realize you've crept up behind them and tied a firecracker onto their tail. *Bang!*

from behind, their attention is distracted, and they're yours.'

'Oh, sure,' Conor challenged her. 'But who said I wanted to make love to you?'

'You did,' smiled Magda. 'You're a man, aren't you? You've been saying it ever since we sat down. Not with words, but here.' And she gently tapped her temples with her fingertips.

Conor didn't know what to make of her. Maybe she was telling him the truth. Maybe she was still working for Dennis Evelyn Branch. There was no doubt that she was a world-class hypnotist, and hypnotism was almost as good as firepower, as he had seen from Sidney's performance at the Richmond Inn. In fact, sometimes it was better, because it left no fingerprints, no fibers, no gunpowder burns, no forensic evidence of any kind.

You need her, he thought. He wasn't entirely sure why. More than likely it was an idea which she had planted in his mind herself. But it seemed like common sense to take her to Norway. Maybe he needed her sophistication, and her ability to talk to anybody with ease. Maybe he needed her weirdness. More than anything else, maybe he needed her moral support. Emotionally, he was limping, at the moment. Lacey had left an empty space in his existence and maybe Magda Slanic had the strength to fill it.

After a long moment of indecision, he said, 'We're leaving for Oslo tonight. Eleanor Bronsky and me. I'll book an extra ticket for you – that's always supposing you want to come. I don't know what the risks are going to be and how long we're going to be there, so pack plenty of clothes. Meet us here at five o'clock. If you're not here, we'll go without you. No waiting.'

'I'll be here, don't you worry.'

'Sir – have you finished with this table yet?' the waiter wanted to know. 'We're really backed up here and we have a whole lot of people waiting to eat.'

Conor stood up, and helped Magda up, too. He gave the waiter $10 and said, 'I want to thank you. I hope you never realize what you've helped us to do here today.'

Only two hours after they had eaten dinner on the plane, the sky began to lighten outside the windows. Conor raised the blind and looked out over an endless continent of cloud. Not far away, another 747 was heading eastward, too, its lights flashing in the premature dawn. Beside him, Eleanor was asleep, wrapped in a blanket. Across the aisle, Magda was reading a book on mystical diets. She was wearing half-glasses, which made her look unexpectedly studious and vulnerable.

An hour before they landed in Oslo, they were given plastic cartons of reconstituted orange juice and damp croissants with strawberry jelly.

'You should have flown to Europe in the days of the Stratocruisers,' Eleanor protested. 'In those days you had a hot breakfast and the silverware was silverware, not plastic.'

'Sure,' said Conor. 'But how long did it take you?'

'That didn't matter. It was the style that mattered, not the speed. In those days you wouldn't dream of traveling in anything but your very best clothes. Shelly Winters always used to travel in her mink. Now look at these people: jeans, sneakers, sweatshirts. Sometimes I wish I could have died before people started to dress like this.'

They arrived at Gardermoen airport twenty minutes early. Outside, the sun was shining and the sky was immaculate blue, but when they left the aircraft they immediately felt the difference in temperature. It was a warm August morning: 60 degrees, expected to rise to 69 degrees by lunchtime. There was a smell of pinewood everywhere, and brine from the Oslofiord.

As they drove into the city in the back of a Saab taxi, Conor felt as if he had arrived in a travel documentary, with neat houses and tiny yards and fir trees all around them. The highway skirted the Bestumkil, a wide inlet the color of dark blue marking ink, with tiny splashes of foam around the edges. Sailboats were already on the water, and water-skiers, too.

'They're out early,' Conor remarked.

The taxi driver nodded. 'The summer is so short, we have to make the best of every hour.'

He turned off before he reached the Oslotunnel, the underpass that carries the E18 underneath the harbor area and the old town, and took them past the Radhus, Oslo's city hall, a huge russet building with two stolid square towers. Then he drove them through the busy, sunny streets to Kristian IV's Gate, where Conor had booked them two suites at the Bristol.

'This is *extremely* grand,' said Eleanor, as the taxi driver helped them with their suitcases. They walked into the lobby, all polished marble and gleaming glass and gilding, with fresh flowers everywhere.

'We won't be staying here for long,' said Conor. 'Apart from the fact that it's five hundred bucks a night, I want to try and find an apartment we can rent, someplace inconspicuous.'

'That's a pity,' said Magda. 'I could easily become accustomed to living in a place like this.'

Their suites were just as luxurious. Thick blue carpets, enormous beds, velvet drapery, complimentary baskets of fruit waiting for them. Conor opened the french windows in his living room and stepped out onto the balcony. The sun was bright, the wind was cool. He could see past the Domkirke with its eighteenth-century clocktower, the oldest in Norway, all the way to Bjorvika, the eastern harbor.

Magda and Eleanor went to their room to unpack; but it wasn't long before Eleanor came back. She sat on the end of the bed eating a fig while Conor hung his shirts in the closet.

'Do you think it was a good idea, bringing Magda with us?'

'I don't know. But my feeling is that she can help us.'

'Do you really trust her?'

'No, I don't. But I think her self-interest coincides with ours, and I think that's good enough.'

They could hear the echoing shuffle of hundreds of feet as tourists walked along Kristian IV's Gate below them; and the murmur of mass conversation. An occasional toot from the harbor, and the cries of seagulls. On the polished walnut bureau a vase of white lilies stood beneath a stern bearded portrait of Harald Harfagre, the first king of Norway. Next to it, Conor's wallet, and a scattering of Norwegian loose change, kroner and öre.

'Don't allow yourself to become cynical,' said Eleanor. 'Cynicism can eat you away, like acid. I should know.'

She pressed her hand against her chest and winced. 'Angina?' he asked her, and she nodded.

'Did you bring your medication?'

She nodded. 'Enough for a week. But I'm going to need a fresh prescription.'

'Don't worry, I'll find you a doctor. We could be here a long time. I don't want anything happening to you.'

Eleanor stood up and held out her arms and Conor hugged her. 'What am I doing here?' she asked him. 'What are we all doing here?'

A seagull perched on the balcony railing, and stayed there, crying, and turning its head, and crying again.

'I guess we're here to save some souls,' said Conor.

25

The following afternoon was even cooler, with a light southwesterly breeze blowing in from Oslofiord, and a watery sunshine that came and went, came and went, like the days passing in a dream.

Conor had spent the morning calling up letting agencies; and they had two apartments to look at – one in Torshov, overlooking the park, and another on Helgesens Gate, in Grunerlokka. Both were only a few minutes away from Dennis Evelyn Branch's address on Hammerfestgata. They had a *koldtbord* lunch at the Engebret Café on Bankplassen – a selection of dried, salted and smoked meats, as well as pickled herring and *fiskeboller* – fishballs in a béchamel sauce – and heaps of plain boiled potatoes sprinkled with dill.

'I hope I'm going to be able to survive on this diet,' said Eleanor.

'It's very good for your health,' Magda told her.

'Unlike Dennis Evelyn Branch.'

They took the subway out to Carl Berners Plass. The train was quiet and brightly lit and almost surrealistically clean. They were relentlessly stared at all the way by three unsmiling men with deepset eyes and troll-like beards and a young blond woman with round glasses and pigtails and sensible shoes. Conor had to admit that they probably made an unusual trio in a country like Norway. Magda, as usual, was dressed in black, with her hair swept up; and Eleanor was wearing Calvin Klein jeans and a stunningly expensive turquoise silk blouse from Yves St Laurent on Madison Avenue.

Conor had opted for a blue check shirt and sand-colored cords. 'You look as if you're going off to cut down trees,' Eleanor had commented.

Hammerfestgata was a short street of gray, 1960s apartment blocks. Rows of lime trees lined the sidewalk, and a single man was walking a nondescript dog. As they approached number 17, the sun went in, giving them the feeling that they were walking into a black-and-white photograph.

They reached the apartment building and pushed their way into the entrance hall. The floor was polished marble composite and the walls were painted beige. There was scarcely any smell, only a hint of vinegar and cigarette smoke. Conor went over to the row of mailboxes and looked at the name-cards.

'Rustad, Jensen, Schei,' said Eleanor. 'It could be any one of these.'

'Yes, but look. Here's the name of the letting agency. Ole Wergeland, on Sars Gate. We can have a word with them.'

They were about to leave when a middle-aged

woman came struggling up to the front door with an armful of shopping. Conor opened the door for her and caught one of her bags.

'Here. We don't want pickled cucumbers all over the floor.'

'Thank you,' she said, in the clear, barely accented English that most Norwegians could speak. 'I always try to carry too much.'

As she went toward the elevator, Conor said, 'Wait up a moment. Maybe you can help us. We're looking for an American who lives here. White hair, white face, kind of thin.'

The woman nodded. 'Yes, there is one American, anyway. A man with white hair. He has different people coming and going. I can't keep track. Once, a man with a beard. I see them sometimes and we say hello, but that's all. I've never seen the woman.'

'The woman? What woman?'

'Just as I say, I've never seen her. But sometimes late at night I hear her talking.'

'Must be a pretty loud talker.'

'Well, I don't like to put my nose into anybody else's business. But, shouting.'

'You don't ever hear what she's shouting about?'

The woman shook her head, giving Conor the impression that even if she did know, she was too discreet to tell him.

'What number apartment do they live in?' he asked.

She pointed to a mailbox with the name *Udgaard* on it. 'That was the name of the old man who lived in the apartment before the American. They never changed his name. He collected butterflies. He died.

It was very sad. Nobody came to the funeral.'

'Thank you for that,' said Conor.

The woman looked wary. 'There won't be any trouble, will there?'

Magda smiled at her. 'You don't have to worry. All you have to do is think of what you bought today. Everything is fine. What are you cooking for supper?'

'*Klippfisk*,' she said.

'That's one of your favorites?'

'*Ja.*'

Magda stepped forward and touched the woman's right temple. 'You're going to enjoy yourself tonight. You're going to feel happy and relaxed, aren't you? You're going to cook a good meal and everybody is going to enjoy it.'

'*Ja.*'

'And

'You're going to forget that you met us. You're going to forget that we asked you about the Americans. You're going to feel peaceful and calm

'And very, very content.'

'*Ja.*'

'I'm going to wake you up now,' said Magda. 'You won't know who we are. You won't remember what we said. You'll simply get into the elevator and go up to your apartment and start cooking supper. You'll wake up when I count to three. One, two, three.'

The woman stared at them. She hesitated, readjusting her shopping bags. Then she retreated into the elevator and pressed the button. Conor watched her as the doors closed, and he had never seen a woman look so perplexed in her life. He had probably looked the same way, when Ramon had hypnotized him at Spurr's.

They left the building and walked along Langgata to Helgesens Gate. The sun brightened and faded, and then brightened again. Helgesens Gate was busy with traffic but the apartment block was only three years old, with a shiny entrance lobby, chrome-plated handrails on the stairs, and a tiled mural of an ocean liner surrounded by seagulls.

A tiny woman with hugely magnifying eyeglasses and a haircut like a silver mushroom showed them around the apartment. It was big and airy and immaculately clean, with white leather couches and glass-topped tables.

'The owner is a professor and his wife,' the woman told them. 'He is gone to Boston University in America. She is gone to Sudan, to look after the thin children.'

'I like it,' said Magda, swirling around in the middle of the living room. 'It has good *feng shui*.'

'It has a bidet, too,' said the tiny woman, proudly.

At the weekend, they moved out of the Bristol to Helgesens Gate. They missed the luxury, but they had already formed an unusual but comfortable *ménage*. Eleanor was still suspicious of Magda but Magda seemed to accept her suspicion quite calmly. Every morning she brought Eleanor a cup of coffee in bed and every evening she poured her a glass of ice-cold *akvavit* from the freezer compartment because she said it was good for her heart.

She began to talk a little about her childhood in Romania and how she had emigrated to the US. She had been taught simple hypnosis at the age of 13 by a friend of her father, an old man with no teeth who smelled of tobacco and liked to dandle her on his knee. He could remember Codreanu's Iron Guard in 1938 and how they had strangled anybody who opposed them. He had learned hypnosis himself from a traveling circus performer who called himself the Great Cantemir; and he had used hypnosis to save himself when he was threatened with garrotting by drunken soldiers.

'Hypnosis is a great power,' she said. 'A very great savior. When you don't have hope, it can give you hope. When you have no way to turn, it can show you a path. There is no mystery. Hypnosis opens up your mind, that's all, and shows you what strength you have; what bravery.'

They kept watch on Dennis Evelyn Branch's apartment block from a small café, the Baltazar, on the corner of Hammerfestgata and Trondheimsveien. Conor had bought a Norwegian mobile phone, so that they could keep in touch with each other during the long hours of their surveillance. On sunny days the café's proprietor put white plastic seats out on the sidewalk, with red-and-white striped umbrellas. He didn't seem to mind that Conor and Eleanor and Magda sat there all morning and most of the afternoon, drinking coffee and occasionally ordering *polser* hot dogs or *flatbrod* with salami and herring.

Nobody resembling Dennis Evelyn Branch entered or left the apartment all weekend. Conor was beginning to think that they might be wasting their time in Oslo. After all, they had no guarantee that Dennis Evelyn Branch was here at all. But at 11:04 on Monday morning, a plain white Volvo panel van drew up outside the apartment building, and after a while two men came out of the front door. One of them was bearded, with a red T-shirt and jeans and a brown leather cap. The other wore a black sweater with a hood and black pants. Conor couldn't see his face but his head seemed unusually big and he was sure that he glimpsed a wisp of white hair.

'That's our man,' said Conor. 'I'm sure of it.'

They watched as the van driver and the man in the brown leather cap carried several large cardboard boxes into the apartment building. The man in the black hooded sweater didn't carry anything, although he looked inside one or two of the boxes as if he were checking their contents. After ten minutes the van drove away.

'Well, I wonder what that was all about,' said Eleanor.

'There's only one way to find out, and that's to go take a look.'

'In that case we'll have to wait until they go out.'

'Either that, or break in while they're asleep.'

'You couldn't do that, could you?'

'I used to be a cop, remember? I can still pick locks.'

But it was only a few minutes before the two men emerged from the apartment building again. They stood on the sidewalk as if they were waiting for somebody. Their faces were shadowed by the lime trees so it was still difficult for Conor to make a positive ID.

'Maybe I should walk past, try to induce them,' Magda suggested.

'Too risky. If that *is* Dennis Evelyn Branch, he probably has a pretty good idea of what you look like.'

In any event there wasn't time. A silver Lexus came around the corner, its tires softly squealing. It stopped right next to the two men and they both climbed in, the white-haired man sitting in the front passenger seat. The driver was a woman with long dark hair and orange Ray-Bans. She drove off quickly, and the car's tires squealed again as she turned into Langgata.

'Three of them,' said Eleanor. 'Maybe that means they've left their apartment empty.'

'It's worth a try.'

They left their coffee and crossed the street. They entered the apartment building and checked the number for Udgaard: apartment 206. They took the elevator up to the second floor without saying a word.

Apartment 206 was down at the far end of the corridor, next to a window that looked out over the street. The apartment building was totally silent. No music, no televisions, no children playing. They padded along the heather-mixture carpet until they reached the door. Conor rang the bell.

No response. They waited and listened for over a minute and then Conor rang the bell again. Outside the window the clouds sailed by on their way to Russia and the Arctic Circle. Still no response.

Conor took out his keyring and opened the black leather pouch in which he kept his lockpicks. He fiddled with the door for a moment. It wasn't a difficult lock: only a three-lever household affair, but the type was unfamiliar. After two or three minutes, however, he managed to open it, and the door to apartment 206 swung open.

The living room was stacked with all of the boxes that had arrived this morning, as well as dozens more. There were six or seven cartons with the Corning logo on them, and the legend Scientific Glassware, Handle With Care. There were other trade names, too, which Conor couldn't identify. Bechtüngsglasfabrik GmBh; Logosystems Inc.; Waalmans Industrie; Schneider BioSeals.

The rest of the apartment was almost bare. The kitchen had no food in it, only a large can of Douwe Egberts coffee and three bottles of Norwegian spring water. None of the saucepans looked as if they had been used, and there was a musty smell in the dishwasher. In the main bedroom there was nothing but a large bed covered by a green duck-down quilt and a single nightstand with a glass of water and a bible. Magda opened the closets. 'Two dresses, three skirts, a couple of sweaters.' She peered at the labels. 'All very expensive. But what revolting taste. I mean, this purple thing is Chanel, but look at it. I wouldn't wear it to my own execution.'

There weren't many men's clothes, either. Two coats, two pairs of pants, three folded sweaters, all in somber grays and blacks and browns.

The second bedroom was far more cluttered and the single bed was unmade. A small china troll stood on the wooden chair which served as a nightstand. A Norwegian-language motoring magazine *Autobil* had been dropped on the floor. Inside the closet the clothes smelled of cigarette smoke and they all bore chainstore labels. 'My God, a reindeer sweater,' said Magda, picking it up and dropping it again with undisguised disgust.

'Go through all the pockets,' said Conor. 'Look under the beds, too; and underneath the mattresses.'

He went across the hallway to the bathroom. He saw himself in the mirrored medicine cabinet over the washbasin, tired and still bruised, but it was like meeting somebody that he hadn't seen for over a year. Conor the detective. Same intent look. Same quick, questioning eyes. He opened the medicine cabinet over the washbasin. It contained a woman's razor, a small pack of band-aids and a half-used tube of Bepanthol emollient cream. No medication, no cosmetics, no eyebrow pencils, no sexual lubricants.

'What do you think?' asked Eleanor, appearing in the bathroom door.

'I'm not entirely sure . . . but I think this place is nothing but a staging-post – someplace these people could stay while they waited for their money to arrive from New York. Someplace to store their equipment, whatever it is. My feeling is that they won't be here much longer.'

He went back into the living room. He was cautious about opening any of the boxes because they were all sealed and he didn't want Dennis Evelyn Branch to suspect that anybody had been here – not until he knew what he was planning. But Magda had mentioned that Victor Labrea talked about 'biohazards' and much of the equipment was marked with company names that suggested biological screening. Micro-Org, s.a. Protective Air Systems, Inc.

'So what do we do now?' asked Magda. 'Maybe we smash everything?'

'There's no point in doing that. They probably have more than enough money to replace it all. What we need to do is keep them under surveillance and follow them wherever they go – especially if they try to move any of this stuff away from here.'

'So, what do you think they are doing?' asked Magda. 'What is worth killing people for – killing poor Ramon.'

'I think they've found a way to convert every man, woman and child on this planet to the Global Message Movement. Join us, repudiate your own religion, or we'll kill you.'

'Am I understanding you right?' said Eleanor. She had a fresh cigarette in her holder, but she didn't light it. 'You're talking about *germ warfare?*'

'What do you think all of this equipment is for – growing tomatoes?'

'Of course not. But how can one man make the world change its religion? Think of the Taliban. Most of them would rather die than convert to Christianity.'

'Sure. But look around you. It seems pretty plain to me that he thinks it's achievable. That's the difference between a man like Dennis Evelyn Branch and people like you and me. You and me, we'd think that the whole idea of trying to convert everybody in the world to the same fundamentalist religion was absurd. Impossible.

'But Dennis Evelyn Branch doesn't see it that way. As far as he's concerned, he's always right and anybody who disagrees with him is in the wrong. If he kills a few hundred people, then that will be *our* fault, for not recognizing his religion, for not giving him air time, for defying a direct instruction from God. You can't win with people like him. You can't reason with them. The only thing you can do is stop them. Dead.'

'So what now?' asked Magda.

'We have to keep on watching him, that's all. See where he moves all of this stuff.'

'I was afraid you were going to say that.'

'You don't have to stay if you don't want to. You can always go back home.'

'What then? Wait for them to find me? Wait for them to kill me?'

Conor took her arm. 'Come on,' he said. 'Let's get out of here before they come back. There's no point in tempting fate.'

They kept watch on 17 Hammerfestgata for over three weeks. By mid-September, the air was beginning to grow cold and the nights started to draw in. Occasionally they saw Dennis Evelyn Branch leaving the apartment block; and occasionally they saw the dark-haired woman and the man in the brown leather cap. But they never saw any of the boxes moved and they never saw any other visitors.

They began to grow frustrated and irritable with each other. Magda couldn't stand Eleanor's smoking and used to throw open the living-room windows every time she lit up. That hadn't been such a dramatic gesture when the weather was warm, but now the temperature was dropping daily, and whenever she opened the windows a chilly draft blew through the entire apartment.

The bland Norwegian food quickly became a daily punishment. Eleanor said that if she had to eat another pickled herring she would commit seppuku all over the *koldtbord*. They tried reindeer at the Restaurant Blom and salmon at Raymond's Mat Og Vinhus and in desperation they even went to a restaurant on Kirkeveien called Curry and Ketchup. The endless servings of fish and more fish and plain boiled potatoes sprinkled with dill made Conor long for a real Irish stew or a big pot of bacon and cabbage, or even some of Lacey's Swedish meatballs.

They played cards. Magda could read the Tarot and predicted that Eleanor would find the love of her life, while Conor was facing a critical and dangerous choice. As for herself? 'I have to decide if I want security or passion.'

'Supposing they do nothing for months?' Eleanor asked Conor, on the last day of September. It was 5:15 p.m. and already it was dark outside. They had noticed an air of encroaching gloom amongst all of the Norwegians they knew. At first they had laughed about it, but now they were beginning to feel the same way. Winter was coming: hours of darkness and sub-zero temperatures, and nothing to eat but fish. And no relief until May next year.

Conor said, 'They're going to make a move soon. I can feel it. If they weren't going to do anything, why did they ship in all those boxes? And that apartment

374

. . . how long is anybody going to stay in a place like that, with only a couple of changes of clothes?'

The next day, October 1, they sat for most of the day in the Café Baltazar talking to the owner, Bjornstjerne. He couldn't have been older than 35 or 36, but he was prematurely gray, with deep shadows under his pale blue eyes, and a scraggly little gray mustache. They had never told him why they had spent nearly every day for a whole month sitting in his café looking out of the window, and he had never asked.

'You like *gravet laks*?' he wanted to know.

'I think I've had enough fish for one lifetime,' said Eleanor.

'It's very good. You can have some to taste, for free. You're my best customers now.'

'You ever wondered what we're doing here?' Conor asked him.

'No business of mine. So long as you pay your bills.'

'Seriously – aren't you even curious?'

'Well,' said Bjornstjerne, with a wink, 'I think you could be spies.'

'In a way, yes. Almost right.'

'*Ja*? Spies? But what can you find to spy on, around here?'

'That apartment block, across the street. There are three Americans living there.'

'That's right, *ja*, I've seen them. They came in here two or three times. Just for a Coca-Cola and a sandwich. I thought they were strange. Not friendly.'

'I guess that just about sums them up.'

'You know them? I wanted to talk to them. My

375

apartment is upstairs here, you know, and they wake me up so many times. Always slamming their doors at two o'clock in the morning. Sometimes three o'clock.'

'Slamming their doors? What doors?'

'The doors of their van. Carrying boxes. Bringing boxes in. Taking boxes away.'

Conor thought: *shit*. No wonder we haven't seen them. They've been shifting their equipment in the early hours of the morning. And of course we haven't been able to keep up round-the-clock surveillance.

'Did you see them last night?'

'No, not last night. But the night before that. They made a lot of noise, and took away a lot of boxes. They drove off and I haven't seen them back since then.'

'It sounds like they're gone,' said Magda. 'How are we going to find them now?'

'I don't know. God, I wish I was still in the police department. I could ask the Oslo cops to trace that van's registration plate. I could lay my hands on their telephone records.'

'Maybe they left some kind of clue in their apartment,' Eleanor suggested. 'It would be worth taking a look.'

Conor checked his watch. 'Let's wait till it's dark. Bjornstjerne hasn't seen them come back, but they could have slipped in when he wasn't looking. The poor guy's got a business to run, after all.'

'You want another beer?' asked Bjornstjerne. 'How about some *gravet laks*? Just try a little. Best fish you ever tasted.'

★   ★   ★

They waited in the café until twilight. An evening mist turned the streetlights into thistledown. Nobody left the apartment block, nobody came to visit. At last Conor said, 'I'm going to have to risk it. I'm going to take a look inside.'

'What if Branch is still there?' asked Magda.

'Then I'll improvise. Maybe I'll make out that I want to join them. After all, if I've been accused of extorting all of that money, I might as well have my share of it.'

Eleanor took hold of his hand. 'You will be careful, won't you, Conor? I couldn't bear it if anything happened to you.'

He looked at her with a question in his eyes but she turned away and sat down, and gave him a brief, flickering smile.

'I should come with you,' said Magda. 'You know, back-up, that's what you say, isn't it?'

'OK . . . but do whatever I tell you to do. No grand gestures. You're not on the stage of the Shubert Theater, you're out on the streets.'

' "Down these mean streets a man must go, who is not himself mean," ' Eleanor quoted.

' "A man who is neither tarnished nor afraid," ' added Magda.

'Where did you learn that?' Conor asked her.

'Well, I have been in many places, done many things.'

Something about the way she said it made him feel that she was being evasive. All the same, he needed all the support he could get. He took her arm and they walked out of the Café Baltazar and across the street.

Apartment 206 was empty. All the boxes had gone, both of the beds were stripped. The china troll had been taken away and the wooden chair was tipped over on the floor.

Conor searched through every room. The closets were empty. There was nothing to indicate where Dennis Evelyn Branch and his associates might have gone. Not even a scribble on a scrap of paper.

Conor was still searching through the kitchen drawers when he heard the front door open. He paused and listened, and said, 'Magda? Is that you?'

Before Magda could answer, the man in the brown leather cap appeared in the kitchen doorway, pointing a small automatic pistol at him.

'Who are you? What do you do here? Put up your hands.'

26

'We were told this apartment was for rent,' said Conor. 'My wife and I just came around to take a look at it.'

The man's eyes darted suspiciously from side to side. 'It's not free. Somebody lives here still.'

'No,' said Conor, 'that can't be right. The rental agency told us that it was free from today.'

'Well, a mistake,' the man replied. 'You have to leave here now.'

'We've come a long way. All the way from Bergen. You're absolutely *sure* this isn't for rent?'

'A mistake, sorry.' The man put his gun back in his windcheater pocket. 'You will have to speak to the agent.'

At that moment Magda came into the kitchen. 'Well . . .' she smiled. 'Are you from the rental agency?'

'No, no. I was telling your husband. A mistake.'

'A *mistake?*' said Magda, with exaggerated shock.

'Seems like it isn't free,' Conor told her. 'This gentleman must have thought we were burglars or

379

something. We're really very sorry. I'll get back to the agents and tell them what klutzes they are.'

It was then that Conor really saw Magda at work: or, rather, Hetti. She reached out and clasped the man's hand in a handshake; while at the same time she touched his shoulder in the kind of gesture that only intimate friends would make.

'Maybe you forget something,' she said, in a voice as slippery as satin. 'What did you forget?'

The man stared at her and it was obvious from his eyes that she had completely hypnotized him. He swallowed, and then he said, 'I forgot my sweater. I left my sweater in the bottom of the closet.'

'So you have to get your sweater?'

'It's going to be very cold. I have to get my sweater.'

'Can *I* ask him questions?' Conor interrupted.

'Sure you can. Just make sure that they're very calm and inductive. Don't try to cross swords with him, if you know what I mean. He may wake up. Even worse, he may tell you a whole pack of lies. And – yes, before you ask – people *can* lie under hypnosis. Everybody is a storyteller, in their own way.'

Conor came closer. The young Norwegian had a pale, gummy-colored complexion, and a noticeable squint.

'So what's your name?' Conor asked him.

'Toralf Kielland.'

'That's a good name, Toralf. That's a name to be proud of.'

'My father's name.'

'So you forgot your sweater, Toralf?'

380

'*Ja*, it cost me a lot of money. It's the new Olympic design.'

'You could have left it here, couldn't you, if you're still living here?'

Toralf blinked in uncertainty. Magda said, 'Is this something you've been told to keep a secret?'

'Yes.' And in a different voice, whiplike, snappy, ' "*Don't say anything to anyone.*" '

'So what is it?' asked Magda. 'You're going away for a while?'

' "*Don't say anything to anyone.*" '

'Who was it, Toralf? Who told you not to say anything to anyone?'

'I don't remember. "*Don't say anything to anyone.*" '

'Listen to that accent,' put in Conor. ' "Don't say any-*thung* to *any – wern.*" Western Texas, if you ask me.'

Magda said, 'I want you to relax, Toralf. Right now you're worried. Right now you're feeling very tense. But if you let yourself go deeper, if you really relax, you won't have to worry about telling us anything. It won't be you at all. You – you'll be asleep. Your mind can talk to us by itself. Your mind trusts us, Toralf. Your mind knows that we can keep your secret perfectly safe.'

Toralf's eyes closed. His head tilted back a little. His mouth opened and he began to breathe deeply and harshly.

'Where are you going, Toralf?' Conor asked him. 'Why do you need to take your sweater?'

At first Toralf said nothing, but then Magda

approached him and took off his leather cap. She started to stroke his forehead with the tip of her middle finger, and ssh him. 'Where are you going, Toralf? Where are you taking all of those boxes? Mr Branch wouldn't mind you telling us. Dennis wants us to know. You want to please Mr Branch, don't you?'

'He says to call him Dennis. He says everybody is equal under God.'

'Well, he's quite right. You're equal and I'm equal and my friend here, he's equal, too. And because we're equal, he wants us to know what you know. He wants you to tell us where you're going.'

Toralf twitched his head and began to look agitated. As a precaution, Conor stepped forward and lifted the gun out of his pocket, a little Browning .22. It wasn't a guaranteed manstopper but you wouldn't want a bullet between the eyes. Magda raised one finger to indicate that he should stay as still as possible. She was taking him deeper and deeper and she didn't want his trance disrupted.

'Come on, Toralf. You don't want to keep Dennis waiting, do you? He wants you to tell us where you're going and he wants you to tell us quick.'

Toralf staggered and swayed. He swayed so much that Conor thought he was going to fall over. He opened his mouth three or four times without saying anything, but then he whispered, '*Tromso.*'

'You're going to Tromso? That's way up north. I mean, that's way, *way* up north. Why are you going to Tromso?'

'God told Dennis what he must do. Dennis has to go to Tromso.'

382

'And why does Dennis have to go to Tromso?'

'To find the sword. Dennis has to find the sword.'

'The sword? What sword?'

Toralf extended both arms as if he were holding a double-handed broadsword and made a sweeping gesture from side to side. 'The sword of the angels. To cut down the sinners.'

'Are you going to Tromso, too?'

'Of course. Dennis has promised to give me the glory.'

'Kid's brainwashed,' said Conor. 'Swords, angels, glory. Jesus Christ. Ask him how he's getting to Tromso.'

'We fly,' said Toralf. 'Dennis chartered a plane from Wideroe. We leave twenty-one hundred. *"Don't say anything to anyone."* '

'I don't think he's going to tell us much more,' said Magda. 'I don't think he *knows* much more.'

'In that case you'd better wake him up and send him on his way.'

Magda leaned close to Toralf's ear and whispered something to him. Conor paced around the empty apartment feeling tired and gritty-eyed and angry at himself for allowing Dennis Evelyn Branch to escape him so easily. At least they knew where he was going, but they still didn't know for sure what he intended to do, or how close he was to doing it. What was the sword, to cut down the sinners? And where did Dennis Evelyn Branch think that he was going to find it?

'When I count to three, you will wake up,' Magda told Toralf. 'One – two – three – you're awake!'

Toralf opened his eyes, and immediately smiled at

them. 'Well,' he said, cheerfully, 'I'm sorry I disturbed you. I'd better pick up my sweater and get going.'

He went into the bedroom, whistling a little tune. He came back with his sweater under his arm and shook them both by the hand. Conor looked at Magda and shook his head in disbelief.

'Come on, we'd better leave, too,' said Conor, once Toralf had gone. 'It looks like we're on our way to Tromso tomorrow.'

They waited for the elevator to come back up. Conor said, 'What did you say to him?'

'I told him to forget he ever saw us, and I told him to forget he ever had a gun.'

'And he will?'

'Of course. One of my greatest talents is post-hypnotic suggestion. I could hypnotize a man, and then three weeks later, at precisely four o'clock, I could make him prick his finger with a pin.'

They stepped out of the apartment building into the street. There was a black VW Jetta parked at the curb. It hadn't been there when they first arrived, so presumably it was Toralf's. Conor looked left and right and saw Toralf with his shoulders hunched, walking toward Trondheimsveien.

'Where the hell is he going?'

Magda shrugged and turned away. There was something about the way she did it that aroused Conor's suspicions. He took hold of her shoulder and demanded, 'Where's he going, Magda? What have you told him to do?'

'I told him nothing. What do you think I am?'

Conor hesitated for a second. Then he started

384

walking quickly after Toralf, shouting out his name. 'Conor – leave him!' called Magda, but Conor shouted, '*Toralf!*' yet again, and broke into a jog.

Toralf had almost reached the intersection with Trondheimsveien. Conor was only 50 feet behind him, but he didn't seem to hear. Without hesitation, he stepped off the curb and walked into the traffic. It wasn't heavy, but it was fast. Two cars blared their horns at him and another skidded wildly sideways to avoid hitting him.

Conor reached the curb. '*Toralf!*' he yelled. '*Toralf, wake up!*'

But Toralf was oblivious to everything around him. A bus was approaching with the sign JERBANE-TORGET on the front. The driver blew his horn and flashed his lights. But instead of carrying on walking, Toralf stopped, and faced it.

'*Toralf!*' Conor roared at him. But the bus hit him with a crunching thud, and he flew across the street, arms and legs flying, almost as if he were turning celebratory cartwheels. He ended up in the gutter, face down, and by the time Conor reached him his blood was already flowing down a drain. A middle-aged woman was kneeling beside him, one hand helplessly stretched out above his head.

'Don't touch him,' Conor warned her, taking out his phone. 'What's the emergency number?'

'For ambulance, 113.'

Magda had reached him by now. The bus had pulled over to the side of the road and most of the passengers had disembarked and were shuffling around in silent shock. Conor looked up at Magda and said, 'He's dead.'

'Yes,' she replied, with a challenging stare. 'Like Ramon.'

Conor stood up. 'Did you do this?' he demanded.

Magda gave him the ghost of a smile. 'Even if I did, how could you possibly prove it?'

As they flew even further northward, the sun began to set, until it was nothing more than a faint halo of orange light behind the clouds. By the time they crossed the Arctic Circle it was dark, and it was only 4:35 p.m.

Eleanor slept most of the way. Their pursuit of Dennis Evelyn Branch was beginning to take its toll on her, and this morning Conor had tried to persuade her to stay behind in Oslo, or even to go back to New York. But she was adamant. 'I've never given up on anything I've set out to do, not ever, and I'm not going to start now. Besides.'

'Besides what?'

'Just besides, that's all.'

Magda drank two vodka-tonics and stared out of the window at the gathering gloom. 'This is like the end of the world,' she said. 'The place where the Snow Queen and Santa Claus live.'

Conor didn't answer. He was still angry at Magda for Toralf's death. The longer he stayed with her, the less he seemed to know her. Her personality was all shadows and reflections. Yet she was very alluring in a strange, outdated way. He could imagine her in Paris in the days of Toulouse-Lautrec, or Berlin in the 1930s.

He tried to read the NorskAir brochure from the seat-pocket in front of him, but it had a special

Norwegian dullness all its own. 'Massive erosion during the Ice Age scoured the fiords and the lakes, which are the deepest in Europe, and formed a scattering of islands along the coast, over one hundred and fifty thousand of them. There is a treacherous tidal current between the islands, the Maelstrom, which was said in legend to suck ships down to the bottom of the sea.

'Along with storms, avalanches and floods, such dangerous natural phenomena led to a wealth of supernatural stories about trolls and giants. Norse mythology also had its destructive gods, like Thor, with his mighty hammer; and Woden, who took the bravest of the dead from the battlefield so that they could enjoy an afterlife of feasting in Valhalla, the Hall of the Slain.

'Most of all, the Norwegian imagination was stimulated by the long dark winters, when story-telling was the only form of entertainment.'

They circled the island of Tromso – a sparse scattering of lights in the Arctic darkness. As they came in to land, the plane was buffeted by a gusty east wind – a wind that blew all the way from northern Russia. The ground crew who waved the aircraft on to its stand were bundled up like polar explorers.

Inside the small terminal building, it was uncomfortably warm and glaringly lit. A few passengers were sitting around waiting for flights to Stavanger or Bergen – miners in jeans and reindeer sweaters and tired-looking businessmen in fur-collared parkas. There was also a family of Sami, or Lapps, in traditional costume, their faces burnished by a lifetime of summer sun and winter cold.

'Where do we go from here?' asked Eleanor, lighting a cigarette and inhaling deeply.

'First of all we find out where Branch and his people are staying.'

'Oh, yes? And how do we do that?'

Conor walked across to the Wideroe airline desk, where a blond girl in a gray sweater was laughing with a balding, dark-haired man.

'Excuse me . . . I'm looking for a customer of mine. He flew up here today from Oslo. I was supposed to give him some schematics for his equipment but I was held up in traffic and I missed him.'

'What name?' asked the girl, checking her computer screen.

'Branch. Dennis Evelyn Branch. But he may have been traveling under his company name, GMM.'

The girl rattled her keyboard. 'Sorry. There was nobody on that flight called Branch. No GMM, either.'

'Well, he had a whole lot of equipment with him. Boxes. Laboratory glassware, that kind of stuff.'

'Oh, *ja*,' the man put in. 'I remember him. The handlers dropped one of the boxes and there was a big argument. They had to fill out insurance forms, all that kind of thing.' He went to a gray steel filing cabinet behind the desk and pulled out the second drawer. 'Here it is . . . William Graham. Northern Scientific, s.a.'

What a nerve, thought Conor. *An evangelist extremist traveling under the pseudonym 'Billy Graham'.*

'Do you have an address?' he asked.

'Sure. Breivika Havnegata 22.' He took out a map

of Tromso island and pointed to it.

'One more favor,' said Conor. 'Can you recommend a good hotel?'

Outside the terminal building it was so chilly that Eleanor wrapped her scarf around the lower part of her face, so that only her eyes looked out. The wind made a thin, penetrating noise like somebody whistling between their teeth. All three of them had invested in winter coats and scarves and gloves before they left Oslo. It wouldn't be long before northern Norway was plunged into months of cold and overwhelming darkness.

A taciturn taxi driver in a dirty white bobble-hat took them to the Walhalla Hotel. He continued to hold out the palm of his hand until he considered that Conor had given him a sufficient gratuity. He even handed back 73 öre, which he obviously considered to be an insult.

'Asshole,' said Eleanor, vindictively, as he drove away; and both Conor and Magda looked at her in surprise. 'Well,' she shrugged. 'You don't stop having opinions, when you grow older.'

The Walhalla had been described by the girl at the Wideroe desk as the 'finest hotel in Tromso'. It was a bland 1970s building with a wooden-floored lobby and a row of subtly lit alcoves containing painted murals of northern Norway: reindeer, Lapps, the Jostedalsbreen glacier, and the North Cape, the *Nordkapp*, the very extremity of Europe.

There was a Troll Bar with fake icicles and trolls and a Viking Restaurant with a longship and shields. Conor could see guests helping themselves from the usual *koldtbord*, as well as *fiskebollor* and *lutefisk* – fish marinaded in lye – which he had already decided was a challenge to the palate rather than a meal.

They were checked in by a man in a brown nylon shirt who never smiled. Eleanor went directly to her room for a shower. 'I'm bushed,' she said, kissing Conor on the cheek. 'I'll see you in the morning,' she said, tenderly. Conor went along to his own room and unpacked, and then went down to meet Magda in the Troll Bar. He couldn't think of sleeping, not just yet. His head felt as if it were full of broken glass. By the time he got there, Magda was already sitting on one of the hairy reindeer-hide barstools, dressed in a tight black turtleneck sweater and tight black leggings, flirting with a huge muscleman with cropped blond hair and eyes like the arrow slits in a medieval castle.

'Conor – this is Birger. He's an iron miner.'

Conor shook hands. 'How's it going, Birger?'

'Well, sir, winter's coming. Very depressing.'

'So, what's the answer to that?'

'Two answers. Women, and *akvavit*.'

'Ha! Ha!' said Magda, and slapped his shoulder.

'Actually, I don't usually stay for the winter. I go to Italy, to work in the iron mines. The pay's not so good but the weather's warmer.'

'So what's holding you back this year?'

'There's a rumor going around that somebody wants a special job done, and that they're prepared to pay three times the going rate, plus a five thousand krone bonus if it's finished on time.'

'Oh, yes? What special job?'

'I don't know exactly. Up north.'

390

They were already 210 miles north of the Arctic Circle, and Conor found the idea of going even further 'up north' to be almost unimaginable.

'It's some kind of excavation,' said Birger. 'They approached another miner I know. They said they were looking for men who didn't have families and who didn't mind taking a risk.'

Conor beckoned to the waitress. 'What's it to be? *Akvavit?*'

'Well, no, I'll have a Budweiser if you don't mind.'

'Make that two,' said Conor. Then he turned to Birger and said, 'These people . . . the ones who want this excavation done. Do you have any idea who they are?'

Birger shook his head, but said, 'My friend said they're new here in Tromso. This is not such a small city, forty thousand people, but the herring people know everything that's happening in the harbor and the canneries; and the teaching people know everything that's happening at the university; and the holy people know everything that's happening at the cathedral. The people who study the Aurora Borealis – well, they're a little bit cuckoo but they know everything that's happening at the place where they keep a watch on the Northern Lights. So you only have to know one of each of them and you know everything that's happening in the whole of Tromso.'

'Do you think you could ask your friend where I could contact them?'

Birger swallowed his beer, leaving himself with a foam mustache. 'Why do you want to know? You don't look much like a miner.'

'Me? No. But I have a lot of experience when it comes to digging.'

'Ah! Archeologist!'

'Something like that.'

*   *   *

Conor and Magda had an early dinner together in the Aurora Restaurant. Candles twinkled on every table in red glass lamps, and a trio played plangent instrumental versions of old Barbra Streisand songs. A fresh-faced young waitress with thick ankles asked Conor if he would like to try *molje*, one of northern Norway's specialties, but it turned out to be fish, liver and cod's roe, and Conor decided against it.

Instead he chose a plateful of fried Sami reindeer with mashed potato, mountain cranberries and gravy, which was the most appetizing meal he had eaten since he arrived in Norway. Magda had a small salad with eggs and beetroot and yellow cloudberries.

Conor said, 'I asked the desk clerk for a weather forecast. The temperature tomorrow is supposed to be way up in the threes.'

'They always say that revenge tastes better when it's cold.'

'I find it difficult to believe that revenge is all you want out of this. You weren't exactly complimentary about Ramon, after all.'

'It doesn't matter what I thought about Ramon. Nobody should be allowed to murder him and get away with it. Anyhow, I want the money that I was promised.'

'And how much was that?'

'If everything went well, a million.'

392

'You know that if I manage to retrieve the money, it'll have to go back to the people who paid it.'

'One pathetic little million won't make a difference. Or even two pathetic little millions. One for me and one for you. You deserve it, don't you think, after everything that's happened to you? You've lost your home, your job, your freedom.'

She reached across the checkered tablecloth and held his hand. Her fingers were cold, her silver rings colder still. 'You've even lost your woman.'

They held each other's gaze for a long, long time. Conor wasn't at all sure what it meant; or what he felt about her. But then she smiled and looked away and said, 'I'd better go to bed. We have some bad men to find in the morning, don't we?'

27

Breivika Havnegata 22 turned out to be one of half a dozen single-story wooden buildings in a small scrubby industrial park three miles north of the city center, next to a junior school. The children were out in the playground with their woolly hats and gloves, screaming and laughing. Through the birch trees, Conor could see the slate-black water of Tromsoysundet, the fiord that separated Tromso from the mainland. The air was chilly and the sky was a milky pearl.

He walked casually past the front of number 22. Three rental cars were parked outside it, two new Volvo S80s and a Saab GT Turbo. The building's windows were blanked out with pale yellow venetian blinds, and the only sign on the door was a weathered cardboard notice which obviously told callers that Kjell Bertinussen Silkscreen Printers had moved to Trondheim. He walked on to the next building, Arvid Sveen Foto, and climbed the wooden steps to the front door. As he went inside he glanced back to the entrance to the industrial park, where Eleanor and Magda were waiting in their own rental car, a dark green Opel.

Eleanor gave him a wave.

Inside the building, a middle-aged woman with elaborate braids and glass-brick eyeglasses greeted him in Norwegian. There was a strong smell of developing fluid around; and through a half-open door, Conor caught sight of a pretty blond girl in another room, working on a digital photo-scanner. In profile she reminded him so much of Lacey that he stopped; and for a moment he was disoriented and didn't hear what the receptionist was saying to him.

'I'm sorry,' he said. 'You speak English?'

'Yes, a little. Yes.'

'I've been looking for Kjell Bertinussen, the printers.'

'Before, they were here,' the woman explained, pointing in the direction of the next building. 'But no more. They have gone. Five, six months. I'm sorry I don't know the telephone number.'

'Maybe I should go next door and ask them.'

'Next door they never open.'

'I'm sorry?'

'They never open. They come, they go. But they never open.' She made a knocking gesture; and then she shrugged.

'I see. Do you know what they do? Do you know what they make?'

'I don't know. I don't know.' She pulled a face to indicate that she didn't like them and she didn't want anything to do with them.

It was then that the pretty blond girl appeared at the door. She had the same clear eyes as Lacey, the same strong Scandinavian face. She wore a pale blue skinny-ribbed sweater with a silver charm necklace hanging around her neck, and a very short navy blue skirt.

'Excuse me, do you have a difficulty?' she wanted to know.

'Hey – nothing really. I was looking for the printers who used to work out of the building next door. Just a few brochures. Nothing special.'

'Oh, yes?' She looked as if she didn't believe him.

'I was wondering if the people next door might be able to tell me where they've gone.'

'Not them. They won't tell you anything.'

'Oh, no?'

'They won't speak to anybody. We try to be friendly when they first come here. We take them cakes and coffee. They tell us, *vuff*! stay away. That's a polite translation. They told us to mind our own business.'

'That's too bad. Maybe they'll talk to me.'

'I don't think so. I don't know what they're doing in there, but they don't want anybody to know what it is.'

'Any ideas?'

The girl came up to the counter. She had a small pattern of pale freckles across the bridge of her nose, and Conor could see that she had been biting her fingernails.

'It's some kind of research. I think biological. When they first start I can see inside their laboratory from my window at the back but now it's all covered up. I see monkeys in cages. White rats, too. Even a dog once. Then one night when I am working late there is a big, big panic. I can see them run around and I can hear them shout. After a while comes a van and parks very close to the door but I see them carry out a man on a stretcher. Maybe he's dead, maybe not. I can't tell for sure and I think it's more wisdom not to ask.'

'Anything else?'

'Yes . . . they are very busy this week. Cars and vans coming and going. Big boxes and cases and lights, too, like they make movies with. I try to make a joke about the noise to one of the men, but they don't joke, those people. Whatever it is they're doing, it's very serious.'

Conor produced his ID picture of Dennis Evelyn Branch. 'You seen anybody who looks like this?'

She frowned at it and shook her head. 'No. But they're all different people, and sometimes they hide their faces with the scarf or the ski-mask. There is also one person in a wheelchair. Always covered with a blanket. Not a big person, maybe a child or a woman.'

A woman? Conor thought about the woman in Dennis Evelyn Branch's apartment in Oslo, who had never been seen, but who had been heard shouting. He put the photo back in his wallet. 'Can I ask you something? Can I ask you when these people finish up at night?'

'Very late, mostly. Once we have an urgent job here and we don't finish till midnight. They are still there when we leave. And they start very early, too. They're always here before I am. Always.'

'Given a guess, what do you think they're actually doing in there?'

'You're not looking for Kjell Bertinussen, are you?' she challenged him. 'You're interested only in them.'

Conor didn't say anything, but he gave her his reply with his eyes.

'Well,' she said, 'you can find out what they're doing in there very easily.'

'Oh, yes? And how would I do that?'

She went back to her desk and took out a small brown envelope. She dropped it into the palm of his hand. Inside was the key to a five-lever deadlock.

'Ivar Bertinussen gives it to me, when he goes. You know, in case the pipes burst, or somebody wants to look at the building.'

'And you're prepared to give this to me? How do you know I'm not a thief?'

She smiled. 'You're not a thief. You have a good man's face.'

'Tell me your name,' said Conor.

'Ola Bergsmo.'

'Well, Ola Bergsmo, I want to let you know that you may have done the whole world a very great service by giving me this key.'

'I don't like them, those men, that's all. And I think that they are making experiments on animals. I hate people who make animals suffer. I believe in kindness to every living creature. I am a vegetarian, and I never wear a fur coat, only natural fiber.'

Conor thought of the reindeer he had eaten for last night's supper. 'Glad to hear it,' he told her. 'These days, most people don't believe in anything.'

★　　★　　★

That night, Conor drove out to Breivika Havnegata shortly after 10 p.m. and parked in the shadow of the school bicycle shed. The lights at number 22 were still shining through the venetian blinds, and the three cars were still parked outside.

The temperature was only 1 degree, and after half an hour most of the warmth inside the Opel had dissipated. Conor couldn't run the engine in case somebody heard it, or saw the exhaust fumes billowing out.

At eight minutes to eleven, a man in a black hooded windbreaker came out of the building, hurried down the steps, climbed into the Saab Turbo and drove quickly away, its tires squealing, heading in the direction of Terminalveien. Conor wiped the condensation off the inside of the windshield. Maybe the rest of them would be leaving soon. He felt as if he would never be warm again.

A few minutes after 1 a.m., the front door of the building opened and a wide triangle of yellow light fell across the road. It was closed again; and then reopened. Two men came out carrying a large cardboard box, which they stored inside the back of one of the Volvos. They stood talking for a while, and then they went back inside.

By 2.30 a.m. it was clear that nobody else was going to leave the building, not tonight. He started the Opel's engine and drove out of the industrial park as quietly as he could, although he was sure that he saw somebody parting the venetian blinds and peering out into the darkness.

399

They met Birger in the Troll Bar at lunchtime. He was looking pleased with himself and he bought them all a drink.

'My friend called me and we went together to the Radisson Hotel to meet the people who want to make the excavation. Very strange, all of them. They were all wearing black and some of them had crosses around their necks, like priests. They asked me a lot of questions. Did I have a family? Did I have insurance? Where did I live? They even wanted to know my blood group.'

'How many were there?'

'Five, altogether. One looked as if he was the boss man but he sat in a corner and didn't speak.'

Conor produced his picture of Dennis Evelyn Branch. 'Did he look anything like this?'

Birger held it close to the table lamp. 'Yes. Very white face, very white hair. And little blue sunglasses. Where did you get this? Do you *know* these people?'

'Did they give you the job?'

'You bet. Why do you think I'm buying drinks? Ten thousand krone a day, for however long it takes. Plus everything found – food, someplace to stay. Plus the bonus at the end of it.'

'That's good money. Worth postponing your trip to Italy. Where are they going to be digging?'

'I'm sorry. I'm not supposed to tell you that. They said this was a very secret expedition, something to do with NATO. Nobody must know where we're going.'

'Can't you give us a tiny little clue?' asked

Magda, leaning toward him and picking a loose thread from his brown checkered shirt.

Birger said, 'Sorry. They said anybody who talked about the expedition would be fired, snap! just like that.'

Magda glanced at Conor and he knew what she had in mind. She ran her finger all the way down Birger's sleeve and stroked his hand. 'You must be so excited about going so far.'

'Well, it's not so far, really.'

'Is it north or is it south?'

'North.'

'Oh, dear . . . even colder. Will there be polar bears?'

Magda kept stroking Birger's hand and his trance was gradually deepening, but all the same she was waiting until he was well under her control before she asked him the critical question: what was the name of the place he was going to? Branch's people had specifically asked him not to reveal it, and Conor knew that a dramatic conflict of instructions could easily awaken him.

'When are you leaving, Birger? Is it very soon?'

'Tomorrow morning. Seven-thirty sharp. As soon as it's light.'

'How will you go? By ship, perhaps? Or airplane? Or maybe by train?'

Birger was about to answer when a girl in a maroon suit marched into the bar and called out, 'Mr Storvik! Mr Storvik! Telephone for Mr Storvik!'

Instantly, Birger's eyes blinked into focus and he stared at Magda as if he had never seen her before in his life. 'What?' Birger said, in bewilderment.

'Mr Storvik! Telephone!'

'That's me,' he said, blundering to his feet.

'You can take it at the bar,' smiled the girl, and went marching off. Conor, Eleanor and Magda waited while he talked, his head nodding as he did so. Eventually he came back and said, 'You'll have to excuse me. I have to go now. They want to fit me for some protective clothing.'

Conor stood up and shook his hand. 'Good luck, Birger. Let's hope you don't need it.'

'Ah, but think of all that money!' Birger retorted, rubbing his hands.

'So they're going tomorrow morning and it's some-place further north but we don't know where it is or why they're going there.'

'Yes,' said Conor. 'But if Birger and his pals are going to need protective clothing, then it must have something to do with this biohazard that Victor Labrea kept on talking about.'

'You need protective clothing for all manner of things,' said Eleanor. 'Cold, heat, radioactivity, acids, soil pollution, *water* pollution—'

'All right, I think we get the picture. If only I could get into that goddamned building and see what they're doing there.'

Magda said, 'If they never answer their door we can't hypnotize them or use burundanga.'

'You brought some burundanga with you?'

'Only a little. We didn't have very much left. But you never know . . . I thought it might be useful.'

'Well, I suggest something theatrical,' said

Eleanor, lighting another cigarette. 'A spectacular diversion, to keep our friends busy while Conor gets into the building.'

'What exactly do you propose?' asked Magda. 'That I walk up and down Lofotgate with nothing on?'

'That would work,' said Conor.

They had lunch in the Domus Café overlooking the harbor. Across the sound they could see the snow-covered peak of Storsteinen, with its cable cars climbing up and down like tiny spiders. It was a weird, blue, half-lit day – not as blue as the time in the middle of the winter when the sun sinks below the horizon for two months on end – '*morketia*' – with only the moon and the snow to see by – but unsettling all the same.

By the time they reached Breivika Havnegata it was growing dark, and a chilly southeasterly wind was blowing. The two Volvos and the Saab were parked outside, as well as two white panel vans.

They parked out of sight behind a red-painted boatshed. Magda gave Conor the small foil package of burundanga. 'If you have to use it, make sure you blow it well away from you, hard, directly into the person's face. Make sure you don't breathe any of it yourself, or else you'll be playing zombies, too.'

Conor climbed out of the car and walked toward number 22. He stood at the side of the building, out of sight of the windows and the front door. Magda shifted over to the driver's seat, while Eleanor stuffed up the sleeve of her coat a long strip of candystriped cotton, torn from a hotel pillowcase. 'You know, I've always wanted to do this,' she smiled. 'They did it in the movie version of *Scarface & Son*. You couldn't have done it on the stage, of course.'

'Eleanor – be very careful, Eleanor,' Magda warned her. 'These people will kill you without even thinking twice.'

'I'll be careful, dear. I have a very special reason to be careful.'

She eased herself out of the car, buttoning up her thick black coat, and then reached back inside for the thin brass-capped walking-stick which they had bought that afternoon in a souvenir shop. She began to walk toward number 22 with an exaggerated hobble, using the stick to support herself. The venetian blind was parted by two fingers and two eyes stared out, but Eleanor looked no more threatening than any other old biddy with arthritic knees, and after a moment's hesitation the blind snapped shut.

Eleanor passed so close to Conor that he could have touched her arm, but she didn't even glance at him. She stepped off the curb and made her way between the two parked Volvos. She paused beside the one on her left – her back turned to the building to hide what she was doing, in case anybody decided to take a second look at her. With a narrow penknife blade, she sprang the lock on the filler cap: she had practised on nine similar Volvos in the parking tunnel in the city center. Then she pulled the long strip of pillowcase out of her sleeve and pushed it into the fuel tank, using the walking-stick like a ramrod to push it well down. She left only two inches of cotton protruding. Then she closed the cover and hobbled off.

Her walk didn't take her far. She circled behind the birch trees, and in three or four minutes – once the cotton was saturated in gas – she came hobbling back. She looked around to make sure that nobody was watching. Then she reopened the cover and forced her walking-stick into the tank to keep its protective flap wide open. She flipped her lighter and touched it against the cotton wick.

Her hobble suddenly became a very hurried walk. Her walk became a jog. A long tongue of orange flame streamed out of the Volvo's gas tank. It grew higher and higher and it began to make a fierce roaring noise like a blowtorch. The parking lot became brightly illuminated and orange reflections danced on every window around.

From inside number 22 Conor heard a yelp like a trodden-on dog. The door was flung open and a man came jumping down the steps. He tried to approach the Volvo but the heat was already overwhelming and its rear windows cracked and popped. 'Shit!' he kept shouting. 'Shit, shit, shit!'

Two more men burst out onto the steps. 'Go get the goddamned fire extinguisher!' one of them yelled. American, without a doubt, and a Southerner by the way he said '*fah*'. He turned in the lurid light of the burning car and Conor saw the deathly white face of Dennis Evelyn Branch.

'My wallet's in there!' the first man screamed. 'My passport, my traveler's checks! Everything! My clothes!'

One of the men dragged out a fire extinguisher. He

broke the seal and started to spray water all over the rear end of the blazing Volvo. The fire instantly spat and jumped, and the man on the steps screamed, 'Not water! You can't use water! Don't you know shit?'

Another man emerged. 'That car's going to blow! Get that van out of here, pronto!'

The next second, the Volvo's gas tank exploded. Although he was hidden around the side of the building, Conor could feel the huge hot blast of expanding air. A fiery plastic bumper was thrown high into the air, and landed in the parking lot more than thirty feet away. Fragments of metal and glass came showering down everywhere. A burning door landed in a tree, and continued to burn, shriveling the leaves. The man with the fire extinguisher was blown to the ground with his shirt on fire. He was kicking and screaming, 'Put me out! Put me out!' Another man thumped at his back with the doormat from the building's front steps.

The second Volvo was burning now; and so was the van. 'You're going to have to call 110!' shouted a voice that sounded Norwegian.

'What, are you crazy? And have the whole place crawling with cops?'

'You don't think that somebody's going to call the fire service anyhow? Look at this place, it's like daylight!'

'I don't believe it,' said Dennis Evelyn Branch. 'I can see it with my own eyes, but I just don't believe it. Marcus – how much equipment we got in that van?'

'Ten bio suits, three two-way radios, a whole stack

of containment boxes, a couple of Nikons. General stuff, like body bags and candy bars.'

'O Lord, what did I do to deserve this punishment?' Dennis Evelyn Branch appealed, in a high, hysterical voice. 'O Lord, I'm begging of you now, if you want me to do your work, then send down a storm of rain. Send down a hailstorm if you have to. But put out this fire, Lord, any way you will. For my sake. For your sake.'

There was a moment's pause. Dennis Evelyn Branch cried out, '*Please*, Lord!' but the Lord wasn't impressed. The panel van blew up with an ear-splitting bang and tumbled backward across the parking lot, over and over. The second Volvo blew up, too, jumping sideways into a border filled with flowering shrubs. The shrubs immediately caught fire like the burning bush in the Bible, and so did the wood-chippings in the border, with a strong whiff of barbecue. A single blazing wheel rolled drunkenly away toward the trees and disappeared from sight.

The heat from the three burning vehicles was immense. They groaned and crackled and splintered. The men stood and watched them, shielding their faces with their hands.

'This here, this is arson,' Dennis Evelyn Branch declared. 'Don't you try to tell me this wasn't arson. Don't no vehicle catch on fire spontaneous. What, *whamm!* just like that? I don't think so. This here's somebody with a deliberate intention to prevent us from doing the Lord's work, passing on His holy message, you believe me.'

'Believe you, reverend,' said the man beside him.

In the distance, Conor heard the braying-donkey

noise of Norwegian firetrucks. He looked out and saw that the Southerner and his companions were all preoccupied with their blazing cars. He took a deep breath, and then he risked it: mounting the steps toward the building three at a time. He reached the door, put his hand on the doorhandle, and it was locked.

Don't panic, he told himself. *And whatever you do, don't look around.*

He took the key out of his pocket, jabbed it in the lock, twisted, and stepped inside. None of the men turned around: they were all too busy with the burning chaos in the parking lot.

Inside the building there was a plain reception lobby, much like the building next door, except that this one was stacked with dozens of boxes and wooden crates. Behind the desk a large-scale map of northern Norway had been pinned, from Narvik to Spitsbergen, with a criss-cross pattern of red ribbons stretched across it with thumbtacks.

Conor studied the map closely, but so many towns and villages were marked that it was impossible for him to work out where tomorrow's destination was. He left the lobby and pushed his way through a heavy wooden fire-door. He found himself in a short corridor with three more doors leading off it to the left.

He tried the first door but it was locked. The second door opened into a storeroom, where more boxes were stacked, as well as assorted oddments of lighting equipment and reels of heavy-duty electrical cable. The third door took him into a brightly lit laboratory.

He closed the door behind him and took a look around. There were workbenches along two walls and two more parallel benches in the center, both of them crowded with chemical glassware, gas burners, binocular microscopes, gas chromograph spectrometers, two top-of-the-range IBM computers and rows and rows of test-tubes.

There was a smell of chemicals and animals. On the workbench opposite stood a dozen wire cages. Only two of them were occupied: one by three white rats, and the other by a small rhesus monkey which appeared to be asleep or drugged. Conor peered into the cage and said, '*Psst!*' but the monkey didn't stir.

The far wall had another door in it, and a large unlit window. Conor approached the window and shaded his eyes with his hand so that he could see inside. There was another room, much smaller, with a single iron-framed bed in it, and a plain desk with a desklamp and a wooden chair.

He tried the door. This, too, was locked – and with a much more sophisticated lock. It was stenciled with the single word QUARANTINE. So Magda had been right about the biohazard. The question was: what kind of biohazard was it?

He made a quick search of all the drawers and filing cabinets, although he didn't really know what he was looking for. He tore a sheet of paper off a pad and copied down the labels of all the test-tubes. Even if he didn't understand what he had found, a biologist might.

There were two plain cardboard folders on the workbench, too. He flicked through them but they were crammed, in tiny handwriting, with biological formulae. He jotted down their titles. *Apia* and *Longyearbyen.*

He was taking a last look around when the door opened. One of the men was standing there, a tall Norwegian, his face reddened by the heat of the burning cars.

'Who the hell are you?' he demanded. 'Who let you in here?'

Conor held out his hand. 'Hi. Sorry to keep you so long.'

'What are you talking about? I don't know you from Adam.'

'Sure you do. Don't you remember that time in Oslo?'

'I don't know what the hell you're talking about. You can't come in here.'

Conor took hold of his hand and gripped it tight. Then he slowly released it, sliding his fingers away in the way that Sidney had taught him. 'You remember. It was summer. The sun was shining. You met me at that café on Stortorvet. You said you could always trust me. You still trust me, don't you?'

The man blinked at him, uncertain. Conor didn't know if he had managed to put him into any kind of trance or not. He might simply have been confused. The firetrucks had arrived outside and there was shouting and clattering.

'Listen, I have to leave you for a moment,' said Conor. 'You feel quite relaxed standing there, don't you? You don't mind waiting because it'll give you time to think about yourself. You've been under stress lately, haven't you? You need to spend some time working out your problems.'

410

He laid his hand on the man's shoulder. The man stared at him with green, troubled eyes. His eyebrows were as blond as a pig's. For one long second, Conor thought that he was going to hit him. But then he stepped back and allowed Conor to pass.

'Just remember . . . think about relaxing. Think about clearing your mind. Your problems – they're like a messy tangled-up bundle of string. Try to unravel it.'

He walked back along the corridor leaving the Norwegian standing obediently in the doorway. He opened the front door and it was still pandemonium outside. Three firetrucks had turned up, and firefighters were spraying foam all over the wreckage of the two Volvos and the burning van. Foam blew in the wind and caught in the bushes. Police had just arrived, too, and two of them were talking to Dennis Evelyn Branch. Branch half turned toward Conor as he left the building, but then one of the policemen must have asked him a question because he turned away again.

'Well?' asked Eleanor breathlessly, as Conor climbed back into the car. 'Wasn't that just *spectacular?*'

'You should get a job in special effects,' said Conor.

Magda started the engine and turned the Opel around. 'Did you get what you wanted?'

'Not exactly. I didn't really have enough time. But I've noted down the names of some of the chemicals they're using and the titles of a couple of files. I'm hoping that they may be able to help us.'

'Maybe I should try hypnotizing Birger again.'

411

'Yes, maybe. But don't worry. We'll think of something.'

'Well, I hope it involves blowing up more cars,' said Eleanor. 'I haven't enjoyed myself so much in *years*.'

28

They called Birger's room six or seven times that evening, but there was no reply. They even went up and knocked on the door. 'Maybe he's checked out already,' said Eleanor. Magda shook her head. 'He's probably spending the night with some whore, celebrating his new job. Men, you know? Sometimes they disgust me.'

The next morning Eleanor checked with all of the air carriers – Braathens, Norving, NorskAir and Wideroe – but none of them had a private charter flight out of Tromso to any destination to the north. She called Troms Fylkes Dampskibsselskap, too, the main shipping company, and they were equally unhelpful.

Conor said, 'We're going to lose our grip on this situation, unless we do something fast.'

Magda picked the cloudberries out of her cornflakes, and arranged them around the edge of her plate. 'So what do you suggest? We send out sniffer dogs?'

'Better than that. What's the time? I'm going up to the university and see if there's somebody who can tell me what these chemicals are, and what these names mean.'

'Do you want me to come with you?' asked Eleanor.

'Sure . . . that would be nice. Magda, why don't you call the auto rental concessions? Check if anybody rented out a panel van and a couple of cars? You could always pretend that you were some secretary, and that one of your bosses had left something behind – you know, a briefcase full of urgent documents, something like that.'

'You want me to be a *secretary*?' said Magda, haughtily.

'If it helped us to find what Dennis Evelyn Branch is up to, I'd expect you to be a restroom attendant.'

'Oh, I see. While you and Eleanor go off to the university to rub shoulders with the intelligentsia?'

Conor took hold of her (very cold) hand. 'Magda . . . we have to find these people. God knows what's going to happen if we don't.'

Professor Jorn Haraldsen welcomed them into an office that was almost psychotically tidy. It had a large bright window overlooking a sculpture garden, in which several hefty stone women stood around as if they were waiting for somebody to bring them their clothes back.

On the left-hand wall of Professor Haraldsen's office hung a large abstract photograph of something crimson and blobby. The right-hand wall was lined with books and every book had been covered in speckled blue paper to match the carpet. Professor Haraldsen's desk was completely clear except for a rough lump of volcanic rock. Professor Haraldsen himself was slightly built, gray-haired, with the face of an ageing imp. He wore a brown knitted sweater with a zip fastener, brown locknit pants and extraordinary brown earth shoes. He looked as if he skied and bicycled and skinny-dipped in freezing-cold fiords.

'How do you think I can help you?' he asked, perching on the edge of his desk. 'I have to tell you, I don't receive many requests from the public at large.'

Conor handed him the sheet of paper with the names scrawled on it. 'I just want to know if these mean anything to you. If there's any connection between them.'

Professor Haraldsen took a pair of half-glasses out of his sweater pocket and scrutinized the list with his nose wrinkled in concentration.

'Ah, well, yes. Amantadine. That's a drug which has been giving some promising results in the treatment of influenza, particularly in the early stages. So are some of these other drugs. Two of these – cyanodine and heliocyclatine – I've never heard of.'

'So what does this suggest to you? That somebody's trying to find a cure for the flu?'

'It most certainly looks like it. Especially if you consider these two other names, *Apia* and *Longyearbyen*. Both of them have associations with the great Spanish flu pandemic of 1918–19. Without any doubt, the greatest natural disaster in recorded history.

'Apia was a small harbor in Upolu, Western Samoa, in the South Pacific. At the height of the pandemic, in November 1918, a ship from New Zealand arrived in Apia carrying several dozen passengers who were suffering from the flu.

'Most of the natives of the South Pacific had never been exposed to any kind of influenza virus before, so they had never been able to build up immunity to it. But in 1918, US Navy ships took the virus to the Society Islands, where it killed over a tenth of the population. And after that ship put in at Apia, seven and a half thousand Western Samoans died within six weeks – which had the dubious distinction of being the highest per capita devastation of the whole pandemic.

'I find it extraordinary that people today seem to know so little about the Spanish influenza, or the terrible havoc that it caused all round the world. Nearly six hundred and seventy-five thousand Americans died – as many as you lost in both world wars put together, as well as Korea and Vietnam. In Britain, a quarter of a million. Here we lost whole communities of Sami – the people we used to call the Lapps – wiped out for ever. Throughout the world, the pandemic killed maybe as many as fifty million people.'

He paused, and then he said, 'It was an incredibly deadly virus, incredibly swift to act. You could wake up in the morning feeling fine and be dead by lunchtime. People dropped dead in the streets. You can always recognize the symptoms of Spanish influenza – vividly discolored faces, blackened feet and bloody fluid overflowing out of the lungs.

'If somebody is trying to find a cure for it, then they should be congratulated, and given all the help

416

that we can offer them. After all, there is a strong possibility that it could reappear – and what could we do about it if it did?'

'I'm not so sure that their main objective is to find a cure,' said Conor.

Professor Haraldsen took off his glasses and blinked at him. 'I don't understand. Why else would they wish to study it? And, obviously, they are trying to locate living samples of it.'

'How do you know that?'

'This other name you gave me, Longyearbyen. You know where this is, Longyearbyen?'

'I don't have the first idea.'

'It's on Spitsbergen, in the Svalbard archipelago, which is half-way between the coast of northern Norway and the North Pole. About five hundred and eighty kilometers north of here. It's the chief Norwegian settlement. Population, maybe twelve hundred hardy souls. Coalminers, mostly; and scientists. You wouldn't want to live there unless you had to.

'Longyearbyen was named after an American, J.M. Longyear, who was the first person to mine coal there, in 1905 or thereabouts.'

'So what does it have to do with flu?'

'Absolutely everything. In September of 1918, seven young Norwegian miners died in Longyearbyen after they had contracted the Spanish influenza here in Tromso. The townspeople of Longyearbyen were very worried that they would catch the virus themselves, so they buried the bodies deep beneath the tundra in the permafrost, which never thaws out.'

417

'That would have killed the virus, wouldn't it?' asked Eleanor.

Professor Haraldsen shook his head. 'It would have had the opposite effect. It would have put it into hibernation; or what in science fiction stories they call "suspended animation". Just like the crew of a starship, who are frozen or have their metabolism artificially slowed down so that they can travel for years without growing any older, so this Spanish influenza virus has been travelling through time also without ageing, ready at any time for reawakening.

'In 1918, medical science wasn't advanced enough to preserve any samples of the whole virus. But we can assume that the bodies of those seven young men have remained frozen solid for the past eighty years; and that they have been well enough preserved to give us tissue samples from which we can isolate a whole live virus.'

He hopped down from his desk and walked across to the blobby photograph on the wall. 'You see this? It's a magnification of the "bird flu" virus which broke out in Hong Kong in 1996. It caused the death of a three-year-old boy; and it was only by killing all of the chickens in Hong Kong that the authorities managed to eliminate it. One point three million chickens! Maybe that seems extreme. But I have no doubt in my mind at all that they almost certainly saved the world from another 1918.

'Before this happened, nobody thought that the virus could jump the species barrier from bird to human. But the flu virus is able to shuffle its genetic codes like a quick-change artist. So you can never know when and where it's going to break out next. It can start with events as unpredictable as the westward migration of infected wild ducks from China. In 1917, the flu broke out in America, but it was carried eastward into Germany and Scandinavia and Eastern Europe by troop movements. These days, if it broke out again, it could so easily be carried around the world by long-haul flights. We take every outbreak of flu very seriously. The World Health Organization has a whole network of flu surveillance experts; and of course you Americans have the Center for Disease Control and Prevention in Atlanta.

'But you've worried me now. You say that somebody is trying to isolate the 1918 virus for some reason other than a cure? What reason could that be?'

'We think that it's possible somebody intends to use a flu virus as a biological weapon.'

'You're talking about who? The Iraqis? We know they have anthrax and the Marburg virus. But the Spanish flu? That would be madness. That would wipe out millions and millions. They could have no control over it.'

'I don't think they're very worried about having control over it, except to protect themselves. They're not Iraqis. They're a breakaway evangelical movement that believes that everybody in the world should convert to their own particular brand of Christianity.'

'When you say *everybody*—?'

'That's precisely what I mean. Everybody. You. Me. The Catholics. The Jews. The Muslims. The

419

Shintoists. The Buddhists. Every religion and every sect of every religion that you can think of.'

'But how can they expect this? It's insanity. What will happen if people refuse?'

'In that case,' put in Eleanor, dryly, 'the whole world will be heaped a hundred deep with martyrs.'

Professor Haraldsen sat down at his desk. He rubbed his chin as if he were trying to decide if he needed a shave. 'This isn't a very, very bad taste joke?' he asked, after a while; although he could obviously tell by Conor's expression that he was deadly serious.

Conor said, 'You're a professor of epidemiology. Don't tell me you don't have any clout with the medical authorities? Surely you can stop Branch and his people from digging up those graves at Longyearbyen?'

'Well, yes. I can try.'

'Then I suggest that you try – because God knows what's going to happen to this world if you don't.'

Professor Haraldsen lifted a phone out of his desk drawer and punched out a number. He waited for a long while, trying to give Conor and Eleanor sympathetic smiles while he did so. At last he was connected to somebody. 'Willy! Yes! Jorn Haraldsen! How are you? Well, fine. I'm really fine. Yes, yes, we must try to go back to the Narvik Skisenter soon! Yes, not to fall over this time! Listen, Willy, I have a question about Longyearbyen. Yes, the Spanish flu business.'

He covered the receiver with his hand and said, 'Willy Bry. He's in charge of all the public health situations in northern Norway. Very good man.

420

Very thorough. Big man. Beard. But he skis like a girl.'

Willy Bry came back on the phone. Professor Haraldsen asked him question after question about Longyearbyen and nodded a lot and kept saying 'uh-huh' and 'uh-huh' and 'uh-*huh*?' As he did so, he made some quick incomprehensible notes with a mechanical pencil. Finally he said, 'OK, Willy. Thanks. Yes. Thanks.' He returned the phone to his desk drawer and closed it. Then he turned to Conor and Eleanor. 'Only one expedition has been given permission to excavate the cemetery at Longyearbyen. The health authorities have been very strict. Nobody else will be permitted to go near the cemetery. They have some soldiers on duty there already.'

'So whose expedition is this?'

'It's a joint project funded by Canada, Britain and Norway. It should begin excavation in seven weeks. The expedition leader is Dr Kirsty Duncan, she's Canadian. A medical geographer and climatologist. And a very dedicated woman, not to be deflected, if you know what I mean.

'Even so, the authorities will not permit her under any circumstances to take the bodies out of the cemetery: they have to be examined underneath a dome of protective covering, one hundred per cent sealed. Everybody on the team will have to wear full protective clothing. You know, the spacesuits.

'If there is any difficulty in removing the bodies from the graves, they will have to be examined in their coffins, where they lie. Afterward, their coffins will have to be sealed and buried again, just as deep.

'They will take out samples from the bodies with a special tool, which is like a hollow drill bit for taking oil samples. All of this material must be kept strictly quarantined.'

'Your friend didn't mention anybody called Branch?'

'Branch? No. No name like that.'

'And he's sure that nobody else can get near to the cemetery?'

'As I said, Willy Bry is a very thorough man.'

Conor stood up and held out his hand. 'I want to thank you for all of your help, Professor Haraldsen. If I can get back to you whenever I need to . . . ?'

'Of course. These are very important matters. A virus can live for many, many years. In Uppsala, in Sweden, in 1966, a team of archeologists dug up a mass grave from the days of the Black Death. Nine of them died within three weeks. Think of that. A disease surviving for six and half centuries.'

'Just one more thing,' said Conor.

'Of course. Anything.'

'Show us where Longyearbyen is, on the map.'

'My God. You don't want to *go* there, do you?'

Conor couldn't eat any more wolffish and pushed his plate away. 'It looks like Branch and his people plan to dig up those bodies before the Canadians can get there.'

'But you heard what your professor said. Nobody else except the official expedition is allowed near the cemetery.'

'I'm not too sure that a man like Branch is going to let the Norwegian authorities stand in his way.'

422

'So what can we do that an army guard can't do?'

'I don't know. But I feel very uneasy about sitting here doing nothing. Besides, don't forget that we didn't come simply to stop Branch from infecting the planet with influenza. We came here to recover Davina Gambit's money, and all the other millions that people had to cough up to save their reputations; and to prove that I'm innocent, too.'

'We also came to punish Branch for killing our friends,' Magda added. 'To give him just as much hurt as he gave to us.'

Eleanor said nothing but looked at Conor and raised one eyebrow. She took out a pack of cigarettes, pushed one into her holder and lit it, but a waitress immediately came over and pointed to the no smoking sign.

'I'm an American,' she protested. 'I'm supposed to know what Royking Forbudt means? Sounds like some second-rate cabaret artiste.'

Conor said, 'Tomorrow morning I think we ought to split up. You and Magda fly back to Oslo, I'll find a way to get myself to Longyearbyen. I don't exactly know what I'm planning to do yet, but I need to lay my hands on Branch before he digs up those bodies and leaves. The only way I'm going to be able to force him to give all that money back is if I have him alive.

'I don't want him arrested by the Norwegians, either. If that happens, they won't let me anywhere near him. In fact they'll probably arrest me, too, if the NYPD have posted my name on the Interpol database.'

'And what, pray, are we going to do in Oslo?'

423

'Wait. Please, that's all you can do. Wait until I call you and tell you that I've got my gun pointing at Dennis Evelyn Branch's brain, and that he's willing to release all of the money in his bank account.'

Eleanor said, 'You realize how ridiculous this idea is, don't you? What chance do you think you have of landing on some remote island in the middle of no place at all, catching Dennis Evelyn Branch and putting a gun to his head? My God, Conor, you're not James Bond.'

'I told you: that's only a rough outline of what I'm going to do. I can fill in the details when I get there. Improvise.'

'I only knew two people who were any good at improvisation. One was Dean Martin and the other was Lucille Ball.'

That afternoon he found a helicopter charter company on Strandgata. He was greeted by two matching young men in tinted aviator glasses and shortsleeved pilot's shirts. They brought out their map. Yes, they could fly him to Spitsbergen. No trouble at all, so long as the weather didn't close in. But when he said that he needed his arrival to be secret, they were horrified. You would have thought that he had asked them to commit sodomy in the street. Didn't he realize it was against safety regulations not to inform Tromso air-traffic control of any flights, and it was forbidden to land aircraft anywhere on the Svalbard archipelago without special permission? Besides, it was too dangerous to land in the Longyear valley, in the dark, without

424

lights. They would have to refuel before they returned to Tromso, wouldn't they? How could they do that, if their arrival was going to be secret? Why did it have to be secret? What was he carrying? Was he a drug-runner? Perhaps they should tell the police what he had asked them to?

'OK, OK,' said Conor, raising both hands to silence them. 'Forget I ever came in here. Forget everything.'

All the same, they were still pouting in outrage as he left their office and headed toward the harbor. One of them was making heavy weather of refolding the map.

At last, in a stifling wooden shed close to the Nordjeteen, where scores of herring-boats clanked at anchor, he found a fisherman who was prepared to land him on the south shore of Isfiorden, to the east of Longyearbyen harbor, so that nobody would know that he had come ashore. The man wore a peaked cap and a blue padded waterproof suit that rustled whenever he moved. Everything smelled of fish and tobacco. On the wall of his little shed was a calendar with a photograph of the Empire State Building on it. Conor, for a moment, felt a sharp pang of homesickness.

After their evening meal in the Aurora Restaurant, they had a last drink in the bar and then went up to their rooms. Conor was still searching through the TV channels when there was a soft knock at his door. He opened it up and it was Eleanor.

'Do you want another drink?' he asked her. 'I think I still have some vodka left in the mini-bar.'

'No, no. I've had enough for tonight. I shouldn't drink at all, the pills I'm taking.'

'How about an orange juice?'

She shook her head. The light from the television flickered across her face as if she were a character in a 1930s movie. 'The thing of it is, I've come to ask you not to go.'

'Don't get me wrong, Eleanor. I'm not going because I relish the idea.'

'It's far too much of a risk. You don't speak Norwegian, you won't know anybody there. And you know how ruthless Branch and his people can be.'

'Eleanor, I have to go. Branch extorted tens of millions of dollars and I have to get it back. I have to get my reputation back. I have to get my life back.'

'Your life is worth more than any amount of money. And you don't have to retrieve all those millions of dollars to prove that you're innocent. I'll help you. I mean it. I know some of the best lawyers in New York.'

'And supposing Branch digs up this virus and spreads it all around the world? Supposing Professor Haraldsen's right, and it can kill countless millions of people? How will I feel about that?'

'Conor,' said Eleanor, taking hold of his hand between both of her hands. 'It's not your responsibility to stop him. You've done enough. Come back to Oslo with us tomorrow morning and we'll fly straight back to the States.'

Conor thought about tomorrow. Tomorrow he had arranged to meet the fisherman down by the harbor at six o'clock sharp, long before it grew light.

Then he was faced with nearly two days of sailing toward the Svalbard archipelago, on sea scattered with ice floes. He had asked the fisherman about Longyearbyen and without taking out his cigarette the fisherman had said: 'One large coal mine, four small hotels, five restaurants, twenty shops, and all the snow you could want.' And after that: Dennis Evelyn Branch.

He would have given almost anything not to go.

'Eleanor . . . it's too much of a cliché to say that a man's got to do what a man's got to do. But this is one of those times. I've lost a lot these past few weeks. My child, my lover, my friends, whole pieces of the person that I thought I was. I'll have to say that I've nearly lost my religion, too, which is kind of ironic, when you consider what I'm going to be doing. But don't ask me to lose my soul.'

Eleanor's lips tightened and her eyes filled with tears. 'I would never ask you to do that. But I can't tell you how much you mean to me. I couldn't bear it if anything happened to you.'

He didn't say anything, but gave her a questioning look.

'I suppose you'll think that I'm just a sentimental old woman. But when you walked into my office you reminded me so much of my son, James. You're taller than him, darker than him, but there's so much about you that's just the same. Reckless, but always determined to do the right thing. And the way you look sometimes, when you've got something on your mind. I can almost see James looking out of your eyes.'

'You don't get to see him any more?'

'He's dead. Died two and a half years ago, at the age of thirty-one. His horse threw him, and he broke his back.'

'I'm sorry.'

Eleanor wiped her eyes. 'It can't be helped. Crying isn't going to bring him back. But I want you to know that you've given me so much pleasure . . . so much of what I've missed. Why do you think I'm here? I called Davina Gambit before we went to see her, and asked her to insist that I come along. When I told her why, she told me that she lost a child, too, a long time ago, and that she quite understood.'

'I still have to go to Longyearbyen tomorrow.'

'I know,' she said. 'I'm just being selfish. For one ridiculous moment I thought that I could get my life all back together again . . . with Sidney, and you. The life that I should have had, but never did.'

She paused, and then she said, 'James was Sidney's child. I never told him that I was going to have a baby. He would have run off even quicker! And, if you don't mind, I'd rather you didn't tell him now.'

'Eleanor . . .' Conor began, but she pressed her fingertip against his lips.

'You don't have to say anything. Just promise me you won't do anything too dangerous.' She paused, and sniffled. 'God . . . I wish I was Magda. I could hypnotize you into coming back to New York with me.'

There was a knock at the door. It was Magda, in a black satin nightdress, her long black hair shining

428

on her ice-white shoulders. She smelled of some very strong, dominant perfume. 'I came to say goodbye,' she said. 'I don't want you to remember me the way I look when I've just woken up.'

She looked at Eleanor and frowned. 'Is everything OK? What's happened?'

Eleanor smiled. 'Nothing, dear. Just saying our goodbyes.'

On Thursday morning, 473 miles north of Tromso, the sun appeared through the fog as a wan yellow smudge. Per Rakke, the fisherman, coughed and said, 'We'll have plenty of cover today. What about some coffee? There's a flask over there.'

Conor was sitting by the misted-up cabin window, looking out at the choppy metallic waves. The strong current was flowing diagonally across the bows of Per Rakke's 35-foot fishing boat, so that it dipped and lurched sideways with every swell. Sometime during the night they had started to run into fragments of broken ice: Conor had heard them tumbling against the hull. Now there were larger lumps all around them, and soon after the sun came up Conor saw an iceberg the size of a small family house in Queens.

The cabin stank of fish and diesel oil and Per Rakke's strong cigarettes, and Conor was beginning to wonder if it had been wise of him to eat that breakfast of bread and cheese so hurriedly.

At least he was warm. He was wearing thick black canvas jeans and insulated boots, and a huge off-white parka with a fur-lined hood. He had zipped Toralf's .22 pistol in his pocket. It had a full clip but he had been tempted to buy more ammunition for it. In the end, though, he had decided against it. Norway had strict handgun laws and he hadn't wanted to attract the attention of the Troms county police.

Occasionally another fishing boat would pass them in the fog; or they would sail close to a bleak snow-capped skerry. It wasn't hard to see why Norwegian folk stories were crowded with tales of sea serpents and sirens and the ghosts of Viking long-boats.

'It's warm today,' said Per Rakke. 'You should come up here in the winter. It's so cold that the smoke freezes as soon as it comes out of the funnel. If you're not careful a puff of smoke can drop on your head and kill you.'

'I'll keep an eye out,' Conor smiled. 'What's the ambient temperature now?'

'Six degrees below.'

'What's that in Fahrenheit?'

'It's easy. You double the Celsius figure and add twenty-nine. So, seventeen degrees Fahrenheit.'

Conor poured Per Rakke some coffee. The fisher-man swallowed it in three blistering gulps, bulging out his cheeks as he drank. 'You hungry? There's some pickled herring in that bag.'

The boat dropped sharply into a trough, and spray splattered against the windows. 'Maybe later,' said Conor.

'Well, *ja*, OK. All the more for me.'

As the afternoon wore on, they sailed up the western coast of Spitsbergen, keeping its snow-covered peaks faintly visible through the freezing fog. They entered Isfiorden with lumps of glacial ice knocking against the hull. Per Rakke steered his boat close in to the southern side of the fiord and slowed his engine to a hoarse, asthmatic chug. On the north side, vaguely, Conor could see spectral white mountains, and scores of glaciers, each of them calving icebergs into the sea.

They passed Longyearbyen harbor – a smattering of lights on their starboard side. Conor could see a row of skeletal pylons along the shore and asked Per Rakke what they were. 'Those are the cable cars that used to carry the coal from the mine to the wharf. The *kibb*.'

They couldn't have been making more than three knots when – without warning – a black granite headland came looming out of the fog. Per Rakke spun the fishing boat's wheel and began to bring her about. 'This is the nearest I can sail to the harbor without anybody seeing us,' he said. 'It's only an hour to walk from here. Not more.'

Conor opened the cabin door and stepped out onto the slippery deck. There was very little wind but the fog was bone-cracking cold, and his breath smoked. The shoreline here rose almost vertically out of the sea, and the upper reaches of the crags were draped in snow. Seagulls screamed around the boat, even though they had no catch aboard. Maybe they had caught the scent of Per Rakke's breath, thought Conor.

'Where can I go ashore?' he called out.

'There's a place beyond that point. The rocks slope gently right down to the sea. You'll be able to land the rubber boat there, no trouble at all.'

No trouble at all? thought Conor as they rounded the point. The place where the rocks were supposed to slope gently down to the sea was a tumble of enormous granite boulders, leading up to a narrow crevice. The tide continually rushed around the point, thick with broken fragments of ice the size of dining-tables for twelve. 'There,' said Per Rakke. 'Perfect. Almost like a holiday beach.'

'If you say so,' said Conor. He waited by the rail while Per Rakke brought the fishing boat within seventy feet of the shore. A seagull hovered so close to him that he could have touched it and he wondered whose soul it was. Per Rakke dropped anchor and then he came forward with a wet cigarette stuck to his lower lip. A faded orange raft was lashed to the deck. He tugged the straps free and pulled the toggle. With a sharp hiss and a succession of crumpling bangs the raft inflated, filling the foredeck. Per Rakke handed Conor two polyurethane paddles and said, 'Row this way, toward the point. The current is very strong. It will sweep you onto the shore. If you can't make it the first time, I'll pull you back on the line, so that you can try again.'

'Some holiday beach. What happens when I get ashore?'

'Then I pull the raft back; and then, my friend, then you're on your own. I've given you Aslak Bølstad's address . . . when you've finished whatever it is you're doing, you go to him. He'll find you someone to bring you back to Tromso.'

'OK,' said Conor, without much optimism. He went into the cabin and collected his backpack. It

432

contained two changes of clothing, some Lindt chocolate bars and a thermal blanket.

He helped Per Rakke topple the raft off the fore-deck into the sea. Then he swung his leg over the side and started to climb down the netting which Per Rakke had hung out for him. He hesitated for a moment and Per Rakke said, 'By the way, there's one thing I forgot to mention. Polar bears.'

'Polar bears? You're kidding me.'

'Of course not. There are more than two and a half thousand on Svalbard. They're very dangerous. The chief predator, you understand. You don't usually see them near the town, but if you do, don't try to run away. Just fire your pistol in the air to frighten it off.'

'Shouldn't I shoot it?'

'With that little gun? No, you'll only make it mad. Something else, too: don't try to chase a polar bear. When they run they get hot very quick and that makes them mad, too.'

Conor looked with apprehension toward the shore. 'Thanks for the warning,' he said. 'Just hand me the paddles, will you?'

It took two or three attempts before Conor could climb into the raft. The current kept swinging it away from the side of the fishing boat and spinning it around in circles. Huge lumps of ice kept nudging against it. At last, however, he managed to get one foot in, and then the other, and throw himself into a sitting position without capsizing it. It swung around even more violently, and the bottom humped up as if Jaws had struck it from underneath. 'Your paddles!' shouted Per Rakke, making wild crablike gestures with his arms. 'Use your paddles!'

Conor untangled his paddles and thrust them into the water. Up on the foredeck of the fishing boat, it hadn't seemed as if there was very much of a swell, but down here he felt as if he were going to be swamped at any moment. His face was stung by freezing spray, and every second wave slopped into the raft and gurgled noisily from one side to the other. He managed to control the raft's frustrating rotation by jamming one of his paddles against the side of the fishing boat, and then he started to row toward the point.

The only rowing he had ever done was at high school, and on the lake in Central Park – leisurely oar-pulling followed by long moments of rest. Rowing toward the shore of Isfiorden against the fast-flowing current of the Arctic Ocean was something different. He had to paddle relentlessly to keep the raft from spinning out of control, and it seemed as if he were being pitched in six different directions at once. He was only half-way toward the point before he was exhausted, his shoulders aching and his heart thumping and his breath coming in tortured wheezes.

As he neared the point, a faster current caught him. He was hurtled toward the jagged granite rocks at almost twenty knots, whirling and bucking and spinning around as he did so. He was surrounded by a white calamity of broken ice.

'– *out!*' he heard, from Per Rakke, his hands cupped around his mouth.

'*What?*' he screamed back.

434

'*Watch out! The rocks!*' and he made a jabbing gesture with both hands.

Conor was spun around again, and then the raft was caught by a surging wave and lifted toward the rocks. He raised his paddle and imitated Per Rakke, jabbing against the granite to prevent the raft being dragged up against it. The shock through his arms was so violent that the paddle was torn out of his hands. But the raft caught the incoming current and was swirled away from the point and in toward the 'holiday beach'.

Conor no longer had any control over the raft. With a loud thump of rubbery complaint, it was swept onto the rocks that littered the shoreline. Conor was thrown sideways and fell against the side, grazing his face on the seams. He felt the surf seething beneath him, regathering its strength, and he realized that if he didn't get out now, he would have to be hauled back to the fishing boat to try the whole bruising performance all over again. He stood up, dancing to keep his balance. Then he rolled over the side of the raft onto the shore, just as a huge icy-cold wave crashed over him. He staggered to his feet, his eyes stinging and his nose filled up with freezing brine. He leaned against a rock, knee deep in water, barking like a seal.

The orange raft was whirled off into the gloom, amongst the ice floes. Per Rakke began to haul it in with the electric winch that he used to bring his nets up. Conor managed to suppress his coughing and climb up onto the rocks, with cold water squelching in his boots. He turned and looked back to the fiord, but Per Rakke was running without

435

lights and his fishing boat had already melted into the fog.

Conor began the slow climb up the ravine, his feet rattling on the rocks, stopping from time to time to cough. The temperature was down to minus 3, and he couldn't help thinking of Eleanor holding his hand between hers and begging him not to go.

29

Once he reached the head of the ravine he stopped and rested. He had always assumed that he was fit, but climbing up through 200 feet of loose granite boulders had almost completely exhausted him. It was dark now but there was an old luminosity in the fog and he could make out the shapes of the surrounding crags. He judged that it was a two-and-a-half-mile walk over the hills to the town of Longyearbyen itself, passing close to the cemetery.

He gave himself ten minutes to recover, and then he started off again. He left the broken boulders behind and started to walk across hard, moss-covered tundra. It was always so cold here that nothing else could grow except lichens and stunted alpine bushes and little purple saxifrage. Even in the middle of summer, the soil thawed to a depth of less than a meter.

After a while, he felt the wind beginning to rise. It made a fluffing noise in his ears, and the bad news was that it was blowing against the back of his head. A north-east wind, directly from the polar ice cap, with no stopovers. The temperature noticeably dropped, and the fog began to sidle away like a company of ghosts. The luminosity grew steadily, and he could see now that it was the reflected light of the moon, shining off the huge silvery glaciers. It wasn't long before he could see the hill behind the cemetery, with snow covering its upper slopes.

At the foot of the hill he saw an array of five or six bright lights twinkling. They were almost exactly in the configuration of the constellation Hydra, like the moles on Magda's back. He heard a faint drilling sound, too, but the wind kept snatching it away.

The wind blew harder and harder. He tightened the strings around his hood and kept his right hand raised as he walked to keep the cold out of his eyes. The seawater in his boots felt as if it had turned into crushed ice, and his toes seemed to have gone AWOL.

The constellation of lights disappeared as he descended into a valley, and it was over twenty minutes later before they reappeared, much closer this time. He was less than quarter of a mile from the cemetery and he could see that Dennis Evelyn Branch was already here in force. Under the glare of the floodlights, six or seven large Arctic tents were pitched. Three diesel generators, thickly jacketed against the cold, were providing the power. Two Mercedes trucks were parked nearby, as well as a Toyota Landcruiser and a Caterpillar excavator with a narrow-gauge shovel, the kind they used to dig drainage trenches and graves.

Seven white wooden crosses were stacked forlornly against one of the trucks – and, where they had stood, two men with jackhammers were hacking

438

up the tundra in dark, frozen lumps. Several other men were hammering spikes into the ground all around the excavation site, and it looked to Conor as if they were erecting the framework for the virus-proof dome.

Conor stayed well beyond the perimeter of the cemetery, ducking low behind the hillocks. A few flakes of snow tumbled in the air, and whirled around the floodlights like moths. The men continued drilling and banging, and occasionally one of them would shout something in Norwegian.

So much for Professor Haraldsen's friend, thought Conor, and his reassurance that nobody would be allowed near the cemetery except for the official expedition. Where were the Norwegian army guards? Where were the health officials?

He watched the excavation work for more than quarter of an hour. In that time, the prefabricated framework for the dome was almost completed. Rolls of heavy-duty nylon sheeting were carried from one of the Mercedes trucks and laid down beside it. The snow was thickening but that didn't seem to deter Dennis Evelyn Branch's workforce at all. They worked at frantic speed, drilling and digging and erecting aluminum struts. Conor tried to pick out Birger, but the men were all so muffled up that it was impossible to tell them apart.

Trying not to lose his footing on the frozen moss, he made his way down the sloping hillside that led to the town. It was clustered by the harbor, a snug collection of wooden buildings that looked like something out of a fairytale, with warm lights twinkling and smoke rising from dozens of chimneys and, across Isfiorden, the immense pale glaciers gleaming.

As he descended the hill, he could see that there was intense activity around the harbor. Floodlights illuminated a small cargo ship with a bright red funnel, and long boxes were being unloaded onto the dock. A Jeep described impatient circles in the rapidly settling snow. The wind sizzled against the back of Conor's hood, and his feet began to itch unbearably.

He was limping by the time he reached the edge of town. He passed two deserted houses and a lumberyard. Then he found himself crossing a wide, snowswept street. Not far away, a dog was barking, and there was a strong smell of coal in the air. The street was criss-crossed with tire tracks, but there didn't seem to be anybody around. He didn't really know what to do next. He had to find out what Dennis Evelyn Branch was doing; but equally importantly, he had to find himself someplace to stay for the night. He passed a wooden shed with its padlock hanging undone, but in this weather it would be suicide to sleep in an outbuilding. With a north-east wind like this blowing, the temperature could easily drop to minus 10 degrees Celsius, or even lower.

Behind him, he heard the sound of an automobile engine. He turned, and the Jeep that had been driving circles on the dockside suddenly appeared at the end of the street and sped toward him. Its lights were blazing and its windshield wipers were furiously flapping against the snow. Conor immediately turned his face away. No point in taking chances. He

440

glanced in at the front passenger window as it sped past, and he was sure that he saw the sharp, intent profile of Dennis Evelyn Branch himself, in a black fur hat. The Jeep left a fine cloud of snow and the smell of gasoline, and then it was gone, up toward the cemetery.

Around the next corner, Conor unexpectedly found the Puffin Bar, a long wooden building with multicolored lights dangling around its veranda. The wheezing of Norwegian folk music came from inside, mingled with the stamping of feet and shouts of hilarity. Conor knew that it was a risk, going inside. It was more than likely that one or two of Dennis Evelyn Branch's subcontractors would be drinking in here.

But he was freezing, and exhausted, and he needed badly to go to the bathroom. He pulled open the door and stepped inside, and pulled open yet another door, and was met by light and warmth and people talking and drinking and laughing. Along the left side of the room ran a polished pine bar, with barstools; and the right side was taken up with tables with bright red tablecloths. At the very end of the room three young men in jeans and yellow shirts were playing a fiddle and a bass and a piano-accordion. This certainly wasn't a New York bar: the cigarette smoke was so thick that it had practically reached knee level. The clientele was almost entirely under thirty, and male: muscular miners with fuzzy beards and permanently blackened fingernails. At one table in the corner sat a group of serious young men in new plaid shirts and Calvin Klein jeans who were probably climatologists or conservationists or oil engineers. They were drinking Haakon lager out of the bottle and tapping their feet out of time. At the next table sat three raucous middle-aged women with their roots showing, and one young girl of seventeen or eighteen who had that mysterious blond Norwegian beauty that reminded Conor so much of Lacey: pale eyes, pale eyebrows, a small straight nose, and pouting pink lips.

'*Ja?*' the barman asked him, with a gappy grin.

'Toilet?' said Conor.

'Oh sure. Through to the back, past the musicians, off to the left.'

'Thanks. And I'll have a whiskey, if you don't mind. Any brand. Double.'

He went to the cramped, cold bathroom and had the longest pee in the history of pees, his eyes closed, his shoulders slumped. While he did so, without disrespect, he said a prayer of thanks that he had arrived here safely, and that God had protected him. When he had finished he took off his parka and brushed off the melted snow. Underneath he was wearing a thick black rollneck sweater and a black wool-mixture shirt. Sitting on the toilet seat, he took off his boots and his soaking socks. He dried the inside of his boots with paper towels, changed his socks, and returned to the bar feeling slightly more human.

Somebody was waiting for him at the bar, a ruddy-faced man with a black peaked leather cap and a thick black beard, brambled with gray.

'This one's on me,' he said, passing Conor his double Scotch. 'Welcome to Longyearbyen.'

'Thanks,' said Conor, and tipped it back in one.

442

He just hoped that it would penetrate down to his feet. He held out his hand and said, 'Jack Grady. Nice to know you.'

'Pal Rustad. Nice to know *you*, Mr Grady. And all of your friends. I think you will make this a very good winter for us, for a change.'

'Well, we hope so,' said Conor, although he didn't have any idea what the bearded man was talking about. 'We always aim to please.'

'Personally, I don't think you'll find anything,' said the man, pouring himself a shotglass of *akvavit* from a bottle on the bar. 'After eighty years? It's not possible. You can't keep anything alive for eighty years.'

'You never know, do you?' said Conor. 'It's worth a try.'

'Well, it will be worth it for us, when all of the TV and the newspapers come here. Everybody here will make some money.'

'The TV? The newspapers? When are you expecting them?'

'I don't know. Maybe next week sometime. This is just the advance party, yes?'

'The advance party?' Conor suddenly realized how Dennis Evelyn Branch had explained his arrival here, several weeks before Kirsty Duncan's expedition. He must have simply shipped in all of his equipment and pretended that he and his people were here to clear the ground. He had enough money, after all, to forge any documentation that was needed, and to bribe any Norwegian shippers who needed bribing.

'You're taking a break?' asked Pal Rustad. 'All of

443

the rest of your people are up at the cemetery. They said you were going to be working day and night.'

'Oh, yes, sure. But my specialty is micro-organisms. They won't need me till they've finished digging.'

'I still don't think you'll find anything,' Pal Rustad commented. 'Let sleeping dogs lie, that's what I say.'

The party in the bar went on till way past three in the morning. The fiddlers were replaced by the Norwegian version of a barber-shop quartet, singing what sounded like very ribald songs. 'They say, I want to sail my longboat up your fiord, my darling one,' the bearded man translated. Conor nodded and said, 'Very subtle.'

He ate an elk steak garnished with boiled potatoes and sauerkraut. The meat was tough but it had a good strong gamey flavor and he was very hungry. His bearded friend introduced him to a big, hand-some dark-haired woman in a *bunad*, a traditional Norwegian costume with an embroidered vest and a long black skirt. Her dress was very feminine but she looked as if she were quite capable of throwing him across the room.

'Everybody is happy that you come here,' she grinned. 'It was such a good surprise.'

'I'll bet,' said Conor. He looked at his watch. 'Is there anyplace that I can sleep for a couple of hours? I don't have to go up to the cemetery till later and I'm bushed. Tired, that is.'

'You're not staying at the Polar Hotel, like the rest of them?'

'Well, I have to share with three other guys, and you know . . . it's not very restful.'

The woman turned to the barman and spoke to him rapidly in Norwegian. 'He says you can sleep in the back. There's a couch.'

The barman looked at him expectantly. Conor said, 'What?' He hoped the woman didn't think that he wanted to sleep with *her*. But then he suddenly realized what the barman was waiting for. He took out his wallet and gave him 1,000 krone.

'Sleep good,' said the barman, making his hands into an imaginary pillow.

He was woken by a scratching noise. He sat up, straining his ears. The party in the bar must have finished a long time ago, because the room was pitch dark and totally silent. He listened and listened, and there it was again. *Scratch – scrrattch – scratch.*

Cautiously he felt for his rucksack, slid open the zipper and took out his waterproof flashlight. He waited until he heard the scratching again, then he switched it on. A huge elk head was staring at him, with massive antlers and black glassy eyes. '*Ah!*' he shouted, and jumped away – even as he realized that it was nothing more than a head, hanging from the wall on a wooden shield.

'Asshole,' he told himself. Quickly he flicked the flashlight beam from one side of the room to the other. At last he saw a scruffy gray dog fast asleep in the far corner, almost indistinguishable from the shaggy reindeer pelt that he was lying on. The dog must have been dreaming of chasing something, because his front paws kept scratching against the wooden wall in a fitful running movement.

Conor checked his watch. It was 5:35 – time he was leaving, anyhow. He felt bruised all over, but at least he was warm and fed and reasonably refreshed. In the freezing-cold men's room he washed his face and stared at himself in the misted-up mirror over the washbasin. He wondered if James Bond had ever felt lonely.

He walked through the bar and let himself out. The whole town was quiet and blanketed in snow, but even from here he could hear the grinding of the Caterpillar excavator and occasional bursts of jack-hammering. His boots squeaked in the snow as he made his way along the street and started to climb the hill. It wasn't long before the cemetery came into view. The site of the exhumation was completely covered now by a semi-transparent nylon dome, over fifty feet across, illuminated from within by flood-lights. Shadowy figures in protective white spacesuits were moving around inside it, so that it looked like a recently landed UFO, with its alien crew.

The snow was falling more lightly now, but the north-easterly wind was still keen, and it made the tents rumble and flap. As he neared the cemetery, Conor skirted around in back of them, keeping himself well out of the light. He opened up the nearest tent and cautiously peered inside. There was nobody there, but there were stacks of black plastic boxes marked Biohazard, as well as a trestle table crowded with scientific equipment that Conor couldn't even put a name to.

He tried the next tent. There was nobody in this one, either, only crates of drilling equipment and reels of cable and boxes of spare halogen lamps. As he approached the third tent, however, a man suddenly stepped out of it, dressed in a bulky protective suit complete with oxygen tanks, and carrying his helmet under his arm. He was a big man, the same height as Conor but very much bulkier, with a black woolly hat and the slitted eyes of a Sami.

'*Hej*!' he shouted, and rattled off a guttural burst of irascible Norwegian, which Conor took to mean that he should get the hell out of here before he was ripped in very small digestible pieces and fed to the polar bears.

'Sorry,' said Conor. 'No speaka da Norsk.'

The man came toward him with a threatening look. He waved his hand two or three times to shoo Conor away.

Conor said, 'OK, I'm going. But look – I've got something for you!' He tugged off one of his gloves with his teeth and unzippered one of his pockets. The man watched him, perplexed, as he took out the small foil pack of burundanga that Magda had given him, and beckoned him closer. The man took two or three steps forward. Conor edged around so that the wind was behind him, opened the foil, and blew the dust directly into the man's face.

Burundanga had put Conor into a trance, instantly, but he had never seen it used on anyone else and for one moment he didn't believe that it was going to work. The man flapped his hand in front of his face, coughed, then stood completely still, staring at Conor with the blankest expression that he had ever seen.

Conor stepped back. Then he stepped closer. 'Can you hear me?' he said. He prodded the man in the chest. The man stayed where he was, his eyes focused on something that Conor couldn't even imagine.

He couldn't give the man verbal instructions, but he took hold of his arm and said, 'Come on, buddy, this way,' and led him across to the tent full of drilling equipment. Obedient as a Labrador, the man shuffled along beside him, and waited patiently while Conor opened up the tent-flap. Once they were inside, Conor said, 'Stay still, OK?' while he closed the flap behind them. Then he stood in front of the man and mimed to him that he should take off his protective suit. At once – and without any protest at all – the man unfastened the seals at his wrists, took off his gloves, and proceeded to undress. Conor helped him to lift off his oxygen tanks, and even let him hold onto his shoulder to balance himself while he climbed out of his pants. Underneath the suit he was wearing a soiled gray sweater and a pair of thick black tracksuit bottoms tucked into two pairs of cheesy, sweat-stained socks. Conor just prayed that he wasn't lousy.

He guided the man to a pile of crates at the far end of the tent, all stenciled BUGGE DRILLS A/S. He indicated to the man that he should sit down on one of the crates and stay where he was. Then he took off his parka and struggled into the protective suit himself. He zipped all the zippers and popped all the poppers and fastened all the seals. It took him two or three minutes to figure out how the helmet locked onto his head, but eventually it closed with a well-engineered *ker-lick*. He twisted the knob of his oxygen regulator and took three deep, pressurized breaths.

He said another prayer: Mary, Mother of God, please make sure that I have put on this suit properly, and that I don't get infected with the Spanish influenza. Because many people need me, even those people who think they don't, amen. And even those people who would rather see me dead, double-amen.

He went back to the man on the crates, and guided him to the far end of the tent. He mimed that he should lie down in the narrow space between two boxes of compressor parts; and then, when he had haltingly done so, Conor covered him up with a sheet of brown plastic wrapping material. He didn't know how to tell him in Norwegian that he shouldn't wake up for at least a couple of hours, but from what Sidney had said, the effects of burundanga could last for days.

Conor left the tent and trudged toward the nylon dome. Another man in a protective suit was waiting for him and beckoned him to hurry up. He broke into a heavy trot.

The Jeep was parked close to the entrance to the dome. Standing beside it were two hard-looking men in black salopettes, and Dennis Evelyn Branch himself. Branch was wearing a black fur hat with ear-flaps and a sable coat that came almost down to the ground. His face was even whiter than the snow, and his sunglasses as dark as writing-ink. Although Conor was sure that he wouldn't recognize him behind the gold-tinted glass of his helmet, he kept his gloved hand raised to shield his face, as if he were dazzled by the floodlights.

'What kept him so damned long?' Branch said to one of the men in salopettes. 'I want all of the bodies out of here in four hours flat.'

The man said something to Conor in Norwegian. Conor rubbed his stomach as if to indicate that he had felt ill.

'I can't believe it,' said Branch, turning away. 'I'm trying to spread the Lord's Word around the world and it all has to be put on hold while this character goes to the bathroom.'

Conor was ushered into the nylon dome. It was dazzlingly bright inside. Most of the excavation had been completed now. Seven parallel trenches, twenty feet deep, had been jackhammered out of the solid tundra, and seven coffins exposed. They were of plain, cheap wood, but the permafrost had preserved them perfectly, so they looked as freshly made as they did when they had been lowered into the ground.

There were seven men in the dome in protective suits, excluding himself, and they were gathered round the furthest grave with aluminum ladders and nylon ropes and a heap of black zip-up body bags. Conor went over to join them, even though he didn't have any idea what he was supposed to do. He was worried about the body bags, though. Hadn't Professor Haraldsen told them that the Norwegian authorities had refused to allow the bodies out of the

450

cemetery? They were supposed to take quarantined samples, not whole cadavers.

One of the men positioned an aluminum extension ladder down the side of the trench and began to climb down it. Another man said something angry to Conor and pointed to the bottom of the trench, so he presumed that he was meant to climb down there, too. He picked up one of the ladders and arranged it on the opposite side of the trench. He was about to climb down when the man shouted at him again and handed him a long-handled crowbar. He gave a thumbs-up, took it, and made his way awkwardly down the aluminum rungs. Inside his helmet it was impossible to see where to put his feet, and halfway down he slipped and caught his sleeve on top of the lower half of the ladder. He heard two or three of the other men shouting at him, but he didn't look up. He was sweating now and his mouth was dry. He knew what could happen if he compromised his protective suit.

He reached the bottom of the grave. The other man had a crowbar too, and he wedged the sharp end of it underneath the coffin lid and waited. Conor took the hint and forced his crowbar under the lid on the opposite side. Slowly, the two of them eased the lid upward until the nails came creaking out, working their way toward the foot of the coffin until the lid was completely loosened. They laid down their crowbars and lifted the lid between them – taking extravagant care not to puncture their gloves on any splinters or protruding nails – and rested it vertically against the side of the excavation.

Conor turned – and there, in the nightshirt that he

451

had died in, his eyes closed, his face puffy-looking but peaceful, lay young Tormod Albrigsten, looking no different from that day in 1918 when he had slithered down the gangplank of the *Forsete* and held out his hand to Arne Gabrielsen.

For almost a minute, everybody in the dome stared down at Tormod in awed silence. He looked as if he might open his eyes at any moment and climb out of the coffin. Conor had seen more dead bodies than he cared to remember, but he had never seen anybody who looked like this, as if he were simply sleeping. Yet he was probably more than a hundred years old.

Suddenly somebody shouted an order and the spell was broken. One of the men lowered down a body bag. This wasn't one of the standard-issue cadaver containment receptacles that the coroner's department used in New York. It was made of some rubbery material and it had a press-together airtight seal as well as a zipper. Conor's companion picked it up and held it out with both hands. He looked at Conor and frowned. Then he shouted at him, and although he couldn't understand Norwegian, Conor caught the word '*akvavit*' and got the gist: the man was accusing him of being drunk.

Impatiently the man shook the body bag at him. Conor looked down at Tormod's body and realized what was expected of him. He bent down and eased his hands into the side of the coffin, and lifted Tormod out.

The body was surprisingly heavy. Not only that, it was utterly rigid, frozen solid, so that it looked as if Tormod were being levitated by a stage magician, his arms by his sides and his legs horizontal. His bare feet were still blotchy from the Spanish influenza, his toes slightly curled.

Conor's companion arranged the body bag in the bottom of the coffin and Conor lowered Tormod into it. They wrapped the bag around him, fastened the airtight seal and pulled up the zipper. Then Conor took the head end while his companion took the feet. They climbed up their ladders on opposite sides of the grave, carrying Tormod between them, as stiff as a board.

Tormod's body was taken away; and then Conor and his companion climbed down into the next grave to repeat the operation. This time they discovered the body of young Ole, who had worked in a quarry. He still had his blond downy mustache. Seeing these boys, Conor was beginning to get some idea of the enormity of what Dennis Evelyn Branch was planning to do. These weren't nameless millions: these were somebody's children. Ole was still wearing a nightshirt which his mother must have made for him, sometime during the First World War.

It took a little over an hour to lift out all seven bodies. As soon as the last one had been carried out of the dome, Conor was handed a shovel and the men began to push all the broken-up soil back into the graves. When they had roughly filled them up, they began to pull the nylon sheeting off the dome and dismantle the framework.

It was snowing again: much more thickly now, almost a blizzard.

453

The floodlights were switched off, one by one, and Conor saw swimming after-images in front of his eyes. The generators were shut down, too. The men in protective suits took off their helmets and started to walk back to the tents. Dennis Evelyn Branch and his two bodyguards went with them. Conor kept his helmet on and hung behind. He had been looking for a chance to catch Branch on his own. In an out-and-out confrontation he would have no hope at all. Even if Branch's men weren't armed, he was hopelessly outnumbered, and he would be lucky to get as far as Branch's Jeep.

He was beginning to think that Eleanor had been right. Only two people had ever been any good at improvisation, and neither of them was him.

He stared to circle away from the tent where everybody else was going – back to the drilling-equipment store where he had left his parka. But the last of the men in protective suits turned around and gave him a wave and called out to him. 'Per!' Then, more insistently, '*Per!*'

He hesitated, but the man called yet again, and he had to follow. He pushed his way in through the tent-flaps still wearing his helmet. Inside, it was dimly lit and stiflingly hot. All of the miners were gathered here now, as well as two or three other men, all of them dressed in black, and two young Norwegians who looked like students. Lab technicians, maybe, Conor guessed.

He saw now how Dennis Evelyn Branch had been able to excavate the cemetery without interference. In the half-darkness at the far end of the tent, five young Norwegian soldiers were sitting in a line on the floor with their cropped heads bowed, cowed and pale. They were being watched over by one of the men that Conor had seen at Breivika Havnegata, the one whose Volvo had burned. He was holding a Belgian FN rifle loosely across his knees and repeatedly yawning.

Dennis Evelyn Branch stepped stiff-legged into the center of the tent with his hands buried deep into the pockets of his coat. He had taken off his black fur cap, and his bone-white hair stuck up wildly.

'My friends, you've done real well here today! You've done us all proud! We're two hours ahead of schedule and that means that we're two hours nearer to the day when the Word of the Lord will be spread around the globe!'

He stalked to the left; he stalked to the right. He never took his hands out of his pockets but the sharpness of his voice made up for all of the arm-waving and the pointing that most evangelists used to stir up their congregations.

'What we did here tonight was ethical and it was scientific. We took almost all of the precautions that the Norwegian health authorities demanded of Dr Duncan's expedition; so nobody can accuse us of fecklessness or of unnecessarily risking the lives of innocent people. All right, the Norwegians didn't want us to take the bodies away with us, but that's what we're going to do, because we have a higher purpose. Not just scientific knowledge, but Christian purity. And if we simply took samples and left the rest of the bodies here, then the chances are that Dr Duncan would work out some kind of a cure for this virus, some kind of an antidote, which is not God's intention.

'God's intention was to give me the means whereby this entire planet can become Christian; and devoted to Christian morality and Christian principles. God gave the same means to Moses in Egypt. "And all the first-born in the land of Egypt shall die, from the first-born of the Pharaoh who sits on his throne, to the first-born of the slave girl who is behind the millstones; and all the first-born of beasts. Moreover there shall be a great cry in all the land of Egypt, such as there has not been before and shall never be again . . ."

'Thus says the Lord, *"Let my people go, that they may serve me."* '

'And that is what I say to the Catholics in Rome, and the Hindus in Delhi, and the Shi'ites in Iran. That is what I say to the faithless Communists in China and the Taoists in Tokyo. I say let the Lord's people go, that they may serve Him. I say, let His people go.'

His voice had been rising higher and higher, and suddenly he was almost screaming. *'Let His people go, that's what I say! Let His people go!*

'Because this planet is going to Hell in a handcart. This planet is doomed! This planet is corrupted to the core like a rotten apple. Unless the peoples of this planet wake up to the Word of the Lord . . . unless the peoples of this planet say, "Hallelujah! Hallelujah! I understand the one true way!" And unless the peoples of this planet junk their Sivas and their Buddhas and their plastic Virgin Marys . . . what hope do we have? What hope of salvation?

456

'Are you going to walk up to the gates of Heaven with a Winn-Dixie bag crammed with rosaries and incense and 3-D pictures of Jesus, and say, "Let me in, Lord, because I'm religious and here's the proof"? That stuff, that isn't religious! That's idolatry! That's worse than idolatry! Being religious is being pure in heart, and having faith in things which you don't have evidence for, and giving of everything you have. More than anything else, being religious is casting pride aside. Humbling yourself, before God. Recognizing in your heart of hearts that you are just the same as every other human being on this planet, no better, no worse. That Sarawak woman in Indonesia, living in her hut, are you any better than her? That leprous beggar outside the Bombay railroad station, how about him? What makes you any better than him?

'Your pride, that's all. Your pride. And God will judge your pride, when it comes to the Day of Reckoning, and those that are proud shall be cast down into the fiery furnace, and those that are truly humble shall sit on the right hand of God.'

Dennis Evelyn Branch lifted his head as if he expected applause, and whoops of encouragement, but when he was greeted by shuffling indifference and a smattering of smokers' coughs he suddenly realized that he was talking to a group of dog-tired Norwegian miners who couldn't understand a word he was saying, and a few students who had probably been enticed to help him by the money he was prepared to pay, rather than his rhetoric.

'Good job then,' he said, anticlimactically. 'Sammy, let's get out of here.'

457

He went for the exit and his protectors followed close behind. Conor realized that this was going to be his only chance. He shouldered his way close behind them out of the tent, and reached into his pocket for Toralf's pistol. Outside, in the pelting snow, Dennis Evelyn Branch was less than twenty feet away, headed for his Jeep, his bodyguards on either side.

Conor unlocked his helmet and tossed it across the snow. The wind was so cold that it took his breath away. He lifted the pistol, aimed it directly at Branch's head and yelled out, '*Freeze!*'

Branch took two or three steps before he understood what Conor had shouted at him. He slowed, and turned around, his hands still deep in his pockets. Conor walked right up to him, less than ten feet away, so that there wouldn't be any chance of missing. The two bodyguards kept their hands hovering high, and well in sight. They didn't want Branch to be summarily shot because they dived too quickly for their guns.

'Take out every weapon you're carrying and drop them on the ground,' Conor ordered, without looking at either of them. His attention was fixed on the spot between Branch's eyebrows. When they hesitated, he shouted, '*Now!*'

There was a reluctant clatter; a Colt .45 automatic, a Beretta, two combat knives and a ninja flail. The snow began to bury them almost immediately.

'Back off,' Conor demanded, and they stepped away, their hands in the air. 'Back off and stay backed off.'

Dennis Evelyn Branch remained where he was,

with his hands still jammed in his pockets. The snow blew between them like a plague of albino locusts. 'I'm not going to pretend this is some kind of pleasure, Mr O'Neil. What the hell do you think you're doing here?'

Conor came even closer. 'I'm your nemesis, reverend. I'm the person who was sent by God to make sure that you didn't take His name in vain.'

Dennis Evelyn Branch looked at him narrowly. 'I warn you, mister, you've done enough interfering in my business, and when you're interfering in my business you're interfering in the Lord's business, and the Lord don't have any truck with unbelievers or those who choose a wayward path.'

'Walk toward the Jeep,' said Conor.

Branch stayed where he was, but Conor stiffened his arm and took a deliberate bead on his head. 'Let me tell you something: if I kill you here and now, it's not going to make my life any worse than it is already. And at least it'll give me the satisfaction of rubbing out the lunatic who made it that way.'

Dennis Evelyn Branch gradually broke into a smile. 'I should have guessed that you were after me, now, shouldn't I, when Toralf didn't show up? And I suppose it was you who burned out all of my vehicles, back in Tromso? Am I right? Go on, tell me, am I right?'

Conor said, 'Walk toward the Jeep.'

'Oh, come on, now. I can understand that you're *aggrieved*. I mean, maybe I went too far with the cockroaches and I apologize for that. But you can understand why we had to take your lady friend, can't you? And after all, you've had your revenge for that. The last I heard, Victor won't be talking again, not without a synthesizer. You're angry, for sure. But we can come to some kind of arrangement, can't we? After all, I respect you. I respect you very much. You came all the way to Spitsbergen to hunt me down, that's something else. Seventy-eight degrees north, Jesus. You must have faith in yourself. And – you know – once you have faith in yourself – that's just the first step. Faith in yourself leads to faith in the Lord.'

'Walk toward the Jeep,' Conor repeated. 'If you don't walk toward the Jeep now, I swear to God that I will kill you where you stand.'

'OK,' said Branch. 'You want me to walk, I'll walk.'

As soon as Branch had turned around, Conor said, 'Hands out of your pockets. Slow, wide, where I can see them.'

'I'm not carrying a weapon, Captain O'Neil. I'm a minister of religion. Besides that, my hands are cold. I left my gloves in the vehicle.'

'Lift your hands out where I can see them. I'm not going to tell you again.'

Branch did as he was told, holding his hands high up in the air, as if he were making a benediction. Conor came close up behind him and quickly patted his pockets. 'OK . . . you can put them back now.'

Branch continued to walk toward the Jeep and Conor followed him only a foot behind. There were still half a dozen construction workers noisily slinging the last pieces of framework into the backs of their Mercedes trucks, but none of them took any particular notice of Conor and Branch. Like all of the vehicles, the Jeep's engine was idling, and its windows were misted up – not on the inside, but the outside.

'OK, climb in,' Conor ordered, opening the passenger door. Branch gave him a long meaningful look and said, 'You're sure you want to do this? I mean, if you're going to stop, now's the time to do it.'

'Climb in,' Conor repeated. Branch made a *moue* and did what he was told. 'Right now – slide over to the driver's seat. You do know how to drive, don't you?'

'Only since I was five years old. My daddy taught me.'

'In that case, drive back down into town. I'll tell you what to do, once we're there.'

Branch shifted the Jeep into gear. 'You realize how hopeless this is. I don't personally carry a weapon but my adherents – well, they like to make sure that nothing untoward is going to happen to me. When they know that you've taken me hostage, they're going to be mighty wrathful.'

Conor looked back toward Branch's two bodyguards. Neither of them had moved; and their hands were still raised. 'Your so-called adherents have to catch up with us first,' he said. 'Now drive.'

He reached around for his seatbelt. As he did so, he heard a disturbance in the back of the Jeep. He tried to turn to see what it was, but then something whipped over the top of his head and caught him around the neck. He dropped the gun and tried to tug it away, but it was a thin braided wire, a garrotte,

461

and it cut so fiercely into his Adam's apple that he couldn't even cry out.

He was pulled back against the headrest, choking and gasping. He pulled at the wire again and again but his fingertips couldn't get any purchase. Branch leaned over toward him with his pink eyes wide and a grin on his face. 'You didn't think that you could interfere with a mission ordained by the Lord thy God, did you, Mr O'Neil? You didn't think that you could stand in the way of the Apocalypse?'

Conor struggled and twisted but the garrotte was thin and unrelenting and he knew that he was going to die. Waves of black light moved in front of his eyes. He could see that Branch was still talking but he couldn't hear him any more. He didn't even have enough breath to ask for absolution for all of his sins, and to beg God to take him into Heaven.

30

He opened his eyes. The ceiling above him was white and blank. Artificial light was falling on him from his left-hand side, and he could see shadows flickering to and fro.

His throat felt agonizing, like the worst tonsillitis that he had ever suffered. He reached his hand up and felt a thin indentation all the way across his larynx, so that his skin was ridged. He coughed, and he had to sit up when he coughed, in case he choked.

The door opened while he was still coughing, and Dennis Evelyn Branch came in. He was wearing a black skinny-ribbed polo-neck sweater and tight black pants. He must have showered quite recently because his white hair was wet and his skin looked damp. He stood a few feet away from Conor, his over-large head looking like an eerily handsome Mardi Gras mask.

'Did you really think you were dead?' he asked him.

Conor couldn't answer, just kept on coughing.

'You kept calling out for a priest, do you know that? As if one of your priests could absolve you.'

Conor lay back on the bed. It was plain, with an iron frame and no pillows or blankets. Branch walked around and stood over him, and Conor couldn't help thinking that he had never seen an expression like that on anybody's face before. Wild, beatific, destructive – so convinced of the reality of a life beyond life that he was prepared to do anything to get what he wanted.

'What time is it?' asked Conor.

Branch checked his wristwatch. 'Around seven p.m.'

'What day?'

'Sunday. You've been sleeping for a while.'

Conor tried to prop himself up on one elbow, but the room tilted so wildly that he had to lie back down again in case he fell off the bed. 'You've drugged me,' he said.

'Of course we've drugged you. We didn't want any trouble, did we? You did the same thing to poor old Knut, so what do you expect?'

'Burundanga?'

'That's the stuff. Total obedience in a bottle.'

Conor didn't say anything for a while, but waited for the beating in his head to subside. 'So where am I?' he asked, at last.

'You don't recognize this place? You're back in Tromso, in GMM's laboratory. Most of my adherents were all for shooting you and burying you in one of those graves in Longyearbyen cemetery, but I had a much better idea. I thought, let's use him as an experiment. Let him be the first to try out the Spanish flu virus. I mean, what an honor that would be, wouldn't it? To be the first person infected by a

464

virus that died out over eight decades ago. A virus that's going to change to spiritual life of every man, woman and child on the planet Earth.'

'You're crazy if you think you can get away with this.'

'Oh no I'm not. I may be a whole lot of things and – boy – doesn't the Lord keep reminding me that I'm less than perfect? But when you have a vision like mine directly from God, and I'm talking *directly* from God here, speaking intimately in my ear while I'm standing there shaving – when you have a vision like that you can get away with anything. And I mean *anything*.'

He suddenly stopped, frowned, and said, 'Would you like a drink of water? You sound like you could use a drink of water.' He went over to the stainless-steel washbasin and poured one out. Then he sat on the bed next to Conor and helped him with his scaly hand to lift up his head so that he could drink it.

'I'm sorry you were personally hurt,' he said. 'That wasn't my intention. But you can't divert the waters of time, my friend. You can't question the ordinance of God. This great revolution is going to happen and nobody on earth can stop it.'

Conor croaked, 'You're really going to let this virus loose?'

Branch looked serious. 'I hope not. I mean that most sincerely from the bottom of my heart. It is not my intention to cast the shadow of death all across the face of the earth; but I promise you sincerely that I will if I have to. It's a plague, but it's the plague of angels. I'm going to ask the leaders of all the false religions in the world to acknowledge the purity and

465

the supremacy of the Global Message Movement, the one way to God, and if they freely and willingly do that, well, that'll be an end to it.'

'You mean you'll destroy the virus?'

'Not exactly destroy it *as such*. After all, it's a living thing sent from God to work His will. So we'll just put it back on ice in case anybody starts getting any wild ideas about going back to their erring ways.'

'So you're going to impose your religious bigotry on the whole world by blackmail? Do you really think that's what God wants you to do?'

'Religious bigotry? What are you talking about, religious bigotry? The Global Message Movement is the only true way! Nobody is going to get to Heaven by any other path! Do you drive to Shreveport to get to Austin? Every nation on this earth speaks in different tongues, but there's only one true tongue, the Word of God. Look at our so-called United Nations! It's nothing but the Tower of Babel!'

Conor didn't know what to say. Dennis Evelyn Branch was obviously beyond any kind of logic; but then he had come across so many people who were just the same. How could he argue with Luigi Guttuso when he wistfully wished that crime wasn't against the law? How could he tell officers like Drew Slyman that extorting money from extortioners didn't amount to justice?

'What are you going to do now?' he asked.

Branch paced from one side of the room to the other. 'We've isolated the whole Spanish influenza virus. At least we believe we have. Now we're ready to try it out. You understand that we have to try it out. We can't threaten the entire population of the earth with something that doesn't work, can we? And you'll be living proof that it does. Well, hunh, *dead* proof. We can ship your body to New York and they'll be able to see for themselves what killed you. Then, it's up to them.'

He was still talking when the door opened again and a tall dark figure stepped into the room. Conor raised himself up, shielding his eyes against the light. The figure came toward him and stroked his cheek. He recognized the perfume; and then he recognized the zinc-white face.

'Hello, Conor,' she said, in the silkiest of voices.

'*Magda?*'

'Oh, you mustn't be upset, Conor. I was never very good with allegiances. I didn't go back to Oslo with Eleanor. I knew that you wouldn't be able to stop Dennis on your own. He has too many loyal followers; too much money; and a vision from God. It's hard to argue with a vision from God.'

'I thought you said that he wanted to kill you.'

'Only when I wasn't being compliant. Dennis will never hurt you, if you're compliant.'

Branch nodded, and nodded again. '*For though we walk in the flesh, we do not war according to the flesh. For the weapons of our warfare are not of the flesh, but divinely powerful for the destruction of fortresses. We are destroying speculations and every lofty thing raised up against the knowledge of God, and we are taking every thought captive to the obedience of Christ.*'

'Amen,' smiled Magda.

'I thought you wanted your revenge on this man,' said Conor. 'I thought you wanted your million dollars.'

Magda stood up straight. 'I realized that there are more important things in this world, Conor, than revenge, and dollars. Each of us has a duty to God.'

Branch opened the door and beckoned. Two men in white biohazard suits came in, although neither wore a helmet. Branch said, 'You can strip him and strap him down now.'

Conor rolled off the bed onto the floor but he was far too woozy from the effects of the burundanga. The two men heaved him back onto it and immediately started to wrench open his shirt and unbuckle his belt. Magda watched with a tilted smile on her face as they pulled off his shirt and his T-shirt and dragged down his pants and his undershorts. When he was naked, except for his socks, they strapped his wrists and his ankles onto the bed-rails so that he was unable to move.

'Fuck you,' he said, panting.

Magda leaned over him and gave him a dreamless smile. Her long black satin sleeves trailed against his penis, making him shiver. 'You always wanted me, didn't you?' she breathed. 'And I always wanted you. It wasn't to be, was it? But at least I've been able to see what I've been missing.'

She ran her long fingernails across his chest, lightly scratching him. He turned his head sideways and refused to look at her.

'Take off his socks,' said an unfamiliar voice. It was dry as an old gate opening. 'I want to see his feet go black.'

Magda moved away and Conor slowly turned back again. Somebody was sitting in the doorway, half silhouetted against the light. There was a moment's pause, and then a high electric whine. The figure came forward – a nodding figure in a wheelchair. It drove right up to the side of the bed and suddenly appeared in the bright light that shone over Conor's head.

Conor stared at it in shock. It was a woman, white-faced and pink-eyed like Dennis Evelyn Branch. In spite of its total lack of color, her face was exquisite, with perfectly arched eyebrows and pale pouting lips. It could have been the face of an angel or a saint. Her head, however, was huge, swollen by encephalitis, and tufted here and there with sparse white clumps of hair. Her arms and legs looked like the limbs of a giant mantis, fleshless and useless; yet she wore a short red satin dress that was deeply cut to the cleavage between her chalk-white breasts. Around her neck she wore a crucifix studded with rubies.

She unfolded one of her arms and laid a bony, attenuated hand on Conor's chest. He flinched in revulsion at her touch.

'If your heart ain't beating like a frog with its legs chopped off,' she said, in that same dry drawl. 'You're not *scared* of nothing, are you?'

Conor stared at her. Her face was so beautiful that the rest of her body looked even more grotesque than it really was; and the sexual blatancy of her dress only added to the horror. What man would ever think of going to bed with her, except in his darkest nightmares?

She was propped in a Scandinavian Mobility electric wheelchair, $35,000 worth, state of the art. She could move herself forward and sideways with complete precision. She could circle around the room and then sit utterly still, which was what she did now.

'Do you know who I am?' she asked Conor, her pink eyes unblinking.

Conor didn't answer.

'Do you know who I *am*?' she suddenly raged, her mantis-like arms flapping up and spit flying from her lips.

Conor gave her an infinitesimal shake of his head. 'No,' he croaked. 'I don't know who you are.'

'I'm the lady who was sitting in the back seat of Dennis's Jeep when you tried to abduct him. I'm the lady who wound a wire around your neck and brought you to order.' She wiped her mouth with the back of her hand and smiled. 'I like things to go to plan, sir. I like things to go orderly. And you – you were definitely not part of my plan, and you were not orderly, no sir.'

Her wheelchair went *neeee*, and she edged herself sideways. It went *neeee* again and she positioned herself so that she was staring directly into Conor's face. He tried hard not to look at her bulbous forehead, and the blue vein that he could see pulsing beneath her translucent skin.

The woman waited for a long time, silent. Then at last she said, 'In every life, Mr O'Neil, a little rain must fall; but in my life a little more rain fell than you might consider fair.

'I believe you've already guessed who I am, but you're such a stubborn self-important bastard you don't want to admit it, do you? I'm going to take such pleasure in what I'm going to do to you now.

It's not often that a biochemist gets the chance to inflict such terrible pain and such overwhelming panic in the course of legitimate research.'

She held out her bony hand and Magda, who was standing close behind her, took it between hers, as if she were pressing a leaf-skeleton between the pages of a book. 'You want to take a last look at this character, Magda?' she said. 'This is the last time you're going to see him looking so healthy. In less than twenty minutes' time he's going to be gagging to death on his own lung fluids.'

Conor looked at Magda but her dead-black eyes still gave nothing away. The woman in the wheel-chair pulled her hand away and performed a slow 180-degree circle until she had her back to Conor. 'Come on, now,' she coaxed. 'You know who I am. You *know* who I am, but you just don't want to give me the satisfaction, do you?'

'It doesn't matter what name evil goes under. It's still evil.'

The woman turned around. Her expression was bright and fierce. 'You think I'm evil? I'm doing the Lord's work here, in spite of the burden that the Lord inflicted on me in my mother's womb. I'm looking forward to the next life, sir, when I get my reward for spreading His Holy Word from one corner of the globe to the other. I'm looking forward to opening my eyes and finding that my legs and arms are straight and strong, and that my hair is long and soft and silky, and that I'm just as beautiful as any other woman who walked the earth.'

She took a deep, tortured breath. 'My mother gave birth to twins. She had German measles when she was pregnant, and both twins were born weak and sickly. But one twin was so deformed that the midwife couldn't believe that it was human, and that twin was me.

'My mother had run away from my father when she first discovered she was pregnant and she tried to have us aborted. She was only fourteen and my father was thirty-five. He was a man of God but he was a tyrant by nature. His manly pride was wounded: no woman ever ran away from *him*. He had my mother hunted down like an animal by members of his congregation and it was our bad luck that they found her before she could have us flushed out of her.

'When he first saw us twins in the hospital my father was horrified. He said we were the spawn of Satan, me especially. He wanted the doctors to smother me and throw my body in the incinerator, like an unwanted puppy. The doctors said they wouldn't do that, but they wouldn't feed me, either. But I survived. I survived for three days, and in the end my father had a vision that I was sent by God for some great purpose, and he ordered me nourished.

'All the same, he insisted that nobody should know about me; that I should never be seen. I might have been sent for some great purpose, but all the same he thought I was something shameful and a punishment sent direct from Almighty God. And that's the way I was brought up: in secret, behind blinds, without friends or family around me. My brother was christened Dennis and I was christened Evelyn, but my brother was always called by both of our names to remind him that he was a twin.'

472

She wheeled herself a little way away, out of the light, so that Conor could only see the white, tufted dome of her head, and not her face. 'Dennis grew up like Father. A dedicated believer in the scriptures and the power of God. I was different. I wanted to find out how God had caused me so much suffering, and why. When I was thirteen years old I started to study science, and in particular I started to study viral infections, like the rubella virus that turned me into what I am.

'Dennis was always devoted to me. Dennis believed what Father believed: that I was sent on earth for a purpose, that I had been deformed by a virus for a reason. Dennis brought the outside world into my room and showed me that I could make a difference to it, that I could change its history, as deformed as I was.

'He studied science at college and he enrolled in a university course in microbiology, and he did that for me. *He* went to the classes and tape-recorded all the lectures while *I* stayed at home and wrote all of his theses and showed him how to do all of the lab work. He carried on with his Bible studies, of course. He was always Bible-hungry. But he lived my life for me, too, that's how dedicated he was. He never forgot that he was Dennis *Evelyn* Branch.'

Conor didn't say a word. He tugged at the straps holding his wrists but they were far too tight for him to pull himself free.

Evelyn Branch said, 'We saw the world and we saw how corrupt it was and we decided that we were the ones who were chosen to change it. We declared war on atheism and false religions. I built some bombs and Dennis planted them. Then I showed him something else that I'd been interested in, too. Ways of making yourself invisible.'

'You're raving,' said Conor.

'No, I'm not, and you know I'm not. Sitting alone in my room I had dreamed for years of going outside into the streets and mixing with other people, so long as they couldn't see me. That's why I studied hypnotism, and all the other ways of affecting people's perception. Hypnotism, and drugs like burundanga. I'm even working on a powder made of gallium and arsenic that can stop light dead in its tracks, the same way that fog does. If a man could coat himself in a powder like this, you simply wouldn't be able to see him. An invisible man.

'It was when I was studying hypnotism that I first came across the names of Hypnos and Hetti. I read about their technique, and I was able to teach Dennis some basic hypnotic induction, and that's how he planted his bombs without anybody seeing him. It helped him in his sermons, too. He can virtually hypnotize an audience when he wants to, *clinically* hypnotize them, so that they're powerless to leave the room.

'But a few acts of religious terror weren't enough. In fact they usually made things worse – whipped up blind hostility, and prejudice. Dennis wanted the whole world to see the true way to Heaven, and that's how the idea of the Global Message Movement came into his head. And that's how the idea of reviving the Spanish influenza came into *my* head.'

'You don't seriously believe that God would want you to do that!'

'Yes, I do. My brother and I, we were chosen.'

'But if you release this virus, millions of people are going to die. Millions!'

'It's the will of the Lord, Mr O'Neil.'

Dennis Branch came forward and laid a hand on his sister's vulture-like shoulder. 'Think it's time we got this show on the road, don't you, Evelyn?'

Evelyn nodded. 'You'd better go through to the lab now, Magda. We don't want *you* to catch Mr O'Neil's little bug now, do we?'

Dennis stood over Conor and said, 'I know this isn't a voluntary sacrifice you're making here, Mr O'Neil. But it's a sacrifice that's going to promote the spiritual well-being of the entire human race, and when the message of God has reached from pole to pole, and the Global Message Movement is the crown of all religion here on earth, I'm going to make sure that you're remembered for ever, and honored for giving up your life.'

Conor said nothing. He found it hard to believe what was happening. It was only when Magda bent over and kissed his forehead that he realized that he was about to die.

Magda left, followed by Dennis. Three lab assistants came in through the double doors, all of them wearing protective suits and helmets. They carried a fourth, empty suit, and an aluminum box stenciled with a red skull-and-crossbones.

Two of them lifted Evelyn Branch from her wheelchair while the other slid her dangling legs into the bottom of the suit. They fastened the seals, locked on her helmet, and adjusted her airflow. Lying in front of them naked, Conor felt utterly vulnerable.

One of the assistants carefully laid the aluminum box in Evelyn's lap, and then all three of them left and closed the doors behind them. Evelyn came whining back in her wheelchair. Inside the distorting bowl of her helmet, she looked more like a fairground freak than she had before. She unlocked the box, opened the lid, and brought out a tiny glass vial of clear liquid.

'Spanish influenza virus, 1918 strain. As virulent as ever, I hope. I'll be surprised if you last longer than forty-five minutes.'

She took out a hypodermic needle, pressed the plunger, and inserted the needle into the vial of virus. 'You'll feel a little bunged up at first, as if you've caught a headcold. Then you'll start shivering and coughing and spitting up blood. After that you'll be gasping for air, because your lungs will be filled up with fluid. I shouldn't let it frighten you. It's no worse than drowning, and at least you don't have to get wet.'

She approached Conor with the hypodermic. She squeezed his left arm with her spidery fingers to make the veins stand out.

Conor said, 'I guess it's no good asking you not to do this.'

Evelyn lifted her eyes. 'Are you a religious man, Mr O'Neil?'

'Yes, I am.'

'You're here, strapped to this table, about to die from the effects of one of the most appalling viruses known to man, and yet you still believe in God?'

'Yes, I do.'

'Are you a Catholic, Mr O'Neil?'

476

Conor nodded.

Evelyn looked toward the observation window where Dennis Branch was standing, his forearm resting against the glass.

'If I were to say to you that if you renounced your Catholicism here and now, and followed the teaching of the Global Message Movement, you could go free – what would you say to that?'

'I'd say that you were lying.'

The point of the hypodermic needle was less than a half inch away from Conor's bulging blue vein. 'I'm not lying, Mr O'Neil. All you have to do is renounce the teaching of Rome, and pledge your allegiance to the ministry of the Global Message, and that's it. No injection. You get up, you get dressed, you go home.'

'Are you testing your virus or are you testing my faith?'

Evelyn Branch gave him a wide-eyed, beatific smile. 'It looks like I could be testing both, doesn't it?'

Conor closed his eyes. In the darkness behind his eyelids, he thought: *What if I renounce my religion? There's nothing to stop me from confessing my sin after this is all over, and asking for God's forgiveness. God must understand what I'm facing here. I'm facing death – and not only my own death, but the likely death of millions of others. If I'm the only one who can save them, what right do I have to behave like a martyr? Better to fall from grace than to let so many die.*

'Well?' asked Evelyn Branch. 'What's it to be?'

'If I renounce my religion . . . if you let me go . . . who's to say that you aren't going to use somebody else as a guinea-pig?'

477

'That's irrelevant, at least as far as you're concerned. This is your choice, nothing to do with anybody else. If you don't embrace the Global Message Movement, then you're going to die, and that's all there is to it.'

'All right, 'said Conor; and his mouth felt as if it were full of ashes. 'I embrace it.'

Dennis Branch banged the window in glee. Evelyn Branch said, just to make sure, 'You embrace the Global Message Movement and you turn your back on the Roman Catholic Church?'

Conor was breathing so deeply now that he was hyperventilating. 'Yes,' he said, even though he knew in his heart that God would never forgive him for this.

Evelyn Branch didn't take the needle away. She remained tense: one hand clutched tight around Conor's upper arm. 'Excellent test. Worked perfect, didn't it? You're a strong man, of very strong principles, I know that. But you're prepared to abandon your faith in order to stay alive, and I can't say that I blame you.

'Dennis will be glad to know that devout Catholics are prepared to surrender their so-called beliefs so easily, in the face of death. Let's hope it works with Buddhists and Hindus and Muslims, too.'

Conor stared through the window and knew that he had renounced his faith in vain. Dennis Branch had taken off his blue sunglasses and was staring back at him with his pink eyes wide open and his face filled with triumph. The world will fall before me. The world will turn its back on false religion, and

478

follow me to God. And I shall lead you all to Heaven, every one.

'I hope you go to Hell, both of you,' said Conor.

Evelyn Branch squeezed Conor's arm even tighter, and pushed the hypodermic needle up against his skin so that it was making an indentation.

Conor said, 'Holy Mary, Mother of God, forgive me for having renounced my faith in you. In my heart I never did. Forgive me for my cowardice, O Lord. Forgive me all of my sins and trespasses. I love you, God, regardless.'

It was then that an extraordinary thing happened. Evelyn Branch's hand began to shake, and then to shudder. She stared at Conor through her helmet and her eyes were bulging with strain. *God*, thought Conor, *she's having an epileptic seizure.* But she wasn't thrashing about or foaming at the mouth or choking. She was struggling with herself. She was trying to push the hypodermic plunger into Conor's vein but for some reason she simply couldn't.

'*What?*' she shouted at Conor, her voice muffled by her bio-helmet.

There was nothing else that Conor could do. He jerked at his straps – but they were far too strong. He saw Evelyn Branch lift the hypodermic away from his arm, and twist in her electric wheelchair. He heard Dennis's tinny voice over the intercom, shouting, 'Evelyn? Evelyn? What's the matter, Evelyn?'

Evelyn lifted her head and her mouth was stretched wide open – like a woman trying to battle with every demon that had ever scorned her or humiliated her. She raised her left hand, protected in two layers of rubber gloves; and then she raised her right hand, with the hypodermic still in it, and pointed it toward the ball of her thumb.

'Evelyn!' screamed Dennis, through the intercom. 'Evelyn, listen to me! What the hell are you trying to do there, Evelyn? Drop the syringe! Hear what I say? Drop the syringe and get yourself out of there, *pronto!*'

Evelyn ignored him, or didn't even hear him. She sat tilted at an angle in her wheelchair. She looked as if she might have had a minor stroke – one eye closed, the tell-tale sign of apoplexy or a mental struggle so ferocious that it was threatening to drive her mad. Slowly, with quivering fingers, she moved the point of the hypodermic needle closer and closer to the ball of her thumb, until she was a millimeter away from pricking it.

'You shouldn't do this,' said Conor. 'If you so much as scratch yourself, that's it. That's the big tortilla. I don't know what's happening inside of your mind, but try to see what you're doing.'

Evelyn stared at him. 'Jesus,' she said. 'You're a saint, after all. If I were you, I would tell me to stick this needle right in my thumb and God damn you to hell.'

'Think what you're doing,' said Conor.

'I'm doing what I'm told. When you're told to do something, you have to do it, you know that. Unless you're God, of course, or Dennis.'

'Who told you what to do?' Conor demanded.

Evelyn didn't answer, but turned toward the observation window. Dennis was staring at her in horror; but behind him stood Magda, with a thin-lipped, satisfied smile. *Shit,* thought Conor. *She hypnotized her. She always said that she was unequaled at post-hypnotic suggestion, and that's what she must have done to Evelyn.*

'Don't do it,' said Conor. But almost in defiance, Evelyn slid the needle through the double layer of gloves that protected her thumb, so that a bead of dark red blood sprang out. She squeezed the syringe and the virus disappeared into her bloodstream. She continued to stare at Conor for almost fifteen seconds, her eyes wandering. Then her head dropped forward, and she collapsed.

'*Evelyn!*' wailed Dennis, beating his fists on the glass. The hypodermic dropped to the floor and rolled away. The three lab assistants hurriedly put on their helmets again and opened up the doors. They unstrapped Conor from the bed and one of them slapped him on the shoulder and said, 'Out! Quick as you can!' Conor heaved himself onto the floor and an assistant helped him to limp barefoot out of the quarantine room. Magda was waiting for him. 'I have your clothes here,' she said. She laid her arms around his shoulders: after all, she was tall enough. She led him through to a small room at the back of the laboratory where his clothes had been tossed onto a chair.

He dressed, leaning against the wall to support himself. He felt weak and shivery, as if he had a pounding hangover. 'It was you, wasn't it?' he whispered. '*You* made Evelyn prick herself.'

'You think I could do a thing like that? Evelyn knows how dangerous that virus is. Maybe I could hypnotize somebody into eating a raw

481

potato, thinking it's an apple. But it isn't so easy to hypnotize somebody into killing themselves.'

'So what are you trying to tell me? That you didn't stay here to save my life? That you came back here to work for Dennis Branch?'

'No,' said Magda. 'I stayed here because I didn't think you were ever coming back. If you disappeared, if you were dead, what was the point of my going back to Oslo? I didn't even stay for my revenge. Revenge is too much of a luxury. I stayed for my money, that's all.'

'Did you know about Evelyn?'

She shook her head. 'Not until now. Not until I came back here. They're a very strange pair.'

'They're not just strange, they're maniacs. If I don't stop them, they're going to wipe out half the population of the world.'

'You? How can you stop them? You're not a police detective any more, are you? I saw you today and you were just an ordinary man with no clothes on. Besides, do you want to get yourself killed?'

They were still hoarsely whispering when Dennis Branch appeared in the doorway. He was breathing deeply and harshly, and he fixed Conor with a look of absolute hatred.

'That's my twin sister in there, Mr O'Neil! That's my twin sister! You're going to watch her get sick! You're going to watch her die! You're going to see what I'm going to do to the world, and then I'm going to kill you, too, with the same virus, and then you're going to know what it feels like!'

'You told Toralf that you were looking for a sword,' said Conor. 'A sword to cut down the unbelievers! Well, just you remember that those who live by the sword shall die by the sword.'

Dennis said, 'If you quote the Bible to me, Mr O'Neil, you'd better quote it right. Matthew chapter twenty-six verse fifty-two: "*All they that take the sword shall perish with the sword.*" And remember what else Matthew said. "He saved others, himself he cannot save." '

31

At first they thought that the virus might not have survived its eighty-year sleep in the snow. Evelyn lay on the bed in a black T-shirt and black drawstring pants, her globe-like head resting against the pillow, her eyes restless. She slept for two or three hours – a disturbed sleep, sweating and murmuring and waving her weakened arms in the air. Conor had been positioned in a hard plastic chair right in front of the window, his wrists tied together. He was so exhausted that he could hardly keep his eyes open, but Dennis kept viciously prodding him in the shoulder-blades and saying, 'Watch! Watch, you bastard! That's me dying in there, too! And soon it's going to be you!'

After fifteen minutes, a bright streak of blood suddenly ran from Evelyn's nose. Within twenty minutes she was trembling wildly. Her face darkened until it was the color of raw calves' liver and her feet turned almost black. She coughed, and covered her T-shirt in a livid bib of blood.

Dennis stood rigidly behind Conor's chair and stared, scarcely blinking, at every grotesque minute of his twin sister's dying. Magda had left the laboratory. She said she couldn't bear to watch. But three lab assistants stayed behind to monitor Evelyn's vital signs. The door to the quarantine room remained sealed; except at 2:48 a.m. when a fully suited assistant took Evelyn a plastic bottle of water and a shot of morphine to ease her pain.

Her end came at 3:11 a.m., with horrifying suddenness, in the same way that the victims of the Spanish influenza had died in 1918. She began to choke and clutch at her throat. One of the assistants came up to Dennis and said, 'She's going, sir. I'm sorry. There's nothing else we can do.'

Dennis jabbed Conor in the shoulders again. 'Watch this, Mr O'Neil, because this is the way that you're going to go.'

Then he raised both arms, and said, '*Now hear this, all you who forget God, lest I tear you in pieces, and there be none to deliver. He who offers a sacrifice of thanksgiving honors me; and to him who orders his way aright, I shall show the salvation of God.*'

Evelyn coughed one more cough. Then – over the intercom – like a locust struggling to escape from a glass jar – they heard her death-rattle.

Dennis lowered his arms and wrapped them tight around his chest. He let out a howl of anguish that was barely human. Then he sank to his knees and pressed his forehead against the floor, sobbing. One of the assistants laid a hand on his shoulder and tried to help him onto his feet, but he twisted himself away.

'Come on,' said another assistant. 'We'd better get the body bagged up.'

485

Conor tried to stand up but the assistant warned him, 'Stay where you are. I don't think that Mr Branch has finished with you yet.' Another assistant went to stand in front of the door, just in case Conor got any ideas about trying to escape. Conor looked around him. There was nothing in reach that he could see to cut the cords around his wrists, only flasks and test-tubes and bottles of chemicals. He could break one, he supposed, but it would take him far too long to saw through the cord.

Two of the assistants put on helmets and went into the quarantine room, carrying a body bag with them. Dennis Branch stayed on the floor, still weeping, but much more quietly now, with occasional rib-racking gasps for breath.

' "*O God in the greatness of thy loving kindness deliver me from the mire and do not let me sink. May the flood of water not overwhelm me and may the pit not shut its mouth on me.*" '

The two assistants lifted Evelyn's bagged-up body onto a stretcher and one of them opened the inner door. He was having trouble opening the outer door, however, so the third assistant came to help him.

But Conor had been reading the labels on the chemicals close by. He suddenly heaved himself out of his chair and snatched a triangular flask of concentrated sulfuric acid from the laboratory bench beside him. Dennis Branch said, 'What—?' and looked up to see what was happening. As he did so, Conor swung his arms over his head so that the bottle of acid was directly in front of his face. With both thumbs, Conor pried off the stopper, which dropped to the floor and smashed.

'Up!' Conor demanded. 'Up on your feet or you get a faceful!'

Dennis stayed where he was, his eyes rimmed with red, his cheeks streaked with tears.

'*Up!*' Conor repeated; and to make his point he jerked his hands up and splashed a few drops of the acid on Dennis's chin.

'Jesus Christ!' shouted Dennis. 'Jesus Christ, are you crazy?' There was a strong smell of scorched flesh and wisps of smoke curled around his chin.

'Just get up and you won't have to find out *how* crazy.'

'Christ that hurts,' said Dennis. 'No – don't do it again. I'll get up. God, you don't know how much that hurts.'

The laboratory assistants stood uncertainly in the doorway of the quarantine room, still holding Evelyn's body. Conor said, 'All of you – get back inside.'

'But I don't have my helmet,' protested the third assistant.

'Get back inside, unless you want to be personally responsible for Mr Branch losing his face.'

The assistants shuffled back into the quarantine room. Conor nudged Dennis in front of him until they reached the door. 'Lock it,' he ordered. Dennis, reluctantly, locked it. 'Right, now you lead the way.'

Together they edged their way out of the laboratory and along the corridor toward the reception area. The sulfuric acid wallowed from side to side in its bottle and Dennis said, 'Don't spill it, O'Neil. If you spill it, then I swear that God will wreak His vengeance on you for all eternity.'

'Don't tell me you're prepared to sacrifice the human race, but not your own face.'

'I need my face for my mission. My congregation has to look at my face and believe that it's a likeness of the Lord.'

'The Lord comes in many different likenesses, Mr Branch. Black, white, yellow and red. Who's to say that a man with a burned-off face doesn't resemble the Lord?'

They reached the front doors. Conor said, 'Open them. We're leaving.'

Dennis did as he was told, but as they awkwardly maneuvered their way through the doors into the freezing cold wind, Dennis swung up his right arm. He knocked the flask of acid from underneath. The acid splattered onto the steps, and some of it splashed against Conor's wrists, burning him like fire. Instinctively, he wrenched his hands upward, striking Dennis on the side of the jaw. Dennis staggered sideways, missed his footing on the icy steps and hit his head against the brickwork. He tried to get up, but Conor kicked him just behind the right ear, and he rolled down the last three steps into the snow.

The doors opened again. It was Magda, staring at him in amazement. 'What's happened? What are you doing?'

'I'm getting the hell out of here, and I'm taking Mr Branch here with me. Are you coming?'

'Wait – I'll get the keys to the car.'

She went back into the building and she seemed to be gone forever. Conor stood in the biting cold, shivering, occasionally glancing down at Dennis to make sure that he was still unconscious. Eventually Magda reappeared, swinging the keys. 'I had to get the spare set out of the laboratory. You've locked them in! They were shouting at me like wild animals!'

Magda unlocked the blue Volvo 440 parked directly outside the building. Conor took hold of Dennis's coat collar and dragged him across to the open door. 'Here!' he said. 'Give me a hand to lift him onto the back seat!'

Just as Magda was walking around the car, however, the doors to the laboratory building opened and an unshaven man came barging out, holding a gun.

'What do you think you're doing?' he shouted. 'Stop! Put up your hands!'

'Mr Branch wasn't feeling too good,' said Conor. 'We were trying to get him to the hospital.'

The man came down the steps. 'What do you mean? What are you doing? What the hell's happened to him?'

He knelt down beside Dennis and lifted his head. Blood dripped glutinously out of his ear and made a spotted red pattern on the snow. 'He's been hurt. You've knocked him out.'

Conor said, 'You're right. Why don't you join the club?' and swung the Volvo's rear door so that it collided with the man's shoulder and sent him sprawling. The man lifted himself up, but slipped on the ice. He lifted himself again and fired at them twice. One bullet shattered the Volvo's rear window and the second banged into the door. Conor shouted to Magda: 'Into the car! Go!'

He managed to heave himself into the passenger seat. Magda climbed in next to him and started the engine. The man fired again and Conor felt a thump in the Volvo's trunk. They backed up with whinnying tires and then slewed off into the darkness with the man still shouting at them.

They drove for almost ten minutes before either of them spoke. Conor kept pushing in the car's cigar lighter so that he could burn away the cords around his wrists.

'How are we going to get Ms Gambit's money back now?' asked Magda.

'Plan C.'

'Oh, yes? And what is Plan C?'

'Plan C is we go back to Oslo and inform the Norwegian police what Dennis Branch and his people are trying to pull. Up until the time he dug up those graves at Longyearbyen he hadn't committed any criminal offense on Norwegian soil; but now he has – and a pretty damned serious one, too. From what I've been reading, the Norwegian conservation people go ape if you pick up some old bone from the beach, let alone seven whole bodies.'

'So then what?'

'They'll arrest him and sequester his funds. The Norwegian police will contact the NYPD and eventually everybody will get their money back.'

'And what about me? What about *my* money? Why do you think I came all the way to this Godforsaken country? Why do you think I've been eating nothing but fish every day? Breakfast, lunch, dinner – fish! I'm turning into a mermaid!'

490

'Was that really all that you came for? The money?'

'Of course. Why else should I come?'

'I don't know. You change your allegiances so quickly.' Conor pushed in the cigar lighter again.

'I never had allegiance to Dennis Branch. I only had allegiance to myself. What was the point of being loyal to you, if you were dead?'

Conor glanced at her. 'You *did* hypnotize Evelyn, didn't you?'

Magda didn't answer, but pulled down the sun-visor and inspected her eye make-up in the vanity mirror.

They drove toward the sparkling lights of Tromso, their snow chains whirring on the frozen road. On their left was the inky blackness of Tromsoysundet; on their right the snow-blanketed mountains which formed the backbone of Tromsoya island, threaded with kilometer after kilometer of floodlit ski-trails. The snow itself was blowing quite lightly from the east.

Strangely – after having traveled so far north to Longyearbyen – Conor felt as if he were returning to civilization.

There was a Braathens SAFE flight to Oslo at 6:30 a.m. Both Conor and Magda slept as the 737 flew southward, leaving the Arctic Circle behind them. They didn't see the ghostly greenish flicker of the Northern Lights, over the land where seven young men had been buried for so long.

491

The story was already in the *International Herald Tribune* by the time they reached Oslo airport. Conor read it in the back of the taxi on the way to their apartment on Helgesens Gate.

The bodies of seven victims of the Spanish influenza pandemic of 1918 were stolen from their graves on Spitsbergen in a robbery that was described by the authorities as 'an obscene act of vandalism with potentially catastrophic consequences'.

Sysselmannen, the Governor of the Svalbard archipelago, said that his office had agreed last year to an exhumation of the bodies by a leading Canadian scientist, Dr Kirsty Duncan. Since the bodies had been frozen solid since their death, it was thought that they might contain samples of the deadly influenza virus, which killed more than 22 million people worldwide.

When a number of well-equipped technicians and engineers arrived at Longyearbyen last week the Governor was deceived by forged papers and e-mail messages into thinking that it was an advance party of the official expedition.

'They observed all of the safety criteria that had been agreed between myself, Dr Duncan and the health authorities,' said the Governor. 'They seemed to behave very responsibly. They were very careful to follow all the regulations regarding driving their vehicles on thawed ground, and to do as little damage to the environment as possible. They stole the bodies but they left the cemetery exactly as they found it, with all the grave markers returned to their original positions, so at first our suspicions were not aroused. It was only when Dr Duncan called us to confirm her arrival that we realized something was wrong.'

It turned out that the so-called 'advance party' had no connection at all with Dr Duncan, who says that she is 'devastated and deeply alarmed' by the grave-robbery. What worries her most of all is that every body was removed in its entirety, which her expedition was specifically prohibited from doing.

'There is potentially a terrible risk if infected tissue is not kept under category-4 control. Not only that, we now have no way of obtaining samples of the whole virus ourselves, so that we can find a way of vaccinating ourselves against it.'

At the moment, police and military intelligence have no idea who might have stolen the bodies or why. One suggestion is that the expedition was planned and financed by Saddam Hussein in order to extend his biological arsenal. A less apocalyptic explanation is that it was set up by a team of rival scientists, since the whole Spanish virus is the flu researcher's 'holy grail' and there is not only great scientific kudos attached to finding it but huge financial rewards for anybody who can develop an effective vaccine.

In 1997, Dr Johan Hultin, a 77-year-old

493

pathologist from San Francisco, single-handedly recovered tissue from a mass grave in Alaska which enabled government laboratories to isolate parts of the 1918 flu virus. Dr Hultin had been trying to recover the live virus from a mission station in Alaska which had been wiped out in 1918 after a flu-infected postman on a dog sledge visited the community. Eighty per cent of the population died within a week and by the time help was sent out to them, huskies were eating their bodies.

There is no suggestion that Dr Hultin was involved in the Longyearbyen exhumation, but there are several other flu researchers who might have been tempted to pre-empt Dr Duncan's project. The cost of the expedition must have run into millions of dollars – so the choice of possible perpetrator is limited.

Police are contacting government laboratories and microbiological research centers all round the world to see if they can shed any light on the most ghoulish grave-robbery since the tomb of Tutankhamen.

'Definitely time to blow the whistle,' said Conor.

Magda said, 'I hope you don't regret it. You shouldn't think that Dennis Branch is insane, you know. You're dealing with a man who believes that he can really save the world. What is the moral difference between him and the Spanish missionaries who forced *your* religion on the Incas, and wiped them out with their diseases?'

'I'm not interested in ethics, Magda. I just want to

494

stop this man from exterminating half the world.'

Magda leaned across the taxi's back seat and kissed him on the lips. She tasted of Chanel lip color. Afterward, she didn't move back, but continued to stare at him from less than two or three inches away, so that he found it impossible to focus on her. 'You're growing older,' she said. 'The world is changing faster and faster. Wouldn't you like to make love to me?'

'Magda, I need your help, not your body.'

'You know what I have found out, in life? You never know what you need, until you try it.'

They had called Eleanor from Tromso and she was waiting for them when they arrived back at their apartment at Helgesens Gate. Candles were twinkling in every room and there was a strong savory smell coming from the kitchen. 'Chicken casserole,' said Eleanor. 'I thought you'd probably be sick of all that elk.'

Conor put his arms around her and held her close.

'I was so scared,' she told him. 'I thought you were never going to come back to me.'

'Eleanor, I can never be James.'

'I know that,' she said, and kissed him, and patted his arm. 'I know that now.'

They sat around the kitchen table that night and Conor told Eleanor about the grave-robbery in Longyearbyen; and the way that Evelyn Branch had died. Eleanor said, 'He's serious, isn't he? He'd rather wipe out the world than allow anybody to think differently. I've met a whole lot of people like that. Usually they don't have the means to exert their power – not like Dennis Branch and his virus. But they would do, given the chance. Absolute belief in yourself isn't a virtue, no matter what rewards it may bring you. It's a disease.'

'I suppose you have some evidence to back that up?' said Magda, pushing away her plate of half-eaten casserole.

'Oh, sure,' said Eleanor. 'I was married to some, once.'

Conor called Oslo police headquarters. They kept him waiting for almost five minutes, listening to a selection of unfamiliar ringing tones. Eventually a brisk detective came on the line. He sounded as if he had just brushed his teeth.

'This is Captain Ingstad. How can I help you, sir?'

'I believe that *I* can help *you*. I have some information regarding the exhumation of bodies at Longyearbyen.'

'Oh, yes? You must tell me who you are.'

'It doesn't matter who I am. I know who dug them up and I know where they took them. The rest is up to you.'

'You're American, yes? I don't understand how you are involved in this matter.'

'Just take it from me that I am,' said Conor. He tried to put himself in the Norwegian detective's position: he would have been equally suspicious if some anonymous foreigner had called up and told him that he knew his business better than he did. He explained about Dennis and Evelyn Branch and the Global Message Movement. He told him about the laboratory at Breivika Havnegata. 'I don't know

496

how much you're going to find there. The birds have probably flown the nest. But, believe me, it's true.'

'You must tell me who you are. If what you are saying is true, then I am sure that we can come to some arrangement.'

How many times have I said those selfsame words, thought Conor. 'I'm sorry, detective,' he said, and broke the connection.

That night, he slept deeply and dreamed that he was floating on an ice floe. He was bitterly cold but he couldn't move, because the ice floe was melting fast and he was on the verge of tipping into the water. He circled around and around, and above his head the stars circled around and around, the scattered constellations of the northern hemisphere.

He dreamed that the ice floe suddenly rocked; and dipped; and that something began to rear out of the water; something huge and tall and white, like a phantom. He opened his eyes and it was a polar bear, standing erect, its claws raised, its eyes burning like incandescent lumps of coal.

Don't try to shoot it, he said. *Don't try to run away from it. Don't run after it, whatever you do.* He felt somebody putting their cool arms around him and saying, 'Ssh, ssh . . .' He was sweating and shaking, and he didn't know whether he was asleep or awake. But gradually he was able to focus, and he could recognize the bedroom ceiling, and the triangle of sodium light from the street outside.

He turned his head and Magda was lying beside him, stroking his hair with one hand and stroking his hip with the other. Her face was so pale that she was almost invisible against the pillow but her eyes were as black as cut-out pieces of the night sky, going on to infinity. Her skin was smooth as her voice was smooth. Smooth as the tip of a silk scarf, being slowly drawn between the cleft of his buttocks and up his spine.

'You were having a nightmare,' she breathed. 'I heard you shouting, so I came in to see what I could do.'

He tried to touch her but she deflected his hand. He tried again and she deflected him again. Her fingertips ran down his side until they reached his hips. Her touch was exquisite, like pleasure and irritation, both at the same time. His penis began to stiffen in spite of himself, and her fingernails formed a birdcage around his glans, teasing, pricking.

'You see?' she said. 'No hypnotism.'

She slid herself beneath him, almost magically, and as he turned over she took hold of his penis and guided it between her legs. His hands were free now, he could feel her – Magda Slanic, the stage hypnotist. She had no body hair at all. Her vulva was smooth as a nectarine. Her breasts were small but they were very firm, and when he cupped them in the palms of his hands he realized that they were pierced with nipple rings.

Her mouth opened wide and her tongue slid all over his face, even sticking his eyelashes together. He lifted his head slightly and she licked his throat.

'Come on,' she whispered, opening her thighs wider. 'You can have me now, Conor, and I will give you feelings like you've never felt before.'

She parted her vulva with both hands, opened it

498

up wide like a pink slippery fruit. She placed the swollen head of Conor's penis against it, and said, 'Now . . . all you have to do is sink inside.'

There was an instant when Conor almost gave in to temptation. He opened his saliva-sticky eyelids and looked down at Magda's white, sculptured face. She was beautiful in an alien way and the feeling of her skin was so erotic that it made his nerve-ends effervesce. But in those slanted black eyes of hers he saw absolutely nothing but self-interest. Even the physical pleasure that she was giving him was entirely for her own satisfaction.

And there was something else: the cock was about to crow thrice. He had compromised his integrity to ask for help from Luigi Guttuso. He had denied his religion. Now he was about to betray Lacey, too.

He leaned forward and kissed Magda on her forehead. It was as cold as ivory. She said nothing: she could obviously guess by his kiss that he wasn't going to make love to her. She lay unmoving while he climbed off her and sat on the edge of the bed. She didn't try to touch him again.

'I'm sorry,' he said. 'It's me, not you.'

'You're feeling guilty. You have such honor, it makes me want to bite you.'

'Honor? I wish.'

She knelt up close behind him. He could feel her nipple rings against his back. 'Yes, you have honor. Bravery is nothing but the child of luck and stupidity. But honor. Honor is the child of suffering and faith.'

He turned his head and looked at her. 'Are you really Romanian?' he asked her.

499

'I am what I want to be. Now, you'd better get some sleep.'

At 10:17 a.m. the next morning, Conor called Captain Ingstad again.

'Well, it seems that your information was correct,' said Captain Ingstad. 'I just wish I knew who you were and how you found out such things.'

'You contacted the police at Tromso?'

'Of course; and they discovered the laboratory exactly as you said. Except that there was nobody there and it was burned to the ground. They found the bodies from Longyearbyen there, too, or what was left of them. They had all been doused in some kind of accelerant, and there is nothing left but ashes.'

'No sign of Dennis Branch?'

'As I said, there was nobody there. I myself went to the bank this morning and checked the account. All of the funds were withdrawn on Friday and the account closed.'

'Did the bank have any idea where the money went?'

'I'm not really supposed to tell you anything. But most of it went to Switzerland and the rest was divided between many different countries throughout the world, even the People's Republic of China. Quite a large amount went to New York.'

'And you don't have any idea where Dennis Branch might have gone?'

'None at all. There are so many ways for people to leave Norway without the authorities having any record. So many small airfields. So many fiords. You could drive into Sweden and nobody would know. Then a ferry from Göteborg to Frederikshavn, and in a day's drive you could be in Brussels.'

Conor said, 'OK, I get the picture. Thanks for your help, anyhow.'

'You still won't tell me who you are? You see, I have the suspicion that you are police.'

'What makes you think that?'

'You know what they say about police. It's not a calling, it's a nationality.'

32

They spent the rest of the day quietly, although Conor couldn't get Dennis Branch off his mind. If he had sent a large sum of money to New York then it was possible that he intended to go there. In fact, he could be there already. But he might simply have been sending funds to Victor Labrea to support the Global Message Movement; or paying Victor Labrea off.

After lunch, Eleanor and Magda went shopping for clothes along Karl Johans Gate, while Conor went walking around Oslo alone. He came at last to the Domkirke, the cathedral. It wasn't a Roman church, but it was still the house of God and he had something to settle. He walked through the huge bronze doors illustrating the Beatitudes, and into the cool interior. The cathedral was decorated in grays, blues, greens and gilt, against dazzling white. Very Scandinavian, and nothing like the high Gothic grandeur of St Patrick's. The only sound was the echoing shuffle of a few off-season tourists, and an occasional voice sounding as if it were underwater.

He knelt down in a pew. The watery October sun came slanting through the stained-glass windows. He closed his eyes and said a prayer for his family and for Lacey; and then he asked for God's forgiveness for having so easily renounced his religion.

Gradually he lifted his eyes and saw the paintings on the ceilings. They were tempestuous biblical scenes such as the Flood and the destruction of Sodom and Gomorrah, as well as calm, uplifting pictures from the life of Christ. The cathedral organ quietly began to play, a Norwegian hymn, melodic and calm, as luminous as one of the distant glaciers that he had seen on Isfiorfden. He understood then that he was forgiven for what he had said to Evelyn Branch; and that he was readmitted to the grace of God. In fact, he had never left it.

He remembered the story of the man who walked across the desert of his life with Jesus beside him; and turned around to look at the footprints they had left behind. 'Look how many times you left me, Lord,' he said, resentfully. 'Whenever I was going through really bad times, there is only one set of footprints.' And Jesus said, 'My son, whenever you were going through really bad times, I was carrying you.'

They returned to their apartment that afternoon when it was just growing dark. Eleanor drew the drapes while Magda switched on the television. Conor opened one of the bottles of chardonnay that he had bought at the local Vinmonopolet, the state-controlled liquor store, for about four times what it would have cost him in New York.

'Just to go out and have a decent whiskey sour,'

complained Eleanor. 'I mean, how does anybody ever get smashed here?'

'They distil their own,' said Magda. 'Cherry *akvavit*, lemon *akvavit*, every flavor you can think of. It's illegal but everybody does it.'

'Rather Philadelphia than here,' said Eleanor, misquoting W.C. Fields.

'It's snowing again,' said Magda; and sure enough it was.

They were still talking and bantering when a CNN news bulletin came on the screen. '. . . Internet message that threatens the entire world with a deadly influenza virus.'

'Turn it up,' urged Conor, and Magda immediately increased the volume.

Serious-faced, CNN's David Channon said, 'The warning appeared on the Worldwide Web at precisely five o'clock this morning Eastern Standard Time. It takes the form of a long personal announcement by Dennis Evelyn Branch, the leader of a breakaway Baptist cult from western Texas, the Global Message Movement.

'Dennis Evelyn Branch claims that he and his followers were responsible for the exhumation last week of seven young men who died eighty years ago on the remote island of Spitsbergen, five hundred and eighty kilometers north of the Arctic Circle. They say that they recovered frozen samples of the Spanish flu virus which swept the world in 1918, killing more people than the combined populations of Washington, DC and New York City.

'They will release this deadly virus Wednesday, October twentieth, at eleven-thirty a.m., at an unspecified location, unless they have a written assurance from the leaders of all the world's major religions that they will renounce their own rituals and their own beliefs and accept the doctrines of the Global Message Movement.'

They sat and flicked from channel to channel. The news of Dennis Branch's ultimatum was on every satellite station across Europe. They picked up Sky News from Britain where a representative of the Archbishop of Canterbury was calling the ultimatum 'a particularly tasteless hoax'. They picked up Italy, where the Pope had issued a statement saying that 'you cannot bargain with your beliefs', which gave Conor a moment of uncertainty. From Cape Town, Archbishop Desmond Tutu said that 'the Word of the Lord does not belong to any one sect . . . it belongs to all of us, to interpret as we understand it'.

At 10 p.m., however, a new message appeared on the Internet – a slowly rotating globe with a cross superimposed on it – and a voiceover in Dennis Evelyn Branch's familiar whipcrack drawl. 'This is Dennis Evelyn Branch of the Global Message Movement. Those epidemiologists who know about the Spanish flu virus will understand that this is not a hoax. This is reality.'

A series of furry crimson blobs appeared on the screen, and hovered there for over a minute. Then the message continued. 'Any half-competent influenza researcher will recognize that for what it is: the whole Spanish flu virus. I have it. I have this virus, and my assistants have been able to replicate it, and the deal is country simple. Either I hear from the following leaders from the following religions within forty-one hours and thirty minutes, declaring their irrevocable conversion to the Global Message Movement, or else you will be getting to know this virus a whole lot closer up.

'You think that you're united. You think that you're a global community. But all of your global community is based on greed and pride and envy and prejudice. You show love for each other only if it fills your pockets! Your religions! What do you ever do but persecute each other, torture each other, tear down each other's churches? The Catholics hate the Protestants and the Protestants hate the Jews and the Jews hate the Muslims and the Muslims hate the Hindus.

'I don't hate any of you, even the Pentecostalists. But I do believe that every one of you is wrong. The way to the Lord is through the words of the Lord. The words of the Lord as spoken to me, clearly and directly in my ear. The way to the Lord is through me and my church, and it's the only way.

'If your child takes the wrong path on his way to school, and heads toward the creek instead, what do you do? You say, "Son, you're going the wrong way," and you'd be failing in your duty if you didn't, because that child of yours could fall in that creek and be drowned. So if he heads that way again, you have to be stern with him. You have to reprimand him. And that's all I'm doing with this virus.

'You have become a disparate world. You like to pretend that you're united, but the only tower that you have built for yourselves is a second Tower of Babel. And remember what happened to those who built the first Tower of Babel. *"The Lord scattered them over the face of the whole earth."*

'The difference is that when *you* are scattered over the face of the whole world this second time, you're going to be carrying something apocalyptic with you. You're going to be carrying the seeds of your own destruction.'

The globe faded out, to be followed by a seemingly endless roll of religions and religious groups, with the names of their bishops or their deacons or their pastors. 'Jesus,' said Magda. 'This looks like the credits for *Titanic.*'

Conor watched the list in silence. He hadn't really believed until now that Dennis Branch would actually spread the Spanish influenza, but now he was convinced. He felt something that he had never felt before – a deep sense of dread.

'If only we knew where he *was*,' remarked Eleanor, taking out another cigarette. She had bought herself a long knitted dress today, in charcoal gray, and she had braided her hair, like a Norwegian woman. She looked different, exotic, as if she had become a character in one of Ibsen's plays.

'Maybe we do,' said Conor. 'He mentioned the Tower of Babel, didn't he?'

'I'm sorry, Conor, but the Tower of Babel is a myth.'

'Sure, but he also mentioned it back in Tromso. He said that every nation spoke a different language, and that as far as he was concerned, the United Nations headquarters was the Tower of Babel.'

'The United Nations? Do you think *that's* where he is? Back in New York?'

507

'Surely immigration would have stopped him,' said Magda. 'He's a wanted man.'

'Of course, but now he's a very wealthy wanted man. He could have entered the States from anyplace at all. By helicopter from Canada . . . by speedboat from Cuba.'

Conor picked up the phone and asked for International Directory Enquiries. Then he dialed 001 – 212 745 1234. 'Hi . . . I'm planning on a visit to the UN headquarters. Can you tell me if the General Assembly or the Security Council are meeting this week? I see. Sure. And I can get tickets? Right, thank you very much.'

He put down the phone. 'There's a Special Session of the General Assembly on Wednesday at 10:30 a.m., to discuss international religious terrorism in general, and Dennis Branch's threat in particular.'

'That *must* be his moment,' said Eleanor. 'He has the same instincts as a theatrical producer. Look at the way he used Magda and Ramon to raise money for him. Look at the way he exhumed those bodies on Spitsbergen. Everything that Dennis Branch does is a drama, played out for an audience. That's the way he preaches, that's the way he arouses his congregation. All my life I've known men like him – producers, directors – men who have to control everything around them.'

Conor said, 'I just hope we're right. I don't want to fly back to New York to find out that he's in the European Community headquarters in Brussels; or Paris; or God knows where.'

'What choice do we have?' asked Eleanor.

*   *   *

They arrived at Newark on Tuesday afternoon. It was a chilly fall day, and it was raining hard. Conor called Luigi Guttuso as they rode in their taxi into Manhattan, and asked if it was OK for them to use the apartment on Bleecker Street for a few more days.

'Why do you want to stay in New York? You should use my beach-house in Sarasota.'

'That's very generous of you, Luigi, but Bleecker Street will do fine.'

'I'll have some champagne sent over. It's the best.'

'Luigi, I don't want to be beholden to you.'

'You're not beholden. Who says you're beholden? You're my brother.'

That's what I was afraid of, thought Conor, and switched off the phone.

As soon as they got back to the Bleecker Street apartment, Conor tried to ring Lacey, but there was no reply, only the answerphone. He took some consolation from the fact that she hadn't yet deleted his name from the welcome message.

Eleanor called the hospital to see how Sidney was, only to be told that he had been discharged and had gone back home.

'His doctor said he was making a wonderful recovery. None of the bullets hit anything vital, and he's as tough as they come.'

She called Staten Island. Sidney took a long, long time to answer, and when he did, Eleanor was too choked up to speak.

At last she managed to say, 'Sidney? How are

509

you, my darling? I just can't wait to see you. How do you feel? Are you walking? Oh, that's marvelous.'

Conor talked to him for a while. He sounded just the same as ever – soft-spoken, droning but resilient beyond his years. 'I want to tell you, Conor, when I felt those bullets hit me, I put myself into a trance. I didn't feel any pain at all. I imagined that I was back at home, lying in my hammock with Mesmer chasing butterflies all around me.

'The doctor said that it helped to save my life. Slowed down my pulse rate, so that I didn't lose so much blood, and kept me from going into shock.'

'We said a few prayers for you, too, Sidney. I hope those helped a little.'

Sidney hesitated for a moment, and then he said, 'Would it be impertinent of me to ask why you've all come back?'

'You've heard about this threat on the Internet,' said Conor, and gave him the briefest of accounts of what had happened in Norway.

'And you think he's here in New York, this Dennis Branch character?'

'Let's say it's an educated guess.'

'Do you need some help tracking him down? You could use a good hypnotist, couldn't you?'

'Well, we have Magda with us.'

'And you trust her?'

'I have to.'

'I could come over and help you. Be glad to, as a matter of fact. I was beginning to think that I was snatched from the jaws of death just so that I could go home and die of boredom.'

'Sidney, I'm sorry. You're still convalescing.'

510

'I'd take it easy. Wouldn't overtax myself, anything like that.'

'Sidney, I really appreciate your offer, but no.'

'I tried, though, didn't I?'

'Yes, Sidney. You tried.'

That night, in the very small hours of the morning, Conor thought he heard a door click. He opened his eyes and frowned into the darkness. He felt too tired to get out of bed and see what it was. The wind, probably. There was a gale blowing outside and a whole chorus of drafts were softly whistling under the floorboards.

He raised his head and listened for a while, but there were no more clicks, and in the end he dropped back onto the pillow.

He dreamed of polar bears again, running after him across the pack-ice.

Eleanor brought him a cup of coffee at a quarter of eight. She pulled back the drapes and said, 'Magda's gone.'

'What?'

'Her bed's empty. Hasn't even been slept in.'

Conor raked his fingers through his tousled hair. 'That's all we need. God – let's hope she's not planning to get in touch with Dennis Branch and tell him that we're here in New York. This could screw up everything.'

Eleanor handed him a note. It was written in sloping, spidery writing, with circles over the i's instead of dots. *Dearest Conor . . . I think now is the time for me to go in search of a new destiny . . .*

I will also think of you with love and respect . . . a man of honor . . . take very good care of yourself . . . Magda.

'It doesn't *sound* as if she's going to rat on us,' said Eleanor.

'No, you're right. But even if she doesn't, I really could have used her talent.'

'You're good at hypnosis, too.'

'Forget it. I'm nowhere near as good as Magda.'

He climbed out of bed, and while Eleanor went into the kitchen to make herself some lemon tea, he showered and dressed. He wore a pale gray shirt and a charcoal sweater. He wanted to look as inconspicuous as possible. It always amazed him that muggers and robbers dress in such highly identifiable clothing, like designer sportswear and distinctive hats. They might just as well have worn name tags. Eleanor wore the same gray dress she had bought in Oslo.

'It's only eight-thirty,' she said. 'Do you want another cup of coffee?'

'I'm jittery enough already, thanks.'

'We could always call Sidney, you know.'

'Come on, Eleanor. Sidney's still recuperating. What if something happens to him? I can't take the responsibility for that.'

'What if millions of people catch the Spanish flu? Can you take the responsibility for *that*?'

Conor sat with his hand over his mouth, thinking. Then he picked up the phone and punched out Sidney's number.

'Sidney? Does your offer still stand?'

'Are you serious?'

'Magda just quit on us. We really need you, Sidney.'

'OK, then. Be glad to. How soon do you need me?'

'As soon as you can. But Sidney, make me one promise. Don't you go dying on me, do you understand? If you die on me I'll never speak to you again.'

They reached United Nations headquarters a few minutes after 10 a.m. and went straight to the information desk in the main lobby. Tickets for the General Assembly were free, but they were only available on a first-come first-served basis. They collected three and made their way to the General Assembly chamber.

Sidney was stooped, and his face was gray, and he was even thinner than he had been before. But he still had the same brightness in his eyes, and he was able to walk quite well with the aid of a stick. He wouldn't shake Conor's hand – 'Don't want to hypnotize *you* today, do I?' – but he smiled and held him close for a moment and said, 'Good to see you, son. Very, very good to see you. I see you've been taking care of my Bipsy for me.'

Eleanor took hold of Sidney's hand and squeezed it, but didn't say anything.

UN headquarters was crowded this morning, with secretaries hurrying this way and that, while crocodiles of Japanese tourists were led across the lobby, chattering and taking photographs of everything, even the ashtrays. The congestion wasn't helped by a group of workmen erecting a large display of blown-up photographs depicting Peace In

Our Time, and a florist in white overalls with BLOSSOM TIME INC. stenciled on the back was working on a huge display of red and white chrysanthemums, arranging them to look like the UN dove, and spraying them with water to liven them up. Occasionally, there were brief flickers of photo-flash outside the main lobby as the delegates arrived. Conor took a long look around the lobby but there was no sign of Dennis Branch anywhere; or of anyone who looked like one of his followers.

'If he *is* here,' said Conor, 'how is he going to introduce the virus?'

'I saw a movie once where some terrorist infected the air-conditioning system,' said Stanley.

'I don't know . . . I suppose it would work if you did it on a plane, with a limited air supply. But in a building this size it seems pretty hit-and-miss. Like Eleanor says, Dennis Branch is out to make a grand theatrical gesture. Waiting for the virus to infiltrate the air supply could take days; and that's if it works at all.'

At 10:25 a.m. they took their seats in the public gallery in the chamber. Conor had only seen the General Assembly on television before, but it looked unusually full, with a high proportion of delegates from the Middle East – Saudi Arabia and Iran and Egypt.

The Special Session opened with a bulletin on the latest threat from the Global Message Movement, read out by the bald-headed Moroccan chairman, Ibn Battuta.

'Dennis Branch warns that he will not extend the deadline of eleven-thirty a.m. today. He says that the

Word of God is non-negotiable. He has given no indication of where he might release the Spanish influenza virus, or how, but we have received preliminary reports from psychological profile experts at the Federal Bureau of Investigation, and from Norwegian investigators on Spitsbergen, and they are in no doubt that he is both capable and likely to carry out his threat.'

Eleanor said, 'Don't you think we ought to warn the security guards?'

'How can we? Supposing we've made a mistake, and he isn't here? We'll all be detained, I'll be arrested as a fugitive, and who's going to stop him then?'

The Special Session continued. The Saudi delegate was furious that the United States never failed to punish Islamic terror groups, but ignored the 'writhing snakepit of murderous extremists within its own boundaries'. The Swedish delegate wanted to know if there was any vaccine that could protect the world population from Spanish influenza, to which Professor Sheldon Farber from the epidemiology department of New York University Medical Center replied, 'No, sir. And even if we had one, we could never produce enough.'

The German delegate asked if this was a 'doomsday scenario'. Professor Farber said, 'If you consider the rapid and painful deaths of a number of people equivalent to the entire populations of New York, Washington and Los Angeles to be a "doomsday scenario" – then, yes, you could call it a "doomsday scenario".'

'It's supposed to happen in less than eleven

minutes,' declared the Argentinian delegate. 'And what are we doing about it?'

'Have any religious leaders anywhere in the world said that they will comply with the demands of the Global Message Movement?' asked the Greek delegate.

Ibn Battuta said, 'I am informed that thirteen different sects have shown some willingness to discuss Mr Branch's demands. I am not at liberty to say who they are, but I can tell you that most of them hold fundamentalist Christian views not very distinct from Mr Branch's own. There has been a statement from one Islamic group that if a single member of its organization dies of Spanish influenza, the streets of the Western world will run red with infidel blood.'

It was 11:28 a.m. Conor kept swiveling his head around, looking for some indication that somebody was attempting to do something unusual. Maybe Branch *had* infected the air-conditioning system, but if he had, and it worked, then it was probably already too late.

One of the Arab delegates abruptly broke into a spasm of coughs. His aide opened the bottle of sparkling mineral water on his desk and poured him a glass. Conor kept an eye on him: it might have been possible for Dennis Branch to infect just one of the delegates, in the expectation that he would spread the virus all the way through the chamber.

The discussions went on, but after only a few minutes Ibn Battuta placed his hand to his forehead and took off his glasses. The Arab started coughing again, almost uncontrollably this time; and then

516

another delegate got to his feet and said, 'Mr Secretary, if you'll excuse me . . .' He swayed for a moment, then his legs buckled and he fell to the floor.

Another delegate started to cough, and then another. The Arab suddenly gave one explosive cough and splattered his agenda papers with bright red blood. A woman delegate screamed.

In less than fifteen minutes, the whole General Assembly chamber was echoing with coughing and groaning and people calling for help in a cacophony of different languages. Even the security men were leaning against the walls, gasping for air.

'We need medics, fast!' called the Canadian delegate. And Professor Farber ordered, 'You must seal off the doors! You mustn't let anybody leave! If this is the Spanish flu virus, then it mustn't get out of here!'

Conor said to Eleanor, 'Time to hit the bricks – now! Sidney – come on, let's go!'

They pushed their way through the growing confusion in the public gallery. Nobody understood what was happening. At least a third of the delegates had collapsed and the remainder were milling around in panic. A blaring alarm started to sound, which made the scene even more apocalyptic.

They reached the doors but a uniformed guard stepped in front of them, blocking their exit.

'Hold up, there! I'm sorry, folks! I'm closing these doors! I just had the order through that nobody leaves!'

Sidney approached him with complete calm and laid a hand on his sleeve. 'You didn't hear that second order, did you, son? Maybe you weren't listening.'

'Second order? What second order?'

'You know us, don't you, son? Our faces are so familiar to you. You've seen us before.'

'I'm not sure that I—'

'Remember those warm sunny days when you were a kid? That's when you met us. We always made you feel so safe, so reassured. We still make you feel good. We're like your grandparents, in a way. Now you remember that second order, don't you? That second order was to let us pass, so that we can make everything right.'

The young officer's eyes darted nervously from side to side, but he was beginning to smile. 'OK, sure,' he said, and stepped back so that they could leave. There was a noisy protest from the crowd of people behind them, and a lot of violent jostling, but the officer held them back.

'Are you sure this is a wise thing to do?' Sidney panted, as they hurried through to the main lobby. 'Supposing we're carrying the virus, too?'

'Well, *I* feel OK, do you? I think those delegates were specifically infected, one by one, although I don't know how.'

They crossed the main lobby, pushing their way through the crowds. But here, too, the doors had already been barred. A klaxon was blaring and people were milling around in complete confusion. Even the girls at the information desk were shrugging and shaking their heads. 'Is there a *fire*?' asked a large woman with a bagful of souvenirs. Outside the building, a grade-school teacher was knocking on the doors to get in, a whole crocodile of children waiting impatiently behind her.

Like a cat seen out of the corner of his eye, Conor glimpsed a thin man in white coveralls turning a corner by the telephones. He saw him for less than a second but he knew who he was. The florist, who had been arranging the dove motif in red and white chrysanthemums, right by the delegates' entrance to the General Assembly chamber. He was dark-haired, and he had been wearing a face mask then, but Conor hadn't really paid him much attention. Maybe his plastic water spray had contained insecticide or biological plant food, something you wouldn't want to breathe in.

Like a virus.

He grabbed Eleanor's arm. 'There – I swear to God that was Dennis Branch.'

'Where? Here? In *person*? You're sure?'

'I *know* it. I had a gut feeling he was going to be here.'

He hurried to the corner. Beyond the telephones were the elevators, but as they approached them, Conor realized that three of them were on their way down, and that the other two had risen too far for Dennis Branch to have caught them in time. On the right-hand side of the elevators was a door to the stairs. It had a hydraulic hinge, and it hadn't quite finished closing yet; and when Conor wrenched it open and listened, he could hear sneakers scuffing on concrete treads.

'He's climbing the stairs. I'll go after him. You take the next elevator. I'll keep in touch with my mobile phone.'

'Don't worry,' said Sidney, lifting his stick. 'You can count on us.'

Conor started to climb the stairs. He was still fit but Dennis Branch must have had legs like an antelope, because Conor could hear him race higher and higher, his footsteps echoing all the way down the stairwell. Conor gripped the handrail and heaved himself up, two and three stairs at a time. *You bastard,* he thought, over and over. *You bastard, I'm going to get you for this.* It was sheer hatred that kept him going.

When he reached the twelfth floor, his telephone rang. Gasping for breath, he stopped to answer it.

'Conor, it's Sidney. We're on the twenty-fifth floor.'

'I'm on twelve. Stay there until I reach you. But don't try anything confrontational.'

'Conor, Eleanor's had a heart attack.'

'Oh, Jesus. She isn't—'

'She says she's OK, Conor, but I've had to call for the paramedics. Listen, I'm sorry. I have to stay with her.'

'Sidney, this is one moment when I really need you.'

'I know that, Conor. But this is one moment when my Bipsy needs me more.'

Conor stood with his head bowed, sweating and breathing hard. O Lord, he thought, these things are certainly sent to try us.

Sidney said, 'Conor? Conor? Can you hear me?'

'Sure, Sidney. I can hear you.'

'Don't lose your concentration, Conor. Don't lose your faith. Confuse him, but flatter him. Distract him, but let him hear what he really wants to hear. You can do it. You have the presence. You have the voice. You have the confidence, too.'

'Sidney—'

'There's no alternative, Conor. I'm not leaving Eleanor for you or Dennis Branch or anybody else. I left her once before and ruined my life. I don't have many years left. I want a chance to live them with the woman I love.'

Conor didn't reply, but switched off his phone and started climbing again. This time, he was powered not only by hatred but by real rage, and he bounded up the stairs without holding the handrail, his face grim, sweat stinging his eyes. His leg muscles felt as if they were blazing, but he kept on climbing, and at last he reached the roof exit on top of the Secretariat Building. He kicked open the door and found himself out in the open, under a scurrying gray sky, with rain spitefully lashing in the wind.

In front of the Secretariat Building, the flags of the United Nations' member states were flying, all 175 of them, and in this wind they made a noise like hundreds of horses galloping. Beyond the flags, Conor could see the PanAm Building and silvery spire of the Chrysler Building; and if he turned north he could see the Lipstick Building where Lacey worked. To the east was the dun-colored waters of the East River, with barges slowly beating their way upstream; and beyond, the housing projects of Queens.

Dennis Branch was standing close to the edge of the roof, his arms spread wide. He had taken off his face mask but he was still wearing a dark-haired wig.

In one hand he was holding the plastic spray bottle which he had been using in the lobby. He didn't turn around as Conor approached.

'I love the Lord because He hears my voice and my supplications. Because He has inclined His ear to me. Therefore I shall call upon Him as long as I live. The cords of death encompass me. I found distress and sorrow. Then I called upon the name of the Lord, "O Lord I beseech Thee, save my life!"'

Conor took two steps toward him and then he suddenly saw how far down it was to the street below. A huge rush of vertigo overwhelmed him, and he stood where he was, breathless, unable to move, unable to speak.

'Well, well, Mr O'Neil. My self-appointed nemesis. A little too late this time, Mr O'Neil.'

Conor couldn't do anything but close his eyes. He could feel the wind against his face and he could hear the traffic far below, and even with his eyes closed he was dizzy.

'What's the matter, Mr O'Neil?' Dennis Branch taunted him. 'Lost your nerve, all of a sudden?'

Conor wished to God that Sidney were here. But then he thought of Eleanor, stricken with a heart attack; and when he thought of Eleanor, he remembered what she had said to him. *'Beat them. Beat the bastards. You're Conor O'Neil. Nobody can tell you what to do, and you can do whatever it takes.'*

He took a deep breath and opened his eyes. It was still a long way down to the ground but he did his best to ignore it. He looked steadily at Dennis Branch and said, 'It's over, Dennis.'

'Over? How can it be over? It's just begun. If they

don't renounce their religions after what happened here today, we'll be spreading the virus all over the world. Every major city in every country.'

'Neat idea, that water spray.'

'Not just neat, it's the very best way of spreading an airborne virus. Blossom Time Inc. kindly offered to donate a floral display to commemorate the thirtieth anniversary of the Biological Weapons Convention. Appropriate, yes? Their offer was graciously accepted; and here I am. Who was going to suspect some menial florist trying to make a dove out of white chrysanthemums? Except that when every delegate went past, I sprayed the air in front of him with a fine haze of virus-infected droplets. One breath, and into the nose and throat it went, and into the lungs. Did you see how quickly it worked? That was Evelyn's doing. She tweaked it a little . . . crossed some of the samples with a pneumonia virus that she's been working on for years. Genetic modification, I believe you call it. I call it Evelyn's revenge.'

'Well, you sure made your point,' said Conor, thrusting his hands into his pockets against the cold. 'Nobody's going to dare to gainsay you now. Nor the Word of the Lord.'

Dennis turned around. 'I feel good, Mr O'Neil. I have to admit it.'

'So what are you going to do now?'

'I'm waiting for my ride. In precisely three minutes from now, a helicopter will be arriving to take me on my way.'

'You took a risk, doing this yourself. You could have got one of your minions to do it for you.'

523

Dennis shook his head. 'This is for Evelyn. I had to make sure that there were no mistakes. Besides, it wouldn't have been right to delegate anybody else to do it. This is my movement, this is my holy struggle, and if I can't stand right at the head of my army and smite the unbelievers with my own sword, then what kind of a leader am I?

'Did Christ send somebody else to die on the cross in His place? No, He did not. He took the risks and He suffered the consequences, and that's why Christ is the King of Heaven. This virus is my terrible swift sword, Mr O'Neil, and I was the one who had to wield it.'

Conor said, 'They're dying down there, Dennis. They're coughing and they're choking and they're dying.'

'And so will millions more, before I'm through. Better to be dead, than follow a false prophet.'

'You know something,' said Conor, 'I never met anybody with your kind of vision before. I never met anybody with such belief in himself.'

For a split second, Conor thought that he might have flattered Dennis too much. But Dennis came up to him and laid his hand on his shoulder and gave him the broadest of smiles. 'You're feeling relaxed now, aren't you, Mr O'Neil? You're feeling good. You're feeling that you've done everything you possibly can to stop me, so – even though you've failed – you're satisfied that you've done your best.'

Conor looked into his eyes and suddenly realized that Dennis was trying to induce a hypnotic trance. In *him*, while he was trying to induce one in Dennis.

He tried to think of what Magda had told him.

Don't concentrate. Don't answer questions. Try to distract the would-be hypnotist by turning his mind back in on himself.

He looked out over the river, and then he looked back again. 'When I think what you're doing here, Dennis . . . converting an entire planet to one true religion . . . well, there's only one word for it. Messianic. That's you. You're the new Messiah. Everybody's been waiting for a second coming and I'll bet you never realized until now that you were it.'

Dennis's smile puckered in appreciation. Conor had diverted his attention by making him think about his favorite subject: himself. 'I think I might have misjudged you, Mr O'Neil. You understand me, don't you? In fact I think you understand me better than I understand myself. Did you know that one in four adult Americans believes that the Messiah will return in their lifetime? Did you know that? It's a true statistic. And you're right. I never, ever imagined that it would be me.'

Conor lifted Dennis's right hand off his shoulder and clasped it warmly. 'What happened to Evelyn . . . I'm real sorry about that. I didn't kill her. I guess she just had a compulsion. You must feel like you've lost half of yourself.'

Slowly, he withdrew his fingers through Dennis's fingers, stroking his palm and the inside of his wrist. 'But now you're going to be the new Messiah. You're going to be the leader of every religion in the world. Who knows? With God's blessing, you may be able to bring Evelyn back.'

'You think so? You mean, bring her back to life?'

'Jesus did it. Who's to say that you can't do it?

525

After what you've done today, you've proved your-self, haven't you? You've crowned yourself with a crown of light and a crown of thorns. You can turn water into wine. You can walk across the East River

'And

'You can actually fly.'

Dennis turned back to the edge of the roof. The wind was gusting strongly now, so that he could hardly stand straight. Over toward JFK, planes were circling in to land. And further to the south, a helicopter was approaching – only a speck so far, but Conor could already hear the flack-flack-flack of its rotor.

'You're not Satan, are you?' asked Dennis, suddenly suspicious. 'You're not trying to tempt me, the way that Satan tempted Our Lord? "*And He was in the wilderness forty days being tempted by Satan; and He was with the wild beasts; and the angels were minis-tering unto Him.*"'

'And do you know what that means?' said Conor. 'The angels bore Him up, and He could fly.'

'You're tempting me!' Dennis screamed. 'What are you doing to my head?'

Inside his pocket, Conor was rubbing his fingers against the striking strip on a book of matches that he had brought back from Norway. They were better than the American books, more combustible. He took his hand out and lifted it up, and popped his fingers. A cloud of blue smoke puffed out, and Dennis was transfixed.

'You're the Messiah, Dennis. The world belongs to you. You can do whatever you want. In fact, I'll prove it to you.'

526

Dennis stared at him with his pink eyes bulging. Conor had never seen such a look on any man's face. Rage, defiance, self-sacrifice, yet blazing pride. He really believed that he was the new Messiah. He really thought that he could bring his twin sister back to life; and that once he had done so he could cure Evelyn's deformities and make her walk. He wanted to think that he could heal people by touching their hands. He wanted to walk on water. He wanted to fly.

More than anything else, he wanted everybody on earth to believe in him, too, and to trust in his ministry, and follow him to glory. He wanted to save their souls. Conor realized then, on that windy rooftop, that Dennis was neither false nor devious. He genuinely believed that he could redeem the sins of the world.

'Tomorrow, we're going to repeat our ultimatum,' he said. 'We're going to warn them again. And if they still turn their backs on us, we're going to release the virus all over the world. In Teheran, in Beijing, in Delhi, in Rome. Everywhere. *Cursed is the man who trusts mankind, and makes flesh his strength. Blessed is the man who trusts in the Lord.*'

He was standing now with his toes over the edge of the roof, his head thrown back, his arms extended like wings. Conor was so close that he could have reached out and put his arms around him.

'They will die in their millions,' said Dennis.

The helicopter was only a few hundred feet away now, and curving in toward the roof of the Secretariat Building. 'Show me that you can fly,' said Conor.

Dennis closed his eyes and stepped off the roof and expected to fly. The wind was so strong that for a few seconds he was lifted, like a kite. But then the wind abruptly dropped, and he plummeted out of sight. He didn't even scream. He fell twenty-five stories to FDR Drive and when he hit the road one of his arms flew off, and was run over by a passing taxi.

The helicopter circled, and hesitated, and then it quickly banked away. Conor stood on the roof as the sound of its engine gradually faded across the river. A tugboat let out a long, mournful hoot. Conor looked around one last time, and then he went back downstairs.

33

By the time he reached the main lobby, United Nations Plaza was crowded with ambulances. Most of the public areas had been cleared and police barricades had been set up. Paramedics in respirators were carrying out dead and dying delegates on stretchers. Conor passed a TV reporter who was excitedly telling his cameraman that over eighty General Assembly delegates had been affected by the virus and that nineteen of them had already died, with more fatalities expected within the next few hours.

He tried to find somebody who could tell him anything about Eleanor, but the situation was too chaotic.

He started to walk back to the Village. He didn't want to take a taxi in case he was infected with the Spanish flu. He took care to keep well away from people he passed in the street, but after he had been walking for over half an hour he began to feel confident that he was clear.

A police squad car slowed down and crawled along beside him as he was walking south on Fifth

Avenue, and the two cops inside gave him a long, suspicious look from behind their amber-tinted Ray-Bans, and he remembered that he was still a fugitive, no matter what he had done to save the world from Dennis Evelyn Branch. He crossed over quickly and walked westward on 20th Street.

He returned to the empty apartment on Bleecker Street. The icebox was crammed with bottles of Dom Pérignon and he opened one up and poured himself a mugful. Who cared about being beholden? Then he sat back in an armchair and pried off his loafers and rested his head back and looked at the ceiling.

A spider was spinning an elaborate web on the Italian light-fixture. Conor watched it spin, and tried to forget the way that Dennis Branch had stepped into thin air.

The virus outbreak in the General Assembly chamber was the lead story on the lunchtime news; and so was the death of Dennis Branch. Police were working on the theory that he had suffered a fit of remorse and had taken his own life.

There was some good news: many of the UN delegates had recovered. A specialist from the New York Epidemiology Clinic said that there were signs that the virus, while it was very fast-acting, was also very quick to lose its virulence. 'I'm seeing indications that this virus may have been altered in some way, which could account for its fast-burn characteristic.'

Conor switched off the news and wondered if he was hungry. He could just do with meatloaf and stringbeans, like they always used to serve in the Kaufman Pharmacy. And when he thought of the Kaufman Pharmacy, he suddenly thought of Magda, and her prescription.

He called Morrie. 'Morrie, this is Conor O'Neil. Fine, I'm fine. Listen, Morrie, that woman with the antidepressant prescription. Has she been in again recently?'

'No, but she called me this morning and asked me to send some more pills around to her hotel. She said she was taking a trip and she needed a couple of months' supply. Waldorf-Astoria, room 815.'

'Morrie, you're a star. I'll come round to thank you in person.'

He hailed a taxi and went straight to the Waldorf-Astoria. He took the elevator up to room 815 and knocked on the door.

'Who is it?' It was Mrs Labrea's voice.

'Florist.'

'Florist? I didn't order flowers.'

'Somebody sent you some anyhow. Blossom Time Inc.'

'Blossom Time Inc.?' There was a pause. Then the chain slid back and the door opened. Mrs Labrea peered out into the corridor, wearing a purple Chanel suit. Conor pushed her roughly back into the room.

'What are you doing?' she screamed, flapping at him with her hands. Conor said, 'Shut up,' and slammed the door behind him.

Magda was there, too. She was wearing a long black coat with a fur-trimmed collar, and lace-up boots.

531

In the middle of the room stood seven expensive suitcases, all packed and ready to go.

'Well, what's this?' said Conor. 'Vacation time?'

'Dennis is dead, if you hadn't heard,' Magda replied. 'Without Dennis, there is no Global Message Movement. Not for us, anyway. We were just employees, not believers.'

'So where are you off to?'

'Someplace warm. Someplace where I can forget about all of this. You. Dennis. And Ramon, too.'

'Takes money, that kind of lifestyle.'

'We have money. Just remember that Victor was always in charge of GMM's finances.'

'How is Victor?'

'Terrible, thanks to you,' spat Mrs Labrea. 'He's going to need years of physio. Years!'

'I thought he was facing charges of abduction.'

'Oh, don't be ridiculous. There was absolutely no evidence.'

'It's strange how persuasive money can be,' said Conor. 'Even more persuasive than hypnotism. How much money have you got?'

'You think I'm going to tell you that?' said Mrs Labrea. 'You must be stupider than I thought.'

Conor reached into his coat pocket and took out his gun. He cocked it and pointed it at Mrs Labrea's face.

'Tell him,' said Magda. 'What harm can it do?'

'All right. A little less than forty-seven million, if you must know. Quite a lot of it went on transport, vehicles, research facilities, excavating equipment, pay-offs, that kind of thing.'

'I've come here with a suggestion,' Conor told her.

532

'My suggestion is that you pay all of that money back to the people you extorted it from.'

'Are you serious? They're as good as criminals, those people. Perverts. Swindlers. They must be, otherwise they never would have paid up.'

'The money goes back,' Conor repeated.

'I have a better suggestion,' said Magda, coming forward and taking hold of Conor's free hand. 'I suggest that we take the money, and that in return I send you a notarized affidavit to prove that you had no involvement in any of this. That way, you will be free again. No longer a fugitive. You can go back to your Lacey and live your normal life.'

Conor wasn't sure that he liked the hint of disdain in her voice when she said '*normal*'. But he liked the sound of being taken off the wanted list. And maybe, in a way, Mrs Labrea had a point. If the owners of those safety deposit boxes hadn't had something to hide, why had they paid up so readily?

Maybe he was starting to think the way that Drew Slyman used to think, but he wasn't a cop any more. He had already paid a high enough price for absolute integrity, and so had Sebastian and Ric and Sidney and Eleanor.

'OK then, I'll make you a deal. You take your money. You disappear. But you make sure that you both supply me with an affidavit explaining what happened. You do something more: you find out which of those UN delegates died today and you send at least fifty thousand dollars to each of their families. And you give Davina Gambit her money back, all of it. And there's one other thing.'

Mrs Labrea listened, and her eyes widened. 'That much? You think you deserve it?' But when she saw the look on Conor's face she said, 'All right, fine. If that's what it's going to take.'

'By the way,' Conor added, 'if you fail to do any of these things, I shall find you. That's a cast-iron promise. I shall find you and I shall make sure that you are punished the way you deserve to be punished.'

Magda leaned forward and kissed him; but he flinched away and wiped his cheek with his fingers. 'The same goes for you,' he told her.

Magda smiled. 'I love it when you're corrupt. It excites me.'

Conor looked at her but didn't reply. Then he turned and walked out of the room and along the corridor. In the elevator he had an overwhelming urge to wash his hands.

When he returned to Bleecker Street, there was a message on the answerphone from Sidney.

'Conor? We haven't heard from you so we hope you're OK. Eleanor's in Roosevelt-St Luke's in the cardiac unit. She had a seizure and she's very weak but the specialist says she's got a pretty good chance of recovery. As soon as she's well enough I'm going to take her down to my friend's house in Miami. Give me a call as soon as you can, won't you?

'I'll tell you a coincidence. You remember that Darrell Bussman you were telling me about? He's here, too, in the same hospital. I know that because some of the nurses were talking about him. It seems like he came out of his coma. His sister played him

534

Buddy Greco records for two weeks solid and in the end he woke up and begged her to stop. You should visit him . . . see if he can remember what happened that day with Hypnos and Hetti.'

There was a moment's silence, and then Sidney said, 'By the way, Eleanor sends you her love. She said sorry about James, whatever that means.'

At the end of the message, Conor sat still for a while. Then he reached forward and pressed the button to clear it.

At 6 p.m. he called home, and Lacey answered almost immediately. He couldn't believe how nervous he was. 'Lacey? It's me, Conor. I'm back in New York.'

'Oh, Conor, are you OK? I was so worried about you. I missed you so much. I tried to get in touch with you but nobody knew where you were.'

'How long have you been back in town? I called your folks but I didn't get any reply.'

'I've been back for nearly a week. Mom and Dad had to go to Florida for a dental convention.'

'Is it OK if I come around? I think we need to talk.'

'Of course it's OK. It's your apartment, too. Oh God, I'm so glad to hear from you. You don't have any idea.'

He rang his apartment doorbell a little after 8 p.m. Lacey opened the door almost at once. She was wearing a white embroidered blouse and a long skirt that reminded him of Norway. Her hair was freshly washed and shining.

535

'Here,' he said, holding out a spray of lilies.

She stared at him and didn't say anything. She made no attempt to take the flowers; nor to embrace him.

'What's wrong?' he asked her. 'Is something wrong? Did I come over too soon? Did I interrupt something?'

'You sure did,' said a muffled voice; and out from behind the door stepped a grotesque figure, like the Invisible Man. His head was helmeted with a white surgical pressure-bandage, with holes cut for his reddened eyes. He wore a fawn raincoat and his hands were bandaged, too.

'Hello, O'Neil. Don't you recognize me?'

Conor stared at him in horror. '*Drew*? Drew, is that you?'

'It's what's left of me, O'Neil. I suggest you come inside. I have one or two bones I want to pick with you.'

'Jesus, Drew. I thought you were dead.'

'I thought I was dead, too. You'd better come inside.'

'Drew, listen – this whole business is over. I'm going to be able to prove that I didn't have anything to do with it.'

'Well, I'm sure you can, O'Neil. I'm sure you can. I guess I always knew that you weren't really involved. It just gave me an excuse to get my revenge for the Forty-Ninth Street Golf Club.'

Conor stepped into the apartment and Drew Slyman closed the door behind him. He snatched the flowers from Conor's hand. 'For me?' he said bitterly. 'How thoughtful.' He threw them onto the coffee table and said, 'Sit down.'

'Drew, it's true. I'll have sworn affidavits that I wasn't involved. And Darrell Bussman's come out of his coma. If he can remember being hypnotized—'

Drew Slyman leaned over him. The skin around his eyes was raw, like thin orange-peelings. 'You listen to me, O'Neil. I was found in that hotel with third-degree burns all over my face and my chest and my hands. That was your fault. That's what you did to me. Even my goddamned dick was burned. Ever since I've been out of hospital I've had my friends wiretapping this number and all I ever hoped for was that one day you'd call it. And now you have, and here we are.'

'I'm sorry, Drew. But what can I do about it now?'

Slyman was silent for a long, long time. Then he said, 'Do you know something? I believe you. You always were a moral man, weren't you, a man of your word? You never bent, you never gave in. I admired you for it and then I hated you for it because I could never aspire to be as moral as you.

'You never compromised, did you? Not once.'

He stuffed his bandaged hand into his raincoat pocket and produced a Colt .45 automatic, took off the safety, and cocked it.

'No—!' said Conor, shielding Lacey with his arm. 'Come on, Drew, we can work something out. Some way of helping you.'

'I don't think so,' said Slyman. 'There comes a time when revenge is just about the only answer.'

He lifted the pistol and pointed it directly at

537

Conor's chest. For a long moment, his arm was unwavering. Nobody spoke.

'I don't know whether God will ever forgive me for this,' said Slyman. At that instant the doorbell rang.

'You expecting somebody?' asked Slyman.

'No,' said Lacey. But Conor said, 'Yes.'

'What is it, no or yes?'

'It's yes,' said Conor. 'I arranged for somebody to meet me here.'

'Go on, then, answer it.'

Conor went to the door with Slyman close behind him. He tried to turn around once, but Slyman prodded him in the shoulder-blade with the muzzle of his gun. 'Just answer it, will you?'

He opened the door and it was Magda.

'Conor?' she said, attempting a smile.

'You brought it?' he asked her.

'Yes, I brought it. Can I come in?'

'It's kind of inconvenient right now.'

She stared at him warily with those pitch-black eyes. He stared back at her. He didn't say a word, but he tried to communicate with his mind that something was badly wrong.

'Can't I come in?' she said. 'I really need to use your bathroom.'

'Magda, I'm sorry, but it really isn't—'

'Come on, now, Conor, you're being ridiculous.'

She pushed past him and immediately confronted Drew Slyman. 'My God,' she said. 'What's happening here?'

Slyman prodded Conor away from the door and closed it. 'A little private party,' he said. 'A shooting party, as a matter of fact, courtesy of Drew

538

Slyman, official avenger of disloyalty and injustice.'

'What?' asked Magda, in alarm.

'I'm just settling a couple of accounts with Captain O'Neil here. Pity you insisted on coming in. Anybody who comes in . . . well, I can't let them out alive, can I? Can't have witnesses. I'm not that hard to identify, after all.'

Magda said, 'You must be that officer who was caught in the fire.'

'Give the lady a cigar. Now, sit down, will you, and keep your mouth shut.'

'You must be feeling such pain.'

'Pain? Let me tell you something, until you've been burned alive, you don't know the meaning of the word pain. Now, do what I tell you and sit down. This won't take long.'

'I have a wonderful cure for pain.'

'What? What the hell are you talking about?'

'Just what I said. I have a wonderful cure for pain. It's simple and it's quick, and you will never feel pain again, ever.'

Slyman hesitated, and stared at her with his blood-shot eyes. 'So what is it, this cure?'

'Do you want your skin to feel cool again?'

'Of course I do.'

'Do you want your skin to feel supple again – to wriggle your fingers – to move your toes?'

'Yes,' Slyman nodded.

'Do you want to sleep soundly at night, with no burning sensation to wake you up?'

Slyman nodded again.

Magda went on and on, one repetitive question after another. Her voice was so hypnotic that even

539

Conor found himself shaking his head to keep his concentration, and Lacey's eyelids were drooping.

'You're ready for your cure now, aren't you?' said Magda. 'Nod if you're ready.'

Slyman nodded. His shoulders had sagged and his eyes were totally unfocused.

'Lift your gun and put it in your mouth. That's right. Right inside, pointing upward.'

'No!' said Lacey. 'You can't!'

'Lacey, there's no other way,' Magda said, quietly. 'If I don't do this, he will kill all of us, and himself as well. He's quite ready to do this. He came in here expecting to die. I'm not asking him to do anything that he doesn't want to do already.'

Slyman stood in the middle of the room with the muzzle of his gun in his mouth. Lacey watched him in horrified fascination, gripping the cushions.

Now Magda's voice was even more soothing. 'All you have to do is pull the trigger, and you won't ever feel pain any more. When I say "goodbye, Drew", you'll pull the trigger, do you understand that?'

Slyman nodded.

'Oh, God,' said Lacey; and Conor braced himself. The longest moment in the world went by.

'Goodbye, Drew.'

There was a deafening bang and Slyman's bandaged head turned into a muslin bag full of crushed strawberries.

Conor tried to grab him as he fell, even though there was no point to it. But Slyman rolled out of his arms and lay on the floor with his arms outspread, as if he were crucified, or flying. Lacey sat on the couch

540

with her hand clamped over her mouth, shocked into silence.

Magda waited for a moment and then she came and stood close to Conor. She opened her black crocodile purse and took out two envelopes. Conor stood up, and took them.

'The blue one, that's the affidavit,' said Magda. 'It looks like you're going to need it sooner rather than later, doesn't it?'

Conor tore open the second envelope with hands that were still trembling with shock, and looked inside. It contained a banker's draft for $750,000.

'That's what we agreed?' asked Magda.

'Yes, that's what we agreed.'

She smiled at him. 'The very first time I saw you, Conor O'Neil, I thought you were the kind of man who was looking for something more out of life. Righteousness, it's all very well, isn't it? But I think you've learned that you never get what you want by being righteous.'

She reached out with a long black-painted finger-nail and absent-mindedly stroked his shoulder. Lacey saw her and looked anxiously at Conor to see what he would do.

'Now, of course, you can have anything your heart desires, can't you?' said Magda. '*Anything.*'

She left the apartment silently and closed the door behind her. Conor could hear sirens in the distance. He sat down and looked at Lacey but he couldn't find the words to tell her what he was going to do next.

THE END

All of the hypnotic induction techniques described in this book are genuine and most of them are based on transcriptions of real case histories. It is strongly recommended that you do not attempt to duplicate them without professional guidance.